THE WAY BEYOND

THE WAY BEYOND

by

JEFFERY FARNOL

Sampson Low
London

MADE AND PRINTED IN GREAT BRITAIN BY PURNELL AND SONS, LTD
PAULTON (SOMERSET) AND LONDON

CONTENTS

CONTENTS

CHAPTER I

WHICH OPENS THIS NARRATIVE AND INTRODUCES OLD FRIENDS

OLD SOL, throned in splendour on a cloud, like a jovial and beneficent god, smiled down upon this right pleasant land of Sussex,—shady woods and sparkling rills, wide, flowery meads where somnolent cows, sighfully content, puffed fragrance; wide-sweeping downlands where cloud shadows played across a myriad flowers, and lonely shepherds sought what shade they might . . . a hot, stilly afternoon lulled by the drowsy hum of little unseen wings.

And nowhere did Old Sol beam more warmly than upon a certain ancient manor house and its immediate vicinity; a very aged house this, glorified by successive generations from the simple Saxon steading it had once been into a very thing of beauty,—mellow of brick, heavily timbered, wide of frontage and stately, its many latticed windows set wide open to the fragrant air.

On this goodly homestead most particularly Old Sol seemed to have fixed his huge, beaming orb,—a great, fiery, extremely inquisitive eye that, peeping in at each and every casement, beheld and peered at

Number One: Sir Peter Vibart in his book-lined library, seated at large desk littered with many papers, an open volume before him, and himself very sound asleep.

Number Two: His secretary, young Mr. Mordaunt, seated remotely at another desk and very wide awake, his large eyes turned up in oxlike (yet soulful) contemplation to the carven ceiling beams, his brow furrowed in the throes of composition, a quill pen idle in his fingers, a sheet of fair paper before him.

Number Three: Mr. Jacob Mayhew, the dignified and portly butler, snoring in his pantry and therefore, just at present, not so dignified as usual but just as portly.

Number Four: Tom, the one-legged ex-soldier, tying up posies and talking murmurously to Rose.

Number Five: Rose, my lady's maid, blushing like her namesake and listening to Tom.

Number Six: Young Richard Vibart in his shirt sleeves, waistcoat unbuttoned, hair much ruffled, busied with rapid quill inditing a letter that begins:

"My own and ever adored Rosemary:"

Number Seven: Mrs. Mayhew, the housekeeper, napping demurely in her own little sitting room.

Number Eight: Miss Janet McFarlane, in the stillroom, girt with clashing chatelaine but just now bending (witchlike) over a seething pot with Lucy the stillroom maid.

Number Nine: Charmian, Lady Vibart, in her boudoir, gracefully disposed upon cushioned settee and yawning sleepily over the book she has dropped three times to her own startled awakening. She, persevering, reads a head-line twice, her long lashes droop, the book slips for the fourth time and lies unheeded and she is upon the sweet borderland of sleep when she is roused by gentle rap on the door and in comes Richard's comely, ruffled head.

"Oh, Richard," she sighed, stretching luxuriously, "you may come in, my dear . . . and tell me why you have been sticking your hair into elflocks and Indian wigwams, as your father does when things put him about."

In came Richard, closing the door decorously behind him, but then began to stride up and down the dainty chamber, and being in boots and spurs, he jingled.

"Indeed," murmured Charmian, watching him fondly and askance, "you grow very like your father! But don't ramp, my dear; stop jingling. Now come and sit beside me and when you're ready—tell me who and what and how."

"My dear," he answered, taking her nearest hand to kiss as a matter of course, "briefly, it's the Governor."

"You mean your father, Richard."

"Of course, though he seems more like a governor. He seems to forget that I'm a man."

"Are you, Richard?"

"Indeed, I hope so. I shall be twenty in less than a week."

"So soon!" she sighed. "Well, what of your father?"

"He's been at it again, Mother . . . this Beverley girl, he's trying desperately hard to ram marriage down my throat! Why—— Good Lord, I hardly know her!"

"This is your fault, Richard. Rosamond Beverley is an exceedingly good match."

"But I don't love her——"

"Don't you, my dear?"

"No . . . no, of course not! And never could."

"Oh?" murmured Charmian. "But pray—why 'of course not'?"

"Because . . . oh, well, I . . . I never could . . . not possibly—no!"

"Ah!" murmured Charmian, sitting up suddenly, though gracefully. "You are so extremely negative that I naturally wonder and ask: Who is it, dear?"

"Who is what, Mother?"

"The cause of such very positive negation. Whoever she is, you will tell me she is all that is beautiful, of course, Richard;—but is she worthy? Is she—nice? Who is she? I can find out for myself, as you know—I always do, but I'd rather you told me."

Up jumped young Richard to stride and jingle again, while his lovely mother watched him a little anxiously until, meeting her wistful regard, he answered, a little incoherently:

"Mother dear, I . . . I worship . . . I adore her with all my body and soul! And of course she's worthy . . . holy . . . much too good for me . . . pure as an angel and . . . oh, beautiful . . . beautiful as . . . as Venus!"

"Goodness—me!" murmured Charmian, widening her eyes at him. "But who is she, Richard—who?"

"She's Rosemary, Mother, Rosemary Ford."

"Gracious goodness—me!" ejaculated Charmian, rising suddenly to her feet. "Black George's daughter——"

"Yes, Mother, yes—and I love her with——"

"So you told me."

"And I believe . . . I hope . . . she loves me too——"

"Then you have actually—told her?"

"Dear Mother, I've asked her, begged, implored her to marry me next week——"

"Richard, don't be so idiotically ridiculous! Such mad impetuosity! Such extravagant haste! Such wild precipitation! Have you dared to tell your father this? Have you?"

Richard's proud young head drooped, he shook it despondently, he sighed dismally, avoiding his mother's eyes.

"No, my dear, no!" he confessed miserably. "I've tried to speak more than once . . . I have indeed. But he is so . . . unaware, so . . . so confoundedly aloof and stately that I . . . I get dry in the mouth and quite tongue-tied . . . like a frightened boy, a dolt, a fool, an ass——"

"Precisely, Richard dear! And you will be all of these if you continue to think or even dream of marrying any one so ridiculously soon. And what does Rosemary say to such mad haste and hurricane wooing, poor child?"

"That's just it, Mother,—this is just where you can help me, if you only will. She refuses to give me any answer until I have broken it to you and Father and won your positive consent. So——"

"A sweet girl . . . and very wise!" nodded Charmian. "Yes, very wise indeed! Well, so she should be, being my own god-daughter."

"And so, Mother dear," said Richard, rather shamefacedly but altogether supplicating, "I . . . I came to you with my trouble, as I always do, hoping that . . . perhaps . . . you might . . . Oh, will you speak to Father . . . tell him for me?"

"No, Richard!" said his mother, sitting down again with a certain finality. "Most certainly not, my dearest; being so very grown-up and such a man, you are man enough to do this for yourself, I hope."

"Lord love me!" groaned Richard dolefully.

"Of course He will, my dear, and help you too, though you must do your share. And when you have told Sir Peter, I will talk too."

"Will you, Mother! Oh, my dear, then all will be well; you can do anything with him, of course."

"Of course, Richard."

"Then first, will you . . . would you be so sweet to . . . to have a word with him—now? Just to sound him . . . see how the wind blows? Will you, dear? For . . . oh, Mother, she is my very life——"

"Do you love her . . . truly, Richard? I mean not only for her vivid beauty . . . do you, my son?"

Down before her on his stalwart knees thudded Richard and looking deep into her wise, questioning eyes with eyes steadfast as her own, answered in voice sunk to note of reverence:

"Mother, I swear to God and you that I love her for what she is, more than what she seems,—for her sweet gentleness, her strength, her white purity. I think I have loved her all my life . . . since we played together as children, yet I only found this out since I came back from Europe. Mother, indeed, indeed I love her most truly. . . ."

Very gently Charmian drew this eager young face near, to smooth the ruffled hair, to kiss the eyes so very like her own.

"Such love should prove a blessing, my Richard," said she softly, "and I ask God's blessing on it—now." Then she arose and settling her dainty petticoats with a little, dexterous shake, looked up at her tall son with roguish eye:

"Now," said she, "I'll go and see just how . . . the wind blows."

CHAPTER II

IN WHICH CHARMIAN MEDIATES

AND thus it was that Mr. Mordaunt, warned by gentle rap on the door, hastily covered up "The Epic Amoroso" and rose to bow as "she who walked in beauty" walked into the room.

"Oh, Charles," she whispered, slim fingers on roguish-smiling lip, "I observe Sir Peter so very busy that I dare to think he will not heed you for a little while so—fly, Charles, fly!"

And when Mr. Mordaunt had sighed, bowed and gone, Charmian proceeded to twist her sleeping husband's dark hair into conical spikes (that she called "wigwams") until he stirred, sighed, opened his eyes and sitting up, very hastily, looked at her rather guiltily.

"God bless me!" he exclaimed. "Amazing! I believe I almost dozed——"

"Slumbered, Peter, slept like a great, big, beautiful, innocent baby." Sir Peter, becoming aware of the "wigwams," smoothed them out, frowned, laughed and, drawing her upon his knee, kissed her.

"What a child you are!" said he. And good Lord—woman, how I love you!"

"Which is only to be expected," she laughed, yet looking at him very tenderly, "and quite as it should be, seeing I am your wife and very wedded spouse. But come now, walk me out into the garden; I love sunshine."

"With all my heart!" he answered, reaching her his hand. So forth they went together along broad terrace and down the steps, by trim, winding walks, across smooth lawns, beneath the shade of great old trees until they reached a bowery arbour.

"I have sometimes wondered," said Sir Peter, as they sat down together, "indeed I have pondered frequently upon that very inexplicable assault on me in Paris."

"Paris?" repeated my lady, looking at him beneath lifted brows. "Why, that was ages since."

"Not quite twelve months," he answered, taking himself by the chin. "God bless us, how time flits!"

"It flies, Peter! It rushes, gallops—oh, hatefully!"

"But what so greatly puzzles me," he continued, "is to determine the reason why I was seized and carried off in such a very——"

"Undignified manner, Peter?"

"No, I was about to say—such a highly mysterious fashion, my dear."

"Why, Paris swarms with thieves and robbers."

"Yet these rascals stole nothing, not even my fob seals."

"Mm—yes," murmured Charmian, viewing him askance; "that was a mistake——"

"A . . . mistake?" exclaimed Sir Peter, turning to look his surprise. "A mis——"

"Why, of course, Peter, that robbers should not rob is so very surprising, —and this reminds me! What were you saying to Richard this morning, out there on the terrace?"

"But Charmian, I——"

"Indeed, you looked so preternaturally parental and poor Richard so miserably self-conscious that I am naturally curious to know why."

"Well, my dear," answered Sir Peter, a little ponderously, "I took occasion to touch upon my wishes for his future, that he should think seriously of settling down and——"

"Not marrying?" she enquired. "Of course, you never mentioned the word 'marriage'?"

"Certainly. I said that I hoped he would marry thus early because——"

"Oh, Peter! But you didn't, ah, you didn't say who——"

"'Whom,' my dear soul, the pronoun being in the objective——"

"Oh, drat your grammar! However, you have probably quite ruined all our plans and spoilt things——"

"Spoilt things?" repeated Sir Peter, amazed and a little shocked. "Now my dear, is it likely?"

"Very! You are sometimes so exactly like a bull in a china shop."

"A . . . bull?" exclaimed Sir Peter.

"Yes!" she nodded. "A bull! A very stately bull, but a bull! For instance, you didn't tell the dear boy that I had made up my mind—I mean, that we were determined he should be married early next year?"

"Certainly not!"

"And you didn't so much as hint who—no, whom—I—we—had chosen for him?"

"Why . . . to be sure . . . now you mention it," answered Sir Peter, taking up a book and putting it carefully down again, "I did, and I think very naturally, mention——"

"Not Rosamond? Oh, gracious, merciful heaven! Not Rosamond Beverley?"

"Why, yes," answered Sir Peter, eyeing his lady very much askance, "I did, my dear. To be sure, I did. And pray, why the expletive?" Now at this, Charmian folded her shapely hands, sighed deeply, shook her head and surveyed Sir Peter beneath wrinkled brows and yet more in resigned sorrow than petulant anger; meeting which look, Sir Peter stirred, rather uneasily, and began to rub at his clean-shaven chin.

"And so," she murmured at last, "our poor, dear bull in his stately bullishness has positively wrecked all the china!"

"But . . . my dear . . ."

"As I say, Peter, you have jeopardized our scheme, yes, beyond all hope. You have played the ponderous parent so effectively that you have quite, oh, quite ruined any chance of this marriage."

"But how?" demanded Sir Peter, starting up from his chair. "Charmian, in the blessed name of Reason,—how?"

"Well, for one thing," she sighed, "I understand this son of ours so well——"

"Yes, but so do I. Heavens alive, Charmian, so do I!"

"Of course, Peter dear, but—only as a father, and no mere father can ever possibly know a son so surely as his mother can. Now had you not meddled——"

"Meddled? Good heavens——"

"Meddled, Peter, I would have had them married almost before they knew it. Yes, Richard should have wooed the sweet child to please himself, or imagined so, and not in obedience to any stern parental mandate. As it is—" Charmian sighed and shook her head at him.

"But . . . confound it all——"

"Yes, indeed, Peter, you have confounded all beyond recovery. Richard will never marry Rosamond Beverley now."

"Great heavens!" exclaimed Sir Peter, a little wildly. "Did we not agree that Rosamond is altogether suited,—an unexceptional match? Didn't we?"

"We did, Peter, but Richard didn't and—won't!"

"And why not, pray?"

"Because he is our son——"

"Exactly! And shall therefore obey us. There is such a virtue as filial piety, a son's duty to his parents and I—I am his father——"

"Oh, dear heart," sighed Charmian dolefully, "that's what troubles me——"

"Eh? Troubles you?" Sir Peter nearly gasped.

"Yes, Peter. Because, you see, Richard is so dreadfully like—both of us. And you were always so frightfully dogged, so serenely unshakable, so sedately determined and politely—unreasonable. And I, though tenderly mild, Peter, and so very sweetly meek and gentle, am not altogether destitute of a quite ferocious will——" Here Sir Peter chuckled, laughed and clasped long arms about the lovely speaker.

"You?" he laughed. "On my soul, you are as meek as a thunderstorm and ferocious as a dove—as gentle as a tiger——"

"But resolute as you are, Peter. So it is only to be expected our Richard must be determined as you and wilful as I am, to choose his own course and pursue it, fearless of consequences."

"Hum!" quoth Sir Peter, frowning. "However, he shall not thwart our wishes——"

"Oh, he won't, my dear, he won't," said Charmian; "you see, I have changed my mind."

"Eh? Changed your mind? How . . . what . . ." said Sir Peter in bewilderment.

"Oh, about Rosamond Beverley. I am sure she is not the wife for Richard . . . entirely unsuited in every way, Peter."

"Not the wife . . . unsuited——"

"Perfectly, Peter."

"But . . . but, good Heaven, it was you suggested——"

"Well, I've changed my mind."

"Astounding!" he exclaimed. "Amazing!"

"But true, Peter dear. And, as for Richard, soon he will be of age and must inherit all Sir Richard Anstruther's money . . . he will be a rich man in one little year, Peter!"

Charmian clenched her white fingers upon her husband's arm, for upon the warm, still air was clatter of approaching horse hoofs.

"Peter, who comes, I wonder?"

"Some visitor or messenger. But why that look, dear soul?"

"Don't you remember the last time we walked here and a messenger came galloping? Let us meet—whoever it is."

Stepping out into the broad avenue, they beheld a horseman in smart livery who, touching hat to them, drew rein and tendered Sir Peter a letter.

"From my lord the Earl of Abbeymere, sir,—and no answer," said the messenger, and touching his hat again, rode away.

"Now I wonder," quoth Sir Peter, scowling at the letter. "I wonder what Abbeymere can be writing about?"

"Probably something unneighbourly," sighed Charmian, "that hateful right of way or the poacher you refused to prosecute."

Sir Peter nodded.

"Tom Lethbridge,—the likeable rascal!"

"But he has a very bad name, Peter, and he is a poacher, isn't he?"

"Undoubtedly! But then, so were we, once upon a time. At least, we used to eat the Lady Sophia Sefton's rabbits, you and I, my dear."

"Those dear, wonderful days!" sighed Charmian. "Our little cottage in the Hollow, Peter!"

Sir Peter unfolded the letter, read it once and scowled, read it again and actually swore, whereat Charmian looked enquiry.

"I say, damn the fellow!"

"Certainly, Peter dear, but why?"

Sir Peter crumpled the letter in scornful hand, smoothed it contemptuously and read this:

"My dear Vibart:

"It may interest you to learn that your son Richard is concerned in a (probably vulgar) intrigue with one of my sister Lady Bedingham's domestics. Alas, these young bloods! And yet the lad has judgment, for the she in question is a young, prime piece, a rarely handsome creature to stir the pulses of any male. You may surprise them of a Monday afternoon or Saturday evening in Fallowdean Copse.

"Yours in reasonable amity,

"ABBEYMERE."

"Man's a liar, of course!" quoth Sir Peter, thrusting the letter into his pocket.

"An odious wretch!" nodded Charmian.

"And to-day," mused Sir Peter, gazing down at his immaculately shod feet, "to-day is Monday——"

"Oh, but Peter—my dear," said my lady, glancing at his grim visage almost apprehensively, "you would never stoop to spy upon your own son,—you!"

"God forbid! But where is Richard?"

"Well, it's just possible he rode over to see the Beverleys, or the Vane-Temperleys. However, tear up that vile letter and forget about it, my dear heart."

"Why, yes," said Sir Peter, kissing her suddenly and rising with a certain very youthful alacrity, "I shall certainly go and destroy it at once."

"Go?" repeated Charmian. "Go where? Now, Peter, what do you mean?"

"That Abbeymere shall watch me do it," answered Sir Peter, in voice grim as his look. Then away he strode, light of foot and with head blithely aloft, and yet with such stern resolution in every line of his stately figure that Charmian, rising to follow, sat down again and opening her lips to call him back, sighed instead.

CHAPTER III

CONCERNS ITSELF WITH RICHARD'S FATHER AND THE EARL OF ABBEYMERE

SIR PETER rode slowly through the sleepy village but so lost in thought that he seemed quite heedless of the little, old woman who curtseyed to him so repeatedly, until he had passed her some distance, but then, becoming suddenly aware of her, he instantly reined his mettlesome animal about to salute the aged dame, hat in hand.

"How are you, Mrs. Lethbridge?" he enquired, smiling down into the small, wrinkled face with its rosy cheeks and bright eyes. "Pretty well, I hope?"

"La', and thankee kindly, S'Peter, I be wonnerful spry 'cept for me chacketin' o' nights an' th' axey as ketches me crool in me pore old knees and elbers, and me baccy arl gone an' me pore b'y Tummus, sir."

"Why, now, what's the matter with Tom? Isn't he back home again with you?"

"La', no, dearie sir," sighed the little, old woman, shaking her head woefully; "y' see, th' Ab'mere keepers do ha' swore a afferdavit again 'im,—and arter your honour a-lettin' of 'im off,—took my Tum t' jail, they 'ave, S'Peter, an' left 'is pore, old mother t' starve,—like the 'eartless roffans as they be, sir."

"Lord Abbeymere's keepers?" murmured Sir Peter, frowning. "But Tom was caught on my land."

"Which do be Gospel true, dearie sir, but they Ab'mere keepers do swear as 'e were a-poachin' o' th' Earl's land likewise, which can't nowise be, no'ow. An' if they proves pore Tum guilty this time, sir, they do say as my b'y 'll be sent overseas t' Botany Bay—" here the bright, old eyes were dimmed by sudden tears.

"There, there, my good soul, don't grieve! Hope for the best. I'll speak to the Earl on Tom's behalf . . . and . . . do, pray, get yourself some tobacco to comfort you. . . ." So saying, Sir Peter dove hand into pocket rather hastily and set divers coins in the work-gnarled hand the old creature lifted up to him, and wheeling his impatient horse, left her pouring benedictions on his head.

And now as he traversed this broad road, he viewed the trim cottages and well-cared-for gardens glad-eyed and was yet gladder for the smiling faces that peeped from lattices and doorways with such shy but very evident welcome as he passed. His folk, these and many more, to be watched over and thought for; his the land from the blue line of downs to the sea, a great heritage and grave responsibility, and all to be young Richard's . . . some day. Richard . . . his son . . . the coming Vibart. Sir Peter sighed, knit his brows in anxious thought, then spurring his horse to faster gait, galloped upon his way.

He was still grimly thoughtful when, some while later, he rode between a pair of tall, massive iron gates and was frowning at the great, many-windowed house that seemed to scowl back at him, when he was arrested by a bellowing "view hallo" and turning about, saw in the shade of a tree, a large, cushioned chair on wheels and in this a no less great personage than my lord the Earl of Abbeymere himself.

"What, Vibart, is it you?" he cried. "I mistook ya for an old friend, but y' are welcome none the less, m' dear fellow; the more the merrier,—how do?" Sir Peter rode forward, returning this somewhat boisterous greeting with more than his usual stately dignity, and for a long moment while the Earl smiled up at him, Sir Peter, grave and sombre, looked down on the

Earl. A tall gentleman of commanding presence this, large in gesture, form and feature, though the eyes that twinkled in the large ruddiness of his still comely face, these small, narrow-set eyes, so much at odds with the full-lipped, smiling mouth, the hearty, chuckling voice,—seemed to belie the very largeness of the whole man, as it were; and it was into these eyes that Sir Peter was looking and thought to read malevolence there, even while the smiling mouth chuckled jovial welcome.

"Light down, Vibart; we'll crack a bottle presently and—ha, you Clipsby, —are ya there?"

"At your service, my lord," answered a voice and something pallid, neat and gentlemanlike bowed itself into view.

"Well, find Sir Peter a seat and bid Travers bring wine——"

"Thank you, no," said Sir Peter. "My business will be soon despatched, Abbeymere, and besides, my horse won't stand."

"Business,—tush!" exclaimed the Earl, largely jovial. "Down with ya, m' dear fellow, I insist! Clipsby, take Sir Peter's horse and tell Travers two bottles."

So Sir Peter dismounted, watched by the Earl, who sighed gustily:

"Damme, Vibart, but y' wear well! Nimble as a boy and devil the vestige of a paunch or grey hair! Are ya never cursed wi' gout?"

"Never, thank God!"

"Then it's a damned injustice!" groaned the Earl, glancing down at his own swathed foot. "A very vile injustice, for it's to be supposed you had ancestors! There's Carnaby too, sound as a bell, damme! Y' know Sir Mortimer, I think, friend o' yours, hey?"

"On the contrary, I've never met him."

"But I've heard him speak o' ya . . . or your cousin Maurice, was it?"

"Very probably. But I'm here, Abbeymere, in reference to your——"

"Hold hard now!" cried the Earl, large hand upthrown; "m' dear fellow, I can guess,—you come on behalf o' that young rascal, Tom Lethbridge, hey?"

"Well, this among other matters," nodded Sir Peter. "I understand you have caused him to be apprehended again and——"

"I have, m' dear Vibart, I most certainly have, and must also inform ya that m' duty to the country, m' neighbours and myself requires I press the matter rigorously; indeed I hope to get the rogue transported this time——"

"For poaching a rabbit, my lord?"

"And to strike terror into like hardened reprobates. You, my dear Vibart, being a man o' sentiment, may deem this a little, well—hard, shall we say——"

"I think it entirely damnable! To doom any young man to such hellish suffering for crime so paltry, if indeed crime it be——"

"But, m' dear Vibart, our ancestors, yours and mine, would ha' used him infernally harder——"

"To be sure," nodded Sir Peter, "blinded him, cut off his hands or feet or mercifully hanged him. To-day merely chains, the hell of a convict ship, soul-destroying labour and the whip. By God, Abbeymere, the barbarian dies hard in us, it seems! However, I shall interest myself on your victim's behalf and should he be condemned, shall carry the matter to a higher court. But enough of this, sir; my errand here is to demand the reason of this letter I had from you this morning and, having heard your explanation, to tear it up."

"Good God, Vibart, surely the meaning's plain enough."

"Not to Richard Vibart's father, sir. And as to your suggestion of Fallowdean Copse, pray understand I am not accustomed to spy upon my son. Under these circumstances, I beg you will expound the matter fully."

"Love!" quoth the Earl and chuckled throatily. "Love, my dear neighbour, the Grande Passion universal, and most charming and vital of 'em all. Calf love if ya will, but to the poor calf a very serious business, a soul-shaking agony, a sweet madness may culminate in such fierce desperation to plunge him to damnation. I speak feelingly, Vibart, for not only is your son Richard thus afflicted but my son Iford also. The game's afoot, m' dear sir, one lovely she . . . your son and mine . . . dogs on the scent, snarling on each other wi' snapping fangs——"

"And, according to your letter, a domestic."

"Eh? A domestic? Did I so describe her? Amazing! She is governess to my sister Bedingham's imps and urchins, Vibart. And there's the devil of it, for my sister will stay here for some time and with her this Walking Tantalization, and the more Iford sees of her, the madder he grows and small wonder, for as I say, she is——"

"My lord," said Sir Peter, rising, "I beg to——"

"Wait, man, wait!" cried the Earl. "Hear the vital reason of my letter: sit down, my dear Vibart, and let me tell ya——"

"I can hear as well standing, my lord."

"Well then, Vibart, I wrote to prevent possible bloodshed, an excellent, sufficing reason, hey?"

"Pray be explicit, Abbeymere."

"Well then, to prevent your son and mine from maiming or killing each other. And your Dick's a dead shot, I hear."

Sir Peter sat down again.

"You mean that Lord Iford and Richard have quarrelled?"

"Ay, damme but I do! They never quite hit it off at Oxford, as you may know, but now—egad, matters are desperate, Vibart. Y' see Iford feels that your son's conduct is not—well, altogether sportsmanlike——"

"Pray how so, my lord?" enquired Sir Peter, suddenly grim.

"Well, Iford, having flushed the lovely prey, feels that your Dick is poaching on his preserves, as it were——"

Here once again Sir Peter arose.

"My lord," said he, with a gesture of stately finality, "you need say no more. Lord Iford shall be relieved of all or any imagined rivalry henceforth. And permit me to remark——"

"Wait, Vibart! Yonder comes the butler at last with—ha, damme, and there's m' sister Bedingham in full sail . . . ay, she's seen us!" As he spoke, towards them paced a sleek and portly butler bearing, and with most tender care, two wicker cradles, wherein reposed as many dusty bottles, while after him strode a smart footman carrying tray and glasses; but behind these stately menials, with them but not of them, fluttered a lady befrilled and beflounced, herself a shape of dominating femininity, slightly ponderous, extremely sparkling and vivacious, yet a little overripe.

"Lavinia, my dear," quoth the Earl, with large gesture, "I think you must remember our neighbour, Sir Peter Vibart;—my dear fellow, you've met m' sister, Lady Bedingham!"

"Why, of course, Valentine," said her ladyship, curtseying graciously to Sir Peter's stately bow. "I met Sir Peter on my last visit, for indeed, Sir Peter, I am frequently here, I so adore the sweet country; its peace and bowery seclusion, oh, these are wine of life to me——"

"Especially at the end o' the season when London's a dooced wilderness, eh, Lavvy? And our wine waits!" cried the Earl boisterously. "Fill, Travers, fill, man,—bumpers to Beauty, eh, Vibart?"

"I fear you must pardon me, Abbeymere," answered Sir Peter, drawing on his gloves. "I never take wine in the afternoon."

"Eh? You don't? Good God! Man's a puritan! Any time's the time for such wine as this. Dooce take me, but y' miss a lot, Vibart."

"Possibly," sighed Sir Peter, "but amongst them—gout! Lady Bedingham, I bid you good afternoon! Adieu, Abbeymere——"

"But y' horse, Vibart——"

"I'll go get it, my lord."

And, having made his bows, Sir Peter went forthwith.

"Fellow's a fish!" snorted the Earl, ogling his wine.

"But how elegant!" sighed my Lady Bedingham. "How strangely handsome! What eyes!"

CHAPTER IV

WHICH INTRODUCES THE "CAUSE"

MEANWHILE young Richard, astride his favourite hunter Saladin, was riding by leafy ways; but although the spirited animal bore him gallantly, though the heavens were bright above him and the glad earth green below, his youthful brow (so very like his father's) was dark with anxious thought, his long-lashed eyes (so wonderfully like his lovely mother's) were troubled, and his firm-lipped mouth showed grim.

He went by lanes and grassy tracks, a devious course that he followed unerringly until it brought him at last to a small wood, its grassy depths pierced, here and there, by shafts of sunny radiance; a remote place and very silent, except for the soft rustle of leafage and the sleepy call of some bird.

At the edge of this wood Richard drew rein to glance about and listen eagerly; then he consulted his watch, sighed impatiently and drooping in the saddle, became lost again in thought. And yet his ears were quick to catch the sound of her step, light though it was, for lifting his head suddenly, he turned and, seeing her, forgot all else.

Tall was she, yet not too tall, and moulded on splendid lines from shapely feet to the braids of bronze-red hair that crowned her glowing beauty; a loveliness that glowed indeed with a quick, generous vitality, for her deep, soft eyes, widely spaced, shone beneath their low-arching brows, her cheeks were flushed, her tender-curving lips vividly red; thus, with the kindly old sun to glorify all the warm, voluptuous beauty of her, she seemed to young Richard a radiant goddess rather than mere human creature very much in love. And no wonder!

Mutely they gazed upon each other in an ecstasy beyond words, look answering look so eloquently that joy grew to a pain at last and, trembling, he murmured her name:

"Rosemary!"

Then he was out of the saddle, had caught her hands and, feeling they were trembling also, kissed them.

"Oh, Richard!" she whispered. "Oh, my dear . . . can you . . . ah, do you love me so——?"

"More than my life, Rosemary! So now . . . may I kiss you?"

"And this is why I could . . . worship you," she sighed, touching his dark hair very tenderly: "to plead for what you might take! But first . . . dear love . . . have you told them? Does Sir Peter know that we . . . that you are going to . . . marry me?"

Now at this, Richard's arms fell from her and stepping back, he looked at her with eyes more troubled than ever.

"No," he answered, bowing head almost guiltily, "No, not yet. Ah, believe me," he cried, seeing her stricken look, "I meant to, dear Heart, I tried to speak of it this morning but couldn't—somehow."

"Oh, Richard—are you afraid to speak?" she questioned distressfully. "My dear, are you . . . ashamed of me?"

"No, no! Ah, never that!" he cried passionately. "How can you think me so vile, so contemptible? You know I love you—adore you . . . And God knows I cannot live without you, Rosemary, and won't! I would have told my father all this; indeed I began to, but he—oh, he's so difficult, so damnably stately and remote that he seems of another world and age. But I shall have it out with him to-night, I swear it,—and then . . . marry you, whatever he says."

"And my dear lady, your mother?"

"Ah, God bless her! Rosemary, I told her and the sweet angel blessed our love . . . Oh, Rosemary . . . kiss me!"

"Not yet, oh, not yet, or I shall forget everything, and I have so much to say. Come and sit down under our old tree."

But when they were seated beneath this aged tree, whose spreading boughs had sheltered them so often of late, they could but look and sigh for pure happiness by reason of their very nearness while the horse Saladin, cropping the grass hard by, often lifted his noble crest to roll an eye at them and snort, for these two young things, strange humans, though seated so very close together, still neither kissed nor spoke nor so much as touched hands; what wonder Saladin snorted in equine contempt?

"Rosemary . . . oh, my dearest . . . what is it?"

"You!" she whispered. "Me! Your father and mother! They are such great people . . . so proud of you! And you . . . their one son, and I am . . . only just me! Oh, Dick, when . . . if ever I am your wife, are you sure you won't . . . regret or be . . . ashamed of poor me?"

"Ashamed?" he cried fiercely. "Don't say it! Never think it! See, I'll kneel to you, Rosemary; here now on my knees I thank you for loving me, because . . . oh, my dear, I should be lost without you! I loved you years ago as a child, as a man I adore you, need you, want you,—must and will have you . . . so, Rosemary, be merciful and marry me."

"Oh, wait, my dear!" she pleaded. "For we must not be wed in secret, as if our love were shameful: first you must tell Sir Peter."

"Of course, dear Heart."

"But suppose he forbids us, as I fear—as I know he will, Richard?"

"Why then, we'll be married at once!"

"But—oh, Dick, I'd forgotten,—you're not of age!"

Now at this young Richard clenched his fists and scowled on the universe.

"I shall be—very soon!" said he, at last.

"Not for a whole year and three days, Dick——"

"Then I'll swear I am, and we'll elope, to be sure. Yes, by heaven, we'll elope!" Rosemary shook her head.

"No," she sighed, "we must wait." Now though her voice sounded gentle as ever, there was in the resolute set of her changeful mouth an expression of such purposeful determination that, known of old, now filled him with dismay.

"But—oh, Rosemary—" he began, then, suddenly dumb, glanced up and beheld a young gentleman in scarlet hunting coat, who smiled at them from the edge of the wood.

"Not praying, surely?" he enquired, bowing to Rosemary, hat in hand. "That you should grovel to Beauty, Dick old fellow, is but natural—" Up sprang Richard with look of such passionate menace that the speaker recoiled and instinctively lifted the heavy hunting crop he carried; even so Richard would have been at him but that Rosemary, quick as he, had leapt between them.

"Damn you, Iford!" quoth Richard, fuming.

"The same to you, Dick,—with apologies to Rosemary. And my appearance here is an intrusion quite premeditated and with no apologies to you, Dick." And Lord Iford, lounging against convenient tree, smiled. Unlike his large sire, Lord Iford was slim and delicately made, his face, pinkly smooth beneath curling, golden hair, might have suggested cherubs and innocence but that his large, blue eyes were anything but innocent and held a lack-lustre, almost haggard weariness—except when they dwelt on Rosemary's loveliness, then they glowed; and jealous Richard, quick to look for and perceive this, clenched his fists and spoke on the instant:

"Rosemary, pray stand aside."

"Rosemary," said my lord, "pray stand where you are and avert very probable ruffianism." Slowly she turned and fronting the speaker, changed from sighing, tremulous girl to resolute woman serenely confident; the eyes that had so lately viewed Richard with such melting tenderness were now bright and steadfast, the gentle mouth had a strangely indomitable expression and her voice when she spoke, though soft by nature, was resonant and wholly assured:

"My lord, if you have any respect for me, I beg you will go."

"Confound me, Rosemary," sighed his lordship ruefully, "but what a glorious witch you are! Since you put it so, I can but obey you."

"Iford," cried Richard furiously, "do you go or shall we——"

"Please hush, Richard! Lord Iford will go because I ask."

"At once, my goddess, to please you. Though our Richard is a little over-bearing, you see he is a man of his hands, Rosemary, a boxer and esteemed a crack pistol shot at Oxford . . . and devilish perilous to quarrel with, eh, Dick? Well, we won't quarrel, old fellow, at least not here and now. Some day perhaps I may feel more inclined and then—well, I may surprise you, Dick, and make it—once for all. Until which joyful day, God bless you!" And with smiling reverence to Rosemary, Lord Iford strolled away, while she looked upon him with eyes a little troubled.

"Dick, what did he mean about 'quarrelling once for all'?"

"Anything or nothing. Let's forget the fellow and sit down again."

"Are you so dangerous, Richard?"

"Reasonably. But come, dear Heart——"

"I could almost like him sometimes, Dick."

"Who,—Iford?"

"Yes. And I think—I think he might be dangerous too, Richard,—deadly perhaps."

"Absolutely poisonous!" quoth Richard, hot with swift jealousy. "And yet no, I beg his pardon! Iford's not such a bad fellow."

"Though indeed, Richard, I've seen him—very drunk."

"Well, but—but, dear Heart," stammered Richard, "I'm afraid I've been the same . . . once or twice at Oxford——"

"Oh, but not now, Richard dear."

"Why, no, but—only because I don't like it. Oh, I'm a very ordinary fellow, not half good enough for you, I know. But I—well, I do try to be worthy of your love, Rosemary. You are so good, so pure and wonderful, that I ought to kiss your dear, beautiful feet—and so I will . . . some day."

"Oh, Dick," she murmured, flushing cheek against his, "I'm terribly human really . . . not half so good as I try to seem. Sometimes I feel a dreadful hypocrite and despise myself. . . . And now, Richard, I have to tell you that I'm going away from Abbeymere—soon! At once!"

"Well, I'm glad you are leaving these people, but when, and why so soon?"

"Because," she answered with quick gesture of passionate loathing, "if I were timid and easily frightened, as I suppose a girl ought to be,—well, I should be terrified now."

"Terrified? You, Rosemary!" exclaimed Richard, in smiling disbelief. "I can hardly believe it—unless—" he broke off, scowling suddenly. "Ah, you can't mean because of Iford?"

"No, Dick,—because of his . . . father."

"What? The Earl? Abbeymere? Has the damned old rake dared——"

"Nothing, Richard, nothing actually. He has never done anything, never said anything and yet—and this is what makes it terrible,—I know he is vile! It is in his eyes, his chuckling laugh, the very air about him,—a hateful, gloating evil, a creeping, stealthy menace. And so—I'm going, Dick——"

"To-night!" nodded Richard, his eyes bright and eager. "We'll go this very night."

"We?" she repeated and, meeting his look, uttered a little gasp of ecstasy.

"We! to-night! You shall go with me, my Rosemary."

"Oh! But . . . where?"

"Wherever you will. We'll elope! London, Paris; I've plenty of money and can borrow more."

"No, Dick, ah—no! To-night you must explain to your father and mother, must tell them you are going to marry me.—And then I want you to give this letter to your mother."

"Oh? Yes, very well," said he, taking the letter she tendered and thrusting it into his pocket. "But, if not to-night, then it must be—to-morrow?"

"No, Richard! You forget,—in three days will be your twentieth birth-day."

"Well?"

"Your dear mother! She will want you with her on that day, you know she will."

"Yes, but——"

"There shall be no 'but'!" said Rosemary, sighing, but with her resolute look. "I will not grieve your mother more than I must. You shall keep your birthday with her. To-day is Monday; come to me here at this hour on Thursday and take me . . . wherever you will."

"Rosemary!" he cried, casting himself on his knees before her. "How I worship you! I shall begin to live—on Thursday. With you always beside me, I may do something worth while at last. . . . But always I shall love you—with my last breath . . ." he choked, and in the reverent, young eyes upraised to hers, she saw the glitter of tears and, stooping to kiss them away, wept also. And thus lost in each other and the wonder of their love, how should they be aware of the eyes that watched them so furtively amid the leaves or of the ears that hearkened so avidly?

"And yet four days is a long time!" sighed Richard.

"Yet . . . only four days!" she answered, sighing also.

"Anything may happen—in four days!" quoth Richard, gloomily.

"Four days will soon pass, dear," said she, smiling wistfully.

"I would to God they had."

"And you'll tell your father to-night, Richard dear?"

"The moment I see him."

"And now—I must go."

"Then I'll see you as far as the wicket gate——"

"No, please. I'd rather part here by our old tree."

"And you'll be quite . . . safe? I mean Abbeymere, damn him! I mean you don't think . . . anything could happen——?"

"No, no! Never worry, Richard darling . . . your love is all about me. Good-bye, my own love."

"Until Thursday!" he murmured. "Oh, glorious, heavenly Thursday!" So they kissed each other sighfully because of this dreary infinitude of four days; then standing bareheaded, he watched her go from him, nor moved until all sight and sound of her had vanished and died away.

Then he was seized of a strange, wild impulse to run after her and bear her away to the peace and safety of his father's house, but checked the impulse and, calling to Saladin, swung heavily to saddle and rode away . . . quite forgetting his whip.

CHAPTER V

OF THOMAS LETHBRIDGE, POACHER

SALADIN snorted suddenly, reared violently, almost unseating his rider, after which high-spirited protest the intelligent creature suffered his ruffled feelings to be soothed and stood, albeit a little fretful still, while Richard looked about for his hat which had tumbled off and in this same moment a husky whisper reached him:

"Oh, Must' Richard! Master Dick!" And from the denser boskage hard by a face peered up at him, a very ill-used face, for it showed divers bumps and bruises and one eye puffed and blackened.

"Good Lord!" exclaimed Richard. "Is that you, Tom?"

"Sure-ly, your honour. Saladin do be mighty skittish, for sure," and out from the leaves came a stalwart dark-avised young fellow, his rough clothes mired and torn, his shaggy head bare and a stout cudgel in powerful fist. "Ay, it be pore Tom, sir, and here be your honour's dicer!" And reaching under a bush, Tom retrieved the fallen hat, dusted it carefully on ragged sleeve and handed it up to its owner.

"But what in the world have you been up to, Tom—your face, man?"

"Why, y' see, Must' Dick, I got away from they danged keepers, dannel 'em! And they was three, consequently, do ee see, I took a wallop or so."

"What was the new trouble, more poaching?"

"Well, they danged liars swore as they ketched me wi' a brace o' pheasants——"

"Hum!" quoth Richard. "And had they, Tom? No, never mind. The question is,—what are you going to do?"

"Lay low till I gets a chance, Must' Dick."

"What chance?"

"To clout th' Earl!"

"What? Abbeymere? Don't be a fool, Tom! That would be attempted murder——"

"Well, don't 'e desarve it? Aren't 'e allus been agin me an' me old mother, ah—and worse, dang an' dannel 'im!"

"Well, that's all over now; you are one of my father's people and he'll look after you—so long as you go straight."

"Why, so I will, if they'll lemme alone, sir. Only I do wish wi' arl me 'eart as you'd ha' knocked Lord Iford down an' belted 'im bloody wi' your whip——"

"Good God, Tom! But why?"

"Becos' 'e aren't fit t' live . . . theer aren't a purty woman as be safe from 'e . . . I know! Ah, I know!"

Now at this, Richard swung round in his saddle to gaze back towards Abbeymere Tower in sudden apprehension; and once again was minded to gallop thither.

"There was my sister Anne, she were a purty lass . . . I were a little lad then, but I mind the day as she went—and wheer?"

"Why, Tom, you know she ran off with a tramping gipsy fellow."

"Ay, I knows that's wot they says, Must' Dick, but me old mother tells different and . . . I know! So I be a-goin' to watch—an' creep—an' wait me chance, an' then—" Tom twirled his heavy cudgel, patted it, kissed it, and nodded. "Then, Must' Dick, I be a-goin' to mark 'e for the gurt beast as 'e be——"

"And hang or be transported, Tom——"

"Well, let 'em ketch me first. Ride on, sir, an' I'll go with ee a piece so fur as Bob Medder's cottage."

"So you know Bob Meadows, eh, Tom?"

"Ay, for sure, sir, us do be main friendly ever since 'e grassed me."

"What, knocked you down, Tom, and why?"

"Flat as a flounder, sir—and 'im such a littlish chap! Ye see, Bob spies me a-kissing 'is little maid and, me bein' strange, 'e thinks I mean 'arm—me, as all childer is friends wi',—'ows'ever, Bob floors me. But when the child wep' and tells 'im I'm her friend, Bob picks me up and axes me pardon and me 'eart fair warmed to 'e, for love me eyes, Bob's got a turble wallop!"

"He certainly has!" nodded Richard, with fervour.

"And Bob's a man, Must' Dick! Bob says as he'd ha' finished 'im proper in Paris."

"Finished whom?"

"Why, th' Earl, for sure. An' talkin' of 'e,—wot about that there bootiful young mam o' yourn wi' the red 'air——"

"It isn't red, y' fool!"

"Looks reddish-like to me when the sun ketches it——"

"Auburn, then,—well?"

"Ar, but is it well, sir?"

"Dammit, Tom, what d' ye mean?"

"Why, I means, your honour, is it well—for her—over theer at the gurt 'ouse, an' 'im t' look at 'er an' stare, an' t'other un t' peep an' pry——"

"Tom, what the devil are you suggesting?"

"You've spoke it, sir—the devil! Him——" Richard checked his horse to glance back once again, and spoke on hot impulse.

"Tom—for God's sake, d' you think there can be any danger——"

"Well, theer was my sister Anne, your honour——"

"No!" cried Richard, a little wildly. "No! Damnation, it's unthinkable!" Yet, even as he spoke, he shivered violently and sat staring on vacancy with eyes wide to such sickening horror that Tom ventured to lay comforting hand on his knee.

"Never look so, Must' Dick; there beant no call to worrit—not yet! An' then besides, here be me to keep a eye——"

"Tom, you're crazed, yes—a crazy fool! And, by heaven, you'll make me as bad, if I let you! Stand away! Good luck and good-bye!" And spurring his willing Saladin quite unnecessarily, Richard galloped away like a whirlwind.

CHAPTER VI

TELLETH MERELY OF RICHARD'S FATHER AND RICHARD

AND it thus befell that at the place where by-lane met highroads, headlong Richard very nearly rode down his stately father. However, both managed their rearing horses very featly and with instant address, whereafter Richard, murmuring breathless apologies, took off his hat and bowed to Sir Peter who, bareheaded also, bowed graciously to him ere they rode on together. And when they had progressed some fifty yards:

"Father—" said Richard.

"My dear Richard—" said Sir Peter, both in the same moment; and instantly both were dumb, then:

"I fear I interrupted you, sir," said Richard.

"You were about to say—what, Richard?" enquired Sir Peter.

"Referring to our conversation this morning in regard to Rosamond, sir . . . Rosamond Beverley, though I esteem her very highly, yet, Father, I—I must tell you that I cannot ever think of her as a—possible wife."

"No, Richard?"

"No, sir. Because I . . . it so happens I am in love . . . engaged to . . . going to marry a—a—another lady."

"Richard, you amaze me!"

"Yes, sir, I—I was afraid I should."

And after they had ridden a while in a somewhat ominous silence, Sir

Peter eased his horse to a walk and turned to find his son eyeing him a little apprehensively.

"My dear Dick," said he, keen eyes suddenly gentle, "I shall be first to wish you joy if the lady you have chosen to bear our name be worthy to bear your children and——"

"Thanks, Father, oh, thanks!" cried Richard, glad-voiced. "Then pray congratulate me, for she is indeed the sweetest, loveliest, most beautiful . . . if you could only see her . . . so good, so pure that I . . . oh, I know myself quite, quite unworthy."

"A very right sentiment, Dick——"

"Oh, Father, could you have but heard her dear, soft voice . . . seen her as she stood at the edge of the coppice to bid me good-bye——"

"What coppice, Richard?"

"At Fallowdean, sir. She looked so adorable, so absolutely bewitching . . . yet such an angel, and her dear eyes——"

"Fallowdean?" exclaimed Sir Peter, stiffening. "Can it be possible the preposterous suggestion is fact? My son! . . . A governess?" . . . Richard's ecstatic smile vanished, his brow darkened, his eyes grew keen and stern as Sir Peter's own.

"Sir," said he, chin aloft, "this lady, who would so honour me, does happen to be a governess. And pray—what then?"

Instead of deigning answer, Sir Peter urged his horse to faster gait; Richard perforce did the same and they rode awhile, knee to knee, in silence tense and a little grim. At last, quoth Sir Peter, level gaze straight before him: "Favour me with the name of this lady."

"Why, Father, you and Mother know her, knew her very well once—she is Rosemary—Rosemary Ford, Black George's daughter."

Sir Peter reined up so suddenly that his animal reared.

"God bless my soul!" he exclaimed, "I . . . never dreamed of this, you surely know that I . . . and your mother, of course, hoped that you would choose one in your own class——"

"Wait, sir—wait until you see my Rosemary, how sweet, how perfectly wonderful she is; then you will understand how greatly fortunate I am and how unworthy, of course."

"She owes a very great deal to your mother, Richard."

"She knows this, sir, and is deeply—oh, deeply grateful."

"It was your mother chose her name."

"And of course it suits her perfectly because it is the most beautiful name in all the world."

"When her own mother died, Richard, it was your mother had her educated as if she had been her own daughter."

"My mother is an angel, sir!"

"Not yet, Dick, thank God! Now, bearing all this in mind, how if your angel-like mother should ask you to forego this . . . youthful passion?"

"I . . . oh, Father, I have reason to think she—won't."

"Or to wait a short year or so?"

"Impossible, sir, I am pledged, sworn, betrothed——"

"You wish to marry Rosemary Ford soon, then?"

"No, sir, I am going to marry her on Thursday next."

"Good God!" exclaimed Sir Peter. "You are mad!"

"Sir, I am in love."

"You are a mere boy——"

"Yet old enough for this, sir."

"You are not twenty——"

"On Wednesday, sir. And even to-day am hours older than when you suggested I should speak to Rosamond——"

"But, great heavens, boy, with no idea of your rushing into instant wedlock! Preposterous! Thursday! Three days hence! Most absurd! Does she—Rosemary—agree then to this wild, boyish folly?"

"After three months of my very earnest pleading, suing and supplicating, sir, and on condition that I warned you."

"Warned me indeed! I am shocked, Richard, profoundly shocked! I fondly imagined my son possessed of a more seasoned judgment! To marry at your age! And . . . this girl! Confound it, boy, this very unseemly haste is——"

"Pardon me, sir, I repeat for three weary months I have prayed and implored, pleaded and supplicated——"

"To undertake such responsibilities! And not twenty! How shall you contrive? What are your plans? How will you live and where?"

"We have not yet decided, sir."

"Have you given these vital matters a thought?"

"Well, to be frank, sir,—hardly."

"Of all the crass, confounded folly!" exclaimed Sir Peter. "How in the name of reason—ah, thank the Lord we're home . . . and your mother there on the terrace awaiting us!"

CHAPTER VII

TELLS OF SIRE AND SON AND HOW THE EARL'S
LIFE WAS THREATENED FOR THE SECOND TIME

MY LORD IFORD was, as usual at this hour, slightly drunk and showed it; my lord the Earl, his sire, was exceeding drunk yet showed it never a whit, except in his eyes, of course; and they sat alone, facing each other across the wine.

"No?" enquired son, eyeing sire with expression anything but filial. "No, is it, sir?"

"Emphatically!" nodded the Earl, ogling the wine on his glass. "Not a shilling, my dear boy, not a penny! No! For money, alas, like all other delightful things, is but very transient, ephemeral, like the glory of a rainbow —seen but to vanish!"

B

"And you—you ha' seen a great deal vanish, eh, sir?"

"True, Iford. . . . I had the kingly art of spending with a magnificence, or —shall we say, was cursed with the virtue of a noble prodigality, a stupendous generosity, a quite boundless hospitality. B'gad, I rained benefits like a Jove wherever I went; on friend and foe alike I showered my fortune——"

"And, sir—my mother's also!"

"Ah, ya sainted mother!" sighed the Earl, though his heavy mouth curled and in his narrow eyes leered an imp of such malignancy that his son, watching expectant for this, grew pale while the hand, hidden beneath the table, became a quivering fist. "Ya poor, dear mother——"

"By your leave we—we'll not discuss her——"

"Then, my boy, why remind me of her loss? She died so long ago——"

"And in a damnable loneliness, sir!"

"The poor soul! To be sure, I was abroad——"

"Yes, sir, you generally were. But I was with her . . . a little lad . . . she looked very small in her great bed, but smaller in her coffin. You were not home to see her buried."

"Alas, no——"

"No!" said Lord Iford, and reaching the decanter from beside his sire's elbow, refilled his glass. "She was not beautiful——"

"Oh, my boy! My dear boy, do remember she was ya mother——"

"I do, sir. I remember also that, although such a great heiress, she was very meek and gentle."

"My dear Iford, she was—well, herself,—a truly admirable creature in very many respects, but——"

"Too humble, sir."

"Humility in a woman, or at least in a wife, is altogether excellent, my boy . . . lauded in Holy Writ, I believe—it says there, I think—that such wife is more precious than rubies. Ya mother, I'm happy to affirm was, in this respect, more precious than diamonds or even pearls. A saintly soul, Iford!"

"And, while alive, very much out of place, sir,—quite, quite lost, poor saint!" murmured Lord Iford, fiddling with his wineglass yet very conscious of the eyes that watched him. "'Oh, death, where is thy sting?' This is also in Holy Writ, I believe, sir."

"Ah, yes, dear boy," sighed the Earl at last, "Death may have its compensation for had your mother been spared to this year o' Grace, would she ha' seen in you, her petted offspring, the realization of her ideals; would she ha' been proud of ya? Perhaps. And yet I almost doubt it, my boy, I do indeed. And why? Because she, being small and meek, admired men that were men, tall men strong and masterful, and you are neither one nor the other, my dear Iford; b'gad you don't resemble me in the slightest, now do ya?"

"No," answered my lord, smiling down at his half-empty wineglass. "No, not in the faintest, very remotest degree, sir."

"Which becomes more painfully obvious every day, my boy."

"Indeed, sir?"

"You have never succeeded in anything as yet and——"

"Probably because I have never troubled to, well—to try, sir."

"Oh, but yes, my boy, yes. You have been trying this month and more, ay, and trying devilish hard."

"Really, sir?"

"Ah, really, Iford! To win your two arms full o' this warm, tender loveliness, this shy-sweet innocency shaped like a passionate Venus, and . . . failed, ha?"

"If by such fulsome description you mean Miss Ford——"

"Who else, lad? Here's you been ogling, sighing and dying for her all these weeks and won of her not so much as a kiss, I'll wager." Here Lord Iford raised his golden head to survey the speaker with his mild-seeming, blue eyes; but once again that hidden hand clenched itself.

"And yet, sir," said my lord gently, "despite your somewhat torrid adjectives, I find her somewhat cold."

The Earl chuckled and laughed until his eyes vanished.

"Cold?" he exclaimed. "With that voluptuous shape, those deep, telltale eyes,—cold? Ya poor simpleton, she's Joy incarnate! Had she lived in my day, we'd ha' made her renowned . . . famous."

"Sir, I think you must mean infamous. Also you appear to quite mis-apprehend the matter, for I am wooing this lady——"

"Wooing, d' ya say? Good God! D' ya call it wooing to sit as ya did at table to-night, dumb as a confounded oyster,—hey? D' ya call it wooing to permit her to remain so hoitytoitily aloof—hey? D' ya call—" The Earl paused in no little surprise to perceive that his son was laughing at him, laughter very gentle but so bitterly contemptuous that the Earl shot forward his large chin and squared his great shoulders in that threatening manner that had carried such dire terrors, once upon a time, into two frightened hearts; once upon a time, for now Lord Iford merely laughed and so eloquently that the Earl, sitting back in his large chair, blinked, chuckled and laughed also.

"What then," he enquired, "do I guess wrong then—hey? D' ya mean the sweet, sly minx plays mock-modest in public to be kind in private,—hey, lad, hey? Has she found ya bold enough at last?"

"Not exactly, sir. You see,—tonight, just before we sat to table, I'd been imploring her to marry me."

"Eh—marriage?" The Earl actually gasped, slopping wine in his stark amazement. "Marriage!" he repeated, and now to amazement scorn was added. " 'Imploring' says you! And a governess! Are ya mad? Ha, con-found and curse me, but we managed our women better in my day——"

"Probably!" smiled his son. "But then, of course, sir, your women would be, well—different."

"Hold ya drunken tongue, sir!" cried the Earl, stung to show of fury at last. "Ha, you're a damnable reminder of ya mother."

"My lord, noble sire, you honour me!"

"Bait ya hook wi' marriage, hey? You would! But I tell ya woman is always woman and always to be won—by a proper man! And we managed 'em better in my day because we were men, sir—men, d' ya hear?"

"I know sir," sneered his son, "hard-riding, hard-drinking, hard-fighting— and all the rest of it. Thank my stars I live to-day!"

"Live?" cried the Earl, and laughed. "Live, hey? Why damme, ya hardly exist——"

"However, sir, my existence will soon be shared by—a wife."

"Ha, she accepted ya then: the sly jade jumped at ya title, of course."

"You err again, sir. She refused me."

"Did she so? Then, begad, it is young Vibart, aha! Oh, I happen to know she'll marry Vibart's son——"

"No, sir, she merely—thinks she will.

"Iford, what the devil do ya mean?"

"Simply that I have determined, and arranged, to make her Lady Iford." The Earl took up the heavy, cutglass decanter much as if he would have launched it at his son's curly, golden head, but he proceeded to fill his glass, though the eyes in the large comeliness of his face seemed more malevolent than ever.

"And what then," he demanded; "what o' ya engagement to Cynthia Bellenden? Need I remind ya that a wealthy marriage becomes more imperative?"

"Then, sir, I fear you must think out some other scheme. Yourself, for instance, being so tall and very male, might woo another——"

"Iford, are ya mad, a fool, or merely drunk?"

"Either or all, sir, for I shall certainly marry for love and to please only myself." At this, the Earl, being viciously enraged, chuckled throatily and fell back upon that retort which, as he well knew, could stir this coldly contemptuous son of his as nothing else might.

"My poor Iford," sighed he, "you become more and ever more like your puling, futile, peak-faced mother!"

But this time it seemed the taunt would prove ineffectual, for Lord Iford sat mute, staring down at the wineglass he was turning and turning in slender fingers; at last, slowly, and with eyes still abased, he arose and lolling against the table, spoke in voice almost whispering:

"My mother! My poor, small, ill-used mother, who died so much before her time! Sir, you have mentioned her to-night with a strange frequency,— but not one look of kindness, not one word of remorse for the misery you caused her. Well now, as this dead mother's son sat here listening to your coarse, brutish sneers, he could very joyfully have struck you dead. And, before God, he may yet! Who knows? For, sir, remembering that little, heartbroken mother of mine, I should be quite charmed to see your noble lordship very completely a corpse."

And now, leaning across the table, he stared down at his sire and though his voice had been quite pleasantly modulated, though his pale lips smiled, his wide, blue eyes, mild no longer, glared such look that the Earl shrank appalled, his wineglass fell and shattered on the floor all unheeded, and when at last he found voice, it was neither full-throated nor hearty:

"Iford—you—you—by God—you're—drunk!"

"Right sir, I am. . . . And yet sober enough to hope that great carcass of yours may soon grow . . . corrupt as your soul. In which fervent hope, right noble lord and father,—I will to bed." And turning upon his heels, Lord Iford, very deliberately, though with an occasional stagger, crossed the wide floor to the door and was gone.

CHAPTER VIII

INTRODUCES ONE CLIPSBY, A NONENTITY (ALMOST)

FOR some time after his son had departed, the Earl sat staring blankly down at the remains of his shattered wineglass; indeed these glittering fragments seemed to fascinate him, for with his gaze still fixed there, he groped for the silver table bell and rang it; nor did he so much as glance up when the door opened but merely bade the bowing footman:

"Send Clipsby to me."

And presently the door opened again, closed softly, soft footsteps crossed the floor and a voice murmured:

"Yes, my lord?" Then the Earl raised his large head with a jerk, sat back in his chair and surveyed that which stood before him; a lank shape neither tall nor short, nor dark nor fair, and with form and features so altogether nondescript and unremarkable, a creature so superlatively negative from head to foot as to be almost a nonentity garbed in sober black.

"You may sit down, Clipsby." Pale eyes flickered and a chair became occupied.

"Wine, Clipsby,—help yourself." The decanter tilted wine into a glass and the glass was lifted to a pale, thin-lipped mouth.

"Now in regard to this girl, Clipsby. Tell me again. You saw her with young Vibart, you heard her agree to elope with him—hey?"

"On Thursday next, my lord."

"Well, Thursday sha'n't serve. Thursday's not soon enough. Iford, the crass fool, means to cut in beforehand and marry her himself, and if he does, young Vibart will probably shoot him. Well, such a marriage won't serve me, Clipsby, and—damn him—I don't want him shot for the same reason. So this fool marriage must not and shall not be, d'ya hear?"

"If your lordship so says, then it probably won't be."

"Ha, damme, it shan't be! We must take a hand in this precious game, Clipsby. I must play Providence and rearrange these young lives. . . . Two puppies snarling over luscious titbit,—along comes the old dog . . . snap! And away with the dainty morsel,—ha!"

"Your lordship's metaphor is apt."

"Well now, see here, Clipsby—draw closer! This same tempting piece o' womanhood, this coy Prudery must be tamed, her prideful virtue humbled, ah, so humbled that she must hide herself from eyes censorious, more especially the doting sheep's eyes of her two adoring swains, young Vibart and Iford, damn him! She thus disposed of, these two fool lads having duly mourned their fallen and vanished divinity, shall presently become amenable to their several father's wills, especially my damned fool Iford, hey, Clipsby?"

"Having regard to Miss Bellenden's very considerable fortune, my lord?"

"Precisely. And the scheme promises; we must act at once, you and I. You will therefore——"

"I, my lord? You . . . mean . . .?"

"Exactly! We must use the Abbey again for a night or so."

A gasping murmur:

"Not that, my lord—no—no!" And now a babble of sibilant, horrified whispering: "Ah, not again! Never again! Your lordship promised me! No, no, I cannot! I will not!"

"Silence, ya fool! This is business! And, what's more——"

"No, no—I will not . . . I cannot!"

"Ah, but ya will! And with the same secrecy and whole-hearted devotion as before, eh, Clipsby?"

"You promised, Abbeymere. You swore an oath . . . and . . . I . . . cannot——"

"Well, ya know the alternative? I see ya do. Death is always unpleasant, Clipsby, but more especially when—it is made a public function, ha?" Two thin tremulous hands clasped and wrung each other, a whispering voice spoke:

"Years and years of agonized remorse . . . years and years of faithful service . . . acts committed that are shame to recall! These should earn respite . . . even for me."

"They shall, Clipsby, they shall! This once more and, though I shall grieve ya loss, you shall go, ay, and with a noble competence."

"The same answer—always . . . always the same!"

"That little chamber in the Abbey ruins beside the Mere; egad, we haven't used it for years! How long since that last happy occasion?"

The whispering voice gasped, "Six!"

"So long, hey! Well, to-morrow early, or, better, to-night, make it habitable as possible——"

"Oh, my lord . . . Abbeymere, show mercy! She is . . . so different——"

"Tush, ye fool! She shall come to no real harm. But to-morrow she must disappear, vanish,—until she elect to fly away on the wings o' shame—yet harmed only in her mock-modest self-esteem and proud virtue. Well now, another glass o' wine? No? Then help me to bed."

CHAPTER IX

WHICH TRANSPORTS THE PATIENT READER TO SCENES
FAMILIAR BUT FORGOT AWHILE

IT WAS high noon when Sir Peter drew rein to gaze up at a certain inn sign whereon was painted the lively representation of a bull,—Sir Peter sighed.

And then, borne to him on the warm, drowsy air, came the thud and ring of hammer and anvil. Sir Peter started, his austere mouth grew young with quick smile, his sombre eyes brightened as they glanced round about him upon this well-remembered, too seldom visited scene. . . . This broad highway, white and dusty, that stretched away between gardens abloom with flowers and backed by thatched cottages shaded by tall and aged trees, beyond which peeped the gable of barn or pointed roof of oast house.

Sir Peter walked his horse along this white road to the smithy and stooping, peered in at the low-arched doorway.

And there all alone at his anvil stood Black George, a very son of Anak in his bare-armed might, plying his ponderous hand hammer lightly as of old, but he sang no more and, amid the crisp curls of his Saxon-yellow hair, Peter espied broad streaks of silver; also his comely face, somewhat sooty from the fire, showed marks set there by more than the hand of old Father Time.

Thus Sir Peter, dusty with travel yet slim and elegant astride his tall horse, gazed upon sooty George—this man he had fought with, loved and honoured, heeding those marks of care and sorrow, silvered hair and furrowed brow, with eyes very wistful and kindly. . . . And then Black George looked up, ,in the very middle of a stroke, and stood, heavy hammer poised, while their eyes, the dark and the blue, gazed deep each into each.

And they spoke no word, these two; only the hammer thudded to earth from George's loosened grasp and Sir Peter, swinging lightly from saddle, strode into the smoky dimness of the smithy, and then hands met and wrung each other across that bright, much-used anvil. . . . And it was Black George first found voice:

"A bit grimy I be, Sir Peter!"

"Clean, honest grime, George. And don't call me 'sir'! The old place—looks just the same."

"Ar—pretty much, Peter. Though I fitted a noo 'andle to the sledge—'bout three weeks ago. And—see up theer, agin the beam,—your own old hammer, Peter. Hung it theer, I did, arter you went away and nobody's took it down since. Dusty and rusty it be, but there it be a-goin' to 'ang until,—well till I be done wi' smithing for good. And now let's stable your hoss, Peter; a rare un 'e be! And now set down yonder in the sun and talk."

And presently, the good horse having been duly cared for, down they sat together in the old porch before the inn door, to gaze upon each other with beaming eyes, to pledge each other silently in tankards of foaming ale, and drink together in voiceless communion like the old friends they were. "The years ha' been kind to ee, Peter; you look hearty and straight as a gun barrel. And your lady be well,—eh, Peter?"

"She is, thank God!"

"And your son,—he be likewise well,—eh, Peter?"

"Yes, and thank God again!"

"Ay, the Lord hath dealt kindly by ee, Peter, kinder than wi'—others——"

"You remember my son Richard, of course?"

"Ay, for sure! Don't I mind him being born, Peter, just six months arter Prue give me my Rosemary. Didn't I watch him grow to a lad . . . whiles you lived hereabouts in Kent."

"Have you seen him lately, George?"

"Ar! Leastways, 'bout a year ago. Comes a-ridin' over, 'e did . . . and a fine, comely young gen'leman 'e be—summat like you, Peter, but mighty like his mother."

"I'm glad you think so, George, because . . . well . . . d' you see . . . he wants to marry your daughter Rosemary."

George's tankard fell with a clatter, spilling what remained of its contents, and he stared down at it beneath slow-knitting brows, while Peter viewed him somewhat askance.

"Marry . . . my daughter?" quoth George, and, stooping suddenly, picked up his tankard, turning it over and over in his great fist and staring at it very blankly. "Marry . . . my Rosemary . . . your son?" he repeated slowly.

"Yes, George, old fellow. It seems they love each other very dearly, very truly, and have done so for a great while."

"Oh, have they, Peter."

"So Richard affirms. Under which circumstances his mother and I can urge no objection. I may tell you that in a year's time Richard will inherit a very large fortune, until when, of course, I shall see the young people properly established."

"Properly . . . established!" nodded George, still frowning at the tankard he was turning this way and that.

"So, George, I am here to ask your blessing on this marriage."

Very deliberately George set his tankard in a corner of the settle and, turning upon his companion, spoke in his slow, thoughtful manner:

"No, Peter! I don't nowise give my consent, nor yet my blessing. What I says is—no!"

Sir Peter started and seemed for a moment positively dumb-struck; his black brows drew together in a haughty frown, up went his stately head and he stared into the calm, blue eyes that stared as directly back at him.

"George," said he, at last, "you amaze me!"

"Peter," said George, "you amaze me more, ah—a sight more!" And now for a moment they fronted each other in silence again, stately arrogance against sturdy pride.

"Then . . . you refuse?"

"Ay, I do."

"May I ask why?"

"Ay, for sure, Peter. And for sure I'll try to tell ee, though you'd ought to know wi'out; hows'ever it be this: You are my friend Peter. And I'm George. But you'm likewise a gen'leman baronet. And I'm a blacksmith. And there y'are. And enough too!"

"But, George man, I was also a blacksmith once."

"Ah—once, Peter! But then, though once a blacksmith, you was ever and allus a gen'leman. And me a smith, ever and allus a smith."

"But, confound it, man, Rosemary is a lady and——"

"No, Peter! She be, ever and allus, a blacksmith's lass!"

"She has been splendidly educated."

"Ah, so she has, Peter, a sight too well. Eddication be good so long as it aren't overdone nor go too fur."

"But, my dear George——"

"Lookee, Peter! I be a smith, like my feyther afore me, and theer aren't no smith can ekal me when I be at my best, so I be proud o' being a good smith, proud as any gen'leman can be of his lands or titles, ah—prouder, I think, because what I eats I wins by my labour, Peter, and what I'll be re-membered by, p'raps, when I'm dead and gone, is the work o' these two hands,—like th' owd church screen as you helped me to finish, years ago, Peter."

"Well, George, this is a good, manly pride and altogether admirable, but it should not come between your daughter and my son, the happiness of our children."

"Ay, but, Peter, I be proud o' my Rosemary, prouder o' her than aught i' this world . . . her sweet looks and ways. She be wonderful like her sweet mother sometimes, Peter, though a bit bigger made,—and, well, I be too mortal proud of her to let her be married by any gen'leman, no—not even your son. So, Peter, let's say no more about it."

"But great heavens, George—you cannot dismiss such an affair so lightly or in such confoundedly high-handed fashion."

"Oh? Why not, Peter?"

"Because it is altogether too serious."

"Well, but—I be mortal serious, ah—serious as death!"

"But why on earth are you opposed to such a match?"

"Because my Rosemary be too much my daughter to wed out of her class."

"You are unreasonable, George, utterly unreasonable, and I think very unwise."

"I be what the Lord and my troubles ha' made me, Peter. And I do the best I can."

"But George, old fellow, the Wheel of Life must turn, do what we will to check it. Better then to turn with it, trusting to the Beneficent Power that first set it going."

"Peter, I don't 'ardly get the sense o' that theer."

"Well, George, when we beget children, we liberate forces beyond our conception; we may school them, educate them, set rules and impose laws, but our careful love can guide them only a very little part of the way; beyond that they must, and will, choose their own path."

"You mean up or down—to heaven or hell, Peter?"

"No, I mean to heaven, George, for I believe all paths, though they lead through blackest hell, must climb back to God and salvation . . . at last."

"Well now," said George thoughtfully, "this be a comforting thought, old friend, ay, a turble comforting thought it be . . . myself being, well—no better than I be and my sweet Prue now one o' God's angels and consequently so fur away from me. . . . And to think as I shall reach her again— some day—even through hell. . . . Lord love ee, Peter, 'tis turble heartsome thought if ever I should get took again wi' tearin's an' rages, as I be sometimes still, and more shame to me! So Peter, I be mighty grateful to ee for this thought. But now . . . what's all o' this to do wi' my Rosemary?"

"She's young, George, like my son, and they love each other with a passion that I believe is very deep and pure because it is true. But George, such love denied, being one of the greatest forces of our nature, may work incalculable evil and, instead of blessing, prove a blasting curse."

"Peter, are ye so turble anxious as your gen'leman son shall wed my blacksmith's lass to save 'em from makin' fools o' themselves—or worse?"

Sir Peter leaned back, staring down at his dusty boots and pinching his somewhat prominent chin as was his wont when at all perplexed; at last:

"George," says he, facing round upon his friend, "George, my dear fellow, I have a confession to make. . . . When Dick first told me of this matter, I must admit that I, well—I was as much opposed to this marriage as you are. But when I listened to his wise mother's words and realized this was no boyish infatuation but a man's reverent love, strong and steadfast, why then I knew his choice must be mine also. . . . And now, George, when I see you so much the man you were, though better, of course, and gentled by the years,—here am I, and perhaps a little to my own wonder, very humbly pleading the cause of our children to you and with all my heart—for their sakes, and yours, and—mine."

"How and whyfor . . . yourn, Peter."

"Because to call Black George's child my daughter will be my joy and my honour."

Once more Black George picked up his empty tankard, looked at it and put it down again.

"Honour?" says you. "Honour! My daughter . . . your daughter! Oh, Peter . . . you've said it! For . . . d' ye see, in honouring my Rosemary, you honour the blessed woman as bore her, ah . . . you honour my sweet Prue . . . 'until the morning breaks' . . . And . . . I can't say no more, Peter . . . except . . . yes!" Black George choked, but scorning to hide such emotion from Friendship's eyes, he lifted great head and looking on Peter through his tears, reached forth his two hands.

"And now, Peter," said he, after some while, "come along in; you shall sit in my Prue's own chair and presently we'll drink tea, though I don't much care for the stuff,—but she were powerful fond o' tea . . . peck-ho she used to call it."

CHAPTER X

CONCERNS ITSELF, AMONG OTHER THINGS, WITH KERSEYMERE BREECHES

RICHARD, athrill with vigorous life and the joy of it, galloped his proud Saladin along roads oft travelled of late for he was riding to—HER. In the breast pocket of his coat was the letter written by his beloved mother to this same adored HER, a letter with message of such wise sympathy and loving welcome that as his powerful animal whirled him through the sunny air, young Richard could have shouted for very happiness. And small wonder.

Reaching the confines of Abbeymere, and almost before he knew it, he checked his exuberance and, approaching the tall, iron gates, was surprised to see them shut; so he rang the bell, in response to which summons there now issued from the lodge a comely fellow in neat livery whom he had known these many years and therefore hailed familiarly:

"Good day, Rudge, old fellow! How are you, John?"

"Arternoon, Mr. Vibart, sir!" answered John, unbolting.

"Why must you lock the gates so early, John?"

"Dunno, sir. 'Tis his lordship's orders! no strangers to be admitted this way. But you beant no stranger, sir,—leastways, I s'pose I can let ee in and yet—I dunno. But, Master Richard, sir, I does know one thing!"

"And what's that, John?"

"There be summat up, 'ereabouts."

"Eh? What do you mean?"

"Well, sir, I means as th' owd place be 'aunted. Ah an' small wonder—wot wi' all them old ruins, an' the Mere so black an' gashly as it be! No, I ain't nowise surprised; if goblings and ghosts flit in sich a place, 'tis only to be expected-like. But it does come crool 'ard on me, considering my kerseymere breeches, and them good as noo."

"Why, what's all this of breeches and goblins, John? Just what are you trying to tell me?"

"Well, sir, 'bout three nights agone I seen it first."

"Saw what, John?"

"This here gobling, sir. Went a-flittering acrost the park, it did, and vanished as I watched. Then t'other evening I seen it a-glaring at me from they bushes over agin the wicket gate as leads into Fallowdean Copse! Was you wishful to see Lord Iford, sir, because, if so, 'e ain't in and——"

"No, no, I am here to deliver a letter to—to Miss Ford."

"Ford?" repeated John, scratching his ear thoughtfully. "She be the young governess lady as be along o' my Lady Bedingham and children. Well, sir, she ain't in, neither."

"Oh, confound it! Are you sure, John?"

"Sarten, sir! She be out a-driving wi' her leddyship and children."

"Why then, I'll wait. Will she be long, d' you suppose?"

"Mebbe a hour. Mebbe two. Mebbe arf an hour. Anyways, she'll be back if you waits long enough, sir. Now will ee wait up at th' 'ouse? My lord th' Earl be up and about again, though 'obbling, or will ee set wi' me a piece in me lodge?"

"Thank you, neither. I'll ride round and wait in Fallowdean Copse. Will you tell her she'll find me there?"

"Ay, I'll tell her, Mr. Richard."

"Thanks, John. Let her know the instant she returns, will you?" So saying, Richard, thrust divers coins into John's ready palm and turned his impatient Saladin.

"Why not ride across the park, Mr. Richard; it be a sight nearer."

"But I've plenty of time, deuce take it! And I prefer the open road and lanes, John. My respects to Mrs. Rudge."

Richard nodded, gave Saladin his head, and away they went with thud of flying hoof and creak of leather, and both of them enjoying it like the high-spirited, vigorous young animals they were, though to be sure Richard's joyous exuberance was somewhat damped. Reaching the coppice, and all too soon, he dismounted, left Saladin to crop the grass, stepped into the leafy shade and looked round about upon this secluded spot hallowed by memories of the beloved SHE destined to his love and care . . . some day. Moved by such very loverlike thoughts he came beneath "her tree" and drew off his gauntlet to touch its rugged bole with bare hand for her dear sake and was deliberating just where he should kiss it when his senses were startled and outraged by a hissing whisper almost in his ear:

"Must' Richard! Oh, Master Dick!"

"Deuce take you, Tom! Confound it all!" he exclaimed, peering angrily about. "Where the devil are you now?"

"Why here, sir, for sure!" And from fissure in this same great tree a bright eye peered forth at him. "This be one o' my earths, Mus' Richard! 'tis here as I roosts frequent . . . But your young leddy, sir."

"Yes, yes—what of her, Tom lad—what?"

"Well I aren't sure but there be summat up. I seen 'er a-wipin' of 'er pretty eye 's mornin'! And th' Earl be afoot and about again, dannel 'im!"

"Crying, was she? Good God! Why? What for?"

"And that theer Clipsby allus a-creepin' an' a-crawlin'——"

"Clipsby? The Earl's valet fellow?"

"Ar,—'im! Sir, 'e were a-watchin' of you an' 'er last time as you met here, a-'arkin' an' a-listenin', 'e were."

"Was he, damn him!"

"Ar, 'e were so, sure-ly. I meant to tell an' warn ee, only you galloped off so sudden-like."

"But Tom . . . oh, curse it! Why should she weep, eh, man, eh?"

"Well, your honour, women critters all do, it be so their natur'——"

"Yes, but not hers, no—not hers. Weeping? Oh, damnation! Where was she, Tom?"

"Well, sir, she were a-sittin'—listen, sir! Hark . . . yonder! Some one comes a-creepin'! Lay low!"

Sure enough, Richard heard a vague stir of movement, a stealthy rustle of leaves subsiding now and then, as if the unseen prowler had halted, the better to use eyes and ears. Instinctively Richard became stealthy also and stepping behind the great tree, crouched there, gazing in the direction of these approaching sounds.

And after some while, out from the denser boskage stepped that negative personality called Clipsby. For a moment he stood utterly still, glancing hither and thither with a furtive expectancy; then two powerful hands whirled him about and his pale eyes were blinking at Richard's scowling, young face.

"Damned rat! You'll spy, will you?" demanded Richard, shaking him fiercely. "Peep and pry, will you? Get out before I harm you!" Then Richard hurled him aside so violently that he tripped and fell, lying a moment as if dazed, then he arose, smoothed and reordered his garments with care, which done, he stood a moment utterly still and with bowed head, gazing at Richard from the corners of his eyes; then, speechless still, he turned and crept away. And when all sound of his retreat had hushed to silence, Richard was again startled and this time to find Tom Lethbridge at his elbow.

"Dammit, Tom!" he exclaimed, "You move like a ghost. By George, I believe he's coming back again and in a hurry too—hide, man, hide!" Even as he spoke, Tom had vanished swift and silently as he had appeared, for again was a rustling loud and louder. . . . Richard leapt forward with joyful exclamation for the vision that suddenly blessed his yearning eyes was Rosemary.

For a moment they gazed upon each other, mute and scarce breathing, then, Richard, forgetting all in the world save Rosemary, had her in his arms. . . . But presently, flushed and tremulous from his kisses, she held him away to look deep into his joyful eyes.

"Richard . . . oh, my dear," she whispered, "you—told them. Your dear, wonderful mother writes me she is . . . glad! Calls me . . . her daughter,—me! She is coming herself to fetch me on Thursday morning, driving over in state . . . for me! She herself . . . to take me . . . oh, Richard, how I do love her! And she calls me . . . daughter!"

"I know!" said Richard, kissing those sweet, tearful eyes, "I know! Oh, Rosemary, isn't life glorious?"

"She says we are to have a—real marriage . . . A great affair . . . and in London!"

"Yes! That's the frightful part of it, of course!"

"Frightful?" exclaimed Rosemary, falling into another rapture. "It's just . . . wonderful!"

"Wonderful?" he repeated. "To be compelled to wait until October——?"

"And she wants me with her, Dick, to arrange things . . . imagine it!"

"Yes, to scheme out dresses and what not, giggling bridesmaids and a crowd of fools to stare at us! I say again it's simply perfectly damn frightful!"

"It's just . . . heavenly, Richard!"

"Why do you—good Lord, Rosemary,—do you actually mean to say that you really want all this fearful fuss and confounded botheration—you?"

"Want it, Dick?" she sighed, clasping hands in a very transport. "My darling, I tremble with joy at the mere thought! It seems too wonderful it could ever happen to poor me! Your lovely mother, how I do adore her!"

"Well," quoth Richard, shaking youthful head, "upon my soul, Rosemary, I thought you were above such things!"

"Your dear mother might have told you that all women——"

"She did, she did; but I thought—well, that you were different——"

"But I'm not, Dick. I'm simply just a very female she creature and so— why, whatever are you scowling at so terribly?"

"This!" he answered and, from where it had lain concealed in the grass, he picked up a pistol, a small, beautifully wrought weapon mounted with silver, very handsome and very deadly.

"Yes," nodded Rosemary, "I dropped it."

"You? But it belongs to Abbeymere, the Earl; here is his crest and monogram."

"Well, it's a hateful thing,—put it down!"

"And . . . by God, it's loaded! Rosemary, how did you come by this damnable thing?"

"It was this morning, Dick. I was sitting alone in the arbour, arranging the children's lessons for the day, when Mr. Clipsby came to me——"

"That fellow!"

"Yes, Dick. And he seems such a very solitary, unhappy man that I feel sorry for him. He appeared greatly distressed this morning, but then he always is, and he began by talking about flowers and how cruel to pick them——"

"Flowers!" snorted Richard.

"He knows a great deal about botany, Dick; indeed he is very clever and a wonderful musician——"

"The fellow's a sneaking spy! Did he give you the weapon?"

"Richard, I'll tell you all about it—if you'll allow me. Well then, Mr. Clipsby went on to tell me that Rudge the lodgekeeper had warned him there were rough characters lurking about, burglars perhaps. And then, Dick, he showed me this pistol and told me to keep it by me and fire it off, if anything should happen to frighten me, and so went hurrying away and left the hateful thing before I could prevent. So I brought it along, hoping to meet him and return it."

"Hum!" quoth Richard, frowning down at the pistol. "Do you know how to fire it?"

"Why, of course! I often shot off Grandfather Simon's old horse pistol; you remember it used to hang by the fireplace in the 'Bull.' What a terrible tomboy child I was! I shot a rabbit once, poor thing! A nasty, wild creature I was in those days!"

"But always beautiful—and with your glorious hair—and afraid of nothing, I used to think."

"And then your dear mother sent me to be tamed at the Academy——"

"And now you are going to marry me——"

"In—October, Richard."

"Ha, well! Meantime, I'll take care of this," said Richard thrusting the pistol into his coat-pocket.

And presently they rose and wandered through the little wood, talking together murmurously, pausing frequently to look at each other, to kiss suddenly and wander on again until, turning aside haphazard into a glade, they came upon Abbeymere's Earl looming very large though seated lowly upon a fallen tree. At sight of them, he flourished his hat in wide-armed gesture of greeting and hailed them in his throatiest, heartiest tones:

"Corydon and Phyllis, I salute ye! Happy Daphnis and sly, witching Chloe, be welcome!"

Richard returned this salutation a little stiffly, Rosemary clung tighter to his arm and averting her eyes, breathed distressfully.

"Oho, Youth!" bellowed the Earl jovially. "Aha, Love! Of what avail bolts and bars 'gainst such combination? My gates are locked yet Love comes stealing in! And b'gad, why not? My bold Daphnis, sweet-sly Chloe, creep ye away again where ye may kiss and fondle unseen and may roguish Cupidon bless ye,—away and leave myself to sit and envious sigh——"

"My lord!" exclaimed Richard, then flushed hotly, grew awkward and strangely abashed before this so experienced libertine's meaning looks and throaty chucklings. Then, clapping on his hat, "My lord," said he again, heedless of the pleading hand upon his arm, "here is neither slyness nor secrecy."

"My dear Richard, I do not reproach," chuckled the Earl. "No, no, lad, far from it,—I envy. Love is a sweet sweet, slyly sly and should be! The drooping lash, the conscious blush, the breathless denial, the tender, imploring——"

"Sir," cried Richard, diffidence and awkwardness swept away by quick, fierce anger, "I came to Abbeymere with a letter from my mother——"

"The bewitching Lady Vibart,—oho, for me?"

"No, sir, for Miss Ford who . . . who will shortly do me the honour . . . who is going to marry me."

"What . . . another of you?" chuckled the Earl. "B'gad, quite a remarkable coincidence, odd—deuced odd and queer!"

"How so, my lord?"

"Well, d' ya see, my son Iford assured me, and very recently, that this same so alluring tantalization, Miss Rosemary, is going to marry him."

"Then, sir, he was probably drunk."

"Oh, he was, Richard, he was, of course. But then, my dear boy, Iford drunk develops certain latent powers, a cool intrepidity and surprising assurance and determination that makes me know him for my son. And, like his sire, he has a true eye for beauty, a choice palate for succulencies feminine— so suffer this coy, shrinking loveliness to explain how one may wed two? Miss Rosemary, how say ya?"

"Sir," began Richard passionately, but Rosemary's smooth, clear voice silenced him:

"Surely, my lord, such idle question needs no answer. Pray, Richard, will you come away now or must I go alone?"

So saying, she turned and moved off and Richard perforce went too and with the Earl's throaty merriment ringing in his ears.

"A beastly old villain!" fumed Richard, when they had gone some distance. "He is, as you said, all evil. Yes, I know exactly what you meant now. By heaven, he's even viler than I imagined! Damn him, he makes me feel unclean, somehow. . . . My Rosemary, you sha'n't stay near him another hour; you shall come back home with me."

"But I can't, Dick, I've so much to do first . . . then there's Lady Bedingham and the children; besides, your dear mother is coming for me on Thursday."

"Yes, but . . . that beast! Rosemary, he's the sort of thing I could shoot joyfully! Somebody ought to murder him——"

"Hush, Dick, hush! My dear love . . . don't, ah, don't say such fearful things."

"Well then, come back with me, Rosemary,—now, this moment! Come home . . . to my mother."

"Ah, no, Dick! Dear, it would just spoil everything. Can't you see? Your mother is coming for me on Thursday—for me! Only a few hours really, dear boy. Ah, now don't frown on me! I shall be all right. I don't fear any one or anything any more—not now! No, not even—him! And I'm not alone; there is Lady Bedingham and Mr. Clipsby and——"

"Clipsby!" snorted Richard, "I tell you, Rosemary, the fellow's a sneaking spy, a rat——"

"And yet he seems the gentlest, saddest creature and so much to be pitied . . . except when he plays Beethoven—then he's—oh, wonderful! . . . And there's Saladin waiting for you under our old tree. Will you let me ride him sometimes?"

"Of course, dear Heart, I'll give him to you if you like, or you shall have the pick of the stables; there's a little black mare I've thought will just suit you. . . . Ah, but Rosemary, I don't want to leave you—here!"

"Oh, but you must!" she answered with her gentle though indomitable look. "Only for a few hours, Richard dear. I am just only living for Thursday, and you! Please give my love to your mother and say I can never thank her in words. . . . Good-bye for a little while, my own Richard! Oh, I am the proudest, happiest creature in the whole world!"

CHAPTER XI

WHICH GIVES PARTICULARS OF A FATEFUL NIGHT

RICHARD'S mother having thus made up his father's mind to the match and arranged Richard's affairs thus happily, it followed as a matter of course that Richard, being young and therefore impatient, a lover and therefore very human, immediately plagued himself with new anxieties.

First there was this, to wit: The dreadful possibility that by some frightful cataclysm, some terrific convulsion of nature, Thursday might never dawn. Secondly, when, somewhat reassured by the fact that the old Earth, having rolled on for so many eons of time, might in all probability continue so to roll,—there rose within him a slow-writhing, sickening fear that lifted envenomed head, like loathly serpent, to hiss the nameless evils that might beset HER, this peerless maid of his reverent worship, at the vile hands of Abbeymere's Earl. . . . This cold-eyed, middle-aged rake anent whom were whispered tales so shameless that Richard, lying wakeful, must start up in his bed, sweating in shivering horror. . . . Tales he had heard and laughed at ere now. And remembering how he had laughed and why, Richard clenched fierce hands, wishing with all his powers that certain wild escapades of his own might be wiped from his soul and forgotten. He was unworthy,—therefore, if indeed Thursday should never dawn, it would be but justice. . . .

It was upon this fateful night that, driven well-nigh frantic by such thoughts, Richard leapt from his bed of torment and dressed, impelled by wild and desperate purpose.

It was upon this night also that Sir Peter, on his way to bed, peering by chance from certain window to behold the night's pale beauty, for the moon was wonderfully bright, stood suddenly rigid with surprise, made to call out, checked the impulse, closed the window instead; and presently, booted and spurred, yet light of foot, went hurrying stablewards.

It was also upon this thrice fateful night that my lord, the Earl of Abbeymere, having dismissed that pallid negation named Clipsby, took a lighted lantern and, limping by devious ways, came at last to a small, ancient door set deep within a frowning arch of time-worn masonry, and unlocking this door, stood, lantern aloft, gazing upon a shape of loveliness that, leaping from narrow bed, retreated to the far wall and leaned there, blinking painfully in the sudden light. . . . And meeting the Earl's look, the gloating menace of these narrow eyes, fear and shame were swept away by a dreadful valour and desperate resolution that found words in awful whisper hissed between set white teeth:

"Go back! I have a pistol here. . . . Go back or by the dear God, I'll be your death!"

The Earl, unfearing now as ever, chuckled throatily and went to her. . . .

Meanwhile Sir Peter, greatly wondering and a little anxious, rode through the uncertain light with due care for his horse's knees, and thus at his leisure arrived at a pair of tall, wrought-iron gates and, finding them shut for the night, groped instinctively for the bell pull, hesitated, fell to a muse and finally turning his animal, rode along by the high park wall, peering here and there among the denser shadows until he espied a horse tethered at a place where the wall was low and easier to climb; and riding near, he saw, as he had expected, that this horse was Saladin. So Sir Peter sat a while, chin in hand, staring at this riderless horse. At last he dismounted, fastened his own animal, glanced about, almost furtively and frowning as with distaste, swung himself very nimbly astride this wall and, after a momentary hesitation, dropped lightly on the farther side. Then he set off, walking rapidly, until stark against the sinking moon rose the wide, scowling frontage of Abbeymere, gable and chimney, battlement and turret. . . . Sir Peter halted to listen and stare at this great house that, to his fancy, had always seemed to menace him with threat of hidden evil, but never so direly as in this present hushed and solemn hour.

It was a still, windless night and luminous with the pallid radiance of a dying moon that lit small, fitful fires in the sedgy waters of the dark Mere; that showed, beyond motionless trees, ghostly peep of the ruined Abbey with the jagged outline of the great house itself looming vague and monstrous, with no spark of light in all its many windows,—an ominous sprawling shape that yet drew him on and on across wide lawns and up dim steps until, turning a sharp angle, he beheld a window whence streamed a warm glow; now this window gaped wide open.

So thither went he and, peering within this lighted room, caught his breath and stood appalled,—for the dreadful menace of this house was fulfilled at last and so terribly that Sir Peter saw his world with all his hopes and lofty ambitions crash to irretrievable ruin.

Then, somehow, he was in the room, staring with awful eyes into eyes as awful that stared back at him; speechless, he gazed from his son's pallid face down at the contorted, blood-smeared thing that lay between them, this dead man that, sprawled thus, bulked larger in death than ever be had done in life. And with his gaze on this, Sir Peter spoke in groaning whisper:

"Great God! Oh, Richard—Richard—how was this?"

"Father! . . . Sir, I—hardly know. He . . . oh, but he deserved death . . . worse . . . and,—well, he is dead—dead you see, but—ah—so ghastly!" The pistol he still clutched in shaking hands Sir Peter took gently, saw it blackened by recent discharge and laid it gently on the table. Then, clasped in his father's protecting arm, Richard looked up and, seeing revealed at last all the passion of love in this twitching, haggard face, uttered a great, gasping sob and bowed his head on his father's breast while, for a moment, his young arms clasped and clung yearningly; then he stepped back, saw his father's hand gesture toward that sprawling horror, heard his faint whisper:

"Richard?" The word was a question.

"Yes, sir—yes!" he answered and, with agony in his own eyes, watched the despair this answer wrought.

"You did not—mean to do it?"

"No! No! God knows I didn't, sir."

"His own pistol, Richard!"

"Yes, sir. Yes, I . . . we . . . he made to shoot and I . . . we struggled and . . . sir, what must I do? Will you—shall I ring the bell—alarm the house?" And Richard turned, reaching towards the silver table bell.

"No! No!" gasped Sir Peter, checking him with a wild, vehement movement. "Come home! And . . . you may still call me 'father,' Richard. I am more your father than ever . . . now. Let us go!" Mutely obedient, Richard crossed towards the window.

"But . . . these candles, Father?"

"Leave them . . . alight. . . . And you are forgetting your hat, Richard." Fumbling it clumsily, Richard took up his hat and came to the window.

"Richard, you have dropped your gauntlet!"

Richard took up the fallen glove and stood aside that his father might precede him through the window.

"You first, dear lad!" So Richard stepped forth into the cool night but drew something very stealthily from his pocket and, turning to close the window after his father, contrived to drop that something into the room.

"Never mind the window, Richard,—come!"

And so, swift, silent and mute, more like flitting shades than living men, they went together—away through the deepening shadows. . . .

But in the great, silent house behind them, after some while, was sound of somewhat unsteady footsteps and a voice, a little uncertain, crooning a song; and the words these:

> "Oh—the best of all ways
> For to lengthen our days
> Is to steal a few hours from the night, boys——

Then the door of that death chamber swung open and Lord Iford stood on the threshhold, slim, elegant and slightly drunk as usual.

"Aha—lights!" quoth he. "You're not yet in bed then, worthy sire? Good! For 'the best of all ways to lengthen our days is—'" the crooning voice was suddenly dumb, the lounging, swaying figure steadied, grew tense and utterly still. Then, very deliberately, Lord Iford stepped into the room; slowly he approached and standing above that awful, sprawling shape, looked down into the large blood-spattered visage with strangely impersonal curiosity. Now as he stood lost in this cold and passionless contemplation he seemed, in some indefinable manner, to take on size and stature. And presently, his golden head still downbent, his blue eyes still fixed in this same terrible, wholly untroubled scrutiny, he addressed this ghastly thing, speaking in gentle monotone:

"So, my lord, there you are at last! The death you have invited so frequently and merited so long, has you at last! A violent, ugly death and yet —very swift . . . in a moment of time! Yet my little mother, the gentle creature you killed, died slowly—inch by inch—through long, weary years—

and you—in an instant! So mercifully! Is this justice? I wonder!" He shivered suddenly and the guttering candles flickered in sudden breath of night wind through the open window, and glancing thither, he beheld that which lay there and, crossing the floor with soundless, unhurried steps, he picked up a handkerchief and saw in one corner, deftly embroidered, the initials R.V.

With this in his hand, Lord Iford came back to stare down again into the marred face and at the contorted form with keen, questioning eyes, as if the dead might yet tell him something. Then he sank upon his knee and, in the same emotionless, deliberate way, grasped the stiffening arm, jerked it, pulled it until from beneath that inert bulk he had drawn the clenched right hand; then with soft yet fierce imprecation, he glanced up and round about this silent death chamber with eyes that, questing to and fro, held a wild and fearful horror at last, as, muttering savagely, he drew from these dead, clutching fingers something that he stared at with the same fearful horror, something that he folded as it had been some holy relic and thrust into his bosom.

Then uttering whispered yet frightful imprecation, he leapt up and for a moment seemed as he would stamp and trample the dead beneath vengeful, merciless feet; instead, he crossed to the door, softly closed it, locked it and removing his tight-fitting coat, became very dreadfully busy.

And when this work was accomplished to his entire satisfaction, Lord Iford donned his coat, adjusted hair and cravat delicately before a mirror and unlocking and opening the door, tugged at that bell which, as he knew, rang in Jasper Clipsby's bedroom. After no great lapse of time, his quick ears caught the faint shuffle of approaching feet, fingers tapped softly on the half-open door, then Lord Iford spoke:

"Come in, Clipsby, my father is dead! See here, man, see here!"

A strangled, wailing cry and the shape that had entered the room so quietly shrank back and back to the panelled wall and crouched there, dumb and with staring eyes, fixed and glaring.

"Shocks you, does it, Clipsby? And no wonder! Pretty ghastly! Slumped in the chair so—and still at his wine! And the pistol—see where it dropped from his dying fingers,—here beneath his dangling hand. . . . Look, and the rug beneath his chair—soaked! Must have done it an hour ago, at least, eh, Clipsby? Last man in the world to have killed—himself, eh, Clipsby? Suicide! Amazing! Wake the servants! Rouse the house! Suicide—eh, Clipsby? Astonishing! Stir, man, stir!"

CHAPTER XII

CONCERNS ITSELF WITH A HUSBAND—AND A WIFE

THEY had reached home, the father and son; they stood fronting each other in the dim light of the single candle Richard had lit at the dying fire, and surely never did candle show two more haggard, careworn faces.

"Oh, Father," whispered Richard at last: "it is awful to think—of it—lying there—waiting to be found——"

"Richard—Richard," gasped Sir Peter, covering his face; "it is more awful to think of the consequences to . . . my dear son! Though an accident, yet the world will call it . . . murder. And all my hopes for you . . . my dreams . . . Oh, God help—God teach me how to save him—my boy—my son!" The stately form was bowed, shaken by wild passion of grief; through those clutching fingers tears fell sparkling; and in this dreadful moment Richard saw this austere father of his with a new vision and, feeling the deep sanctity of the kinship that knit them, clasped this father that had so awed him hitherto, hugged him in quick, yearning arms and, agonized with filial love and pity, strove desperately to soothe and comfort.

"Father . . . dear Father, I never dreamed you could love me so . . . never dared think it——"

"Seemed I so remote then, boy? It is sometimes a pain to show my feelings . . . yet you might have guessed! I would give my life for you, Richard."

"I know it now, Father, oh, I know it. I've grown a man to-night. And in that ghastly moment you bade me . . . call you 'Father!' This memory will keep me strong. . . . And Father, for your comfort, believe me no vile . . . intentional murderer. Think the best of me. Oh, believe that I . . . I am to do what you would do . . . trying, before God, to be worthy of you and my dear . . . mother——"

"Ah—your mother!" gasped Sir Peter. "How shall I tell her? What shall I tell her——"

"Everything, Father. Or shall I? Shall we go up to her—now?"

"No, let her sleep. We will tell her to-morrow . . . in the morning. Get you to bed now, Richard, to bed and try to sleep—go!"

"Yes, but you, Father?"

"I shall sit here awhile. Go to bed, dear lad, I want to be alone."

A clock ticked loud in the stillness; a small night wind sighed mournfully; the solitary candle made of the wide chamber a cold and shadowy desolation, but still the forlorn shape huddled in the great elbowchair moved not, the haggard eyes gazed steadfastly at the grey ashes of the dead fire while, for this grieving father, Hope, that thrice blessed Spirit, very nearly died too:

But

in this moment of black despair came sweet and merciful respite. A door opened softly, small slippers brushed the carpet, trailing draperies whispered —and so came Charmian. Her face in its small, coquettishly-belaced night-cap, was rosy with sleep, her deep eyes slumberous as, pausing beside his chair, she yawned behind a finger, then:

"Goodness—me!" she exclaimed. "So cold, Peter! So lonely! And the dratted fire out, of course! I woke up and was lonely, so I came to find you and now—" she yawned again and as she did so, Sir Peter slowly lifted heavy head and looked at her. . . . My lady's teeth snapped the yawn in two (as it were) and she was down before him on her knees, had gathered him to the comfort and shelter of her arms.

"My love . . . dear husband!" she murmured. "What is it? To sit here and agonize all alone! How dare you? What grieves you so, my Peter,—there, there now—tell me!"

And with face hidden against her fragrant loveliness, he told her.

And when the dreadful tale was ended, they clung together for a while, neither speaking.

"Dead!" she whispered at last. "The Earl dead . . . and so dreadfully!"

"By accident, Charmian! It was an accident . . . but . . . by Richard's hand . . . our Richard!" groaned Sir Peter, lifting his head wearily and sinking back in the chair.

"By . . . Richard's hand!" she repeated, folding her arms on Sir Peter's knees and looking up into his face with eyes troubled as his own. "Our Richard! Are you sure—quite sure?"

"He told me so himself!"

"Where is he?"

"I sent him to bed."

"Poor boy, he is better there! Peter, did you hear the shot?"

"No."

"And yet, oh, my dear, you look as if that shot might kill you too, you look so wounded, dear heart—hurt."

"I am, my Charmian. He was my son, my hope . . ."

"And is still, Peter."

"My son, yes. God help him!"

"Peter, I want you to tell me all over again. I want you to describe exactly what you saw when you entered that awful room."

"No, no, it was too—horrible!"

"Please! You must, Peter, you shall! I insist! Every single thing—everything, no matter how trivial it may seem. Now—tell me!"

Sir Peter raised hand to furrowed brow, and seeing how pitifully this strong hand trembled, she could have wept but would not.

"Peter, tell me! You must!"

And so, presently, Sir Peter obeyed her, of course.

"The Earl was lying on his back . . . in a strangely contorted attitude——"

"Contorted how, Peter?"

"Very unnaturally . . . with one arm twisted under him . . . I don't quite understand how he could have fallen so."

"Where was Richard?"

"Crouching over him . . . staring down at him . . . and the pistol in his hand."

"Did he tell you he had shot the Earl; did he say he had shot him, and how?"

"Yes—no . . ."

"What do you mean, Peter?"

"That he . . . suggested it."

"But didn't say so, positively?"

"No, not—not positively."

"Can you remember his actual words?"

"No, I'm afraid not, I was too distressed——"

"Then so far as you recollect, he said the Earl threatened him, they struggled for the pistol and it went off——"

"Yes, Charmian."

"You didn't stay there long, of course?"

"No, I hurried our boy away."

"You heard no sound—footsteps or voices?"

"Nothing."

"Were there any—bloodstains on—on Richard?"

"None that I could see."

"And then, as you told me at first, Peter, you left by the window. Did Richard seem greatly troubled?"

"Terribly! Terribly! He seemed sick, physically ill. His looks were wild, very desperate . . . he even suggested ringing the bell to alarm the house——"

"Did he, Peter—oh, I wonder why! That was madness unless—I wonder?" Here, crouched against her husband's knees, she bowed her head and seemed lost in deep and troublous perplexity. And at the windows was a pale glimmer that was dawn.

"So," she murmured, "he would have—roused the house?" That means he was willing to—give himself up! Oh, Peter! Peter! I've an idea! If only my guess prove true—how we will thank God!"

"Why, Charmian—my dearest, what——"

"Hush, Peter! Tell me, did our boy do anything else that seemed odd . . . or strange? Did he?"

"Why, no. To be sure, he would have forgotten his hat, but considering his state of mind——"

"His—hat, Peter?"

"Yes, dear. I was hurrying him away——"

"And—oh, Peter—he tried to leave his hat,——"

"He was forgetting it, and no wonder, considering——"

"Yes, dear, yes! What else did this son of ours leave?"

"Nothing. Though I remember he dropped his glove——"

"Then his glove! Which you picked up?"

"No, I made him. But—" Sir Peter gasped and stared amazed for, with gesture of joyous exultation, Charmian threw wide her shapely arms, smiling up into her husband's sorrowful, careworn face with a very glory in her eyes.

"Oh, my Richard, my darling!" she murmured. "Smile, Peter, laugh rejoice, ah—thank God for our son! No, no—I am not mad; only sure that I'm right! Yes, I know I'm right! Kiss me, beloved husband, stoop and let me kiss you for giving me such a son . . . as brave and self-sacrificing as his own father! And look, look! To prove I'm right,—there's the dawn, a new day, Peter! 'Though sorrow endure for a night yet joy cometh in the morning'—so kiss me, my blind, dear love that must break his heart when he should rejoice,—kiss me, my poor, sorrowful child, then let us go and wake our son and tell him we've found him out."

"But . . . but," stammered Sir Peter, "Oh, Charmian, my dear, who—what——"

Then, seating herself on her husband's knees, Charmian kissed his tired eyes, smoothed and patted his thick, dark hair and, tenderly murmurous, patiently explained:

"My own Peterman, in that awful day when your cousin Maurice lay murdered in the Hollow and I nearly dead with fear, you took the pistol from my hand and went out all alone to face shame and death for the woman you loved. But Heaven's mercy gave you back to me and in time God gave us a child that has grown into a man so like his dear father that to-day he would do the same—shielding the woman he loves with his life, fronting disgrace and death, because he loves as his noble father loved before him. So, husband, let us kneel and thank God for our Richard."

"Then—you mean—he is innocent—our Richard?"

"Why, of course he is. He suggested ringing the bell to alarm the house. He tried to leave his hat and then his glove! And why do you suppose—why? Are these the acts of terrified guilt? No, Peter—no! Oh, can't you see, this was to divert suspicion to himself . . . to shield one dearer to him than life! I tell you our Richard is guiltless as yourself, Peter. I feel it! I know it!"

"Then, my Charmian, truly do I thank God with all my heart for him and—for you! Oh, Charmian, how I adore you . . . worship you——"

"Ah, my dear," she retorted, laughing and crying together, "how sweetly fulsome you are and—how I love it!"

"But," said Sir Peter, after a lapse, "if Dick is wilfully running such terrible risk, why—then——?"

"Ah, yes," sighed my lady, "what—oh, what of our poor Rosemary? For she is ours now, Peter dear, ours to cherish. Richard has made her so."

"Yes!" sighed Sir Peter. "So then I must go to her, now—at once, Charmian."

"We will both go to her—after breakfast, dear heart, and bring her back with us, no matter what has——"

Charmian stooped suddenly and both turned at sound of a rapping on the windowpane; and thus they saw it was day, the sun's level beams making a glory all about them. They saw also a white head at the window, a wrinkled face peering in at them.

"Why, it's Adam! Whatever can he want, Peter?"

Together they rose and opened the window, whereupon Adam, this ancient man, Sir Peter's head groom and privileged by long years of service, knuckled an eyebrow and looked from one to other, his old eyes very wistful and anxious.

"Sir, an' m' leddy," quoth he, holding out a letter, "I were to give ye this my own self, an' I do 'ope as the dear lad, axing pardon, Master Richard, aren't in no manner o' trouble like." So he gave Sir Peter the letter, watching with the same wistful anxiety while the parents read together these hastily scrawled words:

My ever loved Mother and Father,

He deserved worse death but in this law-ridden country I think it best, all things considered, to vanish, running away like any shameful coward and yet only to prove myself more worthily your son and in my shame prouder than ever of my noble father and beloved mother. And so, my dears, believing that in your hearts you will have faith in me, despite everything, to know that what is done, being done, what I do is for the best. I am

> now and always
> Your grateful, loving son

> > RICHARD.

"And here is proof beyond all doubting!" said Charmian, kissing this hastily scribbled letter.

"Then—Master Richard has gone, Adam?" enquired Sir Peter.

"Yes, sir. Throwed a pebble up at me windy, 'e did, an' wuk me up."

"How long ago?"

" 'Bout two—three hours ago, afore peep o' day, sir."

"Did he ride Saladin?"

"Ah, no, sir,—went afoot, 'e did, ay an' wi' a stick and knapsack jest the same as you done, sir, twenty-odd year ago. You'll mind that mornin', Sir Peter, peep o' day 'twere then, I mind, and you comes to bid good-bye to your 'oss 'Wings' an' me. Give ye a pipe, I did, sir, a nigger's-'ead pipe and sweet as a nut. . . . Didn't give nothing to Master Dick, I didn't. But Lord, 'e give me no time for nowt. 'Adam', says 'e, playful an' yet sadlike, 'Old Adam,' says 'e, 'give this letter to my father and mother with your own 'and,' says 'e,—chucks it up to me through the windy an' then, 'Good-bye, Old Adam,' says 'e, 'my love to everybody,' an' away 'e goes, sir, an' the world all dark, nary glimp o' dawn. . . . I do 'ope, sir an' ma'm, as—" Old Adam paused and glanced over bowed shoulder as borne to them on the fresh sunny air came a rhythmic throb of approaching hoofs. And presently up the stately avenue rode a horseman, at sight of whom Charmian shrank back, uttering a little cry, while Sir Peter stepped forth upon the terrace somewhat hastily, for this early visitor was Lord Iford, himself as trim and debonair as the glossy steed he bestrode, no sign upon his Lordship of this so very fateful night.

"Good morning, Sir Peter!" said he, reining up and taking off his hat; Sir Peter bowed. "I came over thus early, sir, seeing you are our nearest neighbour, to tell you that the Earl my father is dead. Between the hours, as we judge, of eleven and twelve last night, sir, he committed suicide."

"Suicide!" murmured Sir Peter, his pale face showing little of the chaotic feeling that surged within him. "My dear Iford . . . you surprise me."

"I am surprised myself, sir," answered his lordship, shaking his sleek, blond head; "many others will, I think, be surprised also, for my father, sir, as I

fancy you'll agree, was or seemed the very last person in the world to murder
—himself. However, the fact remains. I am on my way to acquaint Squire
Golightly and Sir Percy Merrick——"

"Will you step in a while, Iford?"

"No, I thank you, sir, I'll be going. . . . Oh, by the way, sir, is Richard
about?"

"No."

"Then it doesn't matter, sir. I merely wish to return something that I fancy
must be his property," and from his pocket Lord Iford drew a handkerchief,
stained, here and there, with dreadful splotches. "It is marked R.V., Sir
Peter, Richard's initials, of course. Rather gruesome, I fear," said he, placing
the handkerchief on the broad balustrade of the terrace. "Yes, rather
horrid!" he nodded. "I found it beside my honoured sire's corpse. Good
morning, Sir Peter; pray, my humble regards to Lady Vibart!" Then, with
graceful gesture of hat, Lord Iford rode away, leaving Sir Peter staring down
at that betraying handkerchief with eyes of horror and face more haggard
than ever.

CHAPTER XIII

TELLETH HOW RICHARD BEGAN HIS PILGRIMAGE

HUDDLED disconsolate upon a stile, Richard watched the sun rise upon a
creation new and strange, a world indeed that was for him a bleak desolation,
a place of so much dust and ashes.

But in this black hour of hopelessness and despair, he remembered his
mother's teaching and so, being thus desperate, Richard bowed his sorrowful
young head and prayed.

Now though the Comfort of Prayer be diminished and somewhat out of
fashion in these bustling, brainy days yet, once upon a time, great and mighty
souls were wont to pray naturally as they breathed: A Man of Sorrows by
dusty highways, on lonely mountain top and above a sleeping city, Cranmer
amid the agony of searing flame. And as such prayers (let doubt who will)
can never go unanswered, as witness: The Enduring Miracle of Calvary; the
stark, scarce, almost incredible heroism of the martyrs;—so, when Richard
lifted his head, the world seemed brighter, the kindly sun warmer and his
loneliness not so grievous; for when presently, climbing the stile, he plodded
on again, there went beside him now the unseen Angel of Hope.

It was as he paused on a tree-clad slope to look hence upon the little
hamlet sheltering snugly beneath the Down that from the woodlands behind
him stole a whistle very soft yet clear as note of blackbird, a summons long
familiar; therefore he turned and peering into the wood's pleasant twilight
called softly:

"Tom! Oh, Tom lad, are you there?"

"Me own self, Must' Dick!" And from a thicket remote from where
Richard was looking, appeared the stalwart form of Tom Lethbridge.

"What are you doing hereabouts, Tom?"

"Well, sir, arter wot 'appened last night, I——"

"Ah,—you know of it, then?"

"Ay, summat, sir. So I slips over to the Manor to find ee an' when Adam tells me as you'm off an' away, I guesses as mebbe you'll mek for Lon'on an' by country ways, so I follered and, well—'ere I be."

"And what now, Tom?"

"Why now, sir, I be tekkin' sarvice wi' you, Must' Dick."

"No, no,—impossible!"

"Why then—you for Lon'on, me for Lon'on,—jest for comp'ny's sake, sir."

"But I don't know that I shall go to London."

"Well, anywheres as you say 'll soot me, sir. Hows'ever, seein' as things be as they be, I aren't a-goin' to let ee go alone, sir."

"Nonsense, man."

"Lookee now, Must' Dick, you be lonesome and I be mortal lonesome so —why not be lonesome together? Come now, Mr. Richard sir, don't ee go for to be 'arsh an' me sich a pore, friendless sort o' chap; don't ee!"

"Well, first," sighed Richard, sinking dejectedly upon the springy turf, "sit down, Tom,—here beside me. Now tell me what you know about . . . last night—anything—all—everything you chanced to . . . hear or see."

Tom being seated, plucked a nodding scabious flower, chewed the stem, stared at the sky, the wood behind them, the wide valley below, anywhere but at anxious Richard who, growing impatient. questioned him again:

"Confound it! Can't you answer, Tom? Speak, man, speak! Did you hear . . . see . . . anything at Abbeymere last night, did you?"

"Ay, I did, sir."

"Well, speak out, man! Tell me—what was it you heard?"

"A shot, sir."

"The . . . shot, Tom?"

"Ar! The shot, your honour."

"Where were you, Tom?"

"Pretty nigh th' Abbey ruins, sir."

"You could hardly have heard it from there."

"Ay, but I did, Must' Richard, very plain,—it seemed to come from they gashly ruins, it did."

"Impossible, Tom! The Earl was . . . was killed in the house . . . the library."

"Sir, it sounded to me like 'twere in they ruins."

"Well, I suppose sound travels far on such a still night."

"Mebbe, sir."

"And . . . what did you . . . see?" Once again Tom stared at earth and sky and chewed silently at the scabious stem so long that Richard, eyeing his troubled face apprehensively, put the question more directly:

"Did you see . . . me, Tom?"

"Ar! I did, your honour."

"What . . . was I doing?"

"Sir, you was a-pullin' sommat out o' th' earl's dead fingers."

"What was it, Tom?"

"Looked like a leddy's scarf, sir, a lacey fallal . . . and very bloody it were."

"Yes," murmured Richard, his wide gaze on the blue distance: "yes . . . it was . . . horribly! And so now, Tom, you are of course quite sure, perfectly certain, that I killed the Earl! You are absolutely certain of this, eh, Tom, eh?"

Tom drew the scabious from his mouth, looked at it and put it back again; quoth he:

"Why sir, if your honour says so, I be as sarten sure as ever you could expect——"

"Tom, what else did you see?"

"Nowt, sir."

"Sure?"

"Ar, Must' Dick."

"Tom, look at me,—right in the eye, yes—so! Now, why are you lying to me?" Tom shuffled uneasily, took out the scabious, shook his comely head at it, growled inarticulately and threw it away.

"So then you saw . . . her! You saw Miss Ford also, Tom?"

"Which sir, since you ax me so p'inted-like, I did."

"Where, man—where?"

"Must' Dick, she come a-runnin' out o' they ruins——"

"The old Abbey? At such an hour? Are you sure?"

"And sartin, sir."

"How was she, Tom? How did she look? How did she seem?"

"Fair desprit, sir. She were a-wringin' 'er pretty 'ands, ar,—an' a-sobbin' fit to break a man's 'eart, sir!"

"Merciful God!" groaned Richard. "My beloved Rosemary! And you there, Tom . . . great heavens! Didn't you try to help . . . to comfort her?"

"Sir, she don't know me, an' I were mortal afeard to——"

"Afraid, y' fool? Good God! Why afraid and she . . . so desolate——"

"Must' Dick, I were afeard she might jump into that theer gashly water at sight o' me and drownd her purty self. . . ."

Up leapt Richard to tramp back and forth in very transport of wild anxiety and baffled love.

"My Rosemary . . ." he gasped, "oh, my poor, sweet girl . . . my dear love! Oh, God help her——"

"Amen, sir!" quoth Tom, rising also. "And lookee, them was her very words,—'God help me!' says she, 'Oh, God help me!' an' then, sir, she cried your name——"

"My name? Oh, my name! Did she, Tom, did she?"

"Ar! 'Richard,' says she, 'Oh, Richard!' an' away she goes—running."

"Where, Tom, where? Which way?"

"'Crost the park, sir, but I didn't see wheer."

"How was she dressed? Had she a cloak?"

"Ar! And a liddle bonnet. Likewise a bundle."

"Was this before you saw me or after?"

"Arter, sir."

"And how long after the shot?"

"A matter o' ten minutes, I rackon."

"And what did you think of it all?"

"A precious lot, sir."

"But what, man, what?"

"Well, Must' Dick, I thought as mebbe th' Earl 'ad been up to 'is dirty tricks again, only this time 'e got more than 'e bargained for, at last. . . . Ay, I thought as your young leddy—" here, meeting Richard's wild, bright eye, Tom coughed and stood in silent contemplation of the universe again.

"Well?" Richard demanded, "you thought and are thinking . . . exactly what, Tom? And tell me truly—speak, man!"

"Why, Must' Richard, I only be thinkin' that if you 'adn't told me as 'twas you shot—us knows oo—I'd ha' guessed as 'twas . . . 'er, your young ledd—Gorramitey! . . . Sir . . . wot—" gasped Tom, reeling, for Richard's powerful hands were twisted in his neckcloth.

"Fool . . . fool . . . damned rascal!" panted Richard, shaking him like a madman. "Never say it,—never dare to—think it, or I'll be the—death o' you! She's innocent—d' ye hear? I killed the beast, I—I—d' ye understand?"

"Yes, yes . . . sir. For God's sake—" Richard loosed his strangling hold and stepping back, clasped hands to temples, staring on gasping Tom as if bewildered by his own ferocity.

"Did I—hurt you, Tom?" he enquired breathlessly.

"Purty nigh, sir. An' me not never nowise meanin' no manner o' harm to no one, your honour; Lord love ee, no!"

"But you said she was guilty of his . . . vile blood . . . my Rosemary and she is an angel, Tom, sacred and holy . . . like my mother.— And besides, I did it, y' fool, I killed him . . . by accident, d' ye understand?"

"Ay, I do, Must' Richard, I sartin-sure-ly do! Though, sir, I'm bold to say as if this leddy, ay, or even your own mother 'ad done the deed, it were only wot a right, proper woman should ought to do . . . con-sidering!"

"Yes, Tom,—yes, by God, that's true! Certainly! Killing may be justifiable—necessary—laudable. Even the Law itself admits as much, I think. And yet—it might be reckoned murder, the law's so damned involved and contradictory. . . . So, all things considered, it's best that I killed him— remember this, Tom! If I let you go with me, never forget that you are travelling with the Earl's . . . accidental killer. You'll never forget this?"

"Not likely, sir!" quoth Tom, cherishing his throat. "Lorramitey, I aren't been treated so roughlike since——"

"Why then, Tom, if Providence be truly merciful and just, as I dare to believe, we can only hope and trust, eh?"

"Ar, sir, that's the sperrit! An' now—wot about a bit t' eat?"

"I'd forgotten all about food, Tom. Anyhow, down in the village yonder should be an inn."

"There be, sir,—the Seven Bells."

"What village is that?"

"Jevin'ton, sir."

"Why then, we'll eat there . . . but the great question is where in the world shall we make for to-day?"

"Well, Must' Richard, I've heered a precious lot about Lon'on, d' ye see, so why not Lon'on?"

"To be sure, Tom. All suspected rogues and rascals run to hide in London, and the longer I can evade capture the better . . . yes, I think London is the place for us. Fifty odd miles, Tom . . . say three days' journey, or four, or five, or a week; it doesn't matter when we get there. By the way, how much money have you?"

"All on it, sir, bar ninepence."

"All of what?"

"All as you give me, sir; 'ere be four pound, nineteen shillin' and four-pence. And arl at your sarvice, sir."

"No, no, I have plenty—that is, I ought to have. Let's see. Here we have . . . thirteen pounds and a few shillings—good! We're rich, Tom, as tramping rogues go."

"Why then, sir, wot about a bit o' breakfus?"

"As you will, Tom. I suppose I may as well eat," sighed Richard. So down the steep they trudged together.

CHAPTER XIV

TELLETH OF RICHARD AND BLACK GEORGE AND HOW THEY CLASPED HANDS

The day was young when they reached the village of Sissinghurst but, despite this so early hour, from the smithy came the musical ring of hammer and anvil. Therefore, leaving Tom seated in the porch of The Bull Inn, Richard went to face Black George; but his step was slow and his head drooped. . . . He came to a little window therein, narrow and cobwebbed, through which he peered almost furtively.

Yes, there was George, and all alone as usual, hammer in one hand, in the other a pair of long pincers, whereby he gripped a piece of hammered scrollwork all lovely curves that sprouted leaves (and always in the exactly proper place) a thing of wonder and beauty such as surely might have won praise of those medieval master craftsmen whose artful hammers beat out such miracles of enduring beauty when iron was iron indeed. But Black George was scowling at this very blackly as, thrusting it back into the fire, he began to blow; and now the soft roar of the bellows thrilled Richard as it had done so often in those far-off, happier days.

Then, setting his (very own-father-like) chin, Richard strode round to the open doorway, took off his hat and spoke:

"Good morning, George!"

The bellows groaned to a silence wherein the sweet clear notes of a blackbird rippled melodiously from some near-by tree, while George's blue, deliberate eyes surveyed young Richard, his thick, lustrous hair touzled for lack of the comb he had forgotten, his garments that, despite native elegance and Tom's care, showed travel-stained and with a hay stalk here and there, his dusty boots . . .

"You work very early," said Richard, extremely conscious of George's fixed and wondering stare. "The . . . the sun hasn't been up half an hour——"

"Ay. But I don't sleep proper no more. But—you?"

"That's a beautiful thing you are making, George."

" 'Tis only a part on 't, Maister Richard. 'Tis a canopy-like for my Prue's grave . . . sacred to her memory, 'till the morning breaks.' I been a-workin' at it, off and on, ever since she—died. I be doubting lately if I'll ever finish it. . . . But 'tis wonnerful to see you . . . so early an' so onexpected-like, and I be wondering why, and likewise bids ee right hearty welcome."

And wiping hand on breeches, George stepped forward to give that hand which young Richard made no move to take.

"Wait . . . wait, George!" said he, a little breathlessly. "First I must tell you that I . . . night before last, though it seems ages ago now,—I . . . killed a man."

George's outstretched hand fell and once again his blue eyes surveyed Richard with this slow, pensive gaze.

"Lord!" he murmured, staring deep into the young eyes that stared back unwavering. "You . . . Maister Richard . . . killed . . . a man, eh?"

"Yes, George. I killed him . . . by accident, but . . . I killed him—I!"

"Well but," quoth George, shaking his head in slow, troubled manner, "I've come very nigh killing . . . two or three men . . . afore now! Ay, 'twas only the mercy o' God as prevented,—only God. Well now, why didn't He prevent you? Eh? Was it . . . p'raps—because this man desarved to die?"

"Yes, he deserved death, George! A far worse death——"

"Why then—here be my hand——"

"George, the man . . . I killed . . . was the Earl of Abbeymere."

"Eh? Abbey-mere? Why, Lord love us! That be where my Rosemary be staying . . . wrote me a letter, she did."

"Yes, George, and I love Rosemary . . . more than life!"

"Rosemary? D' ye mean . . ." George's breath seemed to catch, his right hand became a mighty, knotted fist, and when he spoke again, it was in hoarse and dreadful whisper: "Was it for . . . her sake as you . . . killed?"

"Yes!" answered Richard, whispering also. Then a giant's arms were round him, but arms these that cherished, that held him close, then held him away.

"Gi'e me thy hand, Diccon lad! Now sit ee here beside me and tell the how and why on 't."

"We were to have been married, George, after you gave your consent,—married in the autumn——"

"Yes, my Rosemary writ me about this,—well?"

"Well, George, she confessed to me that this man . . . the evil of him . . . frightened her. And after this, one day in the wood we met him and he . . . oh, George, he . . . looked at her as if she were . . . naked! I could have killed him then, he was so vilely suggestive. After this I began to worry—especially at night. George, I grew sick with dread until one night, nearly mad, I dressed and crept out to the stables, saddled my horse and galloped over to Abbeymere. . . . The place was all dark except one window and this was ajar . . . so I opened it and crept into the room . . . and then . . . he . . I——"

"Go on, lad."

"He caught me . . . threatened me with a pistol; we—we struggled for it desperately and it went off—exploded in his face, George, and—he fell dead at—my feet."

"And what of our dear lass, our Rosemary?"

"Ah, George, I would to God I knew! I come hoping to find her safe here with you. So now I must search London . . . all England until I find her or till I'm taken or give myself up in despair."

"Despair?" repeated George fiercely. "No—never! Despair aren't no word for a man and therefore not for thee, Mr. Richard——"

"Ah, don't mister me, George,—not you! Call me Dick, or Diccon, as you used to do years ago." George's great hands tightened almost painfully, then he turned away and coming to his anvil, took up the hammer and beat a small, soft tattoo.

"Diccon boy," said he at last, "then here's what we must do, as I see it; either give yourself up to the law, tell your tale and trust to judge and jury—which I don't nohow advise, or—strip off your fine clothes, change yourself into a country-seeming chap and go a-hiding along o' me. Choose, lad."

"With you, of course! With you, George. But where?"

"The countryside, Diccon. London! Everywhere, till, God willing, us finds our Rosemary."

"No, no—impossible, George! For, d' you see, I shall be hunted as a murderer and you as my accomplice. No!"

"Yes!" nodded George, his blue eyes sparkling. "This be why and wherefore I'm coming along wi' thee Dick . . . to the end . . . no matter wheer or what."

"But George, suppose we are arrested . . . imprisoned?"

"Better so than me thumping away at my old anvil here and no heart in 't. Ever since my Prue went—all these years, boy—I've been—that lonely! Ay—black lonely, Richard! Ah, well! And now . . . there be some oldish things o' Simon's as should fit ee well enough till us can come by better. Let's over to t' 'Bull'; he should be astir by now, ay—lookee, chimney be smokin'."

"First then, George, I've a friend with me, the staunchest, most faithful fellow. . . ." And forthwith Richard described Tom Lethbridge and how and why he was sharing his own desperate fortunes.

Then forth they went together into the early sunlight to the patient Tom who, beholding mighty, gold and silver-headed George, rose up to his feet, opened his eyes very wide and murmured:

"Dannel me!"

But when George reached his hand out in hearty greeting, Tom flushed, smiled and grasped it as heartily.

"Tom Lethbridge," said George, his lined visage unwontedly kindly, "Mr. Richard names ee friend and therefore so must I. What do ee say, Tom man?"

"Master," answered Tom, "I says, Lord love you—with all me 'eart!"

"Why then, friend Tom, come you in wi' us to breakfast."

CHAPTER XV

TELLETH HOW ROSEMARY, THOUGH OF SEX GENTLE, MET CRUEL FORTUNE WITH THE FORTITUDE OF ANY MAN OR (AND WHAT IS MORE) OF ANY WOMAN

WHEN Trouble, like dreadful cloud, blots out the stars of Hope, and the black tide of Adversity roars down upon us like a flood, the poor, stricken soul either casts up despairing arms and sinks to deeps of starker misery or, calling upon the Godhead within, battles against Circumstance, bold to endure, until he wins to light and security at last, strengthened by the very ordeal to a nobler living.

For there can be no trouble bravely endured, no catastrophe valiantly outfaced but to strength is added greater strength and therewith a new kindliness, a wise gentleness and broad charity bred of past suffering.

Thus Rosemary, in her terrified desolation, having wept awhile, having called upon her God and her Richard,—instead of companying with that dark and fallen angel whose name is Despair, dried her tears, checked her wild and headlong flight, turned aside into a little copse, and so came stealing to the shelter of that same great tree that, for her sake, Richard would have kissed once upon a time and which she loved an whereto she now fled for Richard's sake. Here, sinking down beneath its mighty boughs and leaning woeful, desolate head against its rugged bole, she waited for the day; and hearkening to the soft whisper of its myriad leaves, it seemed to her stricken heart as if the dear, great thing were striving to comfort her, wherefore she kissed it out of very gratitude.

Oho, thou Tree of trees, to have felt the soft pressure of those tender, lovely lips!

And being young and healthy and confiding in God His omnipresence, she closed her weary eyes and thus awhile forgot all troublous fears in such

c

blessed slumber that she neither dreamed nor stirred until old Sol shot down a roguish beam to kiss her into wakefulness.

Then up she started and away through the rosy dawn, by misty woodland and dew-spangled down, flitting like some young dryad on tireless feet until she espied a cottage bowered amid the green, a cosy place yet very solitary and throned in a garden amid a very glory of flowers.

Now in this garden a shortish, broad-shouldered, extremely clean-shaven man wrought, cherishing these flowers like the loved and lovely things they were; so busy was this man that he remained wholly unaware of Rosemary until, leaning across the little wicket gate, she called softly:

"Oh, Mr. Meadows!"

At this shy summons, Bob Meadows lifted his head, disclosing a face shorn clean of its Frenchified adornments of whisker and moustachio, a square, somewhat grim visage, lit by fierce, keen eyes that softened wonderfully at sight of the speaker as, pulling off his old hat, he saluted her with a little bowing flourish, quaint as unexpected and very French indeed.

"Why, Miss Rosemary ma'm, good morning!" said he, hurrying forward to open the gate for her. "You'm early abroad, Mamselle; th' owd church clock's only jest chimed four and ... *Mordieu,* how pale you look! And ... *sapristi, tes jolis pieds,*—your little, purty feet, my dear! So wet! And ye look fair wore out! Come in, Miss Rosemary, come in and set ee down. I've lit the fire and kettle's a-singin' on th' 'ob, merry as a cricket—so come in and rest whiles I brews a cup o' tea."

"Oh, Mr. Meadows," sighed Rosemary, "how dear and kind you are!"

"No, no, *ventrebleu*—no!' Tis only human I be. And oho, Lor lummy, won't my little Nan be j'yful to see you,—come in!" Folding her hand tenderly within his arm, he brought her into the cottage where everything, from the mats on raddled floor to the raftered ceiling was bright and shining as a new pin, as sweet and wholesome as the roses that peeped in at the open lattice.

"Now off wi' thy little shoes," quoth he, "and lemme dry 'em in the hearth ... not too near the fire—so! Now a cup o' tea wi' a *soupçon* o' brandy shall do ee a power o' good and won't do me no manner o' harm." And Bob straightway busied himself with that neat and silent precision that characterized him, chatting meanwhile in kindly fashion: "Nothin' like a cup o' tea,—they dunno how to brew it in France! And Lordy-lord, so pale as you be, my dear, ah, and trembling like any aspen."

"Yes, I—I—Mr. Meadows, I'm—running away."

"Oh? From Abbeymere? Well, I ain't surprised. How about a rasher o' bacon or say, two? And eggs, of course——"

"But, Mr. Meadows I——"

"Running off, eh? And no wonder! And buttered toast—eh? Toast it is! I don't like the looks o' they Abbeymere folk, lord nor earl, *nom d'un chien*—no! Sit ye still and rest, my dear, I'm used to housework though my little Nan's comin' on wonderful, sweeps, dusts, helps me wash up, bless her *beaux yeux,* and larning to cook, too; ay, and begins to read better than I can, thanks to you, Miss Rosemary. Now the toast."

While thus he talked and bacon hissed tenderly in pan, Bob took from above the mantel a very glittering and murderous-looking cutlass whereon he deftly spitted a slice of bread which he proceeded to toast while dexterously turning bacon rashers in the pan.

"Yes, Miss Rosemary ma'm, my dear, since you come to stay in these here parts, you've taught my Nan a oncommon lot, wot wi' addition, substraction and I dunno wot. So, my dear young lady—ma'm, wot I'm a-trying to tell you is . . . if you should ever 'appen to be in any sort of difficulty, or say trouble, why then, Miss Rosemary, please to know as Bob Medders is your man, my dear. If you should ever lack—say a roof, here it be! A bed —upstairs! Friends—here's my Nannie and me——"

"Mr. Meadows, I've said you are a dear, and now—now I don't know what to say, or how to thank you," said Rosemary, stretching out her hands to him in quick gratitude. "You make my sorrow . . . easier to bear; the world seems less cruel and I shall be less lonely just because of you . . ." Her soft voice trembled, her deep eyes were misted in sudden tears, but at his look of consternation she winked them away and laughed, though a little unsteadily, whereupon he laid aside cutlass and toast to rise and kiss her two pretty hands as gallantly as any fine gentleman in the land.

"Miss Rosemary," said he, whisking the frying pan from fire to hob and looking down at her with his keen, honest eyes, "I'm old enough to be your father, so why not let's believe I am? You'd be snug and safe here along o' my little Nan and me. And you could make a proper scholard of her and learn me to speak more genteel. I'm a-trying to, heavens 'ard, for Nan's sake."

"No, no . . . but God bless you for asking me . . . indeed, I love you for it," said Rosemary, in choking voice. "But I must go on . . . I must go far away from here. I came to ask you if you would drive me to Lewes in time for the early Mail?"

"Why, for sure," he answered, pouring the tea with a dexterous flourish. "There's hoceans o' time for the Mail so let's ha' breakfast, my dear. Now eat hearty! These be my own eggs,—look at 'em! I mean—laid by my own chickens."

Thus, while they ate, he, quick to anticipate her wants and instant to serve, continued to talk, rolling out great French oaths most unexpectedly ever and anon; and Rosemary, being strong of soul and very sane, pushed the horrors of last night to the background of her mind and, answering smile with smile, ate and drank with hearty young appetite.

"Lessee, now," quoth Bob, refilling his teacup, " 'twill be all of eight weeks since I found you sitting wi' my little Nan in the lane yonder, eh?"

"Nine!" answered Rosemary. "I was telling her the tale of Cinderella."

"She took to you amazing, my dear! On the spot and—no wonder!"

"She looked so wistful, all alone in the lane and so pretty, I just had to kiss her and then, of course, we were friends. And she's so quick and clever——"

"And healthy, eh, Miss Rosemary? Healthy—eh?"

"As a wild flower——"

"No signs o' death about her,—eh?"

"Gracious goodness—no!"

"Then," said Bob, rising, teacup in hand, "God bless Lady Vibart!" and down he sat again.

"Oh, you know her, Mr. Meadows? You know Lady Vibart?"

"Ay, I do! *Sacré nom d'un nom,* I do so! If 'twarn't for her, you wouldn't ha' been able to teach my Nannie so much as you have,—*mordieu,* no! Because she would ha' been in Paris . . . in her grave! *Voilà,* Miss Rosemary! Lookee, my dear! My little Nan was a-perishing, dying afore my eyes . . . in Paris,—*sang Dieu!* Then along come my Lady Vibart . . . and . . . well, here we are! My dear, I ain't a prayerful man, being by natur' a reg'lar *mauvais sujet,*—but I never look at my little Nanette and her growing so strong, s' plump and rosy, but I don't pray—God bless Lady Vibart!"

"Yes, I love her too!" murmured Rosemary, sad-eyed.

But now upon the stair was hurry of light feet and Nanette appeared, somewhat grown since her Paris days, though still a little frail and wistful as ever; she stopped to clasp her hands and utter a soft, rapturous cry at sight of Rosemary and, having dropped her the demurest of curtseys, ran to kiss and be kissed.

And now, because the laughing child was so happy, the sun so radiant and Bob Meadows so smilingly content, Rosemary tried to seem happy also.

Breakfast over, Bob took out a large silver watch to compare it with the slow-ticking grandfather clock in adjacent corner.

"Miss Rosemary, m' dear," quoth he, nodding, "lessay half an hour, say three quarters. No, no, don't ye trouble now, I'll wash up——"

"Oh, but Mr. Meadows——"

"Nary a thing! I'm used to it. Out into the sunshine—both o' ye."

"But—goodness me! Look at my poor gown!" sighed Rosemary.

"Ay, a bit draggled-like!" nodded Bob.

"Oh, and these!" she wailed, staring dismayed, where lay her travel-stained cloak and bonnet. "And I must be presentable, I hope to get another situation to-day. Whatever shall I do?"

"Do, my dear—hum! *Alors!* P'r'aps you'll want to take 'em off . . . a hot iron! Hows'ever, my Nan'll help ye. I'll go tend my hoss and gig." And away he went forthwith; whereupon Rosemary got busy, and with her own quick, skilful fingers and little Nan's deft and able assistance, contrived such feminine magic that when, ready for the journey, they went hand in hand to find Bob hissing over his sleek cob, Rosemary showed so daintily trim and bewitching from small, deep-brimmed bonnet to shapely foot that Bob, wonderstruck, set down currycomb to grope for his vanished moustachio (a habit with him in all mental stress) murmuring:

"*Mordieu! Ventrebleu! Sacrebleu!* If it don't beat everything!"

And presently seated all three in the roomy vehicle, away they went through the early morning, with birds calling to them from every tree and hedgerow, and they themselves silent for the most part since little Nan was sad to say good-bye, Mr. Meadows seemed grimly thoughtful and Rosemary was dreaming mournfully of that which now might never be and that which yet was to be. . . .

They reached Lewes with plenty of time for the Mail and pulling up before the White Hart Inn, Bob clambered down, waiting grimly for Rosemary to kiss his little adopted daughter then, lifting Rosemary to earth in powerful arms, drew her a little apart, looked at her more grimly than before and spoke:

"Miss Rosemary ma'm, I dunno your trouble nor where you be a-goin' and I don't ax. But—Mademoiselle, I do ax you to take this here to help you on your road. *Alors! Non*—not a word!" And into her unwilling hand he forced a comfortably heavy purse.

"But, Mr. Meadows!" she gasped. "Dear Mr. Bob, I—I couldn't——"

"*Pardieu! Nom d'un nom,* I insist!" he muttered ferociously. "And God guard ye, my dear—Good-bye!" Saying which, he patted her hand, kissed it, bowed and flourished his hat all in a moment and was in the act of climbing into his high gig when a lounging person in jaunty hat, whiskers and a monocle was so ill-advised as to emit a horselaugh and the words:

"Aha, a Froggie!" In which moment Mr. Meadows, ever yearning for conflict, had pinned the speaker by coat collar.

"*Lâche scélérat! Sale espèce de cochon!*" he exclaimed fiercely, shaking the person until hat and monocle were dislodged. "I'm English to me backbone, I am! *Alors!* Well, now—wot?"

"N-nothing!" stammered the person, quailing in the powerful grip of this English fist. "N-no offence——"

"Well then don't come none o' your 'Froggies' wi' me or *je vous coupez le gorge . . . pour un sale bête damné!*"

So saying, Mr. Meadows released the person, mounted nimbly into his gig, scowled truculently round about and drove away, leaving Rosemary, purse in hand, gazing after him through a blur of tears.

CHAPTER XVI

WAFTS OUR ROSEMARY TO A NEW WORLD AND EXPERIENCES MORE OR LESS STRANGE

No need is there to fully describe Rosemary's journey or the troubled hurry of her thoughts; or the bold-eyed young gentleman in the corner whose looks became so very bold that she averted her lovely head, thus hiding her beauty in that tantalization—her bonnet; nor in fact to mention anything until, the coach pulling up suddenly at an unexpected crossroads, she almost screamed . . . for Richard's own beloved voice was speaking within a yard of her! Yes, indeed, she very nearly cried out to him in joyful ecstasy of reunion . . . almost! But, being herself, she cowered back into her corner, dumb yet in delicious trepidation lest he see her as the door opened and in bundled a little old dame almost upon her lap. Then the door slammed, horn blew, whip cracked, hoofs clattered . . . And Rosemary, venturing to peep back as the coach rolled away, she saw him standing bareheaded, so comely, so strong and altogether dear,—but, O Heaven!—his adored face so pale, so sad and careworn that, risking life and limb, she would have leapt forth to comfort him for her own sake, yet remained crouching miserably where she was—for his dear sake.

And now the old dame being settled, she and her baggage, to the bold-eyed young gentleman's evident discomfort, she began to speak, pouring forth her breathless story to all and sundry; and thus Rosemary instantly recognized her old acquaintance Mrs. Westly and, knowing her talkative disposition, was more thankful for her deep-brimmed bonnet than ever.

"Footpads, folks—I'm tellin' ye!" quoth Mrs. Westly with unction. "High-waymen! Two on 'em! As would ha' robbed me money and had me life but for the fine young gen'leman as brought me safe! Fit wi' 'em, 'e did, folks, and Oh, my—what a battle! Bleedin' they was most awful and 'specially the robbers, glory be!"

And ah, be sure that Rosemary held her breath for fear and pride and love, of course, while swelled her rounded bosom and paled her cheek.

"Beat 'em proper, 'e did, like a reg'lar fighting heerio, and knocked 'em down and saved me life and money and took off his 'at to me so polite as if I'd been a haristocrat or reel lady! And so 'andsome and sad and all along o' love—lost 'is sweetheart or summat, poor dear! I be 'oping—ah, and to-night, folks, I be a-going to pray the Almighty on me bended knees as he finds and marries her and as she gives him plenty o' babbies, sweet mites. . . ."

And ah, be sure now that Rosemary's deep eyes smarted with brimming tears that never fell, while her heart ached with a yearning grief that yet found no expression!

"There be nothing like babbies to mek a man proud and 'appy-like,—a man as be a man! And my young gen'leman be a proper man. . . ."

Thus Mrs. Westly held forth in the innocence of her heart and more and more to the bold-eyed young gentleman's disgust, until their coach wheels were rattling and rumbling on the cobbled streets of London.

So pass we through the Mighty City to a certain genteel though dingy house in the dingy corner of a genteel square, at the somewhat forbidding front door of which house Rosemary knocked timidly just as old Sol sinking in glory westwards yet contrived to shoot a fugitive beam, like the kindly friend he was, to cherish and comfort her as the door opened to discover a superior, very prim servant maid who, looking the visitor up and down, sniffed delicately and enquired in very superior accents:

"Your pleasure, Miss, if you please?"

"I wish to see Mrs. Humby. Will you kindly say . . . Miss Gray? I have a letter for her," answered Rosemary, smiling in such gentle, friendly manner that in the act of emitting another superior sniff the maid smiled instead.

"If you'll please step this way, Miss," said she and ushered Rosemary into a stately though forbidding room, for the chairs stood all very upright, as if forbidding the idle lounger, the curtains were thick and heavy, forbidding excess of garish light, a portrait on the wall framed heavily a forbidding face.

After some while the door opened to admit a tall lady rather like the room, for she was stately and in a heavy fashion, handsome; her head was piled heavily with braids of hair, her eyebrows were heavy and chin prominent like her nose, a handsome feature with mobile nostrils that drew together now and then as if pinched by invisible fingers; also, when she spoke, her speech was austere and a little ponderous:

"Miss Gray? To what have I the pleasure——"

"Mrs. Humby, your brother, Mr. Clipsby, was good enough to write you this letter in the hope you might be able to employ me in your school."

"A letter? Indeed? And from my poor brother? Favour me!" Rosemary gave the letter which Mrs. Humby opened and read at the heavily curtained window.

"My poor brother Eustace speaks of you very highly, Miss Gray. He eulogises your attainments extremely."

"He is very kind, madam."

"We are a small establishment—but extremely, chastely select. Our scholars, all daughters of gentlefolk, are boarders. But we are small, Miss Gray, as I have mentioned and we have hitherto contrived admirably with but one non-resident mistress and a pupil-teacher Bertha Woolverton. However, I am willing to essay your services, since poor Eustace pleads your cause so eloquently. Are you willing to commence at once—now?"

"Thank you, yes, madam."

"And your luggage, box, impedimenta?"

"They will come on so soon as I write."

"Ah, to be sure, I can offer but moderate stipend."

"However, I shall do my best to earn it, madam."

"Ve-ery good, Miss Gray! Then, if—seven shillings per week will suffice, consider yourself engaged. To be sure, you will live in and partake at table with myself and husband, and this of course is a great consideration."

"Yes, madam."

"Then for the present I shall encharge you with my juniors—five. Pray attend me."

Up a broad flight of stairs heavily carpeted and with ponderous, carved balustrade; up a second flight narrower and steeper, where lush carpet gave place to a harsh matting, and so into a large, airy, comfortless room where a sullen-faced girl was drawing letters on a blackboard for the behoof of five very small persons perched bleakly, legs a-dangle, on a very hard-looking form, and all of them with very prim mouths, very round eyes and uncomfortably stiff in the backs.

"Ladies!" quoth Mrs. Humby sonorously.

Instantly the five slithered from the form and being safely afoot, dropped five very demure little curtseys.

"You will notice, Miss Gray, that despite their tender years, I address them as 'ladies,' thus inculcating personal dignity. . . . Ladies, I present Miss

Gray, your new mistress! Miss Gray, these young ladies beginning at the left are: Edith, aged eight; Susan, aged six, Margaret, aged seven; Clara, aged six;—and little Jane, aged five." Here five more demure little curtseys, this time one after the other.

"Ladies, you may resume your seats. Obey your new instructress. Pray remember you are ladies and—behave! Miss Woolverton, be good enough to attend me." The sullen-faced girl glared at Rosemary, Mrs. Humby performed an elaborate curtsey and swept heavily from the room, followed by Miss Woolverton, scowling darkly.

Then Rosemary turned to meet the uncompromising stare of ten very bright, extremely critical eyes.

"But, my dears," she enquired, "whatever makes you all look so very uncomfortable?" Five little voices piped as one: "Backboards, if you please, ma'm."

"You poor little souls! Don't they hurt you?"

"Only now and then, ma'm."

"Not much, ma'm."

"We're used to them, please, ma'm."

"We has to be, ma'm."

"But they's 'bominable!" quoth little Jane.

"Then, my dears, let me take them off for you."

"Oh, we dassen't, ma'm."

"Mrs. Humby would punish us, ma'm. Mrs. Humby, she says all ladies must wear backboards when they's little——"

"And I's the littlest of all!" sighed little Jane.

"But—if they hurt you, my dears—" Rosemary paused, aware of a mysterious sound that had piqued her curiosity once or twice already,—a thin, twittering that seemed to hover in the air intermittently, a quavering, ineffectual wail rather like the plaint of a debilitated fairy.

"Goodness—me!" exclaimed Rosemary, glancing up and around. "Pray, what is that strange sound, children?"

"Captain Humby, ma'm."

"Dear me! Is the poor gentleman ill?"

"No, ma'm; it's Mrs. Humby's nerves."

"So Captain Humby plays his flute——"

"To soothe her, ma'm."

"Mrs. Humby needs music, ma'm. She says she 'dores it——"

"I don't!" quoth little Jane. "I likes humbugs!"

"Jane means those peppermints with teeny stripes, ma'm, but I like brandyballs the best——"

"That's why I loves Captain Humby," nodded little Jane; "he gives me humbugs . . . on the sly!"

"Well now, my dears, come now and gather round me and let me see how much we know. We will begin by spelling 'cat'—you, Edith!" This small lady squirmed, turned up her eyes, twisted her fingers and faintly suggested:

"K—?" Rosemary shook her head gently, whereat up shot four little arms and their small owners receiving permission, bleated in unison:
"R!"

"No, my dears!" sighed Rosemary. "And what do you say, Jane?" This very diminutive lady raised her too pale little face and declaimed instantly and with the utmost finality:

"D-O-G." Rosemary shook her head again, smiled, and stooping impulsively, kissed the little face so tenderly that the pale cheeks flushed and round her neck crept two thin little arms.

"Ooh!" sighed Jane. "Nobody hasn't kissed me like that since they buried my mama wiv a lot o' black fevvers."

"Jane's an orphant, ma'm," explained Edith.

"And never goes home for holidays, ma'm," chorused the three.

"And you're a bee-oo-tifullest lady!" declared Jane, with solemn nod. Rosemary gasped and drew the small lady upon her knee.

"Dear little Jane!" she murmured. "I wish you had more roses in your cheeks."

"Oh, no, ma'm. Mrs. Humby says I'm a ailing child not long for this vale—" Here was a loud double knock and the door swung open.

"Lollipops, my hearties—stand by!" cried a chirruping voice and in upon them shot a stoutish gentleman, extremely neat as to person and untidy as to hair and cravat. "She's out, children. Slipped her moorings, messmates, so let all be revelry and—hum!" he exclaimed, halting suddenly at sight of Rosemary. "Sink me! Most unexpected! My dear young lady, pray excuse —had no idea——"

"Oh, Captain Humby," cried little Jane. "Ahoy! Humbugs!"

Captain Humby winked and smiled jovially at the children, then surveyed Rosemary with a kind of wistful dismay.

"Excuse me!" he murmured. "If I intrude—will vanish . . . hoist every stitch and scud. . . ."

"No, no, Captain Humby, please stay. See how glad the children are to see you. Oh, it's wonderful! I am—Mary Gray, the new governess."

"No, really? Begad—how do do? Then—if you don't mind—the children —eh?"

"They seem to like you, sir."

"Oh, we do, ma'm!" said Edith.

"All of us!" chimed the three.

"'Specially me!" quoth little Jane. "So, Captain—humbugs!" Now at this, the Captain looked at Rosemary very like a guilty schoolboy and ran nervous fingers through his hair until it showed wilder than ever; quoth he:

"I—my dear young lady, I—strictly between ourselves—when my—Mrs. Humby is absent, I—ha—smuggle the little souls a humbug or so—bull's-eyes and what not with an occasional lollipop. Children love sweetmeats and —if you don't mind—I happen to have one or two stowed about me—so— if you'll allow . . .?"

"Why, Captain Humby, of course. I think it very kind of you."

"Do you, begad? Then—messmates, ahoy! Belay my hearties, avast and stand by!" So saying, he turned to the five children wide-armed, and they, quite forgetting prim demureness, ran to clasp and cling about him with jubilant acclaim while from deep coat pockets he fished five paper cornucopias of sweets.

"Aha, messmates, and there's jam and cake and jelly for tea, ay, and Coxswain Ben to serve us!" chirruped the Captain, perched now on the form and embracing all five of them. "Tea, my hearties, jam and plum cake—ah, pardon—if your new mistress will permit?" Here he contrived a little bow to Rosemary.

"Gladly!" she answered, smiling. Hereupon, seeing his small messmates rapt in joyous comparison of those paper cornucopias, the Captain approached and spoke, murmuring:

"Think perhaps—this intrusion—had better explain." The which he did in the following staccato fashion:

"Mrs. Humby. An admirable woman. But—with a curse. Nerves! They affect her. Frightfully! At which times she's apt to be—difficult! But 'music hath charms to soothe the'—ahem! Hence my flute."

"Yes, I heard you playing, sir——"

"Playing? No, no,—I tootle! I hate to but—I tootle. . . . And here, I think, is Ben with the tea." As he spoke, a single dull thud resounded on the door which Edith flew to open for the passage of a vast, well-laden tray borne by a long man whose lean, woebegone visage was rendered more so by a black patch in place of his left eye.

"Miss Gray," said Captain Humby, as the tray was set down, "this is my coxswain, Ben Piper, an old shipmate o' mine,—Ben, a leg to the lady." Instantly the coxon performed an intricate evolution with his legs suggestive of a hornpipe, at the same moment bobbing bullet head and touching bristly eyebrow.

"Now, my hearties," cried the Captain cheerily, "bring up alongside and fall to! Coxswain, stand by with the cake and I'll man the teapot. . . . Milk and sugar, Miss Gray?"

And now, waited on by the one-eyed but deft-handed coxon, who seemed a prime favourite with the five (now hilarious) small ladies, a merry meal they made of it. And if the tea was thin and the bread and butter thick, what matter when partaken in such right glad company? For the Captain proved so whimsical and the coxswain's one eye so eloquently jovial that presently Rosemary was laughing merrily (almost) as the children.

Tea was over and the Captain and coxswain were together spinning a yarn —to a rapt auditory—concerning the capture of a very man-eating shark when the door swung wide and Mrs. Humby stared in upon them and seemed, for a moment, Gorgonlike, to turn every one and thing to stone, for beneath her gaze was instant silence and a tense, still rigidity.

"Captain Humby!" she exclaimed, the invisible fingers busied with her handsome nose, "Reginald John, I am astounded! I am shocked and deeply mortified! Aurelia, remove these pernicious edibles! This will demand jalap

all round! Jam! Jellies and cakes! Oh, poison! Away with them, Aurelia!"
Instant to obey appeared the superior servant maid who, meeting the coxswain's undaunted, brightly eloquent eye, was suddenly beautified by a
girlish blush.

"You—Benjamin Piper, begone!" quoth Mrs. Humby, terrifically dignified.
"Begone at once, Benjamin, and never dare——"

"Ay, ay, marm!" answered that worthy, ducking head, touching eyebrow
and waggling leg all at once, whereat Mrs. Humby shuddered violently and
turned on her mute spouse.

"As for you, Reginald—" but even as she spoke, the Captain's fluttering
coat tails vanished through the door in his coxswain's wake.

The Navy thus routed, Mrs. Humby bent her heavy brows upon the five
small ladies, who instantly curtseyed as demurely and stood as prim and
innocently round of eye but with five cornucopias (somewhat depleted) hidden
about their small persons.

"Ladies!" moaned Mrs. Humby. "You have upset and displeased me!
The hour verges towards seven o'clock and instead of your half-hour recess
you will instantly to bed! Miss Gray, you have permitted Captain Humby
to engorge your charges with noxious compounds and indigestible dietary,
thus contravening my established rule. But you were unwitting, so I say no
more. Pray attend the young ladies to their dormitory and should feverish
or other symptoms develop—inform me."

Then Mrs. Humby sighed, moaned and rustled grandly away. So presently
Rosemary marshalled her charges to bed and having listened to their prayers
(and the Captain's flute wailing dismally afar) she tucked them up, kissed
them good night (to their joyful wonder) and seated near-by in her own
small bedchamber, poured out her heart in a letter; this—

"My dear Lady Vibart,
"Because of this terrible happening, I know the dreadful consequences
must follow me all my life. So I have fled away where none must ever find
me, especially Richard that I love so much more than life. And so, for
his dear sake and yours, I pray God to make me brave to endure and
strong to bear all that I must. The wicked earl is dead and Richard knows
I killed him and will perhaps tell you how justly. So, my dear Lady Vibart,
you that I have so yearned to call 'Mother' and do love as a daughter,—
please, please, be kind to me in my bitter loneliness and try to love me just
a little. For indeed, life seems to have ended for me almost before it has
begun. And truly, I could not do as I have done if I did not worship
Richard and love you so deeply,—how deeply it is my prayer you may
learn some day, with the truth of it all. And so, knowing myself for what
I really am, I dare to call you 'Mother' for the first and last time. There,
I have written the dear word and kissed it. And so—Good-bye from this
sorrowful creature that so yearned to be
                                        "Your humble, loving daughter
                                                              "ROSEMARY."

CHAPTER XVII

WHICH, BEING SUCH SPEECHFUL CHAPTER, SPEAKS FOR ITSELF

LORD IFORD, or rather the new Earl of Abbeymere, showed surprisingly youthful as he bowed golden head above my lady's hand, though to be sure he bore himself with a very complete assurance and his eyes with their cynical weariness seemed anything but young, therefore it was to these telltale eyes (be sure) that Lady Vibart bent her serene regard as she motioned him to be seated.

"Well, madam," said he, meeting her calm gaze with a smile politely cynical as his look, "I am here!"

"And how very, very good of you!" she murmured, with such strange and unexpected humility that his assurance wilted slightly.

"No, no," he answered. "Lady Vibart, pray believe me, I am honoured."

"It was kind of you to heed a mother's appeal and grant me this interview."

"Oh, but, madam, I——"

"You have made poor Sir Peter and myself so terribly, so very dreadfully aware that you hold our dear son's honour, perhaps his very life, at your mercy."

The young Earl's discomfort became manifest; his blue gaze wavered.

"My dear Lady Vibart, you—you mistake me——"

"Ah, would to heaven I did!" she sighed. "But there can be no mistake about your unfortunate father's terrible murder."

The Earl appeared shaken; he blenched before my lady's sad yet unwavering gaze; he muttered vague protestations and became dumb at her gentle though imperious gesture.

"You know as well as I, my lord, and as certainly as Richard, that this was no suicide, but—you have endeavoured to make Sir Peter and me suspect our own son—why?"

"Madam, I—I certainly returned to your safe keeping the—damning evidence of his handkerchief."

"But you have also declared it a case of suicide. . . . Why?"

Lord Iford became so exceedingly uncomfortable that he started up from his chair and, crossing to the window, stared out across the park until, remembering himself, he murmured an apology and came back to front my lady's gentle though persistent scrutiny.

"Well?" she demanded softly. "Well, Iford,—or should it not be Lord Abbeymere?"

"Neither, madam, neither, I beg?" he answered almost humbly. "In other times, when Richard and I were friends at school and college, you called me Valentine. Lady Vibart, I would be 'Valentine' to you always, if I may?"

"Why, this depends," she murmured, shaking her stately head.

"Pray—on what?"

"On how much these last few years have changed you."

"Alas, madam," he sighed, sitting down again. "This is a world of change!"

"But generally for the better, Iford, or we should return to savagery."

"Madam, I begin to tremble!"

"I rejoice to know it! And please don't be cynical, Iford. You see, I remember your little, gentle mother . . . in those days you were so like her that I loved you too."

"And—now, madam?"

"Now you are—the Earl of Abbeymere!"

"And what beside, madam?"

"A very, very—too, too old young man!"

"Then let us hope I shall grow younger with age, madam."

"And yet," sighed she, "can you hope to even faintly resemble the Valentine that was your mother's joy and comfort? I wonder!"

Now at this, his cold flippancy vanished, his jaded eyes grew bright and wistful.

"Am I so—greatly changed?" he murmured.

"Beyond all expectation!" she nodded.

"And of course—for the worse, you'll tell me?"

"No, I tell you to—ask yourself?"

The young earl sighed, frowned, smiled and, leaning back, crossed slim legs, quite at his ease again.

"Referring to your kind note," said he, "you mentioned a lady's name. . . ."

"Yes, Iford. Rosemary Ford."

"You promised to tell me news of her."

"Oh, I will. You imagine yourself in love with her, of course——"

"Lady Vibart—really madam, I—permit me to say this concerns only myself and——"

"Oh, dear, no! This concerns Rosemary much more and it also concerns me a great deal. You see, I am her godmother and I also love her—very dearly."

"Her—godmother?" exclaimed the Earl, quite forgetting his studied pose.

"Yes, I have known and loved her ever since she was born."

"Why then, Lady Vibart, I—well, suppose I admit the—ah—soft impeachment?"

"I shall instantly doubt the sincerity of your sentiments, Iford."

The young Earl gasped, glared, started indignantly afoot and sat down again, very stiff in the back, all patrician and haughtiness from golden pate to varnished boots.

"Then, madam," he retorted loftily, "I take leave to denounce your ladyship's harsh and too hasty judgment as quite unwarranted and utterly unjust."

"Let us at least hope so, my lord," sighed she, a little wearily. "But really, your affected man-of-the-world airs, your too-aged cynicism, would seem to discourage such hope."

Once more the Earl rose:

"Madam," said he, bowing, "I believe I will bid you good day and—fare-well. I am closing Abbeymere for good. I hope it may rot—every hateful stick and stone of it. . . . So, let us call it—Farewell!"

"As you will, my lord," she sighed, gazing up serenely into the fierce young eyes above her, "but pray believe also that you are causing much unnecessary pain by shielding your father's murderer."

The young Earl fell back a pace, staring down into this calm, beautiful face, his eyes widening with more than apprehension.

"What—madam, what do you—suggest?"

"I mean that you have given out this murder as suicide, but—not to save my son." Here she paused for the Earl's question that came in a breathless stammer:

"Then who—why—why else, madam?"

"To shield one you believe is really guilty."

The young Earl was stricken at last; apprehension waxed to ever-growing horror; he strove for speech, loosened his cravat as if it choked him and finally, sinking back into his chair, put the second question for which she had waited:

"Who—ah, whom do you mean?"

"Rosemary Ford!" answered my lady. "And being so utterly certain of her guilt, my lord, you are as sure of my son's innocence."

"So then—you know?" he gasped. "How? God—What do you know?"

"That she is as guiltless as Richard."

For a moment his lordship sat dumb with stark amazement that changed to relief, to a radiant joy.

"Thank God!" he exclaimed impulsively. "Heaven bless you, Lady Vibart! Now what proof have you? Show me—pray tell me,—what?"

"None!" she answered gently. "Only I know—I am perfectly certain Rosemary is innocent."

"Then perhaps you will tell me—you can name the guilty one?"

"On the contrary—can you not tell me, my lord?"

Thus directly questioned, he at first shook his golden head, then meeting her intent gaze, seemed puzzled, then started forward in his chair to peer at his serene accuser between suddenly narrowed lids; and so for a breathless moment they gazed on each other, eye to eye. Slowly the Earl's tense form relaxed and, leaning back, he was shaken by a fit of silent though rather terrible laughter.

"So then, madam," said he at length, "you must even saddle me with—patricide? It seems you can fit me to any evil—even to such murder as this! And yet—why not? Indeed, you read me so very truly that I'll confess but for the element of time, I should most certainly have killed the Earl——"

"Hush—oh, hush!" she whispered, both protesting hands outstretched against him.

"No, no, madam! You have invited me to speak; now hear me! Knowing what I know, madam, I grieve I was denied the killing of him; I——"

"Hush, boy! There—there! Don't say it—oh, remember he was your—father!"

"But then, I am my mother's son! I know what merciless beast he was—so when I found him dead and learned why—then, my Lady Vibart, I spurned and trampled him where he lay, for—clutched in his dead hand I found—this! Look, madam!" From his breast the Earl drew a wallet and took thence a strip of flowered muslin.

"This, madame," he explained, drawing the fragment through his fingers caressingly, "this was wrenched from the gown Rosemary wore that night. . . . He had savaged her—and so she killed him, very rightly, and thus spared me the joy and horror of it. And now, well—I live only to find her."

"And—then?"

"I shall marry her if—if she will so honour me and my accursed name." Softly Charmian arose and, coming to the speaker, touched his golden head caressingly as she had so often done when he was a small, timid child.

"So then," she murmured sighfully, "you too! Yes, you really love her, Valentine." He was silent a moment, then with quick gesture somehow rather pitiful in its eagerness, he caught that gentle, caressing hand to kiss it almost wildly and looked up at her with eyes softened and beautified by unwonted moisture.

"Am I—indeed Valentine—again, madam?" he enquired brokenly.

"Yes," she murmured, "you are looking at me now with Valentine's eyes! But oh, my dear boy," she sighed, sinking beside him on the settee, "what a tangled skein it all is! You would thus shield Rosemary. Rosemary actually confesses the crime to shield Richard. Richard vows he is guilty to shield Rosemary. . . . However shall we unravel it unless we find the actual slayer?"

"Then, Lady Vibart, you—you know Richard is—or imagines himself—in love with her?"

"Valentine—they are engaged."

"En—gaged?" repeated the Earl, slowly recoiling. "Then you—you and Sir Peter have—actually consented?"

"Yes, Valentine; they will be married in London just so soon as this terrible matter is cleared up."

Languidly and like one very tired the young Earl rose and stood dumbly before Charmian, staring down on her from a dead-white face; and slowly the ardent, almost plaintive youth of a moment since, changed to a desperate man, colder, grimmer and far more terrible than the old lord, his father; and when he spoke, it was in voice soft yet dreadfully changed as his look:

"Lady Vibart, if I be permitted to advise, I should urge you most strongly to do all in your power, by any or every means, to stop this projected union or—I must—and shall!"

"Are you threatening me, Iford?"

"No, no, I am warning you for the sake of—other days. Dear Lady Vibart, I am telling you that my love is of this sort—if she I love should die, I would follow her in death gladly. So then, rather than lose her to any mere man

—hear me, madam—hear me vow to God I will destroy that man, though he be Richard, your son—and this the last act of my life."

Then, unheeding her word and gesture, he turned and sped from the room, almost running.

And presently, standing by the open window, Charmian heard the sudden clatter of his horse's wildly galloping hoofs.

CHAPTER XVIII

WHICH RECOUNTS AN INCIDENT BY THE WAY

"Now if," quoth Black George, surveying Richard's countrified transformation somewhat dubiously, "if your hair was a bit shorter——"

"It shall be—at the first opportunity."

"But my old jacket do fit un sa-prising, eh, Jarge?" chuckled old Simon. "Lordy! To think as Sir Peter's own son should be a-wearin' o' my old coat——!"

"Ay!" nodded George. "Though it do show a bit shortish i' the back, Simon, an' tightish 'ere an' there,—an' so much the better! But Richard, if ee could make them gaitered legs go a bit 'eavier-like an' not cock your chin so lofty. . . . And then—his 'ands, Simon—wot do ee think o' they?"

"Should ought to look rougher-like, Jarge."

"We'll manage that somehow," nodded Richard, turning as Simon's horse and gig were led round from the stable yard. So presently, having shaken Simon's hand, up they mounted, all three, and away they trundled through the lovely land of Kent; and Simon's powerful horse maintained such pace uphill and down that by noon they had reached Tonbridge town. Here Richard proposed they should dine, and what better place than the Chequers, this famous inn?

Now George had scarcely pulled up in the spacious stable yard and Richard sprung down to stretch his cramped legs, than an ostler appeared, leading a splendid pair of bays harnessed to a dainty phaeton, which horses and vehicle he instantly recognized. Glancing instinctively round about, he saw amid the stir and bustle an elegant veiled lady whom he also thought to recognize, for in this same moment she paused to regard him so earnestly that he bared his curly head and bowed, quite forgetting his country guise.

"Richard!" she exclaimed and came towards him, small gauntleted hands outstretched. "More mysteries then, Mr. Vibart?" she enquired, her eyes very bright through her veil. "You are strangely transfigured!"

"By George, I'd forgotten!" he confessed a little ruefully. "Would you have known me?"

"I did!" she nodded. "Almost instantly, of course. You must change your eyes and hair and walk, the carriage of your head as well as your clothes. But how strange that we should meet again so very unexpectedly—and to-day of all days! You my preserver, my knight-errant, and I the ever-distressed damsel, wronged as usual."

"Distressed?" he repeated in smiling disbelief. "What again, Miss Bellenden? Please, how may I serve you?"

"Come and I will show you," she murmured and led him into the spicy dimness of an empty stable.

"Look!" she whispered and with quick, half-shamed, half-passionate gesture, threw back her veil.

Richard choked back an oath and recoiled, for the tender beauty of one cheek was marred by an ugly weal.

"A whip, sir!" she nodded, dropping her veil. "A whip used thus by my gallant cousin, Sir Nicholas Frayne! This was his remonstrance for leaving him on the road and refusing——"

"Where is he?" Richard demanded hoarse-voiced and glancing about rather wildly.

"In London, Mr. Vibart. This happened yesterday."

"The devil!" gasped Richard. "The dastardly, damned scoundrel!"

"Thank you, Richard!" she murmured, red lips smiling beneath her veil. "That has done me a great deal of good. And I showed you because I am a poor creature quite destitute of menfolk—brothers, father or even near cousins except Nicholas, of course,—and I am so helplessly, hatefully revengeful that—oh, Richard, I should like—I yearn that his face should bear such cruel, shameful stigma as mine."

"Never doubt it!" said Richard, catching her hand to his lips. "When I meet—if only I can find him, his whole detestable carcass shall bear worse marks, I promise you."

"Ah—now see what I have done!" cried she, with sudden, wild gesture. "Oh, what selfish wretch am I, to drag you into my quarrel—thrust trouble and danger upon you——"

"Pray believe that you honour me, Miss Bellenden."

"No, no, I endanger your life!—And my name is Cynthia!—So pray do not worry——"

A rumble of wheels in the yard, hoofs that clattering stamped such devil's tattoo as could be caused only by the most thorough of thoroughbreds,—wherefore Miss Bellenden troubled to glance thitherward and, uttering an exclamation, stepped out from the stable.

"Valentine!" she called, as forth of dusty carriage stepped the young Earl of Abbeymere.

"Cynthia!" said he, flourishing hat from yellow head. "Here's an unexpected pleasure——" But, in the act of bowing above her outstretched hand, he stiffened, stared, glared and frowned. "Now what in heaven's name——!" he murmured.

"To be sure!" smiled Cynthia. "This is—my Richard—Mr. Vibart. He is, I fancy, engaged in some theatricals—charades perhaps, but he is also my preserver—he saved my life, Valentine!"

"Oh, indeed?"

"Yes, indeed, sir! Well, is this so slight a matter?"

"God forbid! Mr. Vibart is fortunate—as usual."

"But don't you know each other?"

"Perfectly!" sighed the Earl, bowing to Richard with exaggerated courtesy. "We know each other—too well."

"And therefore," retorted Richard, returning the bow with scowling contempt, "quite well enough."

"Aha!" murmured his lordship, surveying Richard's country attire with cold-eyed derision. "A charade? The effect is diverting, Vibart." Richard clenched his fists and frowned into the speaker's sneering face so fiercely that Cynthia stepped lightly between them.

"Goodness—me!" she exclaimed. "Such ferocity—such hatred! Then you are not friends?"

"Ask Vibart," smiled the Earl.

Richard merely scowled.

"But why ever not?" she demanded. "You, Valentine, tell me why?"

"Oh, for some reason or other, Cynthia, but so perfectly sufficing that whensoever your Richard and preserver desires to quarrel, your Valentine is eager to oblige."

Once again Richard's aspect became so threatening that she spoke on impulse:

"I could show you better cause, Valentine."

"Dear Cynthia, I beg leave to doubt it."

"Then look!" said she softly. "Valentine—look at this!" And for the second time she lifted her veil.

The Earl gazed at the cruel marks, glanced at Richard, at the busy yard and, his gaze thus averted, uttered one word:

"Who?"

"My cousin, Nicholas Frayne. He is a crony of yours, I think?"

"He was! And yet—hardly a crony. Also, I am on my way to London."

"Oh,—you mean?"

"Everything, Cynthia."

"Valentine, I demand to know exactly what you do mean?"

"To shoot him, of course."

"No!" said Richard. "You are quite too late, Iford. Miss Cynthia has honoured me——"

"Vibart," drawled the Earl, as provokingly as possible, "to hear Frayne had shot you dead would quite charm me—naturally. But my friendship for this lady is far older than yours, so have the goodness to mind your own business. And permit me to remind you that I am—Abbeymere, as of course you know very well——"

"You—Abbeymere?" cried Cynthia, interposing. "You the Earl—oh— why, Valentine, how is this?"

"Because," murmured his lordship, "the old Earl's deceased, very suddenly and rather lately."

"Gracious—goodness!" gasped Cynthia. "Your father?"

"Let us say—the late earl, my dear Cynthia. His lordship is lying coffined at this moment. Two days hence he will be interred with all due ceremonial and myself the chief—let us say—mourner—yes, even to gloves and hatband, I shall seem perfectly *de regle*——"

"Valentine!" she exclaimed. "Sometimes I think you have no soul—no heart!"

"I wonder?" he sighed.

"But—your father! And so sudden, Valentine! Pray how did it happen —when?"

"As to the 'how' of it, Cynthia, and also the 'when'—ask Vibart; he can tell you all about it as well as, or rather better, than I."

"But Valentine——"

"Cynthia, my dear, I like stables as I do horses, but just now I propose to dine; will you be pleased to honour me? Vibart too, if he chooses."

"Why then, in a private room, Valentine,—my poor face!"

"Ah, yes, of course. We will dine *à deux*—unless Vibart will join us——"

"Thank you—no!"

"Then pray, child, bid your noble preserver *adieu* and give me your arm."

"Good-bye Richard—my knight-errant!" said Cynthia, catching his clenched hand in both her own, "Iford—I mean Abbeymere—no, Valentine can be a most hateful beast but pray forgive him—for my sake!"

And presently Richard came where George and Tom patiently awaited him and bringing them into a secluded corner of the taproom, dined with them very heartily on bread and cheese and nappy ale.

"So yon was the young noo Earl of Abbeymere, Tom do tell me?"

"Yes, George. How do you like him?"

"I don't!" growled Black George.

"And yet," quoth Richard, shaking his head in frowning perplexity, "confound me but I can't help liking the fellow—somehow—in spite of myself, George."

CHAPTER XIX

WHICH IS, AT LEAST, A CHAPTER OF ACTION

FILLED with such heroic spirit of adventure as fired the valiant souls of old-time mariners and explorers to sail uncharted seas and dare the joyous terrors of the Unknown,—little Jane opened the door. . . . Her wide grey eyes, that always seemed too large for the small, elfin face, cast one glance behind, then the door closed and she sped out and away on that errant course that was to affect so many lives.

She stood hesitant in a narrow, somewhat depressing thoroughfare that led between high, blank walls, but to little Jane, this small adventurer, it was a place marvellous. The first wonder that charmed and lured her was a knife-grinding machine with stone set in a high frame on wheels, whereat was perched a grimy person shooting sparks from a large knife blade very glorious to behold.

Reaching this so engaging personage, little Jane dropped him the stateliest of little curtseys, whereupon the sparks vanished, the rasping stone became still and the personage himself turned to stare down at her through a pair of large, silver-rimmed spectacles.

"Well," quoth he, "dog bite me if I ever did!"

"What, please?" enquired Jane.

"See sich a werry small lady and all by herself too! Oo are ye, ma'am?"

"I'm Jane."

"Oh?" nodded the knife grinder. "And a werry good name too! Mine's Bill."

"Oh?" said Jane thoughtfully in her turn. "Do you like humbugs, Bill?"

"Eh?" quoth he, rubbing whiskery chin, "I dunno as I ever——"

"This!" said Jane, and from beneath her cloak produced a very crumpled and sadly depleted paper cornucopia, whence she daintily extracted and held up a sweetmeat in question. The knife grinder took it, popped it into his wide mouth and nodded.

"Prime!" said he.

"Then please,—more sparks, Bill!"

"At your sarvice, Miss Jane, ma'm!" So once again the grindstone whirred, spinning faster and faster, until from shrieking steel flew sparks in a very cataract. But, even as she watched in an ecstasy, suddenly above the grind of whirring stone and the vague rumble of distant street, clear and high and resistless to childish ears as the Pied Piper's flageolet, rose the shrill, alluring squeak of Mr. Punch.

"Ooh!" exclaimed Jane and, forgetting all dignity, clapped her little hands, turned on dancing feet and sped lightly away. Knife-grinder Bill craned from his perch to stare after her, then, shaking his head, bent again to his labour, munching the humbug. The which sweetmeat had long vanished and Mr. Punch's shrill summons died away when Bill, in the act of testing knife edge on thumb, saw Beauty standing before him so entirely, bewilderingly beautiful yet so pitifully distressed that he gaped—and small wonder!

"Oh, please—please——" said Rosemary, with gesture of entreaty wholly artless and therefore utterly winning, "a little girl—have you seen her? A very little girl in—blue bonnet and pelisse——"

"Yes, lady, yes, that I 'ave," answered Bill, eager to aid such woeful loveliness, "abaht ten minutes it 'ud be. She comes an' gives me a sucker, though she called it a humbug——"

"Yes, yes—oh, that would be she—little Jane——"

"Ay, ma'm, it were, lady. She told me so—and that per-lite, miss, bless 'er little 'eart——"

"Where—which way did she go?"

"Ma'm, she up and run off arter a Punch-'n-Judy show—like a little arrer, ah—quick as a tiddler in a pond, lady. So if you should 'ear Punch a-squeakin', you foller 'im, miss, an' I'll lay as theer you'll find little ma'm Jane. So don't ye worry your pretty——"

"Oh, thank you!" cried Rosemary and fled—out and away into the flurry and turmoil of the busy street. And many were they, amid the bustling throng, who turned for another glance at her vividly arresting beauty and grace of form—more especially one, a tall, dark-avised man driving a high-wheeled stanhope, a boldly handsome person this, who was so smitten that he uttered an oath of startled, rapturous wonder and checked his spirited horse so violently as to quite discompose the elegant youth lolling sleepily beside him into drawling through peevish expostulation:

"Da—amme, Frayne—wh-at the deyvil——"

"There, Jimmy—look! B'gad—Aphrodite herself! Ha—the shape of her!"

"Eh? What? Where?"

"There, man, there! The golden Venus! See her action!"

The languid Jimmy exerted himself to fix his eyeglass and following the direction of his companion's pointing whip, sat up, cocked his hat more rakishly and exclaimed, like knife-grinder Bill, though with very different intonation:

"Prime!"

"She's Perfection!" snarled Sir Nicholas Frayne, with a certain ferocity of admiration. "Ha, Jimmy, 'pon my soul, she might win me back that monkey I lost to Arthur Cleeve last night; b'gad, she shall!"

"Eh? How—how d' ye mean, Nick?"

"Very simply. Cleeve is due at my rooms in half an hour or so and with Syd Buckley. Well—now lookee, Jimmy—we lead the talk to 'Lovely Woman,' our love-sick Arthur will of course sing the praises of his latest conquest——"

"What, his little dancer—Rosine?"

"Yes, yes. Then I demur. The debate grows hot. I bet him a monkey I can show him a rarer, lovelier creature. I produce yonder young goddess. Then you and Syd and I plump solidly for our Venus and—the money's mine."

"Sounds likely enough, Nick, m' boy. But how bring it off? Da-amme, ye can't kidnap the charming creetur in broad daylight—at least, not on a main thoroughfare——"

"Who says so?" demanded Sir Nicholas, his eager gaze ever upon that lovely hurrying form, "I'll find a way—I must!"

"But—on a crowded street, Nick? No, no,—quite impossible, m' tulip! Why, what how,—where's she off to in such dooce of a hurry?"

"She shan't escape me!" smiled Sir Nicholas grimly and touched up his horse; for their beautiful quarry had commenced to run; indeed, Rosemary had caught at last the sound she had been praying to hear,—the high, piping squeak of Mr. Punch. Guided by this right welcome sound, she sped on, heedless of all else, turning corners haphazard until in a quiet back street, remote from roaring traffic, she beheld a motley throng—women, children (and men, of course) grouped about a very superior Punch-and-Judy show brave with striped canvas, paint and gilding with a sign displayed aloft where was emblazoned this legend nobly lettered:

THE ONLY DOUBLEDAY
with
PUNCH & JUDY

Mr. Punch was in the act of trouncing the Beadle as Rosemary gently though firmly edged through the rapt audience until she beheld the object of her frantic search standing entranced close beside a very comfortable, motherly woman, who smiled down at the small, eager face what time she answered Mr. Punch, tootled on the Panspipe affixed conveniently beneath her dimpled chin or thumped the drum—all at the exact and proper moments.

"Jane—oh, Jane!" cried Rosemary. Then the small truant was being kissed, reproached, embraced and kissed again, while Mrs. Doubleday, smiling more kindly than ever, nodded her comely, large-bonneted head.

"Glory be!" quoth she heartily. "Ah, miss, I thought as somebody would come a-looking for her pretty soon,—such a precious little duck! And such old-fashioned ways and all. Followed us quite a piece, a-holding my hand, when not my Dan'l's, and a-talking to us that pretty!" Here Mrs. Doubleday turned to speak through the canvas to her invisible spouse:

"'S all right, Dan'l—the little angel's found." At this Mr. Punch, knocking the Beadle completely out of time, emitted a piercing, joyous squeal that echoed far and wide, so very sudden and loud indeed that a certain high-spirited horse snorted in protest with great clatter of hoofs, whereat rose an angry murmur from the crowd that opened unwillingly to the passage of a high-wheeled stanhope driven by a tall, arrogant personage who, either by accident or design, caused his nervous animal to rear and plunge so violently that the crowd swayed in quick, wild panic and, caught in this surging press, little Jane was swept from Rosemary's hold and fell almost beneath the frightened horse's trampling hoofs. Women shrieked in horror, men shouted fiercely, but, uttering no sound, Rosemary leapt, snatching up that little helpless form, felt a violent shock, reeled blindly, was caught and—dazed, breathless and trembling—found herself in Mrs. Doubleday's sturdy embrace but with little Jane safe in her arms. . . . Then a tall, graceful person was before her, bowing profoundly.

"Magnificent!" exclaimed Sir Nicholas Frayne, hat on heart, his tone (and eyes) schooled to a now reverent admiration. "By heavens, it was positively heroical! But—your little charge—the poor child—ha, by God, she is hurt —bleeding! Suffer me!"

Hands, gentle though very masterful, lifted the child from Rosemary's trembling clasp, passing her up to the monocled gentleman in the high-wheeled curricle.

"Hold her, Jimmy—gently, man—then into the rumble with you! Now, madam,—wonderful, heroic girl—permit me!"

Somehow, and almost before she knew it, Rosemary was seated in the vehicle, with Jane nestling in her arms—a pitiful little creature whose small face showed paler than ever now and stained with blood, at sight of which Rosemary forgot all else:

"Oh, quickly, sir!" she cried, removing Jane's dusty little bonnet. "To Mrs. Humby's School—to Golden Square——"

"Certainly, certainly!" murmured Sir Nicholas, seating himself nimbly beside her; and away they went.

"Oh, Miss Mary dear," sighed Jane, "now must I die and be buried like my mama?"

"No—no!" gasped Rosemary, kissing that pale, wistful little face and dabbing away the dust and blood-flow very tenderly with her handkerchief. "It's only a tiny cut, my darling."

"But you didn't let—the great big horse jump on me!"

"No, of course not, dear."

"But I lost—all my humbugs!"

"I'll buy you more, oh, lots more—so smile, darling!"

Thus Rosemary found no time to so much as glance at the tall, rather sinister figure beside her or the streets through which he drove, until they stopped suddenly; then she looked up to see Sir Nicholas smiling down at her.

"But—this is not Golden Square!" said she, glancing round about at the unfamiliar neighbourhood.

"It is on our way," he answered easily, tossing the reins to the smiling Jimmy and descending to the pavement rather hastily. "But madam, I feel myself the unhappy cause of our dear little maid's mishap and your own natural distress, and you must let me make such small reparation as I may. 'Pon my soul, you're pale as a ghost—a glass of wine to restore your colour —a doctor for the dear child——"

"No, thank you, sir. Jane's hurt is not serious, thank God! Pray drive us on to Golden Square."

"Not yet—I beg!" smiled Sir Nicholas, reaching both hands to aid her down. "At least, do pray take time to compose yourself—and the sweet child should be washed and brushed—so dusty! Her poor little face bathed—see the blood on it!"

So Rosemary, still shaken by her experience, thinking only of little Jane and fearing no evil, presently suffered herself to be ushered into a sumptuous though somewhat untidy chamber, where a grim-mouthed, fish-eyed man-servant supplied her with water, sponge and towels.

Then, deftly, tenderly and gently murmurous, Rosemary bathed and cherished the little, wounded head until this desolate child, all unused to such motherlike care, turned to look up at her in great-eyed wonderment and uttering a soft, rapturous cry, dodged the sponge to lay her small wet face to Rosemary's cheek, murmuring:

"Oh, Miss Mary dear, I do—love you so!"

And how should Rosemary think, just then, of anything else in the world but the clinging arms of this lonely child and the yearning love thus offered to her lonely self? There are women (thank God!) who are mothers born, and thus Rosemary kissed this small, dripping face and, having dried it, kissed it again and again, whispering:

"Jane—oh, little Jane, my dear—I love you too!"

"Charming! Charming—positively!" said Sir Nicholas, closing the door behind him. "And how do we find ourselves now?"

"Better, sir, thank you," answered Rosemary, "and quite ready to go."

"A quaint child, such a demure little person!" smiled Sir Nicholas. "Positively I must kiss her!"

But as he advanced, Jane shrank within Rosemary's ready arm.

"Eh? Won't you kiss me, little lady?"

"Oh, no, thank you, sir," answered Jane, curtseying politely but drawing a fold of Rosemary's cloak about herself. Sir Nicholas laughed and, crossing to a buffet where stood a number of bottles and decanters, he filled a glass and proffered it to Rosemary.

"A sip of sherry and a biscuit, Miss Mary?"

"No, thank you. But how did you know my——"

"Your charming name? The child, Miss Mary. And it is a delightful name, yes, positively, and beautiful as your lovely self. But do pray sit down—come now—this glass of wine——"

"No, thank you."

"Tush! It will do you good. Miss Mary, I insist."

"So do I!" answered Rosemary, turning towards the door.

"Dear me!" he laughed. "Such determined Beauty? Then a cup of tea? A glass of milk for the child?"

"Thank you, sir—no! We have been away too long already. Mrs. Humby will be anxious."

"And pray, who is Mrs. Humby?"

"Sir, this is not your business and——"

"Not in the least, m' dear soul. However, we will allow Mrs. Humby to be anxious—for a little while. I will explain everything to her later on. B'gad I'll—I'll so belaud your heroism! I'll teach her to know and appreciate you for the treasure you are, Miss Mary. So there's really no cause for such haste. Pray sit down again for a moment or two. And try this wine—come now, you must."

Rosemary's slim, dark brows met in a sudden frown, her blue eyes surveyed the speaker very deliberately from head to foot and feature by feature; also, when she spoke, it was in tone apparently untroubled as her look:

"If you will kindly step from the door, sir, Jane and I will go."

"Presently, m' dear soul. First I must send round to the mews for my curricle and——"

"Do not trouble,—we will walk, sir."

"No, no," said he, smiling, "this I cannot permit. . . . You so agitated, deliciously so! And the dear child—injured and so forth,—to allow you to walk would be positively inhuman."

Rosemary's slender though very capable hands clenched, her eyes sparkled angrily, yet her rich, soft voice seemed smoothly serene as she answered:

"You make it very evident how blindly foolish I was to venture here,— but you see, sir, in my agitation I mistook you for a gentleman."

Sir Nicholas bowed; his lean dark face grew suddenly red and as suddenly pale, then he laughed a little stridently and crossing deliberately to the door, leaned there.

And now, despite her brave showing, something in the devouring intensity of his regard chilled her with swift dread and a creeping self-consciousness that shamed her. But in the clasp of Jane's little fingers was mighty comfort and, looking down into the small, elfin face upraised to her own, she read such mute adoration that the child's very weakness made her strong again and she fronted the sinister, lounging figure at the door, calmly undismayed as ever.

"Why are you keeping us here?" she questioned gently.

"For reasons sufficing," he answered as gently, "one of which you may see by looking in the mirror yonder."

"Will you—please—stand from that door?"

"Not yet, Miss Mary. And despite your taunt, pray believe you have absolutely nothing to fear." And yet even while he spoke, his hot eyes so belied his words to that, once again, she felt that creeping chill of dread. . . . And then, high and clear, spake little Jane:

"Miss Mary dear, do you s'pose he'll 'blige us and open the door if we kiss him to?"

Sir Nicholas chuckled.

"Aha!" he exclaimed. "There speaketh wisdom! Out of the mouth of babes,—and so forth. E'gad, Mary—'pon m' soul, I'll make it a bargain——"

He paused suddenly, listening to a sound of voices below.

"Alas!" sighed he, "I fear we shall soon be driving to your Mrs. Humby——"

Feet upon the stair without; an imperative knock. Sir Nicholas frowned, sighed, opened the door and into the room stepped Valentine, Earl of Abbeymere. Beholding Rosemary, he backed suddenly, his weary eyes grew radiant beneath lifting brows and, drawing a deep breath, he glanced from her to Sir Nicholas and back again; and Rosemary noticed he kept his right hand hidden behind him.

"Rosemary!" he murmured, "You? And—here of all places on earth——"

"Oh, my lord," she exclaimed, "take me away—this man——"

"Ah?" murmured his lordship, "Exactly!"

Sir Nicholas laughed, reaching out his hand in greeting.

"What, Valentine?" said he, "D' you know this lady?"

"I have that honour!" answered the Earl, turning to face him, and so was a moment's silence; but something in their attitude warned Rosemary for, beholding the terrible look on his lordship's youthful face, she stooped instinctively and, clasping the child to her bosom, held her there with face hidden.

"Of course," said Sir Nicholas at last, "if—er—Miss Mary happens to be a particular—er—friend of yours——"

"She is, Frayne, she is!" sighed the Earl, cutting him short. "You see, I live in hopes she will be my Countess. . . . But to-day I am here to remind you of Cynthia Bellenden and—this!" With the word, his right hand appeared and in it a riding crop that, whizzing viciously, smote Sir Nicholas across and across the face—cruel blows that cut—that staggered and drew from the stricken man's lips a cry of anguish. . . . Then in upon them ran Mr. Jimmy, his modish languor quite forgotten, and after him two other young exquisites, all three of whom hastened to support and comfort their stricken companion and for a minute or two was clamour of excited questioning, stilled all at once by the Earl's cold, imperious tones:

"Gentlemen, I will explain. Your friend, Sir Nicholas Frayne, used his whip on a woman. I've used mine on him. You will therefore understand that just so soon as you or he can arrange a meeting, it is my very earnest hope and desire to shoot him as dead as possible. Sirs, I bid you good afternoon!"

Then, reaching hand to Rosemary, he led her from that silent room and out into the street where, behind two foam-spattered horses, stood a dusty carriage.

"Rosemary, where will you go?" he enquired, lifting Jane into the vehicle.

"To Golden Square, please, my lord."

"So near?" he sighed. "Then we must drive slowly for I have much to—to talk about."

CHAPTER XX

TELLETH HOW THE EARL FOUND HIM A LITTLE FAIRY GODMOTHER

"First," said Rosemary, sighing with relief as the carriage bore them away, "first I will explain how we came in—that man's house."

"Please—no!" said the Earl, turning to smile with a quite unexpected gentleness at little Jane. "First honour me with an introduction to her small ladyship here. And secondly," he continued, when this ceremony had been performed to Jane's demure satisfaction, "the burning question is, now and always, when will you marry me, Rosemary?"

"Ah, never," she answered, gently. "I have told you so, often. You know it is impossible."

"On the contrary," he answered as gently, "I know it is not only possible but actually imperative—for the sake of—well, let us say—another."

Now at this she turned to regard him with look of swift and dreadful apprehension.

"Who—what do you mean?" she whispered.

"Yes, you have guessed rightly!" he nodded. "For Rosemary, my dear, we are both of us quite aware that the late Earl did not commit suicide. In fact, we know for certain exactly how—and by whose hand he died. You agree?"

"No!" she whispered, shuddering violently. "No——"

"And yet, my poor dear, in your secret heart you are dreadfully sure—

terribly certain he died by the act of—Another! I can read it in your sweet eyes."

"Well, my lord, even were this truly so," answered Rosemary with her resolute expression, "I should still love him more than life!"

"And so it is," sighed the Earl, "yes, my dear—this is precisely why you must—and will—marry—me."

"My lord, is this a threat? Are you suggesting you will betray him?"

"Dear Rosemary, a man who loves as I—might do anything——"

"Then such love is debasing and hateful!" she flamed.

"Be generous and say—merely human," he retorted, with his cynical smile. "And alas! I'm nothing of an angel and very far from a saint. Consequently I am wholly unworthy, and yet—perhaps for this very reason, love you very reverently, Rosemary."

"Listen, my lord! Hear me once and for all."

"Not unless you call me Valentine."

"Then, Valentine," said she, quick-breathing and leaning impulsively towards him, "look at me—into my eyes! Now—suppose I tell you, confess to you that it was I—the guilt—that my hand——"

"Hush!" cried he, with quick, compelling gesture; and thus was silence between them while eyes looked deep into eyes—and it was his own eager, questioning gaze that wavered and fell, and he silent still.

"Well?" she questioned at last.

"I—don't—know!" he answered, passing hand across brow like one amazed and deeply perplexed. "But, Rosemary, were this indeed so, or—could I ever come to believe it of you, I should only love you all the more, were this possible,—yes, love and bless you for ridding the world of such evil——"

"Oh!" gasped Rosemary, recoiling. "Oh, but he was your——"

"Don't say 'father'! I am the son of my little gentle mother. But, my dear, why will you pretend to such an act? Ah, of course,—you know too certainly that he died by the hand of—Another, yes, yes! And this brings us back to my first argument,—that for his sake you must wed me."

Rosemary sighed wearily and leaning back in her corner, turned to stare out of the window while my lord, leaning back in his, stared at her, and little Jane seated very upright between them, small sandalled feet demurely crossed, stared from one to other and, having surveyed his lordship most particularly —his graceful slenderness, youthful face and golden hair, having thus viewed him with the dispassionate, deep-sighted scrutiny of Childhood, thought fit to pronounce judgment on this wise:

"I like this gentleman, Miss Mary dear, so I think you'd better marry him if I was you."

Now at this, the Earl laughed down at the dignified little speaker quite boyishly, then drawing her close, kissed her tenderly and very solemnly.

"Jane," he murmured, putting back her bonnet to caress her smooth, dark hair, "Oh, little Jane, teach her how to love me. Be my little fairy godmother and bewitch her into wedding me."

"Oh, hush!" said Rosemary.

"Weave spells, little fairy godmother, enchant me into a fairy prince for her, and this poor world into a garden of delight—will you?"

"Well," answered Jane, thoughtfully, "I'll ask God 'bout it. I'll say you into my prayers. I'll say—'Please God make them nice an' married an' live happy ever after, amen'. . . . An' oh, I do wish I'd got nice bright hair, like you!"

The Earl was silent and smiling down at the child, made as if to kiss her, but chancing to meet Rosemary's look of shocked consternation, he checked the impulse and laughed instead:

"Well, Rosemary, you hear?" he nodded. "Do what you will your fate is settled and mine also,—to be married and live happy ever after! My little Fairy Godmother will carry the matter to the Supreme Tribunal——"

"For shame!" cried Rosemary angrily. "To make a mockery of such sweet innocence,—you that have faith in nothing! You that—beat men with whips and threaten their lives,—be ashamed!"

"Oh, I am!" he sighed, "that you should find cause to so misjudge me, for I have my beliefs, Rosemary, faiths I would die for—perhaps! But as regards threatening men's lives, well—yes, I have uttered such threats, once or twice, and will again—now, to you, my dear, and pray heed! . . . Guilty or no, you must never wed Richard Vibart. . . . for his lady mother's sake——"

"His—mother . . . ?"

"Lady Vibart!" he nodded. "You see, when I was a child, I loved her quite devotedly, now that I am a man I esteem her very deeply and it would pain me extremely to become the cause of her everlasting grief——"

"How?" she gasped. "Ah—what are you suggesting?"

"Death!" he murmured, twining a tress of little Jane's glossy hair about his finger. "The sudden death of her only son. So, my dear, you must never marry our Richard or—though he kill me in the act, as I think he would, I shall most certainly end him also. Now, why look at me with such horror; does this love of mine——"

"Love?" she exclaimed fiercely. "Such love is only vile selfishness, a hateful affliction—a dark and dreadful menace."

"Yet it is myself," he sighed, "and all that I am."

"Then I pray the merciful God preserve me from it."

"And here's another prayer!" he murmured. "How shall this avail against an innocent child's, the kind petition of my little Fairy Godmother? I wonder!"

"You grow hateful!" Rosemary whispered passionately. "I begin to despise you more and more, my lord."

"Do you, Rosemary? And yet you don't know the half; listen, dear soul!" Here, muffling Jane's sharp little ears against himself with gentle hand, he leaned across to Rosemary and spoke beneath his breath: "I have lately made myself a perjured liar! I have contrived that the late Earl's murder shall seem *felo-de-se*. I have sworn upon Holy Writ so falsely and effectively that, being esteemed by my deluded fellow men a gentleman and person of honour, my false testimony at the late inquest has branded my own flesh and blood a suicide—as you may read in to-day's *Gazette*. So here sit I a shameless perjurer, no whit ashamed, my dear, because I am so,—merely for your sake. Thus you, Rosemary, need hide no longer and our Richard is free to go wherever he will—except your arms. Also, I—ah, confound it! I fear this must be Golden Square to relieve you of me, and much too soon! . . . And so, little Jane, it must be good-bye for the present. Ah, my sweet, small, Fairy Godmother . . . you'll say me into your prayers?"

"Yes, sir . . . oh, yes, every night!"

"And—would you," said he, rather wistfully, "will you kiss me, little Jane?" For answer up came two thin little arms to clasp and cling. And so they kissed. Then a smart, though very dusty footman opened the door and bowed as my lord, with Jane in his arms, stepped from the carriage and, reaching hand to aid Rosemary, murmured:

"I may call to see you here?"

"No, no, my lord, I beg you will not," she answered, murmuring also and avoiding alike his helping hand and pleading eyes.

"However, I have found you," said he, going on beside her, "as I shall always find you—wherever you hide. To-night I go back to Abbeymere; the funeral is to-morrow,—but soon . . . yes, soon as may be, I shall at least see you again, here or somewhere. For love such as mine cannot be denied."

CHAPTER XXI

TELLETH HOW SIR PETER WENT INVESTIGATING

So THE old Earl, being dead, was buried with all due circumstance; and the great house of Abbeymere, empty, silent and desolate, seemed dead as he.

And yet, upon this sunny afternoon, as Sir Peter surveyed its many windows, he fancied they still contrived to leer or scowl at him malignantly like eyes in the face of a newly slain foe.

Therefore as his musing gaze roved to and fro along the wide frontage, Sir Peter frowned also and was silent so long that John Rudge, the lodgekeeper, ventured speech at last:

"Empty as any drum, S' Peter, an' silent as the tomb, sir! Nary soul left—only me an' me mistus. Sarvants all gone, his ludship likewise clean gone an' nowise never like to come back again no more neether, sir."

"But how do you know this, Rudge?" enquired Sir Peter, his gaze still upon the house.

"Why, sir, his ludship told me so his own self. For 'ardly is th' old Earl buried in th' old ruinated chapel yonder, along o' the rest on 'em, and the grandfolkses gone, sir, than Lord Iford . . . I mean the noo Earl, orders the pair 'oss chariot, packs off the sarvants, locks up the house and tosses the keys —these here—to me. 'There y' are, John!' says he. 'A pound a week an' your cottage,' says he; 'some fools may want to look over the cursed place or even buy it. But as for me,' 'e says, shakin' 'is fist at it mighty passionated, 'may it rot an' be damned!' says 'e—axing your honour's pardon. Then 'e jumps into his carriage and away at a gallop, sir."

"To London, Rudge?"

"Ay, to London, sir."

"How many servants were there—in the house, John?"

"Well, sir, years ago I can mind they was aplenty,—thirty-odd they'd be then, ah—mebbe more, but these last years they wasn't only nine or ten, counting of Mr. Clipsby, though 'e weren't not 'ardly wot you might call a sarvant, sir."

"A superior person, John, as I remember him."

"A gen'leman, sir, to my thinkin'—talked like one, dressed like one, walked like one an' played organ or pianner fair bootiful!"

"Yes," murmured Sir Peter thoughtfully. "I remember now—more companion than servant—and I heard him play once, years ago, remarkably . . . hum!"

"But never no more, sir!" sighed John.

"You saw the Earl that night . . . the night he—died, eh, Rudge?"

"Ay, I did, sir. Along about two o'clock i' the morning it would be, or a bit earlier, when Mr. Clipsby comes a-knockin' at my cottage door yonder. 'Me lord wants ye up to the 'ouse, Rudge,' says 'e, breathless-like. 'The Earl's shot hisself——'"

"So . . . he told you that, did he?" enquired Sir Peter. "Did he say anything else?"

"Why, yes, sir, he says to me, says he: 'Did ee see anybody run across the park, John?' says 'e——"

"Strange!" murmured Sir Peter.

"Well—no, sir, ye see there was me breeches! I'd told Mr. Clipsby about 'em a-vanishing away so very mysterious. . . . Hows'ever, up I gets, sir, an' goes a-running to the' 'ouse . . . and theer's th' Earl sure-ly very on-common dead, a-settin' in his armcheer——"

"Sitting in his armchair, was he, John?"

"Ay, sir,—all doubled up like, an' his face black wi' powder an' smeared wi' blood—fair 'orrorsome for to be'old."

"Who else was there?"

"Nary a soul, sir, only Lord Iford an' Mr. Clipsby an' me. 'Lookee at—that, John!' says m'lud, p'inting to his feyther's corpse, 'If ye never see death afore, you sees it now, John!' says 'e. 'Pah! cover it up, Clipsby!' 'e says. But Lord, sir, Mr. Clipsby backs away as if 'e dassent go anigh it, so I takes up a rug and covers the gashly thing. But, 'no, no!' says me lord, 'damme, it looks worse that way!' and 'e whips the rug away so quick an' fiercelike that the corpse pretty night comes a-toppling out o' the cheer—so I puts out me 'and to keep it from falling. But—'let be, John!' says m' lud, fiercer than afore; 'don't ee touch it, a tumble or so won't 'urt it,' 'e says. 'Off wi' you,' says he, 'rouse the grooms, bid one on 'em gallop for Doctor Burgess, and keep the lodge gates closed, John,—like your mouth. Wait for the inkwest,' says 'e, 'an' then tell 'em all you know.' . . . Well, Sir Peter, you was at the inkwest, sir, and heered me testify . . . on oath——"

"Yes, I heard!" murmured Sir Peter, staring away at the house again, perceiving which, John sighed and nodded gloomily:

"Ah, theer be the great, old place, sir, empty at last as any drum and silent as a grave! Theer be the carpets an' furnitur' an' I dunno wot all,—ah, and the family portraits all a-staring wi' their painted eyes at nobody—all except one, Sir Peter, the late dee-seized Earl—his portrait aren't theer becos 'tis burnt—ashes it be, sir!"

"Burnt? How so, John?"

"Sir, 'twere in the Abbey ruins the very morning as they buried him. I— well, I chanced to be thereabouts and sir . . . in that theer lonesome place I hears a voice, ay . . . I hears a voice most on-expected an' a-talkin' quick an' fierce-like. So I creeps apiece nearer and . . . Lord love me, Sir Peter, theer be Lord Iford—I mean the noo Earl—a-burning th' old un, ay, his very own feyther, sir, leastways his picter-portrait, on a little bonfire as ever was. Ay, sir, 'tis Gospel true! Theer stands m'lud, arms folded, a-watching his feyther's portrait burn and a-cursing of it right fearsome!"

"Ah,—then . . . but doubtless the poor young gentleman was drunk, John."

"Well, not so as I could notice, sir; stood steady, 'e did, and spoke very plain, your honour."

"Spoke, John?"

"Sir, 'e did! 'Burn!' says 'e, twixt his teeth like, 'Burn, damn ye!' says 'e, —saving your presence, Sir Peter! 'Burn!' says 'e, 'and I hopes as you'm a-burning in hell fire now—an' forever!' says 'e,—ah, sir, an' wi' sich oathes as fair curdled me blood! . . . Hows'ever, Sir Peter, if you be still minded for to see over the 'ouse, here be the keys. I'll take care o' your hoss, sir."

And now, as Sir Peter approached the great desolate house, before his mind's eye was a vision conjured up by the lodgekeeper's words, a dreadful vision of such unnatural hate and maniacal fury that he halted suddenly, arrested by this appalling conclusion:

The hand that could burn a father's picture might assuredly strike that father from life!

Up marble steps, across broad terrace to the massive door that presently swung wide upon a lofty, pillared hall. Closing this door behind him, Sir Peter glanced round about and thus became vaguely aware of something unfamiliar and very much out of place amid such stately surroundings and saw this for a shabby travelling trunk whereon was pasted a neat label whereon was boldly inscribed:

> Mr. E. Clipsby
> In care of Mrs. Humby
> No. 12 Golden Square
> London.

Through this hall went Sir Peter, his footsteps echoing dismally, along the picture gallery with its rows of staring portraits, across the great ballroom to a long corridor with an arched door at one end.

After a momentary hesitation, he opened this door and stepped into a spacious chamber, this same room that had seen and held the dark secret of such grim and violent death. The stained carpets had been removed and, save for this, all things showed as he remembered them on that most fateful night. ... Motionless he stood there, head bowed as if hearkening for some expected sound to break the awesome, brooding stillness of this desolate mansion, or as though this room might of itself tell him something, while his musing gaze surveyed that part of the floor where once had sprawled a dreadful, blood-smeared, contorted shape. ... At last Sir Peter stirred, sighed, turned abruptly and heard his spurs ring strangely loud as he crossed to a certain shadowy corner where hung a curtain of arras; drawing this aside, he beheld another door, an ancient, stealthy-seeming door, for it was small, narrow and flush with the panelling; moreover it was armed, top and bottom, with formidable bolts. Having pondered this discovery, he opened the door and saw, beyond two worn stone steps, a passage floored and roofed with stone, a vista of groined arches lit by narrow lancets high overhead, and guessed this some part of the ancient and once famous Abbey by the Mere.

Slowly Sir Peter descended these steps and began to traverse this passage, his eyes quick to heed the many evidences of past beauty and grandeur in carven capital and lofty, fluted column. But suddenly the echo of his slow footsteps died away as he paused to stare down at a particular flagstone beneath wrinkling brows; for some while he stood thus, silent and very still, his frowning gaze scanning the age-worn pavement, now here, now there, until he raised his head suddenly, aware of a sound at last, the vague stir of soft and stealthy movement that came and was gone; wherefore his glance quested dark corners for the furtive shapes of flitting rats. Then he went on again, but treading more lightly now, with a strange unwillingness to trouble the pervading stillness with tramp of foot or jingle of spur.

He had progressed thus but a very little way when he checked again, arrested this time by something that twinkled up at him from between two of the flagstones and stooping, he picked up a handsome, cut-steel coat button. He was gazing very pensively at this, when once more his sharp ears caught that vague sound . . . something was moving near-by.

Sir Peter stepped forward, alert, peering, and, set deep within a wondrously sculptured arch, came on another door and this ajar; slowly, cautiously, he pushed it wider and saw this:

A dim, vaulted, medieval chamber; in one corner a chair, a small table and richly carved bedstead; in the opposite corner a tall, old-fashioned press and, staring wide-eyed above this, the pallidly nondescript face of that hitherto negligible person, Eustace Clipsby.

CHAPTER XXII

WHICH IS A CHAPTER OF QUESTION AND ANSWER, AND OF A TRANSFORMATION

SIR PETER halted upon the threshold, surprised and a little challenging; Eustace Clipsby advanced a pace and, bowing ceremoniously, spoke in his pleasant, cultured accents:

"Pray, Sir Peter, may I enquire your pleasure?" And in this moment it seemed to Sir Peter that this person whom he had seen so often in the past, yet never heeded, he now beheld for the first time.

"Mr. Clipsby," said he, advancing into the chamber, "I understood that Abbeymere was quite empty, wholly deserted."

"It was, sir; it is and will be," answered Clipsby serenely. "I am here by my lord's permission to arrange and collect certain articles left behind," and he gestured towards the great bed where, among divers oddments, lay a suit of clothes.

"Then since you are here, Mr. Clipsby, perhaps you will favour me by answering a few questions?"

"To the best of my ability, sir . . . I fear I cannot offer you a chair."

"Thank you, this shall serve," answered Sir Peter and, crossing the stone floor, seated himself upon the bed, his dark eyes down-bent to the worn pavement that had been laid by the reverent hands of sturdy friars long since forgotten dust. "Mr. Clipsby, you had known the late Earl a good many years, I believe?"

"Yes, sir," answered Mr. Clipsby. "But now have I your permission to continue my work?" and he motioned to the sheaves of papers he had been docketing.

"Pray do. I would not waste your time."

And so for a while was silence broken only by the rustle of papers flicked open by dexterous fingers to be scanned quickly, refolded and set aside.

"I remember," continued Sir Peter at last, his gaze still roving, "yes, I recollect Abbeymere once told me that you and he were at Oxford together."

The pale eyes that had been perusing an open document darted askance to flash a glance at the speaker's musing face; then Mr. Clipsby answered in his pleasing voice:

"We were, sir, at Cambridge."

"Cambridge, to be sure!" nodded Sir Peter. "Then, having lived with the family so long and intimately, you should know the present Earl very well."

"Yes, Sir Peter."

"It was he who found his unfortunate father on that very fateful night, Mr. Clipsby."

"It was, sir."

"And yourself, Mr. Clipsby, found them together. Will you favour me with

D

any particulars that struck you as seeming in any way remarkable on that dreadful occasion?"

Mr. Clipsby glanced at the document he held, refolded it, laid it aside, took up another and answered:

"Sir Peter, you were at the inquest, you heard my evidence. I can only repeat, sir, what I said then——"

"That you saw in fact the Earl dead . . . huddled in his armchair, Mr. Clipsby?"

"Such was my evidence, sir, and I have nothing more to add." Here was silence again while Mr. Clipsby's long fingers opened and folded papers and Sir Peter's musing gaze, wandering up from the floor, was focused upon those articles so near him upon the bed.

"Still . . . one wonders!" he murmured at last.

"At what, sir?"

"Well, for instance, it might puzzle any one, Mr. Clipsby, how a dead man should rise upon dead feet and get himself into a chair!" And now his dark gaze met those quick, pale eyes to find them wholly untroubled and steadfast as his own.

"You propound a riddle, Sir Peter."

"Well, yes, it would seem I do."

"And alas, sir, I have no head for riddles!"

"A pity!" sighed Sir Peter, "for there are others."

"Indeed?"

"Oh, yes. One might wonder why certain of the flagstones hereabout have been recently washed?"

"Really, Sir Peter?"

"Beyond all doubt, Mr. Clipsby. Both in the passage outside yonder and in this very . . . interesting room. Surely you can see this for yourself—there! And there again!" Mr. Clipsby leaned to peer at the flagstones thus indicated, glanced at Sir Peter and—bowed.

"Now that you point them out, it would almost appear so," he nodded. "But who would do such strange thing?"

"Who, indeed?" murmured Sir Peter. "And—why?"

Mr. Clipsby merely shook his head dubiously and turned back to the documents before him.

"You will admit," said Sir Peter gently, "that such evidences in such strange, desolate place are at least—suggestive?" Once again Mr. Clipsby turned to front his questioner face to face and Sir Peter, thus meeting the intensity of his pale, indomitable eyes, felt vaguely disquieted by a sense of some very extraordinary change, a flashing vision of unexpected force, a serenely confident power that transformed these pallid, oft-seen features out of all knowledge.

"Pray, Sir Peter, what do they suggest to you?"

"Allow me to counter your question with another. Are you so perfectly assured in your own mind that the late Earl died by his own act?"

Mr. Clipsby sighed a little wearily.

"Sir, you heard my evidence at the inquest. I can say no more."

"And you, Mr. Clipsby, heard me suggest the Earl did not die in his chair, yet you evinced no surprise nor so much as questioned the statement. Pray why?"

"Sir Peter, I accept Lord Iford's statement and the evidence of my own eyes." So saying, Mr. Clipsby turned back to his papers and documents.

"Why, then," quoth Sir Peter, watching these inscrutable features, "concerning Miss Ford——"

The parchment that Mr. Clipsby happened to be looking at crackled, but his face was as expressionless and eyes blankly direct as ever, while he stood waiting for his questioner to proceed.

"You are, of course, acquainted with this young lady?"

"Acquainted, yes, Sir Peter."

"And you are also doubtless aware that on the night, the very hour of Abbeymere's death, she disappeared, and her friends are naturally gravely anxious——"

"Are you so much her friend, sir?"

"More, Clipsby, more! She may be my son's wife one day."

"Then, Sir Peter, it is to be expected she will communicate with you in her own good time."

"Meanwhile, our anxiety on her account grows, Clipsby. Therefore if you know anything—anything, no matter what, that may comfort us, Lady Vibart and myself, I beg you will speak."

"And alas, sir, I have nothing to say."

Sir Peter eyed the speakers impasive face with a gathering frown.

"This, sir, becomes increasingly manifest!" he retorted. "But her sudden inexplicable flight argues a black mystery! Miss Ford saw or heard something so terrible that she fled in panic. The question is,—what?"

"And alas, sir, echo alone answers."

"Echo?" said Sir Peter musingly. "Well, yes—I believe Echo answered—here—to the shot that killed the Earl—here between these age-old walls! I believe the Earl sank and lay dead upon this age-old pavement . . . those three worn flagstones yonder that show evidence of washing. I believe, Mr. Clipsby, could Echo speak of past events, it might discover strange things . . . a rustle and scrape with sound of feet in painful very desperate effort, sounds that go from this chamber out and along the passage to the library, with intervals of restful silence, for Abbeymere was a large man and would be a ponderous burden. It is thus, I think, that Echo might answer."

"Indeed," said Mr. Clipsby, smiling, "it would seem that Echo may become quite eloquent."

"And . . . these clothes," said Sir Peter, gesturing towards the huddle of garments on the bed, "if they were worn by the Earl that night, they should prove eloquent also?"

"As how, sir?"

"Well, the coat I see bears unmistakable stains; also these handsome buttons are quite remarkable and one should be missing. . . ." Here Sir Peter turned the garment with his riding crop while Mr. Clipsby, folding his hands upon the papers before him, watched beneath level brows.

"Yes, as I thought," murmured Sir Peter, "here, as you may see, one button has been . . . wrenched off."

"From which it is to be inferred, sir, that you found it."

Sir Peter arose and, crossing the chamber, laid the button in question upon the desk.

"I found this," he explained, looking into the eyes that looked back into his so steadfastly, "I found this in the passage out yonder, it had fallen between two of the flagstones and both of them have been recently washed."

Mr. Clipsby took up the button, turning it this way and that in the failing light.

"Ah, Sir Peter," he murmured, "now had this but the gift of speech! As it is—here is no more than a mere coat button. . . . What, are you going? Then, Sir Peter, allow me to bid you farewell! Adieu, sir, we are not like to meet again,—at least, not here at Abbeymere." So saying, he bowed and Sir Peter, returning the salute, crossed to the door and, glancing back from the threshold, saw Mr. Clipsby still turned the button this way and that, gazing down at it with a strange, faint smile.

CHAPTER XXIII

IN WHICH THE READER, LIKE THE WRITER, MAY FIND MATTER
FOR SURPRISE

BEHIND Mrs. Humby's School for Ladies, or rather Academy for the Offspring of the Gentry, was a fair-sized garden with a lawn (somewhat pinched and haggard) and a vegetable plot (large and opulent) wherein Benjamin Piper, A.B., erstwhile coxswain to Captain Reginald Humby, R.N., was wont to busy himself, somewhat ferociously and in all weathers, to the vigorous nurture of such right succulent edibles as peas, beans, parsnips, onions, carrots, potatoes and what he termed "sallet raffle."

The coxswain gardened, fair or foul, spade, fork, rake and hoe, like a true seaman, A.B., that is to say—with a will and cheerily-o! and in despite of the piratical depredations of such slimy and stealthy foes as slugs, snails, wire-worms, grubs and the like foes, against whom he waged desperate and unceasing warfare with soot, with salt and any or every lethal weapon as came readiest to hand, more especially a certain stick armed with a long, sharp spike that he dubbed his "belaying pin."

Such earnest, nay indeed such passionate gardener was the coxswain that on moonless nights, when all save trouble and wickedness slept, he was wont to steal forth armed with dark lantern and the belaying pin and thus cut out, capture or destroy these creeping foes at their fiendly work by what he described as "the Element of Surprise."

But even this afternoon a slug more reckless than his fellows and venturing abroad scornful of danger, was espied by the ever-watchful coxswain, who instantly bore down to bring this audacious foe to close action; in other words, Benjamin Piper, A.B., was stalking this destroyer with elaborate caution, his feet were soundless, his one eye gleamed, the spade gripped in knotted hands was lifted slowly for exterminating stroke when—his ears were saluted by a sudden loud and imperious knocking on that weather-beaten door which had opened for little Jane's truant feet not so very many days ago.

The coxswain, at the top of his swing, started, faltered, whispered a hearty curse, set himself anew, smote the slug into nothingness, set by the spade and, loosing the bolts lately affixed by Mrs. Humby's stern mandate, swung the portal wide, then stared, gaped, retreated a step and saluted, finger to eyebrow.

"Sink me, Mr. Eustiss, sir," he exclaimed, "sink and scuttle me, Mr. Clipsby, your honour, I didn't 'ardly know ye, take my Davy if I did, sir!"

"I'm not surprised, Coxswain," answered Mr. Clipsby with pleasant trill of laughter, "not in the least surprised, for I am changed, thank God; the whole world is changed and for the better, Ben, for the better!" So saying, Mr. Clipsby stepped into the sunny garden, but a Clipsby very strangely and most wonderfully transfigured.

From glossy hat to glossy shoes he was all that a modish, dignified, middle-aged gentleman possibly could be; but this marvellous alteration went far beyond and much deeper than mere excellence of raiment, it was in the man himself; a joyous vitality beamed in his pale eyes, it seemed manifest in the curl of his colourless hair; his pallid features showed lines of such virile resolution as transformed it into the face of a new and very potent entity indeed.

"And what," he enquired, leaning gracefully on the jaunty, tasselled cane he carried, "what are you doing here, Coxswain?"

"Was engaged at close quarters with a inseck, a varminous slug——"

"Ha, vermin,—a slug?"

"And a mighty big un, sir."

"And you . . . killed him?"

"Flat as a flounder and dead as a kippered herring, Mr. Eustiss."

"Admirable fellow!" beamed Mr. Clipsby. "There is an untellable satisfaction in killing . . . vermin! It is, I protest and declare, a laudable, a noble, nay—a holy act . . . to kill a slug . . . of any and every kind." Here Mr. Clipsby laughed softly yet with a peculiar joyousness and clapped the coxswain's broad shoulder.

"And how are the folks, Ben,—the Captain and my sister?"

"Sir," answered the coxswain, shaking his head, "when I tells you as the Cap'n's been a-tootin' his flute fair heartbreakin' all the morning, well—you'll understand."

"Her nerves again, Coxswain?"

"Ar! Them narves of hers, Mr. Eustiss, sir, has been actin' reg'lar scandalous o' late."

"And the young lady I sent here, Miss Gray, how is she?"

"Tight, sir,—all trim alow and aloft; ay, she's all ataunto,—but, 'tis her, and bless her pretty eyes,—as is the cause for narves as aforesaid, Mr. Eustiss."

"Then my sister Charlotte must be reasoned with, the matter adjusted at once."

"Ay, ay, sir, but—Mrs. Humby being a craft o' the First Rate, three tier and all heavy metal, wot I asks is—oo's a-going to do same? Ar, oo's a-going to engage her yardarm and yardarm, broadside and broadside,—oo? The Cap'n dassent, I can't, and you, Mr. Eustiss,—well, last time you was alongside, she very nigh blowed you out of the water."

"True enough, Coxswain, but things are changed since then . . . and there is Captain Reginald John crossing the lawn yonder."

"Ay, sir, and did ye ever see sich doleful creetur? And him once sich a prime sailorman, sich a hell-roaring fighter, sich a cheery officer and now—all down by the head, rolling to every sea and——"

"Call him, Ben." Forthwith the coxswain curved hand about shaven lips and hissed in hoarse yet penetrant whisper:

"Cap'n, ahoy!"

The Captain halted in his quick, short, quarterdeck stride, lifted chin from breast and came hastening to them, his flute protruding from the bosom of his neat, blue coat rather like some half-concealed weapon of offence. Beholding Mr. Clipsby, he came to an abrupt halt and, like the coxswain, stared at his visitor from head to foot in speechless amazement.

"Well! Damme!" he exclaimed at last. "I say damme, can this be . . . you yourself, Eustace?"

"Precisely, Reginald John! Myself—at last!" smiled Mr. Clipsby. *"Courage, mon vieux, le diable est mort!"* And stepping lightly forward, he grasped the Captain's hand, shaking it in grip so unexpectedly strong and hearty that Captain Humby actually gasped.

"B—but—who—how—what?" he stammered.

"Freedom!" laughed Mr. Clipsby. "Freedom, my dear fellow! I'm free as air, as bird on bough! And talking of birds, Reginald—listen!" Tucking the handsome cane beneath his arm, Eustace Clipsby whipped the flute from his astounded brother-in-law's breast, set it to lip and began to play a joyous lilting measure as only a master might,—rapid trills of merry liquid notes, sweet and clear as piping thrush, softly melodious as rippling brook,—a song of all free glad tidings . . . then he laughed lightly, tossed the flute into the air, caught it dexterously and thrust it back into the Captain's coat, all in as many moments.

"To-day, Reginald John, I'm fifty-three and my youth is renewed unto me like the eagle's; yea, I could leap and skip as young rams, for to-day—I'm free!"

"Free," repeated the Captain rather dismally, seating himself heavily in the coxswain's wheelbarrow. "Free, but why to-day? You're always free, Eustace, you . . . never married!"

"Not yet," laughed Mr. Clipsby, "but I'm—only a boy of fifty-three. So—who knows?"

"Belay now, brother, belay!" cried the Captain, lifting his hand in eloquent warning. "Talking of matrimony, well—how say you, Coxswain Ben, what's the word, Coxswain?"

"Avast!" quoth the coxswain hoarsely.

"Avast it is!" nodded the Captain gloomily. "Lookee, Eustace, marriage may be only a lottery to some poor fools, but to this fool it's the bilboes, a lee shore, breakers, shipwreck and—absolute confummeration!"

"Which means that you are suffering from nerves,—Charlotte's eh, Reginald John?"

"Ay, ay, damme! And the children's, bless 'em! All a-mope and piping their eyes. Ye see, she's given Miss Gray notice and——"

"Has she? Aha, and for what reason?"

"The dickens only knows! Something or other about a child breaking bounds——"

"'Twas little Miss Jane, love her little 'eart!" explained the coxswain.

"Why, then," said Mr. Clipsby, settling his lustrous hat more firmly, "for this reason we must go reason with Charlotte forthwith. Come, Reginald."

Mr. Clipsby, having reached a certain window, had rattled it wide open, whereat Mrs. Humby—outspread grandly upon cushioned settee, her handsome, stately head tied up in bandage aromatic—emitted a faint scream plaintive and very ladylike, then in tone subdued by suffering yet imperious withal, demanded:

"Who dares? Who is it? What?"

"Nemesis!" answered her brother, clambering through the window. "Woman, your accursed nerves have found you out at last; the fiend Hysteria would hurl you to an abyss of woe where the fang of Remorse should tear you—but for me."

Mrs. Humby emitted another scream, still ladylike, though louder this time and more sustained.

"Eustace!" she gasped, staring on him with wild, half-swooning eyes. "But . . . oh, is this you? So changed! Can it possibly be you? Ah, heaven—it is!" Here, forgetting faintness in contemptuous indignation, she roused herself, pointed imperiously to the door and spake in that terrible voice, at sound of which all had been wont to quail:

"Eustace, begone! Leave me this moment! I command! Hence—instantly!" Mr. Clipsby chuckled and, seating himself beside her, patted the lustrous tresses that crowned her shapely head.

"Charlotte," said he, "don't be a little fool!"

Mrs. Humby gasped; she flashed great eyes at him; she rose majestically and was instantly pulled down again.

"Sit still or be slapped!" said he, in voice more terrible than her own.

"Oh, my gracious heaven!" she ejaculated, quailing slightly. "This is not my poor brother . . . it cannot be! And yet . . . ha, Eustace, how dare you? Such savagery! What means this outrageous——"

"Lottie," he began; Mrs. Humby, like stricken animal, uttered a broken cry, shuddered violently, swayed moaning as if about to swoon and was jerked erect again. "Lottie," he repeated, "cease playing the fool and listen to me; first—off with this rag!" The aromatic bandage was whipped from her temples and cast into distant corner.

"Now heed me, Lottie! Henceforth you won't have a nerve in your whole body to bully folks or plague poor Reginald John any more; their tyranny is ended,—are you listening?"

"Yes, but ah, pray remember I am but a feeble woman Eust——"

"A fiddlestick!"

"A d—delicate creature and——"

"Strong as a horse! And moreover I,—are you listening?"

"Yes, dear Eustace, oh, I am—I am!"

"Very well,—no more nerves! Now, regarding Miss Gray,—she is a young lady of the highest character and I have placed her in your care—I say 'care,' Charlotte—for a very good reason. You will therefore instantly revoke her dismissal and——"

"But Eustace, she——"

"Will therefore remain in your charge until——"

"But dear Eusta——"

"Until her future plans are determined. You will care for her, try to love her, watch over her or—by my soul, Lottie, you will regret it to your dying day. So here she must and shall remain, for the time being."

"Very well, Eustace. Only do please tell me——"

"No more at present. I'm going to play for the children; they must have an hour's recess, my dear."

So saying, he rose and crossed to the door and there Mrs. Humby would have stayed him but, seeing the unwonted fire in his pale, deep-set eyes, the grim set of his lean jaw, she moaned instead, bowing her proud crest in unaccustomed submission and viewing him with look of awed amazement, sighed in murmurous humility:

"I'll summon Miss Wolverton with the young ladies and Miss Gray, of course."

Her so strangely altered brother nodded gaily, blew her a kiss and, opening the door, betook himself to that stately, though forbidding chamber. Here, when he had drawn back the heavy curtains and opened the windows, he swept a heterogeneous collection of ornamental oddments from the tall pianoforte and, seating himself before the instrument, ran his white hands across the keyboard, filling the room, the very house itself with such glorious tumult of rich chords that presently in at the open doorway peeped adventurous Jane's little elfin face, woeful tears now forgotten, and behind her other small ladies less venturesome, but all apeep in joyous wonderment; and beholding them, Eustace Clipsby smiled, calling to them above the luring music:

"Come in, children! Come and dry your tears, for hear now what the music says: 'There is no more sorrow or tears!' Hark what the music tells you,—there now! It says 'Laugh, children, laugh and be glad!' You, Miss Rosemary, yes, pray bring them in—every one. So! Now, my dears, listen to the sweet, grand Spirit of Music ... hear what it sings: 'Fear and trouble, shame and sorrow, shall be all done away. . . . Only Joy shall be, in the end of things,—peace and joy abounding for ever and ever'—listen!"

And so with Rosemary and Miss Woolverton (her sullen face for once seeming almost happy), these children, big and little, sat entranced by the very magic of these hands so sure and masterful upon the keys, that filled the air with melodies grave and gay, tunes familiar, nursery songs glorified into pæans of rapture, blithe yet stately measures that set little feet tapping and small heads swaying until suddenly these magic fingers were stilled and he was smiling round upon them one and all, while Rosemary, hands clasped, gazed upon this so transfigured Clipsby, dumb with an awed amazement.

"There, my dears," said he, rising, "so much for to-day! Now off with you, —out into the sunshine and play, shout, my dears, sing, laugh, dance and— ah, be happy!"

So away they sped, each and every, not at all like Mrs. Humby's demure young ladies, but like the eager young creatures and happy children they were.

CHAPTER XXIV

IN WHICH MR. CLIPSBY CONTINUETH TO SURPRISE

"EVEN yet," said Rosemary, glancing a little askance at her companion, his free, gallant bearing, "I can scarcely believe you are really yourself, Mr. Clipsby."

"My dear," he answered, suddenly grave, "I am like a man freed from a long imprisonment, passionate for life, eager to make up for the weary, wasted years of my vanished youth. For any and every harm I may have committed I would achieve some good act. I would be servant to all distressed, comforting their sorrows, making songs of happiness in sad hearts. Such time as I have left me, such money or gifts as I possess—I would spend them all to benefit whom I may. Thus I have much to do and my time, I think, will be short, so I must be busy—oh, busy!" Here, with movement almost violent, he started afoot and, striding to the open window, stood there a moment, quick breathing; then he was back again, looking down on her with a wistful anxiety that she thought almost pathetic.

"And now," said he gently, "first of all—you, Miss Rosemary. I that have no friends would be friend to all and most of all . . . to you, for you are sad, I know. You are thinner, paler than you were, your eyes large with sorrow, your smile a ghost of itself—why, why? Oh, Miss Rosemary, will you suffer me to help you how I may? Child, will you trust me, confide in me, allow me to share the burden of your troubles,—will you?" Thus speaking, he reached out both hands to her with gesture of such humble yet passionate supplication that instinctively she took those tremulous fingers in her own warm, vital clasp, murmuring:

"But you were always kind, always my good, gentle friend."

"I have striven to be," he answered, murmuring also, "more than you can ever imagine, yes—ah, yes, even when I permitted you to run off that night alone and half distracted,—oh, believe this!"

"I do!" she answered, pressing these nervous hands ere she released them. "What should I have done without you? That night of horror . . . that awful, awful night!"

"When the Earl . . . died!" he nodded.—"Ah, but why tremble, my dear? For consider,—an evil creature ceased from evil; is this a matter to shudder at? Ah, surely not, for Death may have purged him . . . a little! Purified him . . . perhaps. Here then, my child, is no cause for horror but of rejoicing rather! So forget, forget . . . ah, cannot you smile again?"

"Ah—no, no!" she whispered. "I shall never forget; how can I, how may I? He haunts me still . . . I saw him . . . lying dead . . . murdered——"

"But, Miss Rosemary, surely, surely, you know by this time how there was never any suspicion of murder?"

"Never any . . . suspicion——!" Rosemary gasped and was dumb, but looking at him with such wild eyes that instinctively he reached out his arms as if to comfort her, then checking the impulse, sighed and let them fall.

"My dear . . . oh, my dear," said he in shaken voice, "surely you saw it . . . read the account in the newspapers?"

"No, no—I dared not look at them."

"Miss Rosemary, dear child, the inquest proved conclusively that the Earl killed himself."

"Killed . . . himself?" she whispered. "Ah, but I saw! I . . . I thought— oh, dear heaven . . . what have I done?" Then he was on his knees beside her, had caught her hands, speaking in strange, breathless manner:

"Do not grieve . . . have no fear . . . whatever you have done, it is nothing that shall harm you, nothing that shall not be amended. Only confide . . . trust in me and I will help you, even though it cost all that I have of life remaining, all that I am. What was it you saw, child? What was it you did?"

"I wrote to Lady Vibart . . . accusing myself of murdering the Earl."

Mr. Clipsby rose to his feet slowly like one that was old or very weary and stood a long moment looking down on her very oddly.

"You . . . accused yourself!" he repeated. "And . . . to Lady Vibart? Why then, you must have feared—my poor child—you must have felt utterly convinced that your Richard had fulfilled his wild threat against the Earl's life. Yes, of course, this only could explain such reckless, such very lovely action. . . . To accuse yourself! Ah, young Richard is fortunate in such a love! But pray tell me, if you will, what so convinced you of his guilt? Will you tell me all that you remember of that night?"

"Yes, yes," she answered breathlessly, "yes I will . . . come nearer, sit here beside me and I'll tell you all I can remember; to speak of it may perhaps help me to forget." And thus leaning towards him, her gaze on his pale, gentle face, she spoke below her breath:

"It seems like a horrible nightmare," she whispered, shuddering, "vague and all confused yet—frightful! It all begins with a dreadful sick drowsiness some time after tea and Lady Bedingham telling me to go and lie down. I remember stumbling upstairs to my room and falling upon my bed and . . . dreams . . . I remember waking the first time in a strange place, a dim stone chamber with an arching roof . . . a great bed . . . I thought I was still dreaming until I found the pistol, the same one you had given me once before or one like it. Then I grew terribly afraid and screamed. . . . The door wouldn't open so I screamed until the sick faintness took me again. . . . I remember waking a second time . . . and no light . . . I crouched there in the darkness, praying to God but with the pistol clasped to my heart . . . I heard footsteps at last, then the door opened and I saw . . . the Earl. . . . He was carrying a lantern. . . . But I had the pistol and meant to use it; I showed it and told him I would . . . oh, but I was sick and giddy and when . . . the dreadful moment came, I grew weak . . . I dropped the pistol and instead of shooting I fainted. . . ."

"My poor child! Sweet innocent!"

Turning toward this tenderly compassionate murmur, Rosemary stared amazed and caught her breath to see the speaker's face so dreadfully at odds with his tone, the slitted eyes aglare, teeth agleam between lips back-drawn in bestial ferocity; then this awesome face was hidden by a twitching hand . . . the tender voice spoke again:

"But a just and merciful God heard your prayer, child, and smote this would-be destroyer from life!" The veiling hand fell and Eustace Clipsby was smiling at her, his lean, pale face gentle as ever. "So you do not remember seeing . . . anything more . . . hearing any sound, my dear?"

"No, no! When I opened my eyes, the lantern was standing on the old press, the door was wide open and I ran from that hateful place and along a passage . . . a little door was ajar and, peeping through, I saw the library and the Earl lying dead and . . . Richard . . . oh, Richard, was standing over him . . . with that same pistol in his hand——"

"Richard? Richard Vibart?" As if spurred by some resistless force, Mr. Clipsby arose—then stood dumb and utterly still while Rosemary continued:

"I would have gone to him but his father came."

"You mean . . . Sir Peter?"

"Yes, he climbed in through the window. Then . . . I heard Richard confess he had shot the Earl . . . I saw his father's despair and I crept away. Then, thank God, I met you——"

"And Sir Peter believed him guilty . . . his own son?"

"Ah, but then, I believed so too and Richard is my very life!"

"Your life?" he repeated. "Your life?" Then he was before her on his knees, looking at her radiant eyes. "So now, dear child," said he, "ah, you sweet, strong-souled woman, hear me tell you, kneeling thus in the sight of the God before whom I must appear soon, I think,—hear me declare that your Richard is innocent as your sweet self——"

Then Rosemary was kneeling also, head bowed between trembling hands, in a very ecstasy of joy and gratitude.

"Thank God!" she whispered, and now, lifting face and hands to the man who watched her so reverently, "And, oh, thank you too, dear friend; indeed,

indeed, you have helped one poor soul to-day, you have lifted me from hopelessness to . . . oh, to heaven!" And catching his hand, she kissed it ere ever he might prevent.

"My dear . . . oh, my dear!" he stammered, raising her. "Why, Miss Rosemary, I—I—no one in all my wretched life ever——"

"Don't!" she exclaimed. "Don't or I shall cry. . . . And if you look at me so—so humbly I shall kiss—both your hands . . . such wonderful hands! And do—do please call me Rosemary. . . . And oh, you have made me so . . . wonderfully . . . happy."

"Then, Rosemary, I am happy too," he answered, smiling. "And now, please tell me when you sent that letter of confession."

"Two days ago."

"Then I must go to Holm Dene and see Lady Vibart at once. The sooner I do, the sooner you will see your Richard."

"My . . . Richard!" she murmured fondly. "To see him again—Ah, but no!" she cried, starting to her feet. "I cannot see him, I must not, dare not! Viscount Iford—the Earl—has threatened his life and . . . oh, Mr. Clipsby, I'm afraid . . . he is so quick, so . . . smiling and deadly."

"Now God forbid!" exclaimed Clipsby in quick dismay. "Did he utter this threat recently? Has he found you here? Have you seen Valentine lately?"

"Yes . . . oh, yes."

"And he threatened—murder?"

"No—and yet almost as dreadful; he vows Richard shall fight him . . . a duel!"

"A duel!" repeated Mr. Clipsby, passing nervous hand across his deeply furrowed brow. "Licensed murder! No—no! Yet how prevent? Oh, my child, it was to avert such possibility and—yes, to save you from his persecution that I hid you here . . . and now, now that he has found you. . . . Ha, there is such vile blood in him—such wild and reckless evil—that if I must . . . ay, by God, I will——"

"What—ah, what do you mean?" she whispered, shrinking before the speaker's dreadful transformation, that sudden and awful ferocity of look and gesture; and he, as if aware of this, crossed to the window and stood there a moment, his face hidden from her.

Greatly wondering and a little fearful, she went to him and taking his hand that had become a quivering fist, spoke very tenderly sweet:

"Dear Mr. Clipsby, I would not grieve you with my troubles; you have known so much unhappiness that I would comfort you instead . . . but I must go away for Richard's sake, because he is so fierce and reckless too and . . . if they killed each other, as they might, I shall die as well. So I must hide again. . . . Oh, indeed, I am no child afraid of life . . . only I ask you to promise not to make my troubles yours but just to remember me as your grateful, loving friend——"

"Rosemary . . ." The fist she held became a clinging hand, the haggard face he turned on her was gentle now and quivering with emotion, the pale eyes were softened and misted by painful tears.

"Oh, child," he pleaded brokenly, "do not turn from me or . . . spurn my aid. I have been so desperately lonely and now I have . . . dedicated myself to your service; your welfare is my happiness, so trust me, Rosemary, only trust me . . . or I——" Here, sinking upon the window seat, he covered his face; then, moved by divine sympathy and quick compassion, Rosemary stooped to touch his bowed shoulder, his greying hair.

"Dear lonely man," she sighed, "I do and will trust you."

"Then tell me, pray tell me how he . . . how Valentine found you here—in such secure place as this, how?"

So Rosemary recounted the episode of little Jane's truancy and all it had led to, while Mr. Clipsby listened with a strange, painful attention.

"Frayne?" he exclaimed when the story was ended. "Aha, Sir Nicholas Frayne! And now Valentine's threat, can you tell me his exact words?"

"Yes they were these—or nearly: First he said how much it would grieve him to cause Lady Vibart everlasting grief by shooting her son . . . then—oh, that he would certainly kill Richard, even though Richard should kill him in the act."

Eustace Clipsby rose suddenly and stood chin in hand, frowning at the sunny garden in troublous perplexity.

"Oh, Abbeymère!" he murmured. "An evil, evil house! And yet——! My dear, I have known Valentine all his life and, though the son of his father, he is yet so like his gentle, lovely mother that I have sometimes thought and hoped he might make Abbeymère an honoured name one day, if only for her sake. . . . Ah, well, well, however this may be, I can give you this perfect assurance—these two youths shall never shed each other's blood,—never!"

"Ah, but how—oh, how can you be so sure?"

"My dear, God or Nature has set about all created things certain immutable laws and one of these—this: that Violence destroys itself; it has in the past and . . . it shall in the future. So trust me, child, have faith in the future and be comforted."

CHAPTER XXV

WHICH BEING OF NO GREAT INTEREST IS COMMENDABLY BRIEF

REACHING London in the afternoon, Richard, having secured quarters for his companions and himself at the George, paused not for bite or sup but, obsessed by sudden bitter thought, instantly chartered a hackney coach and had himself driven speedily to a more familiar part of the great city; for the thought that harassed him was this: that Valentine the Earl probably knew Rosemary's whereabouts and was on his way to see her,—might indeed be with her at this very moment.

Thus Richard, determined at any cost to be sure of this, was driving apace to the Earl of Abbeymère's town residence.

Before this stately though somewhat gloomy house the hackney coach drew up and, bidding the driver wait, Richard strode up the steps and, attired like a country yeoman, thundered on knocker and tugged at bell exactly like his own hasty, somewhat imperious self. In response to which resounding summons the door was presently opened by a red-faced, pompous person who breathed short and who, at sight of Richard, or rather his clothes, immediately frowned and shook his head violently:

"Downstairs, me feller, the back door for you!" he wheezed and made to shut the door, but Richard's foot had interposed, Richard's hand had seized his collar and Richard's look and tone were so unexpectedly compelling that the man gaped.

"Fool, is your master in? Is the Earl here?"

"No—no; oh, no, sir!"

"Are you expecting him?"

"No, sir; oh, no. His lordship's at Abbeymere for the funeral. There's nobody here, sir, nor likely to be; y' see, this mansion's for sale, ah—and everything in it too." Richard sighed, frowned and loosing the speaker's collar, took forth certain coins and dropped them into the man's ready palm.

"Now," he demanded, "are you sure, quite sure, Lord Abbeymere will not come here to-night?"

"That I am, sir, and certain,—Bible oath!"

"Thank you!" groaned Richard and, descending the steps, stood for a moment staring vaguely about him very much like the lost and bewildered young countryman he seemed. Finally he paid and dismissed his coachman and set out to walk the long miles back to the Borough, his eager eyes scanning every woman's face, his feet pausing now and then or turning aside to follow some form that it seemed might be Hers. . . .

Thus the tireless search for his lost Rosemary had begun,—a search that was to go on and on until he found her, if it took him all his life.

CHAPTER XXVI

TELLETH HOW RICHARD HEARD MR. PUNCH SQUEAK TO GOOD PURPOSE

WEARY, weary days for Richard, tramping the mighty city over, street and square, circus, court and alley; sometimes with his two companions but, of late, oftener alone.

To set forth every morning with hope renewed. . . . The eager quest amid the myriad faces that passed him by, faces but glimpsed to vanish for ever; the unending tireless search for the one face he never saw and yet visioned in his dreams so constantly that, struck by some chance resemblance, he would plunge recklessly through the roaring traffic of these cobbled thoroughfares—hasting, hasting, blood athrob with yearning tremulous hope, only to halt at last and stand in hopeless dejection, jostled to and fro by the busy, heedless throng; and so, as night fell, trudging heavily back to his lodging.

It was upon a certain afternoon that, chancing upon an *à-la-mode* beef shop, he entered and, seated in the nearest box, ordered and consumed a scarcely tasted meal.

The place at this hour was empty and upon the stained tablecloth within his reach lay three or four crumpled newspapers. Instinctively he took up the nearest and, glancing over the close-printed sheet, saw this:

The Late Earl of Abbeymere

On the tenth inst., as reported in our issue of yesterday's date, the Earl of Abbeymere was found dead in his chair, his features blackened by the discharge of a pistol that lay beside him. The Inquest, a report of which is given at length on another page, proved the unhappy nobleman was deeply involved financially and almost at the end of his resources. This dark prospect, it is alleged, preyed on his lordship's mind, with the shocking result that he was driven to the perpetration of this rash and fatal act. His lordship will be interred within the private chapel at Abbeymere where lie so many of his illustrious and noble ancestors.

The newspaper fell from Richard's nerveless fingers and he sat utterly motionless, staring before him with radiant eyes, his whirling thoughts centred upon the one blessed fact.

Suicide! Then his beloved Rosemary was innocent! Her dear hands were spotless! The dark deed that had so shocked and yet for which he had honoured her, she had not committed! His Rosemary was guiltless as himself! Why then, he might shed these rustic clothes . . . take his proper place . . . with power and money enough to set, instead of three, a score, a hundred men scouring London until she was found and safe in his arms . . . upon his heart! Up came his head, back went his shoulders and he was afoot, glad-eyed and eager; he turned to be gone and stood stricken motionless by such sudden dreadful doubt as sickened him.

Suicide? But was this so? Could it possibly be? And deep within his consciousness this unuttered question found voiceless answer:

"No,—never, never! Such men as Abbeymere do not slay themselves."

Richard sat down again, conned the obituary notice through once more, then, turning to the verbatim report of the Inquest, read it every word. . . .

"So Valentine had deliberately perjured himself! And why—why? Valentine had been the chief witness and had testified falsely throughout the enquiry! And—why? Valentine had suppressed all mention of that betraying handkerchief with its monogram R.V., but for no love of Richard Vibart! Then, in heaven's name—why? Unless to shield one he loved far beyond such petty things as truth and honour; and who should this one be but—Rosemary. And Rosemary had been armed! Rosemary knew how to fire a pistol! A shred of Rosemary's lace had been clutched in those dead fingers!"

Richard bowed his head between gripping hands and groaned within himself:

"Rosemary! Beloved! Oh, my dear! Pray God I find you . . . soon!"
And thus he remained oblivious to all but his troublous thoughts until,
aroused by sound between disparaging sniff and apologetic cough, he glanced
up to behold a lone and dismal waiter drooping mournfully hard by.

"Hanything more, sir—if you please?"

"My bill," said Richard; which document being instantly proffered, he paid
it and with tip of such unexpected liberality that the waiter, his low spirits
tempered by amazement, bowed him to the door.

And so to the streets again . . . roaring traffic, clatter of hoofs and grinding
of wheels, tramp and shuffle of countless feet and . . . faces! Everywhere
faces to be hastily scanned, as they flitted by,—to right, to left and across the
busy street; peered at with eager, straining eyes that darted glances here and
there lest any of these innumerable, vanishing faces should pass unseen and,
so passing, be—the Only One.

Evening was at hand when he found himself in a maze of back streets, a
quiet neighbourhood, and reaching a place where three ways met, he hesitated
although careless whither he roved, since any street, square or alley might
show him the beloved shape he sought.

Now as he stood thus, gazing about with weary, lack-lustre eyes, from
somewhere near by rose the sudden shrill, cheery, piping voice of Mr. Punch
and thither instinctively Richard turned.

And presently borne to him came the glad sound of childish laughter with
the deeper tones of their seniors, that grew louder until, rounding a sudden
corner, Richard saw this merry crowd grouped about a Punch-and-Judy show,
brave with striped canvas, paint and gilding and a notable signboard that in
large characters proclaimed to all and sundry:

THE ONLY DOUBLEDAY

with

PUNCH & JUDY

PRIVATE PERFORMANCES   TOWN OR COUNTRY

The performance was almost ended as Richard approached, for the joyous
crowd was dispersing and thus he saw Mrs. Doubleday who, with a final
tootle on the Panspipe and bang of sonorous drum, now rid herself of these
encumbrances the better to aid her spouse, as Mr. Doubleday, suddenly ap-
pearing and having donned THE HAT, proceeded to dismantle his theatre
with great expedition and despatch, while Mrs. Doubleday removed the plump
pony's nosebag, stowed it in the little cart, turned to address her husband and
came face to face with Richard. For a moment she eyed him somewhat
askance then, peering closer, her comely face was brightened by smile of
friendly recognition and welcome.

"Why, bless us!" she exclaimed, grasping his hand. "Is this you, young
gen'leman, and so changed and all! Dan'l, come you; here's the young man
as helped us days ago on the road; step up, Dan'l!"

Mr. Doubleday stepped forthwith; he lifted THE HAT on high, he waved it once, he put it on again and, taking Richard's other hand, shook it so heartily that cheered by the sincerity of their greeting, Richard answered smile with smile.

"My dear young sir," quoth Mr. Doubleday, "the Drama of Puncianello being a strain on the vocal organ and this, moreover, being an occasion, the flowing bowl is indicated. There stands hard by a house of call, a haven for conviviality yclept The Bell. Sir, you must honour us; thither will we repair so soon as our portage be freighted."

"Gladly," answered Richard, "if I may help you to pack up."

Thus very soon the theatre was folded and stowed snugly in the cart and grasping the somnolent pony's bridle, Mr. Doubleday led on down a street and across a street, round a sudden corner into a quiet court and to the cosiest of little taverns; then, the pony's nosebag duly readjusted, down three steps into the neatest of taprooms and through a doorway into the snuggest of snuggeries, where a stout, hoarse-voiced man bade them heartily welcome and, having supplied their several needs, left them cosily together, like the good host that he was; here, seated between Doubleday and spouse, Richard felt himself mightily comforted by their simple-hearted good-fellowship.

"We've finished for the day," said Mrs. Doubleday, beaming over her glass, "and a rare good day it's been,—three pound, eighteen shillings and thrippence, three fardens, Dan'l!"

"Why now, it's been a lovely day, I think, so bright and sunny! Ah, and very eventful too for us, what with a pickpocket a-picking pockets in the middle o' the performance, and a chimbly afire Battle Bridge way, and sweet little lambs being nigh trampled to death under my very nose by black-whiskered villains in gigs——"

"And rescued, Maria, by goddesses new come from Arcadia!"

"Right, Dan'l! A golden goddess as snatched that sweet innocent from right under that great horse's trampling hooves, she did . . . and then I catches her in my arms on my buzzum and kiss her, I did and had to, her lovely pale cheek, her shining golden hair——"

"Auburn,—auburn tresses, Maria!"

"Auburn?" repeated Richard, starting.

"Red-gold, my friend!" sighed Mr. Doubleday into his half-empty tankard, "such tresses glorious as lured young Paris, happy lad, to his lovely doom——"

"Red-gold?" murmured Richard tenderly; then, snatching at a straw, he leaned nearer to question breathlessly:

"Was she tall . . . was she blue-eyed . . . a deep—oh, a wonderful blue?"

"As ocean's unfathomable deeps, young my friend! Ah, as starry firmament at dewy eve——"

"And tall . . . graceful . . . was she tall?"

"As very daughter of the gods! A maid Olympian! A creature divine, being Perfection's self! These orbs ne'er saw her peer nor ever shall again, for——"

"Then it is she!" cried Richard, starting to his feet. "It is Rosemary . . . it must be! Did you learn her name?"

"Nay, sir, she but like a vision dawned and vanished from my dazzled sight——"

"In a gig!" added Mrs. Doubleday excitedly, and forthwith gave a very full and particular account of the incident, aided by the occasional rolling periods of her spouse.

"Did you . . . oh, did you learn where she was living?" stammered Richard.

"Well now, I heard her tell Blackwhiskers to drive to . . . let me see . . . a Square it was . . . not Portman—no! Nor Saint James'! Nor . . . wait a minute,—it was Golden, eh, Dan'l? It was Number Twelve, Golden Square, eh, Dan'l?"

"It was, Maria! Exact and true as usual, your memory waketh mine. Golden Square it was, young sir, Number—why, God bless us!" Richard's quivering hands were upon an ample shoulder of each and he was looking down at them from a face radiantly transfigured.

"God bless you indeed!" he exclaimed fervently. "For I think . . . I hope . . . yes, I believe you have given back to me more than my life. So God bless you always! And if this wonderful thing be really true, you shall see . . . you shall know some day how much you have done for this poor, miserable wretch that was me!" So saying, he kissed Mrs. Doubleday, suddenly and very heartily, seized the hand of her (for once) speechless spouse, shook it, snatched up his hat and stick and sped blithely away.

CHAPTER XXVII

GIVETH SOME ACCOUNT OF AN AFFRAY AND
MR. JASPER SHRIG

TREMULOUS with that eagerness which only Youth is blessed to know, Richard sped upon his way, alternately upborne by hope and harassed by despairful uncertainty. Now being in such frantic haste to reach Number Twelve, Golden Square, and be done with this harrowing suspense one way or the other, it naturally befell that he lost himself. Instead of reaching some main thoroughfare where he might charter a speedy hackney coach, he was plunging ever deeper into an unlovely neighbourhood of back streets, alleys and narrow courts; but on he sped, cursing in a very fury of impatience until, turning a sudden corner, he entered a somewhat gloomy alley, at the farther end of which stood four men. Eager to learn his direction, Richard began to advance towards these fellows then halted suddenly, warned by something furtive and threatening in their aspect, for all four were armed with sticks or bludgeons and one man had stooped to peer cautiously around a corner while his companions crouched near by, and all this with such very evident and sinister purpose that Richard tightened his grip upon the stout ash he carried and instinctively crouched also. . . . Followed a moment of breathless expectancy and then around that corner into the alley stepped a slim, elegant young personage and was instantly surrounded and set upon by the four. But this young gentleman dodged very nimbly and, getting his back to the wall, endeavoured to fight off his assailants with the light cane he bore . . . then his modish hat went flying . . . he was stricken to his knees . . . Richard glimpsed a pale face upturned to the sunny sky and instantly recognized the detested features of Valentine, Earl of Abbeymere, yet in that instant leapt, shouting:

"Hold 'em, Valentine; I'm with you!" And in he went, with flailing stick and thudding fist,—in to a close, desperate battle. . . . Stamping feet, hoarse gasps, reeling shock of blows, and suddenly, high and clear above it all, the Earl's breathless though jubilant cry:

"That you . . . Richard? Good old Dick . . . just in time! Have at 'em——" And now, his assailants staggering before Richard's furious onset, he struggled to his feet, fighting viciously.

So bludgeons rose and fell, slim cane whizzed, stout ash stick thwacked until it broke, and in its stead two powerful fists smote. . . . And while they fought thus side by side, the two against the four, they cheered and panted encouragement at each other as they had done when boys.

A flame shot across Richard's sight, he reeled blindly and went down headlong, to be kicked and trampled a while . . . then to struggle up unwillingly from a numbing, restful blackness, and strive desperately to answer the voice that cried on him so insistently:

"Speak, Dick! Wake—wake up! Dick man—speak!"

So Richard opened swimming eyes, clasped an agony that was his head and spoke:

"Oh . . . curse!"

"And dammem!" cried the Earl, rather wildly. "How are you now, Dick?"

"Eh? Oh . . . pretty well, thanks. They didn't . . . crack your nob too, then?"

"Thanks to you—no, Dick. My dear fellow, can you stand?"

"I'll try! . . . No good! Must wait a bit. Head's deuced queer! Pins infernally wobbly! Who . . . what hit me, Valentine?"

"A cudgel meant for me, Dick,—as, in fact, I believe they all were. However, you ran in and took it and oh, damme, I believe you saved my life! Which makes things devilish awkward . . . considering! So confoundedly contradictory . . . oh, the devil, to owe my life to you!" fumed the Earl, frowning down at the pale, bloodstained face pillowed on his shoulder, while he dabbed at it very gently with his handkerchief.

"Are the rascals . . . gone, Val?"

"Yes, and this is the devilish queer part of it—why should they run? You were stunned, I was on top of you and pretty well done up, and then, instead of finishing me—off they went, took to their confounded heels."

"Very . . . odd!" sighed Richard, stifling a groan.

"Vich, young sir, I wenters to deny!" wheezed a jovial voice above them, "I takes the liberty to say as it vere only to be expected."

Peering upward, Richard made out the speaker for a shortish, plump, aged person neatly clad in wide-brimmed hat, brass-buttoned blue coat, with beneath this, the shorts and top-boots of an earlier generation, a very quaint and altogether arresting figure.

"Oh?" enquired the Earl haughtily. "And pray, why was it to be expected?"

"Vich, young sir," answered the Person, nodding a smoothly round, good-natured face lit by two very quick bright eyes, "since you ax so p'inted, I'll tell ye as them windictives, being Paddy Mears, Chuffy McGuire, Snifty and Toby Niggle,—twigged—me."

"Indeed?" quoth my lord with growing arrogance. "And who might you be? One of them?"

The aged yet rubicund Person, crossed gnarled hands upon the knotted stick he bore and, shaking his head gently, beamed down on his arrogant young questioner more good-naturedly than ever.

"Young gen'leman," quoth he placidly, "scorning that 'ere insinivation, I stretches out my daddle—or as you might say, famble—to your young gen'leman pal, and so soon as us can get him on his stampers, inwites him, and you, if so minded, to step along o' me to the old 'Gun' and taste a drop o' the Vun and Only as my partner brews like nobody else can't. If——"

"The 'Gun'?" exclaimed my Lord, troubling himself to glance up at the speaker again. "I was on my way . . . looking for the Gun Tavern."

"And was likewise expected, sir."

"Indeed?"

"Ar—indeed."

"I want word with a Mr. Shrigrow Sharp, a police fellow. I was told he was to be seen at the 'Gun.'"

"And so 'e is, sir, ven not elsevere."

"You grow impertinent, I think."

"Vell now, p'raps I do."

"Who the dickens are you?"

"Shrig's my monnicker, sir, baptismal Jarsper. Now . . . for yourself, let's see," murmured Mr. Shrig, his bright, roving gaze fixing itself on the young Earl's jewelled cravat, "you—yes, you are a sprig——"

"A what? Confound you!"

"A sprig, sir, a shoot or, let's say, a bud o' nobility as has lately bloomed. From obrervation dooly recorded and de-ductions therefrom drawed, I'm pretty sure and sarten as you are the young, noo Earl of Abbeymere."

"How do you know this?"

"Simple addition, m' lud, two and two being four. And remembering your ludship's late misfort'nate pa, vot I says is—love a duck! And now, m' lud, if your young gen'leman pal feels ekal to it, the sooner ve sluices him out-side and in—the better he'll look and feel."

"Did you know my—the late Earl?"

"Vell, no, m'lud, not 'ardly vot you might call 'know'. But your young pal——"

"Can you stand now, Dick old fellow?"

"Of course . . . yes—" mumbled Dick, aching head between his hands. Hereupon, with Mr. Shrig's able assistance, he contrived to get upon his legs; but the pavement heaved and spun giddily beneath him, a mist seemed all about him, a sickly haze that deepened upon him to a choking darkness. . . .

"Dog bite me!" exclaimed Mr. Shrig. . . .

It was after some interval that Richard became aware of water very cold and sweetly refreshing that stirred the vigorous life within him to slow wakefulness; of a dripping sponge and of the Earl in shirt sleeves plying this sponge with such great assiduity that Richard gasped through the torrent:

"Hold . . . hard . . . Valentine!"

"Ha, damme, old fellow, but that's prime!" exclaimed his lordship, dropping sponge to snatch up a towel. "Can you speak, then? Yes, of course! 'Richard is himself again.' That's famous!"

"But you . . . you've pretty well—drowned me!" gasped Richard.

"And no wonder! You were out, Dick, knocked clean out of time! That cursed bludgeon took you a perfectly damnable crack! Worse than I thought. We got you up once but down you went again and . . . damme, but you looked . . . I thought you'd hopped the vital twig, old fellow . . . and all to help me! That's the most accursed part of it . . . considering!"

"Well but," enquired Richard, feeling his sorely battered head very tenderly, "how did I get here, and . . . where is it?"

"This is a tavern called 'The Gun,' old man. And I got you here with the aid of an aged, rum old buffer in top-boots and a spencer. But now, Dick, the question I'm pondering is,—why was I attacked so murderously?"

"Thieves!" groaned Richard.

"Perhaps! And yet I doubt it. I've been half expecting something of the sort. You see, there is some one, I fancy, who would sleep better if he knew I was dead or thoroughly crippled."

"Who, man, who?"

"That fellow, Nicholas Frayne. I used a whip on him,—both cheeks, old fellow, and he must fight——"

"Ah . . . Miss Cynthia——"

"Exactly! But Frayne happens to know I am pretty deadly with the hair triggers—rather more so than ever you are, Dick—and Frayne doesn't like the idea of risking his precious carcass, as I happen to have learned; so it would be like him to choose this . . . the safer way."

"You mean . . . he would murder you?"

"Why not, my dear fellow? He hates me very perfectly and what is more, he is afraid of me. Anyhow, I am having the fellow watched . . . which is the reason for my visit here. . . . But my present care is to see you safe and snug in bed. Where are you staying, old fellow?"

"Bed?" scoffed Richard, albeit, faintly. "No such thing . . . I shall be well enough. But, speaking of Miss Cynthia Bellenden, pray, are you not . . . engaged to her?"

"No, Dick; oh no!"

"But . . . you have . . . proposed to her?"

"Frequently, my dear fellow, a year ago and solely at the late noble Earl's mandate; you see she is an heiress and he had an eye to her moneybags. . . . But now, what of yourself, Dick; where can I take you?"

"Ah, to be sure," sighed Richard, hands to throbbing head. "Where? I was in a tremendous hurry . . . yes, I was going to find . . . good heavens— Rosemary!" Uttering the name, he started up from his chair, swayed dizzily and sank down again, while the Earl watched him with eyes agleam beneath faintly wrinkling brows.

"Still a trifle weak, eh, Vibart?" said he.

"It will pass," retorted Richard, grim-lipped. "Meanwhile, perhaps you will answer me a question?"

"Perhaps!" nodded my lord, beginning to rearrange his somewhat rumpled cravat before the small looking-glass beside the mantel.

"Do you know," demanded Richard, leaning back heavily in his chair, "do you know where she is . . . Rosemary?"

The Earl having loosed his cravat, retied it with exasperating deliberation and, viewing its effect in the glass, answered gently:

"My dear Vibart, you may be sure I do."

"Then . . . will you tell me . . . her address?"

"My dear Vibart, be perfectly assured that I will—not!"

Once again Richard started up and, swaying upon his feet, clenched passionate fists.

"Now damn you, Abbeymere——" he began.

"Gently! Gently!" admonished the Earl, easing himself into his tight-fitting coat. "What a wild, passionate fellow . . . and with a headache too!"

"Cold—sneering—devil!" gasped Richard, hands clasped to his throbbing temples.

"And yet," sighed the Earl, taking up his battered hat and surveying it very ruefully, "I am very truly grateful for your help and sincerely deplore you should have been so hurt in my cause. But I will not, must not divulge Rosemary's whereabouts because she fled to hide herself from you——"

"Liar!" groaned Richard, sinking so feebly into the chair again that the Earl eyed him with a sudden wistfulness and spoke in tone altered as his look:

"Does your head pain you so much, Dick? Shall I bathe it again?"

"I called you a liar, Valentine."

"Yes, I heard. . . . And you see, Rosemary fully believes you did the killing——"

"Ah!" sighed Richard. "But why . . . and how do you know this?"

"Because she told me as much——"

"Then . . . you have seen her . . . recently?"

"I have enjoyed that felicity. In time to come, I expect to see a great deal more of her,—I am living—hoping to make her my Countess——"

"Never!" cried Richard fiercely. "I'll see you dead first!"

"Oh, no, no!" murmured the Earl, smoothing his ruffled hat, "you would not see me dead, because you would be as dead as I—if it is a duel you are threatening?"

"Of course . . . yes . . ." groaned Richard, closing his eyes to the pain of his throbbing head.

"I'm glad to be assured of this," nodded his lordship, turning back to the looking-glass, "for, as I suggested in regard to Frayne, I have no fancy to die like the late Earl . . . killed like a mad dog, Vibart,—not that way, if you please."

"Ah . . . what the devil do you suggest?"

"The answer, my dear fellow, is a handkerchief with the initials R.V. Pray, what have you to say of it?"

"That . . . at any rate . . . it proves you a perjured liar, Abbeymere." The Earl, putting on his hat before the mirror, smiled at his reflection quite happily.

"It will be a strange fate, Richard, if you and I that were children together and playfellows should have grown up merely to slaughter each other——"

"This rests with yourself, Valentine. Confine . . . your attentions to Miss Cynthia Bellenden and——"

"For, if we fight," went on the Earl serenely, "we shall most certainly exterminate one another, but with—ha, confound it, I've lost my cane—with this singular difference, that I, being the last of my damned race, shall pass with no one to mourn me, except possibly old Clipsby,—but you, Vibart, how vastly otherwise! Consider your gracious mother's tears! Your honoured father's grief! Ponder this, Richard, and if only for their sakes forego this idle dream of Rosemary, this very selfish passion——"

"Insufferable . . . presumptuous fool!" exclaimed Richard, heaving himself out of his chair with such violence that he staggered, tripped and fell heavily.

"Dick!" cried the Earl in quick concern and stooped to lift him; but with passionate gesture Richard spurned this proffered help and contrived to get himself back into the chair unaided.

"Now, now!" quoth the Earl reprovingly. "Be calm, I beg. Sit still awhile, for you are in no fit state to pummel me at present, so do restrain yourself . . . or perhaps I had better remove this invitation that is me. . . . I'll be off——"

"Valentine," said Richard, leaning shakily across the table, "keep away from Rosemary; cease your devilish persecution or——"

"Richard," said the Earl, turning lightly towards the street door, "you should know me well enough to be very certain no threats can ever deter me, so—why waste your breath? Ah, well,—good-bye for the present! I hope you will soon be again your very hale and hearty self. I thank you very truly and most sincerely for having very probably saved my life . . . what a devilish, preposterous, contradictory business it all is! . . . And I've lost my cane and one feels so undressed in town without one's cane! Pray tell our top-booted old hero I will call another time. . . . Adieu, my Richard." And with lips up-curling in faintly mocking smile but with eyes aglow with something very much better, the Earl waved his gloved hand, opened the door and went his way, while pain-racked Richard viewed that door, despairfully eager to be gone also.

"Twelve!" he muttered, striving to rally his failing senses, "Twelve—Golden—Square—" His throbbing head sank heavily between his arms outstretched across the table, and, vaguely wondering at this sick weakness, he sank to a troubled drowsiness.

From this stupor he was aroused somewhat by a hand very large yet gentle . . . big fingers that crept softly among his thick, wet hair . . . voices near at hand yet strangely indistinct:

"Vot d' ye say of it, Corporal?"

"A pretty . . . tidy . . . wallop, Jarsper!"

"Ar! And vot then, pal?"

"He should ought to take a nap, Jarsper, forty winks . . . bed——"

"No!" mumbled Richard, lifting heavy head with an effort. "I'm in—hurry—must go. Shall be all right—a sip of brandy . . ."

"Water would be better——"

"But a glass o' the Vun and Only, best of all!" quoth a hearty voice. "Tak' a sniff o' this, young sir!"

Beneath Richard's nose came a steaming glass whence stole an aroma so subtly delectable that he sipped instinctively, drank avidly and, looking up into the rubicund visage of Mr. Shrig, smiled.

"Bravo!" exclaimed another voice and, glancing round about, Richard saw the speaker for a comely giant whose face, lit by the gentlest of blue eyes, showed the handsomer for the snowy hair that crowned it and the neatly trimmed white whiskers that framed it.

"Sir," said Mr. Shrig, upending the glass that Richard had just emptied, "this here is my pal an' partner, Corporal Richard Roe, late o' the Grenadiers——"

"Twenty-odd year ago, Jarsper!"

"And lost his daddle at Vaterloo——"

"But only my left, sir!" added the Corporal showing the gleaming steel hook that replaced his lost member.

"I—feel honoured!" said Richard, reaching out a somewhat unsteady hand. "My name is Richard too, Richard Vibart."

"Eh? Wibart?" exclaimed Mr. Shrig, with a sort of pounce. "Any relation to Sir Maurice . . . Buck Wibart, as got hisself murdered . . . in a wood?"

"He was my father's cousin."

"Think o' that now! Vell, blow me tight!" exclaimed Mr. Shrig, in a kind of ecstasy, shaking Richard's hand with the utmost heartiness and beaming more jovially than ever. "In a vood, too! Mr. Wibart, vot I say is, if a cove is born to be murdered—pick a vood, sir, birds a-carolling so gay, leaves a-vispering so peaceful, brooks a-babbling—much better than, say, the slime o' the river, or street, back alley, garret or cellar,—no, gimme a vood of a dooy morning or sunset. For though born in the city, I hankers for the country and if ever Windictiveness ketches me in the shape o' bludgeon, bullet or steel, let me corp lay among lilies o' the walley or——" Mr. Shrig paused suddenly and cocked his head, as from the little barroom or tap without, the street door slammed and a bell tinkled.

"A customer, Corporal Dick? I don't think so. Vait a bit! It aren't the time for reg'lars and—Lord, but 'e's a unpatient party, ooever 'e is,—'arkee!" And indeed, the invisible customer was rapping very insistently; and then a voice called:

"Hallo—hallo! Is there anyone about?"

"Somebody's very full o' noos or—fright!" quoth Mr. Shrig, in placid surmise. "And Gimblet not here! Go see, pal Dick, and leave the door ajar." Away strode the gigantic Corporal forthwith into the taproom and was there instantly accosted by that same agitated voice and one that now struck drowsy Richard as being vaguely familiar:

"This cane!" said the voice. "I recognize it . . . I know it well. I found it in the kennel . . . the gutter close by . . . and blood near it . . . splashes of blood! Tell me, is the owner here?"

"Why, sir," answered the Corporal, "he may be and then again—not . . . ye see, there was two on 'em. If you'll wait 'arf a moment, I'll——"

"Hex-cuse me, Mr. Wibart!" quoth Mr. Shrig and rising from his chair with surprising nimbleness hurried out of this cosy kitchen, closing the door behind him.

Aware thus of a soothing rumble of voices, Richard stared dreamily at the dim fire and, the pain of his head easing, nodded slumberously, closed his eyes and opened them with a start to Mr. Shrig's voice:

"Mr. Wibart, sir, there's gen'leman outside says you're precious vell acquainted and begs a vord. How about it, sir?"

"Certainly!" answered Richard, sitting up.

"Thank you!" said a pleasant voice and now Richard beheld the speaker, graceful, middle-aged, perfectly attired, who stood looking down on him with such serene dignity of bearing that instinctively Richard made to rise, but out came a neatly gloved hand to arrest him gently.

"Ah, no, do not trouble. . . . You do not recognize me, Mr. Richard?"

"I—I fear not," Richard stammered, "and yet—why, yes—are you—by George, can it be—Eustace Clipsby?"

"Yes," sighed Mr. Clipsby, coming a step nearer, "and must you frown? Won't you pray believe me your friend——"

"Friend?" repeated Richard, his scowl growing blacker.

"To be sure," murmured Mr. Clipsby, "you treated me rather roughly last time we met; you also denounced me as a 'creeping spy'—as I suppose I was, but for the well-being of one very dear . . . to you."

"Do you mean Rosemary . . . Miss Ford?" cried Richard in sudden eagerness. "Do you . . . oh, can you tell me where she is?"

"Mr. Richard, I will take you to her so soon as you are able——"

"Now!" cried Richard, lunging to his feet. "At once . . . this instant! Only bring me to her and I'll swear you are the best friend I ever had. Come, oh, pray, let us go."

"Certainly, dear Mr. Richard, though I would counsel waiting until you are more yourself; to see you thus might shock her and——" Mr. Clipsby paused suddenly, his keen, watchful gaze on the door for, though the latch had lifted soundlessly, this door was opening furtively inch by inch; and now into the room came a shock of rusty red hair and a pair of eyes, remarkably blue, round and bright, that seemed to take in the spacious kitchen and its occupants at a single comprehensive glance.

" 'Lo!" said a husky voice. "How's the cows, Old Un?"

"Aha!" chuckled Mr. Shrig, clapping hand to thigh. "So there y' are! Come in, Gimblet my lad. Here's luck for ye, luck as has dropped in twice, all along o' Windictiveness in the shape o' bludgeons, four on 'em and the gold-'eaded cane o' your Sprig o' Nobility, my b'y."

"Oh? Has he been here then, Old Un?"

"Ar. His lordship come a-looking for you, my Gimblet, and would now be laying a stiff in the dead-'ouse, ay, a perishing corp but for this here young nob,—so come your ways, my lad. Mr. Wibart and friend," quoth Mr. Shrig, gesturing towards the rusty hair and bright blue eyes still just a-peep beyond the door, "lo and be'old you, my b'y Shrigrow Sharp, as I named in memory o' my ownself and my pal, Corporal Richard Roe o' the Grenadiers, but vot they calls Gimblet at the Office because he's so precious sharp and goes through the criminal mind like a gimblet through so much vood. Step forrard, Gimblet."

Thus adjured, the hair and eyes were followed by a longish, tip-tilted nose, a wide, humorous mouth, and so by degrees until there stood revealed a smallish, bony man, very quick and light of movement, a man who might have been anything from a very horsey horse coper to a lightweight pugilist, for about his scrawny throat was a neckerchief showing white double rings on a blue ground (known among the true milling coves as the blue bird's-eye), his slim, spry legs were encased in cords and gaiters and his wide, humorous mouth was quirked upon a straw.

"There he be, Mr. Wibart and sir!" quoth Mr. Shrig, with a prideful possessiveness. "My very own lad as being the kid o' nobody knows oo, me and the Corporal took in 'and, bred up and trained till to-day, sirs, he stands afore ye the boldest thief taker and the very sharpest cove as ever tracked willainy to the nubbing cheat or vore a red veskit."

"Excepting one, Old Un!" said Mr. Sharp, wagging his red head; "there's only one Jarsper Shrig and won't never be another to compare. But what's been forrard here, Old Un? What's the lay?" Hereupon Mr. Shrig very succinctly described the murderous attack on the Earl, naming the four assailants; to all of the which Mr. Sharp listened in silence and very round of eye, at certain times chewing avidly at the straw that yet seemed never to decrease.

"The question being," added Mr. Shrig in conclusion, "oo set this here Windictiveness afoot?"

"Ar!" nodded Mr. Sharp. "But vot now, Old Un?"

"Now, Gimblet, here's two gen'lemen, Mr. Richard Wibart and friend Mr. Clipsby—baptismal Eustiss, aren't it, sir?"

"It is," nodded Mr. Clipsby, with his gentle smile. "And now may I enquire why Lord Abbeymere should be hereabouts?"

"That you may, sir, and prompt and to the p'int I'll answer you,—because said young Nob, or as you might say, Heavy Toddler, seems to think as 'e may be took off very sudden and onexpected, like his late unfort'nate pa."

"You mean—by suicide? But why should——"

"Mr. Clipsby, sir—no! Not sooicide! I never said no sich vord. The Inkwest may call it fellerdesee, but I think different, sir, and there's some as . . . knows different!"

Here Mr. Clipsby, in the act of putting on his very modish hat, looked at it instead with a strange intensity and put it down again.

"Dear me!" he murmured, in his pleasantly modulated voice. "But my dear Mr. Shrig, why in the world should you, or any one else, doubt the finding of the Inquest?"

"Sir," answered Mr. Shrig, shaking his head, "me 'aving see so much o' huming natur',—its tricks, sir, its wanities and rum dodges, I've growed by natur' wery suspicious o' Natur', d' ye see——"

"Then doubtless you can give me some logical reason for such very strange suspicions in regard to the late Earl's death?"

"Oh, I dunno, sir!" sighed Mr. Shrig plaintively. "Natur's often at odds wi' Reason,—but the reason for this here sooicide don't nohow sound reasonable enough, according to the reports as I've dooly read. . . ."

"Now, Mr. Clipsby, if you're ready, I am!" said Richard impatiently.

"But, Mr. Wibart sir, your neckercher aren't dry yet," Mr. Shrig demurred.

"No matter; it will do."

"And vot's more, sir, added Gimblet, "you're still a bit groggy on your pins."

"I shall be well enough, thanks . . . Mr. Clipsby, pray let us go."

"But—your 'air, sir!" admonished Mr. Shrig. "Your 'air so vet and vild-like! Loan the young gen'leman your comb, pal Dick, and a towel for to dry his napper."

"Right you are, Jarsper!" And the Corporal's long legs vanished incontinent up the precipitous stairs in adjacent corner while Richard chafed to be gone.

"May I enquire," pursued Mr. Clipsby, seating himself beside Mr. Shrig on the high-backed settle, "what exactly you find so . . . unreasonable in the late Lord Abbeymere's suicide?"

"Sir," answered Mr. Shrig, reaching a cherished clay pipe from the rack on the wall at his elbow, "lookee now,—ven any man commits sich a onnat'ral act as self-murder, it's only nat'ral as he should commit said act in the manner as comes most nat'ral to hisself. F' instance! The gent in question shoots hisself stone dead—through the left temple. Vich is Fact Number Vun, I think? You being on the spot, sir, see for yourself—through the left temple, eh, sir?"

"Ye-e-es," murmured Mr. Clipsby, dwelling on the word, "I . . . believe it was."

"Not sure, sir? The left temple! Couldn't you swear to same?"

"Upon my word, Mr. Shrig, I hardly noticed, but I believe it was the left."

"Mr. Clipsby, sir, I know as it was left; 'tis in the evidence, sir,—by the discharge of a pistol ball through the—left temple." Here Mr. Shrig began to fill his pipe with nimble fingers while his bright eyes roved other where, his gaze now on the rug beneath Mr. Clipsby's feet, now on Mr. Clipsby's varnished boots, his flowered waistcoat, his greying hair.

"Well?" murmured Mr. Clipsby at last.

"Vell, sir," sighed Mr. Shrig, "from all as I'm able to larn, or as you might say, diskiver,—I find as said unfort'nate gent vas—right-handed. Vich is Fact Number Two, I think? But you can tell me very certainly, sir, seeing as you knowed deceased, none better, it being dooly in evidence as you lived with his lordship constant, years and years, and could swear on your oath as his lordship vas nat'rally right-handed,—eh, sir?"

"I can. Certainly!" answered Mr. Clipsby gently. "But how shall this signify? A right-handed person may be sufficiently ambidextrous, a man at such desperate moment might use either hand quite naturally."

"Vell," sighed Mr. Shrig, his gaze roving as high as Mr. Clipsby's elegant shirt frill and pausing there, "a man might and then again he might—not! But that there vord—'amby'—might I trouble you for same again, sir?"

"Ambidextrous," repeated Mr. Clipsby, staring abstractedly at the smouldering fire, wherefrom his companion now lifted a small ember with the tongs and proceeded to light his pipe.

"Ambi—dexteerious!" repeated Mr. Shrig between fragrant puffs, rolling out the syllables. "Am—be—dex—teerious! Now that's a vord as is a vord, that is, —eh, Gimblet, my b'y?"

"Ar!" quoth Gimblet, who had sat near by listening, looking, and chewing ceaselessly on the straw that seemed magically never to diminish in the very least . . .

"But that is not my neckerchief," quoth Richard, busily (and very tenderly) combing his hair by aid of the small, bright looking-glass above Corporal Roe's neat desk.

"No, Mr. Vibart, it's mine, sir, my best," answered the old soldier. "Seeing as your own aren't yet fit for active sarvice at present, I beg you'll accept the loan of it, sir."

"Very kind of you!" said Richard, taking up the ornate article in question. "Silk, by George! Thanks, Corporal Roe! I'll return it soon as possible."

"Suit yourself, sir. Whenever you happen to be passing——"

"Ar!" exclaimed Mr. Shrig, rising. "Venever so be, Mr. Wibart, us'll always give ee a velcome at the old 'Gun'—all three on us, with a drop o' the Vun and Only, than vich there never vas any drink to ekal it nohow. . . . And you too, Mr. Clipsby, sir, any time as you feels so inclined—drop in, sir. And now Mr. Wibart, seeing as you'm so anxious to be a-toddling and remembering that there rap on your napper, or as you might say, mazzard—the Gimblet shall go get you a nackney coach . . . and sharp's the vord, Gimblet, my b'y."

"Sharp it is, Old Un!" answered Gimblet and instantly vanished.

But now, as Richard became more himself, his impatience grew to such a pitch that he could remain inactive no longer and, leaving Shrig and Mr.

Clipsby still hobnobbing in the chimney corner, hastened from "The Gun" and along the alley to Grays Inn Lane and stood there so eagerly watchful for the expected conveyance that he was oblivious to all but the passing traffic until roused by the gently diffident voice of the gigantic Corporal.

"Begging your pardon, sir, but that there friend o' yourn, Mr. Clipsby . . . might he be a—very great friend, sir?"

"Clipsby? No—yes," said Richard, his gaze on the ceaseless traffic. "I'm hardly sure. Why do you ask?"

"Well," answered the Corporal, eyeing Richard's averted face with a peculiar intentness, "only because my comrade Jarsper seems to have took to him so very strong."

"Good!" Richard nodded. "Clipsby has always seemed a shy, lonely, old fellow and—ha, there comes the hackney coach at last! Will you be good enough to hurry back and tell him—" But at this moment forth of "The Gun" stepped Mr. Clipsby, closely attended by Jasper Shrig.

Forthwith Richard sprang into the vehicle, bidding Mr. Clipsby hurry and calling on the coachman to drive fast.

So Mr. Shrig wished them a cheery farewell and, with slight yet significant gesture, winked up at the driver, who nodded, chirruped to his horses and away rumbled the coach.

They rode for the most part in silence for Richard was dreaming of Her, picturing just how she would look, what she would say to him, what he should say to her; while Mr. Clipsby seemed lost in a profound abstraction.

When at last they spoke it was together:

"These confounded clothes!" exclaimed Richard.

"That Jasper Shrig interests me!" said Mr. Clipsby.

"To appear before Her . . . like a loutish clod!"

"He was a Bow Street officer years ago, I understand."

"And my head all bruised, Clip, and lumpy as a curst potato! Am I much marked, Clip?"

"Enough to show interesting, Richard. . . . It seems like old times to hear you call me Clip."

"Yes, that was years ago . . . you used to call me 'Dicky.' But things are greatly changed since then. . . . I ought to treat you with more deference——"

"No, no, pray call me Clip. And know that whatever change there may be, in circumstances or the world or ourselves, is and must be—for the better . . . And here we are, I think—yes, this is Golden Square——"

"Aha, then she does live here!"

"Then you knew this?"

"No, I only hoped . . . and by George—there is Number Twelve!" Uttering the words, Richard flung open the door and leapt from the moving vehicle so precipitately that he reeled and only saved himself from a fall by clutching the rails of a front garden. Then Mr. Clipsby was beside him and they were ascending a flight of stone steps; a door was opened by a prim yet pretty maid; ensued a carpeted passage, a small, pleasant room with window open to the glowing west and as if borne upon the radiant glory came a blithe chorus of happy, childish voices. Looking from this window, Richard saw a grass plot where children romped and amid these dancing, elfin shapes, tall and gracious as some young and gentle goddess—Rosemary.

Richard caught his breath and, as he gazed, this so fiercely sought, so yearned-for, beloved form blurred suddenly upon his swimming vision.

"Wait, I'll send her to you," said Mr. Clipsby's gentle voice.

Richard crossed to the mantel and leaned there, head bowed upon his arms, trembling with wild and joyful expectancy; then turned to the sudden opening of the door and seeing her so near—stood speechless. But with sobbing murmur, a cry inarticulate yet more eloquent than any words, she fled to him and was on his breast, his yearning arms fast about her.

CHAPTER XXVIII

SHOWETH HOW RICHARD SWORE AN OATH

THE sun had set an hour ago but the sky was still glorious with his passing where the moon stood like a pale wraith peeping over a certain ivy-clad wall; and surely never in all her length of days had she spied two more ridiculously happy creatures than these that sat together on a bench the coxswain's deft hands had contrived beneath this same wall in a remote corner of the vegetable garden (this famous battle ground).

And of what should they talk but themselves and their own concerns, of their past tribulations and dear hopes of the future? But at last Richard must come back to that dark memory that cast its cold shadow upon even this glad hour of joyous reunion:

"So then," said Richard, glancing from the lovely face beside him to the coxswain's scarlet runners that made this corner a green bower, "he must have been shot while you lay still insensible?"

"Yes," murmured Rosemary.

Saith Richard, his gaze still averted:

"Dear, you never believed he killed himself!"

"Do you Richard?"

"No."

"Oh, Richard, you are so terribly certain of my guilt that, deep down in your heart, you are miserable even with me in your arms. You are so horribly certain that you tried to sacrifice yourself for me, and oh, my dear—can't you see how glad, how happy this makes me,—can't you?"

"No!" he murmured. "No."

"Because," she explained, smiling into his troubled eyes, "knowing you believe me guilty proves to me that you are innocent beyond all doubt, and in spite of your silly confession and running away."

"Why . . . then," said Richard, with a sort of joyous gasp of sudden realization, "if you . . . really thought me guilty . . . it proves . . . oh, Rosemary, my darling! Then I needn't dread the future any more; nothing can harm you, the Law cannot touch you——"

"But, dear," she questioned, "why were you so dreadfully sure I had . . . killed him?"

"A strip of the scarf I had given you! It was caught and twisted about his sleeve buttons. It must have happened when——"

"Yes, I remember!" said Rosemary, shivering. "He struggled with me . . . hatefully——" And now Richard was shivering also; the clasp of his arms was joyous pain.

"The foul beast!" he exclaimed. "Had I been there, I certainly should have killed him——"

"Hush!" she cried, closing his lips with gentle fingers. "Hush, Dick! Somebody did kill him! Thank God it was not you!"

"No," growled Richard, "I got there too late! But who . . . who could have saved you and shot the——"

"Dear love, what matter?"

"Sometimes I have wondered if Valentine——"

"Don't —don't think of it any more. Oh, Richard, let us forget and talk of ourselves and the future! First, does your dear head still pain you?"

"Nothing to matter," he answered, kissing her anxious eyes. "Nothing can ever really matter now that I have you again."

"Mr. Clipsby, the dear, tells me you saved Valentine's life; this was brave and noble of you, my Richard."

"No, no, he would have done the same for me, of course. Valentine is a sportsman, thoroughbred and was my friend once."

"And why not again, Dick?"

"Impossible—quite! I'm done with the fellow and he with me."

"Richard, won't you try to make him your friend again—for my sake?"

"Anything for you, Rosemary, anything in the world . . . and 'pon my soul, there are times when I truly like him. And yet I'm pretty sure Valentine has too much of his father's damnable nature to wish for anyone's friendship, least of all—mine."

"Has he ever threatened your life, Richard,—a duel?"

"My dearest, if you know this, why bid me try to make him my friend?"

"Because there is so very much good in him and he so needs a friend. Mr. Clipsby says the good influence of his sweet mother and the evil of his father are so evenly blent in him that he may be each in turn——"

"Oh, he is!" nodded Richard, "and generally his father."

"Yet Mr. Clipsby is sure the good must eventually triumph if he be given the chance. . . . Anyhow, Richard, you are going to promise, you shall swear to me by our dear love, that you will never—ah, never under any circumstances, suffer him to force a duel upon you. Swear me this, Richard, swear it on your love for me."

"But . . . but, my dear girl," stammered Richard, "suppose he insult me publicly . . . or, by George, even strike me! How then?"

"Endure it for the sake of our love," she answered, meeting his look steady-eyed; now though her voice was so gentle yet, beholding the resolute set of her pretty chin, Richard frowned and set his own grimly.

"But how if I am scorned for cowardice?" he demanded. "Every one would despise me!"

"Endure this also for my sake and I shall know you even braver than the bravest."

"But, Rosemary! Oh, good Lord, this is perfectly impossible——"

"Then so am I!" she retorted, and putting aside his restraining arm, she rose with the high dignity (almost) of his own mother.

"Great heavens, girl, Rosemary, what do you mean?"

"That if you place every one's opinion before mine, you may have—every one—but none of me."

"But oh, my dear . . . darling, don't you see that a man must protect his own honour or be shamed——"

"Yet leave his woman to break her poor heart if he be killed! No, Richard dear, I will never be wife to a man who will lightly peril his life for such an idle, selfish idea, no—oh, never!"

"Now this," cried Richard, leaping to his feet and striding to and fro a little wildly, "this is a perfectly frightful go! It's preposterous! It's ridiculous! And not to be endured!"

Rosemary simply looked at him.

"It's outrageous! Yes, by George, it is!"

Rosemary turned her back upon him.

"Such a vow would turn a man into a—a—transform a man into a vile cur to be kicked, a—a—oh, confound it,—he'd be a mere—thing!"

Rosemary sighed plaintively and her shapely back was eloquent.

"But I . . . if I ever did take such vow . . . I should despise myself!"

"Yet be my dear-loved and honoured . . . husband!" murmured Rosemary and—glanced at him over her shoulder, but with such eyes and such infinite promise of look as may have made and ruined mighty empires ere now. . . . And Richard, being merely Richard, young and a man (almost), leapt to her and seizing her hands, kissed and kissed them, murmuring:

"Why then . . . marry me, Rosemary; marry me, for I'll swear and vow as you will to have you mine for ever."

Then Rosemary's soft arms were about him, her gentle voice in his ear:

"Hold me close, my Richard, close! Your dear heart to mine. Now, standing so, heart to heart before God, swear me you will never peril your life, that is mine too, in any duel, under any circumstances, with any man. Swear me this, Richard, here upon my heart and in God's holy sight."

So Richard swore this oath and kissed her; then, coming back to the bench beneath the ivied wall, they sat down again.

"Yes," said Rosemary thoughtfully, "Mr. Clipsby seems sure the good in Lord Abbeymere will triumph in the end, because all good, he says, must conquer evil, or Time and the World turn backward,—back to savagery and nothingness. . . . He is a wise, strange, wonderful person, Dick."

"Who,—not Valentine?"

"No, Eustace Clipsby."

"Clipsby? Now, there's a strange fellow, by George! I don't know what to make of him, confound me if I do!"

"You mean this sudden wonderful change in him?"

"Yes, dear, it's a perfectly astounding metamorphosis! I've know old Clip all my life, of course, as one knows a tree or a piece of furniture . . . always a silent shadow of a man. As schoolboys, Valentine and I used to mock and make game of him—we were rather devilish urchins,—jeer at his pale face and meek looks and he used to smile and fade away without a word——"

"Oh, Richard,—the poor solitary creature! To mock him!"

"Most boys are small savages."

"And he is lonely still, Richard, and yet so patient and strong . . . such a wonderful musician . . . and he was my good, kind friend."

"Ah, but—is he, dear Heart? What is he? So confoundedly mysterious! But enough of him. Tell me you love me . . . kiss me!" Rosemary did both.

And, thus lost in the growing wonder of their happiness, they were blind to everything else and quite deaf to the stir of leaves that had rustled so stealthily above them more than once.

"Ah, when will you marry me, my Rosemary,—when? After all we have suffered, my mother can't, won't, shall not keep us waiting, so,—when, dearest, when?"

"Whenever you will, Richard."

"Then soon—soon!" he murmured. "To-morrow I will take you to her,—to my mother! To-morrow I will take you—home!"

"Home!" repeated Rosemary tenderly. "Home . . . to our mother——"

"To-morrow!" quoth Richard. "We will start early and——"

"Demanding pardon—twice!" laughed a mocking voice. "But no, I think not——"

The leaves rustled louder than ever and down from the wall leapt the young Earl of Abbeymere, so suddenly that he staggered and all but fell; then recovering, he took off his hat and bowed.

"Apologising twice," said he, smiling, "once for this intrusion and once again for eavesdropping. Yet I intrude, as I eavesdropped, very happily, to forbid, to warn and to——"

Then Richard was upon him, Richard's long arms whirled him back to the wall and his powerful fist clenched to smite that pale, sneering face that neither flinched nor lost its mocking smile; but in this moment, Rosemary had interposed.

"Richard—don't!" she cried, seizing that threatening fist. The Earl laughed grimly.

"You see, Rosemary," said he, "you see why I must kill him, my own dear——"

"Now curse you, Iford," cried Richard in passion-choked voice. "You address my . . . future wife!"

"Let us rather say—our future lovely mourner," the Earl retorted. "Oh, Rosemary," he cried, "Oh, dear my sweet, we, being about to die, salute thee!"

"Ha, by heavens," cried Richard contemptuously, "the poor sot's drunk, as usual! But this sha'n't excuse him. Loose me, Rosemary . . . will you shield the fellow?"

"Richard," she pleaded, "you promised me! . . . Oh, my lord, go—please go!"

"Go?" repeated his lordship, his glowing eyes scanning Rosemary's troubled loveliness. "Call me Valentine and I'll . . . consider it."

"Valentine, I beseech you——"

"No!" cried Richard fiercely, "you shall not plead with the impudent fool. Abbeymere, get out, or by God I'll drag you off and thrash you, d' ye hear me?"

"Too often!" sneered the Earl. "And always snarling empty threats . . . all cursed bark and devil a bite——" Out shot Richard's arm again and Rosemary, leaping to restrain him, was swept aside so violently that she would have fallen —but the Earl caught her, folded her to his breast and kissed her full on the lips; uttering a passionate cry, she broke from him and . . . saw him go down headlong beneath Richard's fist, to lie motionless and half stunned.

"Richard!" she gasped, in horrified whisper. "Oh, Richard—what have you done?"

"Done?" quoth Richard, scowling down on his prostrate enemy. "This is only the beginning——"

"Right—exactly right!" said the Earl, propping himself on an elbow and speaking between bloody lips that smiled still. "This is but the beginning of what I have expected and intended; the end will be smoke and—silence!" So saying, he arose, retrieved his hat, put it on and, drawing out a dainty handkerchief, dabbed his bleeding mouth with tender solicitude.

"Pray, Vibart," he enquired, stooping to pick up his fallen riding crop, "when will suit you to stage our second act—this 'consummation so devoutly to be wished' ?"

"Any time and place," growled Richard. "And now, my noble, sottish lord, have the courtesy to take yourself off or——" But here, Rosemary stepped forward, her lovely face a little pale, yet calm and very purposeful; also Richard saw her round chin was set in that manner he recognized and knew so well of old.

"Richard, my dear," said she, speaking in her ordinary smoothly soft tone and turning her back upon the Earl, "when I exacted that promise from you, made you swear me that sacred oath, that I think his listening lordship may have overheard,—swearing by our love that you would never suffer any man to force a duel upon you, I thought Lord Abbeymere a better man than he proves. But because you are my Richard, your promise still holds, the oath is still binding——"

"Oh, but Rosemary . . . my dear . . . but you . . . you see," stammered Richard, viewing her with troubled eyes, "I . . . I struck him! And a . . . a blow must be answered one way or other and consequently——"

"Consequently, Richard, you are always my honourable man, thank God, and faithful to your word!"

Richard glanced at Rosemary's sweetly resolute face and, bowing his head, uttered a sound between sigh and groan.

"You heard her, Abbeymere?" said he. "Very well then—do what you will, speak as you may, I'll esteem it no more than the senseless act and futile babbling of a drunken fool. But . . . for the blow I struck you, come and take a thump at me." So saying, Richard fronted the Earl, folded his arms and stood waiting.

Lord Abbeymere stood mute and very still, his pale cheek flushing painfully, his cynical self-control so strangely shaken that when at last he spoke it was in an unwonted agitation:

"So you think . . . you'll dare . . . not to fight me?"

"No, I am positively certain."

"Not even if . . . if I have you proclaimed . . . branded . . . a coward in all the clubs?"

"No!" cried Richard fiercely. "No! I won't foul myself with your vile blood, Abbeymere!"

"Then—try this!" gasped the Earl and leapt suddenly with riding crop upraised; but the blow was parried, the whip wrenched away and tossed over the wall; then, pinning him by the collar, Richard held his pale, quivering fury at bay.

"Valentine," said he between gnashing teeth, "yearning to be your death, I promise Rosemary that from this moment you shall be to me as if you were truly dead, and buried and . . . rotting! Is this enough? Now come on, take your blow at me and be off!" Once again Richard crossed his arms and, gazing steadfastly into the Earl's distorted features, waited to be struck.

But the Earl stood motionless and, quite unheeding Richard, kept his haggard gaze on Rosemary.

"Come!" said Richard impatiently. "Hit away and be done with it!" Still the Earl never so much as glanced towards him; and now, almost as if compelled by this persistent gaze, Rosemary turned and, meeting his intense regard with the blue serenity of her Saxon eyes, shook her head at him reprovingly as a sad and tender mother might have done.

"My lord," said she gently, "there is a devil in your eyes, a demon of hate and destruction, yet once or twice I have thought to see an angel there, the kindly good spirit that is the heritage of——"

The Earl laughed stridently:

"My dear soul," said he, "if I didn't love you so much, yes—with such abiding folly, I should find you quite too sweetly detestable."

"I wonder," sighed Rosemary, her gaze still holding his, "are you angel or devil?"

"Who knows?" he laughed. "However, I had rather flourish a red-hot brimstone trident than flutter the downy pinions of an angel. And now, pray go; leave us,—unless you wish to see me pound and pummel our Richard until I tire or he forgets the oath you imposed,—such ridiculous, unmanly and impossible promise and——"

"Valentine!"

With a half-weary, half-petulant gesture, the Earl turned.

"What, you again, Clip!" he exclaimed. "Always on my heels! Always interposing when least expected or desired——"

"Always, Valentine, according to the promise I made your sweet mother——"

"Enough of that!" cried the Earl imperiously. "Here is no time or place for sentiment. Give Miss Rosemary your arm and walk her into the house or wherever——" He started and swung about as, uttering a high-pitched, joyous squeal, out from the tall green mysteries of the coxswain's scarlet runners sped the small, elfin shape of little Jane.

"Mary!" she cried. "Oh, Mary dear, I——" Here, catching sight of tall, scowling Richard, she stood dumb, turned to fly and thus beheld the Earl.

"Ooh!" she exclaimed. "It's you!" and ran to clasp his slim, booted leg. "Oh, I'm glad, glad, glad you've comed back to me at last! And I've made lots an' lots of magic . . . spells, you know. So now you can take me 'hind the beans if you want to an' kiss me. Come away with Jane . . . go with her . . . magician spells you know . . . 'steerious!"

The Earl, looking down at his small suppliant, whispered an oath to himself; then off came his hat to her and he bowed with a flourish.

"Spells—of course!" said he, a little hoarsely. "Fair greetings to thee, dear Fairy Godmother,—greetings and—" his voice broke and he sank upon one knee to clasp this small sedate lady in cherishing arms. "Darling little Jane!" he murmured and, bowing his head to her small shoulder, whispered awhile; and the child, listening to these whispered words, smiled and touched that bowed head with a very small, very motherly hand, answering in her clear treble:

"An' I love you too! Lots, I love you! Oh, more 'n' all the humbugs in all the shops, I do! So I said you into my prayers every night, and I made you some spells; come an' let me show you how,—'cause you see there must be grass an' flowers for my very bestest magic-an'-spells, an' they're awful 'steerious. So will you go with her, please?"

"Yes, show me," said he with a strange eagerness, "show me!" And, lifting her to his shoulder, away he went with his little Fairy Godmother throned triumphant.

"Now upon my soul," said Richard, shaking his head like one very much perplexed; "he is a queer, mad fellow and yet that child actually . . . by George, she kissed him!"

"Yes," said Mr. Clipsby, his deep-set eyes very bright and shining, "and a child, by her very innocence, is dowered with a strange, instinctive sense of good and evil . . . and she kissed him! Listen to her now!" he exclaimed, as from the garden rose another squeal and bubble of childish laughter. "Now who dare think the devil is paramount yonder? A child is very near God and therefore potent for good. . . . But I come from my sister, bidding you sup with us, if you will."

"With all my heart," cried Richard gladly. "And yet—no! There is a friend waits for me; by Gad, I must go! Please tell Mrs. Humby and the

Captain I am coming to thank them and say *adieu*. . . . Rosemary," he continued, as Mr. Clipsy vanished behind the scarlet runners, "my dear, I clean forgot to tell you, your father is in town, at the Tabard——"

"My father?" she repeated. "In London? But this is wonderful!"

"Dear Heart, he came to help me find you."

"And this," sighed she, "is even more wonderful. Yes, Dick . . . he never seems to want me near him. I think when mother died, all his love died with her. I have tried to make him care for me, but he never seems to notice or want me near him. I have written every week but he never answers. And yet . . . he is so lonely but doesn't seem to know it. I think his poor heart is broken . . . dead."

"Anyhow, you shall see him to-morrow, sweetheart. And to-morrow I am taking you home . . . to my mother. To-morrow! Early!"

CHAPTER XXIX

CHIEFLY CONCERNING MR. MORDAUNT'S EYE, AN EPISTLE EXTRAORDINARY AND HOW CHARMIAN PREPARED HER FOR BATTLE

OF young Mr. Mordaunt's two oxlike eyes one showed unmistakable signs of recent hardship and ill usage, for it was swollen, it was discoloured and it mortified him; therefore he wore his hat atilt and kept this shameful and shamed feature as much in the shade as possible, as he rode homewards this bright and sunny morning. Reaching the Holm Dene stables, he dismounted, rather shakily, and leaving the horse with Bob, one of the under-grooms, hurried across the wide, superlatively neat yard towards where Old Adam was sunning himself throned on an upturned bucket, like the aged but extremely competent presiding genius of this spicily fragrant, well-ordered domain.

"Good morning, Mr. Mordaunt sir," said the ancient man, rising to touch hoary eyebrow and glancing keenly and askance at this young gentleman's pale, too sensitive face (and damaged eye of course). "Ay, 'tis a love-elly morning sir, though Farmer Grove do tell me us needs rain; but they farmers is never satisfied——"

"Old Adam, please . . . please sit down again," said Mr. Mordaunt in his quick, nervous manner. "Now, pray look at my eye and tell me . . . is it very noticeable?"

"Well, sir," answered Old Adam, surveying the organ from divers angles, "it are."

"Very annoying!" sighed Mr. Mordaunt, setting his hat more atilt than ever. "Highly distressing!"

"Lord love ee, sir, 'tis only a black eye!" quoth Experienced Age consolingly. "How mout you ha' took it,—if I may ax?"

"From a brutal, foul-tongued fellow at Lewes."

"Aha!" exclaimed Old Adam, frowning in sudden ferocity. "Then 'twas for sayin' summat again' The Fambly, I'll lay."

"It was; yes, Adam; but how did you guess?"

"Sir, there be a lot o' scandalious talk goin' on about Our Fambly o' late. F' instance, at th' old 'Duck i' the Pond,' last evening as ever was, I powered nigh a pint o' good ale over a chap—namin' no names—as spoke agin The Fambly, which chap young Bob theer knocked down for me, immediately arterwards,—me bein' a bit old-like for fisty-work. Ay, there's a lot o' no-account talk going on, sir."

"There is," sighed Mr. Mordaunt, frowning also, "there is indeed. I hope and pray it never comes to her ears!"

"Oo's years, sir?"

"Oh, I . . . I was thinking of . . . of Lady Vibart . . . it would distress her. . . . But now . . . my eye? Is it so dreadfully remarkable? Will it become very black?"

"Sir, that theer black eye o' yourn, though pretty black, aren't nothin' in partic'lar as black eyes go. I've 'ad worse in my time. Bathe it, sir, cold water 's good, but a bit o' raw steak's better. Step up to the house sir, ax Mrs. Mayhew for a gobbet o' raw beef, slap it on, keep it on and nobody never won't be none the wiser nor know nowt about it—to-morrer. . . . And Mr. Mordaunt, sir, seein' as you took said black eye for the good o' The Fambly—lo and behold you, sir, my 'at is off to ee!" And rising from the bucket, Old Adam bared his white locks, saluting the eye with such respect that its owner flushed self-consciously.

"Thanks," said he, returning the aged man's salutation, "thank you, Old Adam. . . . Cold water and beef! I'll do it!" So away he hurried, approaching the house furtively, by indirect paths and roundabout ways; yet was he fated to meet whom he was most anxious to avoid, for, dodging round a tall, clipped hedge, he came face to face with my Lady Vibart, she walked pensive and alone. Off came his hat instinctively but, with rare presence of mind, he bowed sidling and askew, thus presenting his undamaged optic to her regard; but few things might escape those beautiful, quick eyes, for:

"Gracious!" exclaimed my lady, and then: "Goodness me!" and then: "Heavens! Mordaunt, you've never been fighting—you?"

"Alas, madam," he answered, guiltily abashed, "I—I fear I—must confess so. . . ."

"Very reprehensible!" she murmured. "But—how interesting! Let us sit down—here in this shady corner. Now! Tell me all about it." And Charmian was smiling on him so very kindly that he flushed and grew abashed for quite another reason since, remembering that which no eye must ever read, to wit "The Epic Amoroso of the Truth Unutterable," his conscious gaze abased itself and for a moment speech was beyond him.

"I'm quite sure you fought in a good cause," she prompted gently.

"I—I venture to think so, my lady," he stammered. "I had ridden over to Lewes on business for Sir Peter and while there I—I had a—a little unpleasantness."

"You mean some one gave you a black eye, Charles. Who, pray?"

"A Mr. Thomas Vince, madam."

"I know of him, a quite detestable young man. I sincerely hope Mr. Vince's eyes or nose are . . . not quite unscathed, Charles?"

"They are not, my lady. I contrived to . . . to mark him . . . here and there."

"Then, my dear Charles, your swollen eye is vindicated. And why did you come to blows with this person?"

Now here, meeting his lovely questioner's compelling gaze, he grew embarrassed for yet another reason.

"Ah," she murmured, laying white hand on his bowed shoulder. "I apprehend . . . it was to do with us here at Holme Dene, was it not?"

"Yes, madam."

"Did it concern Sir Peter?"

"No, madam . . . not exactly."

"Myself?"

"No, no, my lady; ah, no, indeed."

"Then it concerned Richard, of course. Pray what had this Vince creature to say of my son?"

"Mr. Vince uttered a disparaging remark touching Richard and . . . a Miss Rosemary Ford, a remark I could not allow to pass unnoticed——"

"So you hit him! Hard, Charles?"

"As hard as possible, madam."

"You are a valiant, true-hearted boy, dear Charles. Now come indoors and I will tend your hurt.—Oh, indeed, I have bathed other black eyes before now!

"There!" said my lady, her ministrations ended, "I could not do more or feel prouder of you, Charles, if you were my own dear son, as indeed you might well be. . . . Please, as you go, ask Miss Janet to see me in my boudoir."

"Her Son!" Mr. Mordaunt groaned within the stricken soul of him, sighed deeply, bowed and departed.

Then Charmian hastened to her own chamber and, seated before a some-what littered writing table, began to search through the papers and oddments that littered it until (her dimpled chin showing almost grim) she pounced upon a certain letter heavily sealed, daintily perfumed and directed in a fine Italianate handwriting; she flicked open this dainty epistle with disdainful finger, read it, frowned at it, crumpled it up, smoothed it carefully out, perused it again and exclaimed between white teeth the monosyllabic word:

"Cat!"

She was still frowning at this letter when, with martial clash of silver reticule, Miss Janet strode in, closing the door behind.

"Well, m' dear?" she demanded.

"No,—very, very ill, my dear!" answered Charmian, giving the letter a passionate shake. "Something slimy and evil is afoot, Janet! Viciousness is abroad! Odious scandal has begun to rear its venomous head and bares its poisonous fangs!"

"Oh?" murmured Miss Janet.

"Yes—oh! repeated Charmian. "Oh, Janet and indeed! And for gracious goodness' sake, don't be so Scottish and unemotional, so pestilently passionless! I tell you there's something evil, something black and hateful abroad! And do sit down!"

"Evil?" quoth Miss Janet, seating herself obediently. "Evil, ay. But 'tis no tae be wondered at in this sinfu' worrald, wae's me! But whaur's it the noo, m' dear?"

"Anything or nothing or—everything, Janet. But something vile, exactly what I dare hardly conjecture. But I can feel it, Janet, sense it in the very air wherever and whenever I go."

"Umph—humph!" exclaimed Miss Janet pensively. "Can it possibly have anything to do with that ghastly Abbeymere affair, my dear . . . the . . . death?"

"Probably!" murmured Charmian, gazing at her faithful companion with troubled eyes. This . . . or Richard's sudden disappearance and poor Rosemary's flight—bless her! Yes, viper tongues may be busy on this . . . hateful gossip."

"Mebbe!" nodded Miss Janet. " 'Tis but to be expectit in this unco' censorious worrald."

"Janet, I'm almost sure of it! And more,—I do believe these ugly rumours mostly proceed from that odious feline thing called Bertha Golightly!"

"It'll no surprise me," sighed Miss Janet. "I mind Bertha; she was your junior at school and——"

"A nasty, little, frilly thing that tattled tales of every one," cried Charmian.

"But why are ye sure 'tis Bertha?"

"I'm not sure—yet! I can only suspect. But why did the creature write twice, and with such sugary persistence, pleading with me to take my Peter to her garden party to-day?"

"Did she so?"

"She wrote first a week ago, my dear, and I promptly wrote back, declining and excusing ourselves. The other day she wrote again—here's the letter and more stickily sweet than ever . . . and I've scarcely spoken to the creature for years! Listen to it!" And snatching up the perfumed letter, Charmian read it aloud and with her own interpolations as follows:

"My dear, dear Lady Vibart, or may I not for the sake of past association name you my sweet, sweet Charmian——

"No, ma'm, you may not! Oh, you fulsome, sugar-and-cream idiot!

"I am scribbling these brief lines with my Algernon's hearty endorsement to once again implore you to grace my *fête—champêtre*——

"Nothing so vulgar as a garden party, oh, no, ma'm!"

"All the County will be here and yet incomplete, lacking your charming self and dear, handsome Sir Peter. And then besides——

"Ah—listen, Janet! Here Madame Tabby begins to spit and arch her back!"

"And then besides, my dearest Charmian, as your loving friend, I crave your presence for your own so precious sake. There are little naughty rumours stealing about concerning your dear son Richard, the charming, gallant, darling wretch,—and a certain too beautiful, too, too captivating young g——

"There, Janet! Our sleek and spiteful tabby cat shows her pink tongue and polished claws—and spits verjuice! But there's more and worse yet!

"Then again, Charmian mine, I, as your early companion and loving friend, feel it my heart's duty to beseech your and Sir Peter's presence to smooth away certain doubts and still these soft, whispered rumours concerning the poor, dear Earl of Abbeymere's so very strange, tragical, dreadfully mysterious end. Of course the merest word from Sir Peter can explode, blow away and utterly disperse such airy innuendoes as idle curiosity may have bred.

"And there, I think, the slimy serpent stands confessed, Janet, writhing in her frills and flounces, rearing venomous head, darting her poisoned tongue or——" Charmian crumpled the dainty script once more and immediately smoothed it out again.

"Ay," nodded Miss Janet, "or—what, m' dear?"

"Or be—trodden upon!" hissed Charmian, between snapping white teeth. "And . . . oh, my Janet," sighed she, thrusting out one slim, daintily shod foot, "I'm going to tread and trample—heavily, or know the reason why!"

"Is there ony mair o' yon letter?"

"Merely jam and wind, my dear. Madam Tabby ends thus:

"And so, my sweet, sweet Charmian——"

"Janet,—never, oh, never dare to call me 'sweet'!"

"Never!" quoth Miss Janet, clashing ferociously. "Why would I? What's after 'sweet Charmian' ?"

"This!" answered Charmian, uttering disdainful sound very like a snort:

"I am offering two petitions to Omnipotent Providence,—I pray for fine weather and my own dear Charmian, whose tender image nestles ever in the heart of

> "her most devoted
> truly affectionate
> ever admiring
> "BERTHA GOLIGHTLY.

"P.S. My Algernon sends humble greeting, dying to kiss your hand and is warmly expectant of dear Sir Peter. Oh, do not fail thy Bertha."

"And there," said Charmian, tearing this fragrant missive across and across, "there it is, Janet! This is why I must gird me for battle,—be up and doing."

"Oh! What?" demanded Miss Janet.

"Blunt her claws! Draw her teeth! Twist out her serpent's fangs!"

Thus it befell (after some little while) that Sir Peter, busied with his bailiff John Berry over certain abstruse calculations, was roused therefrom by the opening door and glanced up, frowning a little, to behold such radiant vision that he blinked and, forgetting to frown, caught his breath, while Mr. Berry rose to bow profoundly with stamp and jingle of spurred boots.

"Why, Charmian . . . my dear . . . ?" murmured Sir Peter, rising also. "Whatever——?"

"Oh, John Berry," smiled my lady, curtseying grandly to this square-faced, round-eyed gentleman, "pray tell me, am I well?"

"Madam," he answered fervently, "you are more and far beyond a mere 'well'!"

"Dear Mr. Berry," said she, with giggle of girlish laughter, "you are becoming the absolute courtier. Pray, sir, will you permit Sir Peter's submissive wife to steal him away from you?"

"My lady," answered John Berry, bowing more profoundly than before, "who may resist your ladyship? Surely not I."

"Nor I!" laughed Sir Peter. *"Experientia docet.* Time hath made me something wise. We will finish our business to-morrow, Berry."

"Very good, sir. Madam, your servant. Good afternoon."

And with cheery salutation to husband and wife, John Berry clumped and jingled away.

"And now, dear soul, why all this stately magnificence?" enquired Sir Peter, leaning back in his chair the better to behold her.

"Bertha Golightly and other felines, Peter! And it is thus I shall front and outface the creatures," and then Old Adam came knocking to enquire:

"Will ee have the open or closed carriage, m' lady?"

"Oh, the closed, Adam. And the dapple-greys."

"But, my Dear Heart," enquired Sir Peter, as the old man hobbled away, "where are you off in such lofty estate?"

"To the Golightly affair, of course," she answered, frowning at herself in the looking-glass.

"Great Lord!" exploded Sir Peter. "You never intend to visit those people?"

"No, Peter dear, I didn't say visit; we are merely looking in at their garden party, you and I——"

"I?" he exclaimed in a tone of indignant amazement. "Never in this world! You know what I think of the fellow! Golightly was Abbeymere's creature and we of course never agreed as magistrates—or anything else, for that matter. And of late I find him rather more irritating and bumptious than ever! No, Charmian, no! Certainly not! I am sorry to disappoint you but visit this man I . . . will . . . not. Absolutely no, Charmian!"

"I think I will have you in your newest coat," she murmured, musing over him, as it were, "the blue with silver buttons, Peter, I love you in dark clothes——"

"But, Charmian, I am telling you I'll not call on the man! It is quite, quite impossible! Golightly has contrived to be even more obnoxious of late——"

"Why, of course he has, my Peter. But haven't you noticed a growing change in other of our neighbours lately . . . since Lord Abbeymere's death?"

"Eh? A change?"

"Yes—A strangeness . . . an indefinable something . . . an aloofness. Haven't you remarked this, Peter?"

"Well . . . no, my dear, no——"

"Ah, no, you wouldn't, because of your cattle and cottages and things. You are too tremendously engaged about things that scarcely matter to know anything about things that do . . . and it is high time you learned. And you shall be taught this afternoon! But, my dear, boots and buckskins, of course, will never do! I suggest your strapped pantaloons and pumps, or——"

"Charmian, I . . . am . . . not—going! I detest the fellow heartily——"

"This is exactly why you must go—and shall, dear love! And—not the pantaloons! I prefer you in kerseymeres—they are tight-fitting and you have such exceedingly nice legs, Peter. Come, let us hurry; the carriage will be at the door, and you must change into a frilled shirt—most essential!"

"But . . . great heavens above! Don't I tell you——"

"Frequently, Peter dear. But we must not let the greys stand, they are so fidgety. So come along, dear man; I'll tie your cravat for you myself . . . for go with your poor, meek, supplicating humble person you must and shall! Come . . . Sweetheart!"

Sir Peter frowned, sighed, laughed, kissed her and—went (of course).

CHAPTER XXX

GIVETH SOME DESCRIPTION OF AN AFFRAY FEMININE

MRS. ALGERNON GOLIGHTLY sighed ecstatic; for here, upon her trim and spacious lawn, seated at many little rococo tables busily engaged in the consumption of her tea and other dainty comestibles was THE COUNTY (or rather, some part thereof).

Thus Mrs. Golightly, throned at dainty tea equipage beneath shady tree, with the three chosen friends of her bosom, was at her gayest and showed more sprightly, more girlishly vivacious than usual, as with play of sparkling eyes she glanced from one to another of her chosen three; to wit:

At the Honourable Miss Amelia Poynte, slightly sere and yellow with aristocratic nose so very high-bred that when under any stress it twitched and quivered as if tweaked by invisible fingers; at Lady Priscilla Lylton, tall and commanding in a kind of osseous fashion; at Mrs. Julia Burchard, the little widow, plump, prattling yet romantic.

"Well, my dears," she cooed, dimpling upon all three. "All are here! All! Every one that counts in the County——"

"Except—the one!" sighed Mrs. Burchard.

"Oh, but," gasped Miss Amelia, "one might be sure she would not venture! To run the gauntlet of so many eyes!"

"She refused your invitation, Bertha?" questioned Lady Priscilla.

"She did, darling! Of course! But I wrote again . . . the sweetest letter . . irresistible, I hope and think."

"Then, dear Bertha, you opine she may adventure?"

"My dearest soul, she is a creature may do—anything! Such audacity!" Mrs. Golightly's blue orbs turned themselves heavenwards. "At school my dears, she was so wild! So ungoverned! An imperious minx utterly spoiled by too much money. She was expelled at last for violently assaulting Miss Finch the Principal . . . tore her cap off, my dears . . . pulled her hair, and all on account of a young pupil-teacher—such an ugly, awkward thing and Scotch. . . . And expelled, my dears! With ignominy!"

"Oh, one can well believe it!" gasped Miss Amelia, the invisible fingers busy with her thin-nostrilled nose again. "The airs she gives herself in the County! One wonders how she dare when one remembers what one is hearing—everywhere!"

"Ah!" sighed little Mrs. Burchard romantically. "You mean, of course, her son's elopement with . . . that governess creature! Poor Richard, such a handsome, naughty fellow! They do say the creature he's fled off with is . . . a beauty——"

"Oh, but . . . such audacious boldness!" moaned Miss Amelia. "One blushes even to think——"

"Quite shocking!" exclaimed Lady Priscilla, pausing, teacup at lip, to shudder violently through all her bony structure. "To fly together that same dreadful night, in the fatal, very hour! Flaunting their shame in our very faces!"

"One would like," sighed Miss Amelia, delicate nose a-twitch, "one is curious to hear what his doting mama would find to say in excuse for his blatant, his very . . . well, bare-faced conduct. And it is but right she should explain . . . if she can,—she owes it to the County!"

"And Sir Peter too!" quoth Lady Priscilla. "So remote! So lofty! This might shake even his superlative arrogance——"

"Ah, my darling Pris, do but wait!" cried Mrs. Golightly, laughing with roguish vivacity. "Pride before a fall, you know! My Algernon has lately discovered . . . oh, my own dears! My Algernon means to question him and —demand an answer! And such a question! Indeed one that——" But at this moment appeared an ornate young footman who, bowing stiffly, announced to his mistress in hoarse whisper:

"They'm arrove, madam. Sir Peter and Lady Vibart."

Mrs. Golightly set down the half-emptied cup with a clatter, she glanced at the faces, suddenly tense, of The Three, caught her breath, patted her ringlets and arose:

"Actually!" she murmured. "Oh, my precious dears, of all the imaginable —! Lead on, Thomas!" Then, clasping her hands, she raised her eyes towards heaven, gasped and fluttered away.... And after some while (obedient to whispered mandate) the young footman, stepping forward, announced in voice stentorian:

"Sir Peter ... and ... Lady Vibart!"

The clatter of cups and saucers was magically stilled, the chatter of voices hushed and for a moment was strange and almost painful silence while all eyes stared in the one direction. Then, gliding serenely forward, Charmian, Lady Vibart, favoured the County and her hostess with a slow and graceful curtsey, while Sir Peter, bowing, glanced about him, puzzled and a little indignant.

But now, tossing back her ringlets with girlish abandon, Mrs. Golightly tripped to them, cooing rapturous welcome:

"Oh, Sir Peter ... what pleasure! Dearest Lady Vibart—nay—my own precious Charmian, how positively sweet of you to honour poor us! All the world is here ... our world ... the dear County! You know every one, of course! My naughty Algernon should be here to greet you but—oh, there he is, in solemn conclave with the dear Bishop and General Saxby! Ah, he sees you—he comes!"

Teacups were clattering again and the sunny air humming with politely murmurous talk and modulated laughter as Squire Golightly advanced upon these late visitors.

A pink, a plump yet classical gentleman was the Squire, with a Roman nose of terrific, of portentous possibilities quite unsupported by a small, pouting, rosy mouth and fade-away chin; but his gestures were Roman as his nose and he bore himself like the Greek Ajax, ready and eager to defy the lightning, had there been any.

"Sir Peter," quoth he, posturing classic welcome, "my Lady Vibart, this is —shall I say a glad surprise? Shall I remark—an unexpected pleasure? Be supremely welcome to—The Manor! A neighbourly gathering here, Sir Peter, an assemblage of friends and neighbours. My Lady Vibart, I leave you to the tender care of my dear wife. Sir Peter, will you walk?"

"Yes, yes!" cried Mrs. Golightly, clapping her hands with youthful exuberance of joy. "Go, Sir Peter, begone, you men creatures; I'll care for your darling Charmian, she shall be my Charmian for a little, happy hour."

"Eh, Vibart," quoth the Squire, "our ladies to their tea, we of the sterner sex to ... eh ... to something stronger. This way——"

Murmurs and curious glances a-many; smiles and hearty greetings a few, that Sir Peter returned a little stiffly but that his lady answered with a gracious, very sweet urbanity.

Scraps of murmurous conversation:

"Their son ... young Richard ..."

"Elopement, you know ... ran off ... a servant maid ..."

"No, no, a governess, my dear...."

"But . . . on the fatal night. . . ."

This and more Charmian's quick ears caught as she moved, slow and stately, beside her vivacious, chattering hostess; and thus presently beholding The Three waiting in the leafy shade, couched and entrenched, as it were, behind their teacups, agog and quivering for action, Charmian's ruddy lips parted in slow, languorous smile (that yet showed pearly teeth), up went her stately head, her curling lashes drooped upon eyes that glittered, and she bore down upon The Three like a line-o'-battle ship, as stately, as graceful and very nearly as deadly.

Three ladylike cries of ecstatic welcome, six hands outstretched in eager greeting, lips apout to peck the chill kiss of feminine salutation upon unwilling cheek; then:

"Dear Charmian," quoth Lady Priscilla, bony elbows aquiver, "how surprisingly well you show."

"Truly wonderful! Perfectly amazing, my love!" prattled little Mrs. Burchard; while the invisible finger and thumb seemed to tweak Miss Amelia's thinly sharp nose more spitefully than ever as she gasped in nervous, high-bred manner:

"One is, well . . . naturally surprised, dear . . . under the circumstances, love . . . indeed, all things considered, one wonders how you do it?"

"A kind heaven," sighed Charmian, sinking upon the rustic seat beside her hostess and arranging her silks coquettishly, "has blessed me with an easy conscience, my dears, a contented mind and a most excellent digestion. Yes, whatever my outside may be, my inside is very well."

"Oh . . . my dear!" gasped Mrs. Golightly, eyes wide in youthful innocence. "Oh . . . you mean——?"

"Stomach, my angel!" answered Charmian, full-throated. "My stomach!"

Lady Priscilla recoiled; Miss Amelia emitted a small, ladylike screech; Mrs. Burchard shivered and Mrs. Golightly hid her face.

"Charmian . . . oh, my sweet!" she whispered, peeping through her fingers. "Was that not a trifle . . . just teenily-weenily inclined to be . . . coarse?"

"However," said Charmian, cup at lip, "we all possess stomachs and many of us find them such infliction that they become an affliction to others. But why should my rude health be cause for such surprise?"

"Well," answered Miss Amelia, with a pounce, "under the circumstances one wonders——"

"Dearest Amelia, what circumstances?"

"Amelia alludes," said Lady Priscilla, pouncing in her turn, "to your poor Richard, of course, my dear; his sad entanglement, his reckless elopement with this artful young person——"

"So romantical," sighed Mrs. Burchard, "but alas, so indiscreet! To flee with one so much beneath him socially!"

"Let us hope, my Charmian," wailed Mrs. Golightly, "let us pray, for your own sweet sake, that the poor, dear boy will not be so blind, so cruel, so madly infatuate, so heartlessly reckless as to . . . oh . . . to marry the creature!"

Charmian set down her cup, glanced from one eager, watchful face to the other and laughed joyously:

"Now, my dear things," cried she, "whatever, oh what phantasy, what fairy tale is this?"

"Neither!" snapped Lady Priscilla, bony finger upraised accusingly. "Your Richard has gone, run off, fled with a pretty governess or——"

"Eloped!" sighed Mrs. Burchard.

"And . . . oh, my precious Charmian," cried Mrs. Golightly, "not only has he run off with this too beautiful, too, too seductive governess creature, but . . . they . . . eloped . . . fled . . . on the very night, perhaps even the fatal hour of the poor, dear Earl of Abbeymere's strange and dreadful death! We know it! Every one tells of it! The news is everywhere!"

Charmian's long lashes flickered and drooped, then her bright eyes surveyed The Three with look unwavering and serene as usual.

"Pray," she enquired gently, "does Gossip tell the name of this governess?"

"Certainly!" retorted Lady Priscilla, craggy chin outthrust. "She is named Ford, Rosemary Ford!" Charmian smiled, she tittered, she laughed, and so unfeignedly that her hearers eyed her, and themselves, askance.

"My poor, precious pets," said she, at last, "now see how wildly, how foolishly gossip has led you astray! This dear child, Rosemary Ford, is my own beloved god-daughter——"

"Ah, no—no!" cried Lady Priscilla indignantly, "this young person is, or was, governess to Lavinia Bedingham's children——"

"She was, Priscilla, but she is—my dear godchild Rosemary Ford, of the Sussex Fords, an extremely ancient family settled in the County long before the Conqueror stole it,—and she is engaged to marry my son Richard in a few months' time, I'm happy to say——"

"Marry?" echoed Lady Priscilla.

"Your son——" gasped Miss Amelia.

"Richard!" nodded Charmian.

A moment of amazed silence, then Mrs. Golightly spoke in her most dulcet tones:

"Oh, but, my own dear, what . . . what of these strange tales that she has vanished, that Richard has vanished——"

"Quite true, my dear Bertha. Rosemary is in town to choose her *trousseaux* and bridesmaid's gowns. I shall join her shortly."

"But then, my precious, what of Richard?" said Mrs. Golightly somewhat between her teeth. "What should take him to . . . Abbeymere and on that fatal night? Oh, he was seen, yes, my love,—and Sir Peter also!"

Charmian's heart missed a beat, the hand upon her fan slowly clenched itself as if in sharp agony; then she laughed, sweetly musical as ever.

"Bertha!" she murmured, with an arch smile. "My dear! Is it so strange for young impetuous lover to steal away 'neath the moon to sigh and gaze upon his beloved's window? Or for stern sire, alas grown beyond such sweet folly, to speed after and drag the unhappy swain back to home and bed? Oh, my dear, think on your own long-vanished youth and sigh!"

Mrs. Golightly, perhaps because of this hyphened adjective, glared and sighed rather hissingly. . . .

Meanwhile Sir Peter hearkened to the Church-cum-Army-cum-Landed Interest laying down the law for those (the more benighted) of the community, that vast, indefinable body that so often needed (it would seem) being "kept down" and "in its proper place"—wherever this may be,—until they had strolled and talked themselves into the house, to a chamber where other gentlemen were seated about bottles and glasses that twinked very seductively.

. . . Sir Peter, glass in hand, was bowing his acknowledgments to the little fiery-eyed General when Squire Golightly got upon his legs, his nose more portentously Roman, his attitude more Ajaxian than usual as, raising plump and dimpled hand, he addressed the company:

"My lords and gentlemen——"

"Eh—what now?" bellowed the General, "what the devil's this,—a speech?"

"A few brief—shall I say very brief—words, my dear General——"

"Brief, eh? Good! No oratory, Golightly! I don't trust oratory. Plain speech is my rule, so—no confounded oratory!"

"I beg a few words, gentlemen, on a matter which in some measure touches us all as neighbours and persons of condition in the County, a matter of the utmost, I may say, of the very gravest moment——"

"Sounds dem'd clemmy and churchyardly!" quoth the Honourable Bob Westover, ramming in his monocle.

"Gentlemen and neighbours, I will admit I have convened you here with an ulterior and, I venture to think, a laudable motive——"

"Then out with it!" barked the General. "Get to it! Fire away man!"

"Sirs, it behoves us one and all, nay, becomes our bounden duty to enquire more particularly into the very sudden . . . shall I say death? Shall I say . . . mysterious taking-off of our esteemed neighbour, the late Earl of Abbeymere——"

"But—good God, Golightly," cried the General, "that sorry business is all over, ended—done with! Why dig it up again?"

"My . . . dear . . . General," retorted the Squire, looking round about as if in hopeful expectation of jagged lightning-flash or shattering thunderbolt, "we, as persons of account, should all of us instantly seize metaphorical spades and dig amain for the good of this our County and humanity at large, for I——"

"Meta—what's—a—name spades?" snorted the General. "Ha—the devil! This is oratory!"

"Eh?" quoth the Honourable Bob, blinking. "Dig? Oh, dem!"

"Gen-tlemen!" quoth the Squire, plump hand aloft in classic pose. "Know that I have lately discovered . . . a new witness! A witness who is ready to swear on oath that upon that fatal night of the Earl's demise, he saw two persons stealing into Abbeymere Great House! A witness who observed these two persons very plainly and beyond all possibility of mistake!" Here once again the Squire, as Ajax, glanced round about him, cleared his throat and continued more impressively than ever:

"Now if there be any here amongst us who have, or who desire to offer an explanation, I crave silence for them . . . speak, I beg!"

"Eh . . . eh, what . . . oh, demme, what?" barked the little General, rolling his eyes terrifically. "Any here? Any of—us? Ha—what, Golightly, what the devil d' ye mean?"

"Does no one offer to explain?" questioned the Squire in sombre tone, his eyes staring hard at the ceiling. "What . . . nobody? Then alas, I, being slave to duty, needs must and—will. Gentlemen, I have then, as I say, a witness ready and willing to take oath, at proper time and place, that, upon that dreadful night, in the very hour of the noble lord's ghastly death, he saw two persons, one following some while after the other, mount the terrace at Abbeymere. Gentlemen, he was able to recognize these persons and will swear they were no other than Mr. Richard Vibart and his father—Sir Peter!"

Ensued a moment of stunned silence, a strange and rather dreadful silence; then:

"Good God!" exclaimed the General. "Preposterous! What . . . eh . . . what d' ye say to this confounded rigmarole, Vibart?"

Sir Peter, being utterly dumbfounded, became rather more stately than usual, glancing with keen deliberation from one amazed face to the other of this silent and very uncomfortable assembly.

"Yes, but," demurred the Honourable Bob, fumbling for his tumbled monocle, "first of all—who's your witness, G'lightly—who?"

"A . . . very worthy person, sir——"

"Yes, but—who, Squire—I ask . . . who?"

"A person named . . . Timothy Perkins."

"B' Jove, I remember him; he was Abbeymere's head gamekeeper and discharged for drunkenness and so on——"

"Eh? Good God!" exploded the General. "A . . . ha, demme, a gamekeeper! A drunken rascal! Shame, Golightly, shame, sir——"

"Gentlemen, all this is beside the point," cried the Squire with a sudden almost ferocious triumph. "The real question is—what says Sir Peter Vibart himself—what?"

Very deliberately Sir Peter set down his wineglass and arose; then, turning his back upon the Squire, viewed the expectant company, face after face, with the same level, dispassionate regard and with shapely lips upcurving to slow smile, spoke with that air of gentle yet positive assurance that was his at most times:

"It would seem that, when not drunk, the man Timothy Perkins is a somewhat observant person. Gentlemen, I bid you—Good afternoon——"

"But . . . oh, but—" quavered the Squire, forgetting to be classic . . . "you surely will not leave us without some word of——"

Sir Peter bowed and went.

Thus Charmian presently espied his tall figure moving towards her amid the throng, pausing now and then for word with some friend or acquaintance and yet, despite the smiling, leisured ease of him, something in the set of his shoulders and jut of chin caused her a quick pang of anxiety; therefore it was with her gayest air that she smiled at and beckoned to him with her fan.

"Oh, Peter dear," she sighed plaintively as he made his obeisance to them, "have you come to say we must go? So soon! How quickly such hours fly, for—ah, dear Bertha, you have been so entertaining—indeed, all of you! *Adieu*, my dear things and do pray contrive something as amusing against our next meeting."

Curtseys, smiles (more or less toothy), kisses . . . and away sailed my lady upon her husband's arm; but from between vivid, smiling lips stole a whisper for his ear alone:

"The odious cats; I do wish a large dog would bite them!" And thus beside her very silent husband my lady floated serenely away. But . . .

CHAPTER XXXI

TELLS HOW ROSEMARY CAME HOME

SCARCELY had the carriage door shut them in than, sinking back on the cushions, Charmian sighed wearily and fanned herself violently.

"Oh, Peter," she murmured. "Oh, my dear, another ten minutes and I should either have swooned or scratched some of them! . . . Well, are you quite instructed now; have you seen and heard enough?"

"So much," he answered, frowning at the passing landscape, "that I am in deep perplexity."

"Then now you know that you were seen . . . you and Richard . . . at Abbeymere that dreadful night?"

"Yes, my dear, Golightly had the effrontery to announce the fact——"

"The man you sent to prison, Peter?"

"Yes. He beat his dog to death——"

"Oh, Peter, but this is dreadful!"

"It was,—for the dog!"

"And for you, for you! This man hates you! Oh, my dear, this is quite terribly frightful. That he of all others should have seen you that night! Peter, it's awful!"

"Yes, I suppose it is . . . unfortunate," he murmured.

"Suppose? You know it is, Peter—it's a perfectly fearful complication, it's——"

"Now, my dear, don't begin to worry——"

"Begin? I began days . . . weeks ago! Oh, Peter, whatever are you going to do about it?"

"Nothing, Dear Heart."

"Absurd! Preposterously ridiculous! Do you actually mean to say——"

"Not a thing, my dear! I shall simply permit the sordid matter to . . . blow over . . . pass away——"

"Peter, Peter—it is only a little breeze now but it may grow to a tempest to destroy you . . . and me! So my Peter—act! Strive! Defend yourself before the storm roars down to sweep us both away!"

"My own dear," he murmured, holding her within the strong comfort of his arms, "don't distress yourself so wildly for so little. Your hot imagination runs riot, Sweetheart, and you are crossing bridges before they are well in sight! This afternoon has warned me and I shall be prepared. But I will not stoop to defend myself by any public word or act; it might argue fear and only the guilty are fearful."

"Then what shall you do?"

"Nothing—except it become manifestly needful."

"Peter," she demanded suddenly, "has it ever occurred to you that, after all, the hateful man may actually have shot himself?"

Sir Peter, eyes closed, merely shook his head.

"Well then, has it ever occurred to you to really suspect any one?"

Sir Peter, eyes still closed, answered drowsily, "Yes, dear."

"Oh, my gracious heavens above!" exclaimed Charmian, sitting upright very suddenly and leaning to seize and shake his arm. "Who? My goodness, and you have never so much as given me the least hint! Who, Peter—who?"

Murmured Sir Peter, eyes pertinaciously shut:

"My dear, the personal pronoun, being in the Objective Case, should be 'whom'!"

"Oh, drat your pedantical grammar! Who is it you suspect as the—murderer?"

"My dear soul," he sighed, "it being only the merest suspicion, destitute of all shadow of proof, I cannot possibly say. Instead, if you will have me converse, let me tell you about my Alderneys and——"

"Oh, Peter Vibart," she exclaimed between shut teeth, "you are such a hatefully complacent, dogmatically dogged, odiously secretive wretch that I wonder any poor, deluded woman could be fool enough to ever marry you! Not a word, sir! Be silent and think about that! Or if you can, sleep—sleep and have a hideous nightmare!"

Sir Peter laughed and reached out his arms for her but she held him off and, shutting her fan, used it as a weapon of offence.

"I will . . . not . . . be kissed!" she cried furiously. "Don't touch me with those . . . nasty great . . . arms——"

Gone now was my lady's serene stateliness, vanished was Sir Peter's dignity; his hat was off, his hair dishevelled, his usually rather saturnine features transformed with an almost impish glee; and as they battled thus, the carriage turned in at their own lodge gates, rolled smoothly beneath the shady avenue towards the old house that winked its many lattices in the level beams of sunset, like friendly eyes in jovial welcome. . . .

. . . And then, before the carriage might pull up, the door was plucked open and in upon them toppled a something that seemed all shoulders, arms and eager hands that drew and held them both.

"Mother dear! Father!" cried a joyous voice. "Here I am and . . . here we are again! I couldn't wait——" Charmian uttered a little scream of beatitude.

"Richard!" she cried and, dropping her fan, clasped an arm about each of her men-folk, kissing them alternately. And thus, with their son between them, they reached the wide doorway of the old house, where stood Miss Janet and beside her one who trembled and curtseyed and blushed—and showed therefore only the lovelier.

"Yes, there she is, Father! . . . I've brought her home to you, Mother! . . . waiting to kiss you both! Oh, by George, but it's glorious to be home and with you again! Mother, your hand—so! Father, come and kiss our Rosemary!"

My lady's bonnet was askew, but her eyes were bright with welcome; Sir Peter's hair was on end, but his smile was more eloquent than words. And Rosemary, kissing and kissed, forgot her shyness and yet trembled at Charmian's touch and Sir Peter's firm-clasping hands, for she knew she had indeed reached "home" at last.

CHAPTER XXXII

IN WHICH MR. SHRIG SETS FORTH SUMMARIES OF THE CASE

THEY were seated in the morning room, my lady busied with that embroidery the which (like Penelope's web) never seemed any nearer completion; Rosemary was inditing a long letter to her father, when the door opened and in upon this peaceful scene clashed Miss Janet, her air even more militant than usual.

"And yon's the thirrud!" quoth she, clanking to and fro like a heavy dragon. "Three in twa days! Peeping and prying, I'm tellin' ye, Charmian!"

"Prying on us, Janet? Again! Are you sure?"

"My certie, I am that! Three o' them in twa days! Watching the hoose!" Rosemary's busy quill was suddenly arrested and she glanced from the speaker to her godmother in sudden apprehension.

"And what," enquired Charmian serenely, "what was he like, this third man, Janet dear?"

"A country yokel-looking creature, no' vera big and chewed a straw."

"Did you accost him?"

"I did that! 'Look now, ma man,' I said, 'ye're trespassing and if ye're no' oot the noo and awa', I'll ca' the gardeners and grooms tae wheep ye,' said I."

"Well, did he make any answer?"

"Ay, chewed his straw at me, touchit his hat an' said he didna twig and— would I speak English. So I told him vera plainly if he didn't remove and instantly, I'd have him beaten by sticks and bitten by dogs."

"What then, Janet?"

"He pulled off his hat, m' dear, and oot of his hat took this folded paper, the whilk I read,—ay and 'tis either an unco gallimaufry o' nonsense or—aweel—see what ye make o't." So Charmian took this paper and read aloud there from these words, very carefully written but without punctuation of any sort.

"Dear Mam or Lady or Sir axing the favour of a word at yr convenience or sooner on acc of Sir PV being lately suspicionated of The Capital Act in re Ld A lately deceast yrs to command J Shrig
    The sooner the better agents of a certain party being previous active"

"Goodness—me!" exclaimed Charmian, staring at this document in troubled perplexity. "What an odd letter . . . and a little disquieting!" And she read forth again:

" 'Sir P.V. being lately suspicionated.'

"Heavens, Janet! And this:

" 'Agents of a certain party being previous active.'

"Who is J. Shrig—to know so much of this odious business? Janet, exactly what was he like—the man who gave you this? I must find him—at once!"

"Dear Godmother," said Rosemary breathlessly, "there is a man out there now, a strange man staring up at the house. . . ."

Glancing hastily through the open window, Charmian beheld the man in question, a squat, stoutish person in blue spencer and top-boots, whose hands were crossed upon an extremely nobbly stick while he surveyed the house in keen though leisurely fashion with a pair of very bright eyes set in a smooth, round face.

"Janet, is that the man?"

"No, m' dear, he'll juist be anither o' them,—four in two days! I'll oot an'——" she stopped as, with sound of hasty footsteps, Mr. Mordaunt appeared and now, a little breathless but very determined, confronted the intruder.

"Who are you? What do you want?" he demanded.

The stranger, turning with placid deliberation, raised nobbly stick to the wide brim of his shaggy hat and beaming pleasantly on his indignant young questioner, answered in husky though resonant voice:

"Shrig's me monnicker, sir,—to see Sir Peter Wibart or Lady "

"Sir Peter is out and——"

"Then Lady, sir, or p'raps his son, Mr. Richard——"

"Charles," called my lady, leaning out from the window, "ask Mr. Shrig to approach."

Mr. Shrig advanced forthwith and, taking off his hat, made Charmian an odd little bow that somehow matched his quaint, old world attire.

"Are you the J. Shrig who wrote this letter?" she enquired, viewing him with her level, all-seeing regard.

"That verry i-dentical, ma'm!" he answered, meeting her scrutiny with gaze steadfast as her own. "Jarsper Shrig, Lady, vunce o' Bow Street, now o' 'The Gun,' Gray's Inn Lane, and though retired and pensionated, still with a leery ogle, or as you might say peeper, ma'm, for Windictiveness ver-ever found, be it 'igh or low, town or country, any times, anyveres, ma'm."

Charmian surveyed the speaker with wise feminine eyes that took in every feature of this face, so beaming and rosy (despite grim-lipped mouth), and eyes twinkling with such wistful goodfellowship that her frown vanished and her ruddy lips curved to answering smile.

"Then be welcome," she said, "for I think you are the very man I need."

"Ma'm, I am!" he answered. "This is axackly why you be'old me."

"Then come in, Mr. Shrig, and tell me what kind wind wafted you here. Charles, please show him the way."

So into this dainty chamber clumped Mr. Shrig in his old-fashioned top-boots and at my lady's behest, took a seat, placed beneath it his hat and stick and, looking round upon the three ladies, beamed more rosily than ever.

"Rosemary, if your letter is finished, dear, Mr. Mordaunt will see it franked and posted. And while you are in the village, Charles, please ask Mr. Mason for another skein of crewel silk, like this! And should you chance to see Sir Peter or Richard, tell them I want them home at once. . . . And now," said my lady, as the door closed upon Mr. Mordaunt's slim elegance, "now, Mr. Shrig, please explain this letter of yours and how you are here at Holm Dene so very opportunely?"

"Ma'm," he answered, his bright glance roving, "a few days ago a young Bow Street pal o' mine come into these here parts on business and—I come too. I put up at the White Hart in Lewes. I sat me in the tap. I listened and axed questions. I used me legs, likewise me eyes an' y-ears, and the consequence is—I wrote that theer reader."

"This letter," nodded Charmian; "but before you tell me what it means, I want to assure you that if you can help me . . . a certain matter, you will find me not only very grateful but willing to pay you well. So now let us talk on a business understanding."

"Well, ma'm, business is business and money comes in very useful. But lady, I'm axing you to believe as 'tweren't neither vun nor t'other as drawed me here, but jest a nat'ral love for The Game and being wery 'ard set agin all manner o' Windictiveness. I'm old, ma'm, and not so spry as I vas and p'raps not vorth nobody's money, by me looks. But then—I'm a old dog o' the Law, me lady, vith nose as keen on the scent as ever it vas and—wery much at your sarvice, if so be acceptable."

"Thank you, Mr. Shrig. Then first of all—I have been annoyed lately and very much mystified by strange men haunting the place; they have been noticed lurking in the park, and yesterday one of them even ventured into the garden yonder. Two men, I am told, who creep and vanish,—peeping and prying. And why? Whom are they watching? What do they want? Let your first duty be to find this out for me as soon as possible, Mr. Shrig."

"Ma'm," he answered, his roving glance on the gilded cornice, "I knowed all o' this, days ago. These here men—there's two as you've mebbe seen and two as you ain't, vich makes four on 'em—eight peepers, ma'm—these men is spying constant on Sir Peter Wibart and your young gen'leman son Richard, and all on 'em set thereto by Windictiveness in the shape of a—naming no names—plumpish, 'igh-'anded gent."

"The odious wretch!"

"Ma'm?"

"This will be Squire Golightly, of course!"

"Me lady," quoth Mr. Shrig with gentle, deprecatory wag of head, "I ventur' to suggest, seeing as how,—the vord Windictiveness, naming no names, eh, ma'm?"

"As you will, Mr. Shrig."

"Now then, ma'm, the case o' Windictiveness agin' said Sir P.V. is pretty strong and—a-growing stronger!"

"Oh? How, pray?"

"Me Lady, so fur as me eyes and y-ears has served me, the case stands thus." Here Mr. Shrig drew forth a somewhat battered and very bulbous notebook and opened it at a certain page, continued:

"P'int Number Vun: Sir P.V. and Lord A., though neighbours, has never been friends.—Agreed, ma'm?"

"Yes, Mr. Shrig—heartily! Lord Abbeymere was—but pray continue."

"P'int Number Two: Sir P.V. is rich and spends a mort o' money on his estates;—Lord A. ain't and lets his estates go to rack an' ruin an' tenants ditter.—Agreed, ma'm?"

"Quite true, Mr. Shrig."

"P'int Number Three: For years Sir P.V. and Lord A. have disagreed about a right o' vay. They've also disagreed in politics, religion, on the magistrates bench and off; in short, they ain't never agreed in nothing votsoever.—Yes or no, ma'm?"

"Indeed . . . yes, although——"

"P'int Number Four: Sir P.V. and the Earl of A. has been heered to come to words pretty frequent—partic'larly re. a noo road as Sir P. vas a-cutting of.—Agreed, ma'm?"

"Ye-e-s. I think there was some little friction but no real quarrel, Mr. Shrig."

"P'int Number Five: It is also in evidence that Mr. Richard Wibart threatened said Lord A. vith personal wiolence and has been heered to declare as said Lord A. deserved and ought to be —shot!—Agreed, ma'm?"

"No! No—certainly not! Richard did not! I never heard he had made such dreadful threat. . . . And if ever he did, it was in the righteous heat of the moment and meant nothing! Richard is quite, quite incapable of such wickedness, as you will all agree when you meet him."

"Very likely, ma'm, but then I ain't Justice, and Justice, being so outrageous blind, might not. And a threat agin life, spoke hot or cold, ain't easy forgot and don't never do the threatener no manner o' good!

"P'int Number Six: On the fatal night as the Fact was committed, Mr. R.V. is seen approaching Abbeymere, but—not like a ordinary visitor—by the front door, but furtive and sly—from the rear——"

"Richard is never furtive or sly!"

"Agreed, ma'm! But Justice, not knowing said young gent, might take t'other view—and vould!

"P'int Number Seven: On same fatal night and soon after Mr. R. is seen, Sir P.V. comes a-follering him and—not by the front door neether but, like Mr. R., in very suspicious manner, furtive and sly, creeping cautious arter his son——"

"Mr. Shrig, never in this world! Sir Peter couldn't possibly creep—under any circumstances."

"P'raps not, me lady. Having took a good peep at said gen'leman in Lewes market, I think not, but—I ain't Justice nor yet the judge and jury as may have the trying of him!"

Now at this, Rosemary uttered an inarticulate cry of horror, Miss Janet started so violently that she clashed, while Charmian sat rigid and mute, gazing large-eyed into Mr. Shrig's face, that now seemed very stern and grim indeed.

"You don't . . . you can't think," she faltered, "it can ever come to . . . a trial—Sir Peter! Charged with . . . murder! My dear son! No! No! It is impossible!"

"My lady," said Mr. Shrig, his voice a little huskier, "it is so wery possible that I'm here to do what I can to prewent. For lookee, ma'm! Your husband and son vas at Abbeymere that night—vich is bad enough! But they vas seen —vich is a sight vorse. Can they deny the fact—on oath? No! Vell then, can they explain the fact——"

"Yes—oh, yes! Richard will tell you he went there . . . because he could not sleep . . . he was wildly anxious about Rosemary . . . Miss Ford here, so he rode over——"

"Eh—Miss Ford?" exclaimed Mr. Shrig, his keen gaze now upon Rosemary's pale, anxious loveliness. "So you vas at Abbeymere that night too?"

"Yes, sir," she answered, meeting his fiercely keen gaze with unfaltering regard. "I was staying there as governess to Lady Bedingham's children— the Earl of Abbeymere's sister."

"Ford . . . Rosemary . . ." murmured Mr. Shrig, carefully inscribing the names in his "little book." "Ah!" quoth he, and sat a moment, lips pursed in soundless whistle, and staring at nothing in particular; then turning suddenly upon my lady, "So then, ma'm, Mr. R., being anxious about Miss Ford—vich I'll ax reason for same, later on—Mr. R. rides to Abbeymere and how then?"

"He . . . he wished just to be near her, Mr. Shrig . . . But his father happening to see him gallop off so wildly at such hour, rode after him to . . . to bring him back. . . . So you see, Mr. Shrig, it is all quite reasonable when explained. You see this, don't you? Oh . . . don't you?" Once again Mr. Shrig pursed his shaven lips as if about to whistle, but instead of so doing, shook his head slowly from side to side.

"All I ax, me lady, is—can they prove it? Have they ever a vitness as can svear for 'em?"

"No," answered Charmian, shrinking before the expression of her questioner's face.

"Then, ma'am," said he, gently but remorselessly, "do you, can any o' you, think as any strangers—any judge or jury—could believe sich a tale? No, I see as you don't! And—no more do I!"

"Oh, but . . . the inquest?" gasped Charmian, wringing tremulous hands. "The inquest proved it was suicide."

"That inkwest, ma'm, meant nothing and proved less! A crowner as asks no more than 'e did—according to the reports—a jury o' country lads as vas content to ax nothin' at all! But vun fact did come out in evidence, a fact as first set me a-thinking—ma'am, the deceased Lord A. was shot into the left temple and yet was knowed to be, ever and allus—right-'anded!"

"Then, what . . . what do you suggest?"

"Me lady, 'tis pretty sure and certain as deceased vas shot by some other party."

For a long moment Charmian gazed speechlessly at this stoutish person whose round and placid face seemed but a mask for the astute and penetrating sagacity of the real man, and rising impulsively, she came and reached out her hand to him, saying:

"Mr. Shrig, you have shown and warned me of quite unimagined perils and for this I thank you; now show me how to escape them and my gratitude will be beyond expression."

Mr. Shrig rose, took that soft hand, shook it, dropped it and nodded.

"Lady Wibart," said he, "I took up this here case first of all agin Windictiveness; now I'm a-going to do all as I can for your sake, ma'm. But I must be told all the facts as is known, if I'm to anyvays help your folk—for proof's the vord, ma'am,—Proof! Prove 'em innocent or—some other party guilty."

"Yes, but . . . oh, Mr. Shrig,—how?"

"Ma'm, since you ax so p'inted, I'll answer you full and free, m'lady, I dunno—yet!" Here, sitting down again rather suddenly, he turned and beamed on Rosemary.

"Young ma'm," quoth he, "the question is—how much can you tell us? Since you vas at Abbeymere that 'ere night, you may p'raps have seen or heered summat—the fatal shot f'r instance, eh—come now?"

"I will tell you all I can," she answered, facing him resolutely now, "but I heard no shot."

"Then p'raps you might chanced to ha' seen the body, or as you might say, ca-daver, eh, Miss Ford?"

Rosemary shivered and glanced, mutely questioning, at Charmian.

"Yes, dear child," sighed my lady, seating herself beside Rosemary on the settee, "tell Mr. Shrig all you saw, all you heard,—every hateful detail."

So, clearly and briefly as possible, Rosemary described the incidents of that too eventful night while her listeners sat dumb, all three, until the story was told.

"So!" exclaimed Mr. Shrig, shaking his round, bald head. "So—here's the reason Mr. Richard worrited! And no vonder! And then, Miss Ford, arter you'd peeped at him an' Sir P. stooping over body o' deceased,—vot next?"

"I ran down the passage and out through the Abbey ruins. . . . I ran blindly until I found myself beside the Mere."

"Vy there?"

"I was all distraught and hardly knew what I did."

"And then, Miss?"

"Something frightened me. . . . I heard the sedge rustling and I . . . fancied some one was hiding there . . . eyes watching me——"

"Eyes, Miss? Oo's?"

"I couldn't see, but I felt sure some one was crouching there. I was terrified and ran back to the house. Just as I reached the terrace, I saw Sir Peter and Richard going away and I wanted to run after them, I felt so lonely and terrified . . . but instead I went on to the north wing and, hardly knowing what I did, I threw a handful of gravel up at Mr. Clipsby's window."

"Mr. Eustace Clipsby? Oh! Ar!" nodded Mr. Shrig, beaming quite jovially. "And vy Mr. C.'s vinder?"

"He had always seemed so good, so kind and gentle . . . and I was quite distracted with grief and horror."

"Very nat'ral too!" nodded Mr. Shrig. "And did Mr. C. open said vinder?"

"Yes . . . in a little while."

"And . . . dressed complete, vas he?"

"I didn't notice."

"But not in his nightcap? Not—eh, Miss Rosemary?"

"No."

"And looking sleepy—eh? Just voke up, like?"

"I don't remember . . ."

"Did 'e seem very sa-prised to see you?"

"I can't tell I—I only remember imploring him to come down to me. . . . I told him something dreadful had happened and that I must get away . . . at once."

"Did that sa-prise him?"

"Yes . . . I think so."

"Ha!" quoth Mr. Shrig, rubbing his knees and staring very hard at the rich carpet beneath his dusty boots. "And vy must you be for running off in sich desprit hurry, Miss Rosemary, ma'm—I ax you?"

"Because——" Rosemary paused and glanced appealingly at her godmother, who instantly kissed her, saying:

"Tell him, my own dear, tell him everything."

"Then Mr. Shrig, it was because I was mad enough to think Richard had . . . killed the Earl for my sake and so I meant to run away and divert suspicion to myself—for his sake."

"Noble-ish, Miss Ford, ma'm, but wery oncommonly wrong, miss, wrong. Hows'ever! Did Mr. C. keep you long a-vaiting?"

"No, not long."

"Meaning as he was wery quick?"

"Yes."

"And all dressed proper,—cravat and neckercher?"

"I didn't notice."

"Did 'e go and take a peep at the cadaver?"

"No—oh, no!"

"Oh! Then vot did he do?"

"Helped me to collect and pack the few things I needed . . . gave me all the money he had . . . carried my bundle for me across the park . . . comforted and helped me like the dear, kind friend he is."

"Oh? Friend o' yours, eh, Miss Rosemary?"

"Yes, yes, indeed!"

"And vot then?"

"I hid in a little wood till day came, then caught the early coach for London. Mr. Clipsby had given me a letter to his sister there, who keeps a ladies' school. . . . And that is all I have to tell you, Mr. Shrig."

"Ho!" quoth he, beaming up at the cornice again. "And them eyes by the Mere . . . cat's, dog's or man's, do you think?"

"I . . . can't be sure."

"Might ha' been either, eh?"

"Yes."

"Didn't notice no shape about it?"

"No, only the eyes."

"A pity! Nothing more to tell me, Miss Rosemary?"

"No, I've told you all—everything."

"And you, m' lady?"

"There is one thing," answered Charmian thoughtfully, "something that has surprised me. Sir Peter lately informed me that he suspected some one."

"Oh?" murmured Mr. Shrig. "Ar? Didn't say oo, ma'm, did 'e?"

"Mr. Shrig, he positively refuses to so much as breathe a hint until he can prove—Oh, thank goodness, here they are!" she exclaimed joyfully, as borne on the sunny air came a clatter of hoofs, jingle of bits, cheery voices, a clink of spurs and in through the wide lattice vaulted Richard.

"Mother!" he cried. "Rosemary! Janet . . . bravo and hurrah! Father says we may be married—in a month! Subject to your agreement, Mother. So, dearest—be agreeable and . . . why, who's here . . . is it—yes, Mr. Shrig, isn't it? How are you, Jasper Shrig man; and whatever brings you so far from London Town?"

"You, sir!" answered Mr. Shrig, rising to clasp the hand Richard extended. "Yourself sir, your father and Windictiveness!" Then the door opened and upon the threshold stood Sir Peter.

CHAPTER XXXIII

CONCERNING SIR PETER, HIS CONSCIENCE

"So," quoth Mr. Shrig, shaking his head gloomily, "you refuse, eh, Sir Peter? You refuse to name the party as you suspects, eh, sir?"

"Absolutely!" answered Sir Peter, with his air of serene finality. "Definitely!"

"Vy then," said Mr. Shrig, as serenely persistent, "you might p'raps breathe, or shall us say, visper the shade or shadder of a nint, sir."

Sir Peter's lips quivered to the ghost of a smile as, taking up a quill from the writing table before him, he leaned back in his chair and shook his head.

"No, Mr. Shrig," said he sternly, "to denounce or throw suspicion on any one without positive and actual proof is infamous,—the act of a mere scoundrel——"

"Meaning sir, this here Squire Go-lightly." Sir Peter actually started.

"Eh? Now what do you know of this . . . gentleman, pray?" he demanded.

"More than 'e thinks, sir, and not so much as I could vish. . . . So you can't even drop me a nint . . . careless like?"

"No."

"Oh!" murmured Mr. Shrig, rubbing the knees of his cords and shaking his head reproachfully at the blunt toes of his top-boots. "Not even if I varns you—wery partic'lar, as things can be made to show oncommon black and precious orkard agin you, Sir Peter?"

"No, Shrig! Not even if the authorities should even proceed so far as to apprehend me. Being innocent, I have nothing to fear and——"

"Axing your parding but stop a bit! Sir, jest think o' the many pore innocent folk, men—ay and vomen too—as have kicked their innocent lives out on the gallers tree afore now. Lookee, Sir Peter, you and Mr. Richard are nobs, reg'lar 'eavy toddlers and gen'lemen both, and may be innercent as sucking doves and lambs noo-born—but, the Law is the Law, and if the Law can anyways prove ye guilty—it'll be noose an' jibbet for both on ye! And sir, wot'll your pore lady do then—I ax you?"

Sir Peter's look was still serene, but he fidgeted with the pen in his fingers till, becoming aware of this, he laid it down, rose from his chair and, crossing to the window, stood gazing out at the sunny landscape; and now Mr. Shrig, seeing him thus shaken, questioned him again:

"It wouldn't be this here young sprig, sir, eh—this noo, young Lord Abbeymere as you suspicions?"

"No," answered Sir Peter, gently but without turning. "Oh, no!"

"And you still refuse to name the party as you do suspect, sir?"

"I do, Shrig! For the last time, please understand that under no circumstances will I voice my suspicions without proof positive."

Here, once again, Mr. Shrig pursed his lips, but this time emitted a low and dolorous whistling, while Sir Peter, chafing at such unwonted and dismal sound, continued to gaze out of the window until at last Mr. Shrig broke off in the middle of a doleful note and spoke, almost as mournfully:

"Sir Peter Wibart," quoth he, in sighful reproach, "the Gospels says, sir, someveres, as even the Lord needs them as he'd help to likevise help him by helping theirselves and, sir,—I'm only a wery ordinary huming being as vould help you—if 'e might." Now at this, Sir Peter turned and, beholding Mr. Shrig's rueful visage, his own dark, stern features were brightened and suddenly transfigured by his youthful smile.

"God bless you, Shrig man," said he impulsively. "I believe you would; indeed, I begin to think you will. But how more can I help you to help me and mine? You have heard my son's story and my own explanation of our presence at Abbeymere that night—such as it is! I have even told you how these young people, thinking to shield each other, would have taken the guilt upon themselves. What more can I do?"

"Sir," answered Mr. Shrig, his bright gaze roving up from Sir Peter's gleaming boots to his flowered waistcoat, snowy cravat and the resolute chin and shapely mouth above, "if you won't tell me the party as you suspects, you can tell me the reasons for your suspicioning said party."

"Hum!" quoth Sir Peter and, glancing towards the window again, began to rub his chin.

"You can gimme," said Mr. Shrig, his gaze now upon Sir Peter's profile, the rather arrogant jut of nose and jaw, "your reasons for suspectin' and cause for same, sir."

"Well . . . yes," nodded Sir Peter, as if to his own very active conscience, "I think I can do this . . . certainly. . . . Then, Mr. Shrig, if your eyes are as sharp as they appear to be, you will find my reasons at and in Abbeymere itself, the house."

"Wery good, sir!" said Mr. Shrig, diving for hat and stick. "The sooner, the better."

"Do you mean you'll go at once?"

"This wery moment, sir."

"Such zeal is highly commendable, Shrig. I will give you a note to the man in charge shall afford you admittance to the house and also the ruins of the ancient Abbey by the Mere," said Sir Peter, busy with rapid pen. "Be particular in your inspection of the ruins, Shrig. There are various means of entrance into them, but I suggest you go by the small arras-hung door that leads from the room where the Earl was . . . found dead. Give this note to John Rudge at the gatehouse; you will find him worth while questioning, I fancy."

"Sir Peter," answered Mr. Shrig, stowing the note very carefully within his hat, "everything is vorth questioning in this here vorld,—them as is blessed or cursed with tongues, and things as, not having ever a tongue, can't therefore lie."

"Why then," answered Sir Peter, with another of his rare smiles, "when you have done at Abbeymere, come back and remain with us a while at Holm Dene, if you will."

"Thankee, sir, that's very handsome and I feels dooly honoured. So back again I'll toddle—to-morrer, if convenient to you then, sir. And now, by your leave, I'll be off."

"Then go to the stables and ask old Adam, my head groom, for a conveyance."

"Thankee again, sir, but my gig's awaiting in your stable yard. Good arternoon, Sir Peter!"

"Good-bye for the present, Shrig. I shall be curious to learn how much Abbeymere tells you and what answer the ruins make."

CHAPTER XXXIV

TELLETH HOW MR. SHRIG READ A LETTER AND ASKED QUESTIONS

Now being in the open air and beyond the range of Sir Peter's keen eyes, Mr. Shrig's booted legs abated all hurry and bore him at leisured gait and by roundabout ways where roses bloomed and trim paths radiated from an ancient sundial surrounded by an age-worn stone seat whereon dropped young Mr. Mordaunt and so lost in the perusal of an open letter in his hand as to be wholly unaware of anything else, for Mr. Shrig's top-boots trod with such a careful silence that they enabled their wearer to approach near enough to glimpse the letter over Mr. Mordaunt's bowed shoulder; and having thus contrived to read certain lines of this letter, Mr. Shrig spoke:

"Ax parding, sir, but—your thumb . . ."

Mr. Mordaunt started violently, turned and, beholding the speaker, leapt to his feet.

"What . . . what do you mean?" he stammered.

"Only your thumb, sir. I couldn't exactly make out that 'ere last vord by reason o' your thumb. So if——"

"Do you mean you . . . were prying? Did you dare to read——"

"All except that 'ere last vord, sir."

"Then con-confound such impertinence!" quoth Mr. Mordaunt, very red and stammering with indignation.

"Now now, Mr. Mordaunt, sir, you knows me . . . I'm Shrig, Jarsper, guest o' Sir Peter and here at Holm Dene to serve the Fam'ly and look into matters with the ogle of axperience . . . consequently, young sir, I vants that there letter."

"Do you tell me you are a—guest—here?"

"Ar! And by Sir Peter's own inwitation! And now, young sir, I'll—take this here scripter——" and with the word, Mr. Shrig leaned suddenly forward, twitched the letter deftly from Mr. Mordaunt's fingers and was smiling into that young gentleman's astonished face, all in a moment. Quoth he:

"Now, sir, as mootooal friends o' the Fam'ly, let you an' me set down and con this here over together," and sitting down forthwith, he beckoned Mr. Mordaunt beside him.

"But what . . . how can I be sure you are a friend?"

"Mr. Mordaunt, sir, you 'ave me vord and here under me dicer is me phiz, chivy or signboard—wery good! Now let you an' me go over this here and see vot us makes on it. Hearkee!"

And Mr. Shrig read forth as follows:

"Let Sir Peter Wibart take and instantly heed this warning. Powers are in motion while he sleeps. Messengers ride post to London. An indictment is to be sworn and Sir Peter arrested at any moment. Oh, the shame of it! Sir Peter Wibart arrested for MURDER (you'll notice, Mr. Mordaunt, as the Capital Act is wrote in capitals, sir). Consider the odium, the stigma, the undying scandal. Therefore let him at once (you'll notice as 'at vonce' is underlined, Mr. Mordaunt, sir) save himself if he can, by any or every means. This the advice and warning of a

"FRIEND.

"And vot," enquired Mr. Shrig, staring down at this mysterious screed with round-eyed intentness, "vot d' ye make o' that, sir?"

"I don't know. . . . It seems impossible! Incredible . . . too awful to contemplate! Sir Peter . . . arrested for—murder! Oh, my God, it will kill her——"

"Oo?" enquired Mr. Shrig, still intent on the written words, "kill oo, Mr. Mordaunt, sir?"

"Lady Vibart . . . God help her!"

"A-men!" sighed Mr. Shrig. "But . . . do you 'appen to reckernize this writing, sir—eh?"

"No . . . no, I don't!"

"Vich aren't saprising, con-sidering as 'tis wrote disguised."

"Disguised? But how—how do you know?"

"Axperience, young sir. This here was wrote by a voman—leastways a fe-male, I reckon. The question is—oo? Also—vy? Here's Windictiveness and a voman, a wery orkard combination! A voman and Windictiveness . . . and they both begins with a Wee!"

"Oh, but how does it matter who wrote it——"

"A precious lot, young sir."

"Then Sir Peter must be warned—at once. I'll go to him this instant . . . give me the letter; he must see it immediately . . . come, let us find him——"

"Easy now, easy!" murmured Mr. Shrig, holding up his nobbly stick reprovingly. "Veer's your eyes, sir? Think a bit; ar—let's ponder or, as you might say, roominate. Can't you see as this yer a-nonymouse letter vas wrote to that wery i-dentical purpose, eh, sir?"

"No. What purpose?"

"To make Sir Peter act sudden—an' act wrong! To make him move—and move into danger! To make him commit hisself an' give suspicion summat as may be tvisted to act agin him and look more like—proof. For Proof's the article, young sir,—vithout Proof, and vith a capital P, nobody nor nothing can't do no manner o' real harm. So set ye down, Mr. Mordaunt, and be good enough to answer a few questions—for the good o' the Fam'ly."

"Anything you will!" answered Mr. Mordaunt, seating himself, only to leap up again and pace nervously to and fro. "Anything in the world—to help —the Family——"

"Very good, sir. You are Mordaunt, Charles, private secretary to Sir P. Wibart. Long so?"

"Since I left college, three years ago."

"Are you devoted to said Sir P.?"

"Yes, yes—most truly!"

"To his Lady?"

"I would die for . . . for the Family."

"Wery good again. Ever been to Abbeymere?"

"Once or twice."

"Then you knowed the late Earl, p'raps—by sight?"

"Very well. And I can assure you that he was an overbearing tyrant, a black-hearted villain, with something in his expression . . . almost obscene at times . . . oh, a hateful man!"

"Har!" exclaimed Mr. Shrig. "You didn't axackly cotton to said noble lord, eh? Did you ever hear Mr. Richard Wibart threaten his life?" Mr. Mordaunt took four steps away and four back, then answered, chin aloft:

"Sir, I leave Mr. Richard to answer for himself."

"Wery good indeed!" nodded Mr. Shrig and, setting hand to fob, began to work at himself until, after no little exertion, he had extracted a large silver watch; having duly consulted this somewhat unwieldy timepiece, he proceeded to work it out of sight again.

"Fi' minutes past five. Might your time be the same, sir?"

"Yes, just about."

"Vich makes him fi' minutes late!"

"Are you expecting some one?"

"Ar. He'll be along by an' by. In the meantime, do you 'appen to know a gentleman name o' Clipsby,—Mr. Eustace Clipsby?"

"A gentleman? Well, no . . . at least, if you mean Lord Abbeymere's . . . I hardly know how to rate him; he seemed hardly a servant . . . no, certainly not a servant . . . and yet, such a poor, meek, silent person."

"Oh?" murmured Mr. Shrig, smiling quite benevolently, "'Poor, meek, and silent,' says you. Vould you say as he was afeared o' deceased Earl of A.?"

"Well—no. Oh, no, not afraid but abjectly humble and submissive."

"Did you see said Mr. Clipsby very often?"

"Very seldom."

"And always a meek, mild, wery silent person—eh?"

"Always. But what can he have to do with Sir Peter's very distressing situation?" Beaming upon his anxious young questioner, Mr. Shrig pursed his shaven lips and whistled a pleasing birdlike trill, whereat, and almost instantly, from around an adjacent clipped yew hedge appeared a broadeaved countryman's hat shading a face chiefly remarkable for bright eyes, a pointed, tip-tilted nose and a wide, humorous mouth quirked upon a straw.

"'Lo, Jarsper!" quoth the head.

"Gimblet, how's the cows?" enquired Mr. Shrig, beckoning.

"Flourishing, Old Un, being back in their native pastures."

"Then, me b'y, us'll be a-looking into the milk an' butter business. But firstly—Mr. Mordaunt, sir, this here is Shrigrow Sharp o' the Office, and sharper than any gimblet,—and sir, like me, he is at present a-doing and a-thinking for the Fam'ly. So if you should happen to see him anywheres at any time, don't take no manner o' notice."

"Very well, Mr. Shrig. But now—in regard to that anonymous letter—I should like to hand it to Sir Peter at once and——"

"Sir, I'll take charge o' this for the present, and . . . Mr. Mordaunt, sir, don't say or so much as visper a vord about it to Sir Peter; leave that to me likevise. Sir, if your pit-a-pat, or as you might say 'eart, sir, is half as faithful to the Fam'ly as I reckon it is—not . . . a single . . . vord! Is it a go?" Mr. Mordaunt looked into the speaker's face and read there so much to reassure him that his own anxious features brightened and he reached out his hand, saying:

"Mr. Shrig, I promise."

"Wery good, sir. And if you should 'appen to spy Lady Wibart anyways troubled, visper you in her lovely y-ear and say: 'Jarsper Shrig's got his ogle on Windictiveness—wery vide open indeed.' Good arternoon, sir! And now, Gimblet, let's take a peep at them cows, and sharp's the vord."

"Sharp it is, Old Un!" Then Mr. Shrig touched his hat and strode off beside Gimblet at pace so speedy and with look so assured and purposeful that Mr. Mordaunt, watching in large-eyed concern, felt more comforted than before.

CHAPTER XXXV

DESCRIBETH WHAT BEFELL AT ABBEYMERE

Mounted in his high-wheeled gig, Mr. Shrig saluted Old Adam with his whip, up leapt the Gimblet and away they went. Reaching the open road, Mr. Shrig drove at such a pace that conversation became something of an effort; therefore they rode in silence. Very soon they had reached the great iron gates of Abbeymere but Mr. Shrig drove on at the same speed until they came to a narrow lane, or rather track, that turned abruptly from the highroad, a little-used thoroughfare by the look of it, shut in on the one side by tall trees and wild underbrush and on the other by a high wall, mossgrown and ruinous here and there.

"Whoa-up, Old Un!" quoth Gimblet.

Whereupon Mr. Shrig pulled up opposite a part of this neglected wall whence the coping had fallen, thus making it easy for an active person to climb.

"You should ought to manage that, eh, Jarsper?"

"Ar!" nodded Mr. Shrig, viewing the wall with expert eye. "I'll con-trive,

F

lad, with you to gimme an eave ven and vhere needed. We've plenty o' time for it, eh?"

"Better than an hour, Jarsper."

"Wery good!" quoth Mr. Shrig, drawing a short clay pipe and tinder box from waistcoat pocket. "You've been over the 'ouse and grounds, Gimblet?"

"Every inch, pretty nigh, Jarsper."

"Any bloodstains?"

"Plenty! Lord A. must ha' bled tee-rific,—which, though bad for him, was good for us."

"Ar!" mumbled Mr. Shrig, lighting his pipe. "Blood . . . observed right . . . can be a very good . . . vitness. Now then, viles I take a puff at me steamer, let's hear your report, the deductions as you've drawed and reasons for same."

"Well, Old Un, I argufies as Lord A. was shot to death in the Abbey ruins, in a rum old chamber as needs looking for,—reasons; bloodstains on stone floor, washed away but not quite, as I'll show ye. Body was then conveyed along flagged passage,—proof: four paving stones has been washed there likewise, but on base of wall, two splashes and a smudge as can only be blood, proving very plain as corpus was dragged that way. Three stone steps, leading up from said passage into panelled room of the house, has also been washed but in corner of lowest step—one round bloodspot. In panelled chamber—where according to evidence at inquest, body of deceased was found—a large stain on oak floor beside smallish table."

"Har!" murmured Mr. Shrig, watching the smoke from his pipe dreamily. "I'll take a peep in a bit. Now vot o' t'other matter?"

"The young Earl left London this morning, Old Un——"

"Call him Number Vun, lad."

"And Jarsper, what's more, he rode horseback and—alone!"

"Oh? Any shadders?"

"Two. According to your orders, word was sent to the man Clipsby——"

"Call him Number Two, me b'y."

"Well Jarsper, Number Two not being at home, a message was left."

"Not at 'ome, eh? Now, dash me vig! If Number Two don't turn up—humph! Did you say as Number Vun arrived in Lewes—and safe?"

"Ay, safe and sound, which is rum, Jarsper, and very dusty, which ain't. For, d' ye see, Old Un, after him come them two murderous——"

"Call 'em shadders, Gimblet."

"Well, Number One has a wash and a bottle and then—and here's another rum thing, Jarsper—he leans out o' winder very conspicuous, and them two shadders a-watching him from the stables, and sings out to the ostler, 'Have a horse saddled for me at sunset; I'm riding to Abbeymere,' says he. Think of it, Old Un; he rides from London alone, although warned, and then, not being murdered on the road, tells any one as chances to be listening that he's riding to Abbeymere—at sunset. And I reckon this is the rummest go of all! Looks almost as if he was askin' for trouble, don't it?"

"Not trouble, no—death, Gimblet, death!" said Mr. Shrig, knocking out his pipe very tenderly. "And death ends every trouble; leastways folks thinks so. And now hitch my mare secure, then gimme a leg up atop yon wall. Lordy, but I'm growing too old for sich tricks!"

However, with Gimblet's ready and powerful assistance, Mr. Shrig was very soon perched upon the wall, his booted legs adangle, surveying the scene before him with a profound and lively pleasure; a wilderness of mazy thickets and mighty trees, beyond which dense boskages rose the distant, smokeless chimneys of the great house with the age-old ruins of the Abbey beyond,— broken arch, pillar and crumbling wall, pallid against the dark, still waters of that sedge-girt, gloomy Mere.

"Bee-ootiful!" he murmured in a sort of ecstasy. "In all me born days I never see a place more perfect nor fitter for—The Capital Act!"

"Specially—at sunset, Jarsper!"

"And them shadders, me b'y, they was a-hearkening an' vatching Number Vun at Lewes, eh?"

"They was, Old Un."

"And veer are they now, lad?"

"Still there, Jarsper, tied up very tight and gagged very secure and hid under a pile o' hay in a old loft, where nobody ain't likely to find 'em. Me and Bob caught 'em—onexpected like."

"Wery good, Gimblet! Now help me old bones down off 'n this here wall."

The descent safely accomplished, Mr. Shrig adjusted his hat, resettled his garments and, slipping his hand within the Gimblet's muscular arm, followed whither he was led until they reached a place where, themselves screened from all observation, they could survey the great, old house, courtyard and terrace, and look down the sombre avenue of tall, aged trees.

Very patiently they waited, seldom speaking, their eyes alert and ears straining to catch expected sounds—that came at last . . . the slow, plodding hoof-strokes of a horse.

"Number Vun!" said Mr. Shrig in whisper.

And presently they beheld the young earl of Abbeymere riding towards them, a slimly elegant, youthful shape and yet the very figure of gloom and bitter despondency; for he rode drooping in the saddle, chin on breast, lacklustre eyes bent earthwards, a very old young man ineffably weary.

Reaching the courtyard, he reined in his slow-pacing horse and, lifting heavy head, turned slowly to glance behind and round about him and, while his wide eyes quested thus, he too seemed listening expectantly, as he lifted his head to scowl up at his house that seemed to scowl back at him. Awhile he sat thus, as if waiting for that which should be; at last, with sudden, impatient gesture he dismounted and, leaving his horse to wander where and how it would, mounted the terrace and vanished round the house in the direction of the Abbey ruins.

"What now, Old Un?"

"Fi' minutes!" whispered Mr. Shrig, taking out his large watch; but scarcely had he uttered the words than upon the air throbbed another sound—horse hoofs again and coming at wild and furious gallop.

"Number Two!" whispered Mr. Shrig. The rhythmic hoofbeats rang louder, nearer . . . and speeding up the avenue came Eustace Clipsby who, almost before his foaming spattered horse might check its wild career, had leapt from the saddle and was up the terrace steps, running like a madman.

"Now," quoth Mr. Shrig, "bide here, Gimblet—vatch, listen and—silent as death!" Then Mr. Shrig's stout, booted legs were bearing him stealthily yet with surprising nimbleness up the terrace steps and on—into those stark and grimly ruins, along the stone-flagged passage, through the small door and into that panelled chamber where the dead Earl had left his ghastly mark. With scarce a glance Mr. Shrig traversed this chamber, for beyond was resounding echo of running feet, and then a voice that called desperately:

"Valentine! Valentine—wait!" This answered by another voice high-pitched and passionate:

"Clipsby . . . ha, damn you Clip . . . why must you follow me?"

"According to my oath, Valentine, the promise I made to your mother . . . here in your mother's room."

"My mother's room, yes . . . Come in, oh, come in, man—if you must! . . . Here I was born, as you know, Clip; here she died . . . and here is the only place for me . . . the best and only place for what is to be."

"What do you mean, boy?" Hasty footsteps and Clipsby was facing the Earl and neither dreaming, in such hour and grim desolation of this great, empty house, that keen eyes were watching and sharp ears listening beyond the unclosed door.

The Earl had tossed off his hat and standing thus bareheaded, his golden hair, bright in the sun's last beams, shone strangely like a nimbus, but the face beneath showed wild and haggard, the long-lashed eyes stared wide on vacancy and when he spoke, quick and passionate, there was a strident note in his voice very like terror:

"Oh, Clip . . . Clip, I begin to think I am going . . . mad! Mad, I tell you! I rarely sleep and when I do . . . such cursed dreams! Well, better death than that; better die sane, eh, Clip? A flash, a puff of smoke and . . . rest! And Rosemary . . . she hates and despises me! I saw it in her eyes! So does Richard, damn him! But—why not? God knows I scorn and hate myself— oh, bitterly! I drink to forget and never can forget I am the son of the man I hate dead as I hated him living! His vile blood is in my veins, so . . . why not let it out? Why not end it all? I rather hoped Frayne's rascals would do it for me—on the London road. I expected a shot on my way here. But well, perhaps this is best . . . and what place better suited than my mother's room, here, where I was born . . . where she died . . . in this very chair and my little childish arms fast about her—you remember, Clip?"

"Yes, yes, I remember, Valentine, but——"

"So here it shall be then," cried the Earl, with a strange and awful gaiety, "my last look for her loved face yonder," and he turned where, above the mantel, hung a painting, the portrait of a woman young and small and slim, whose pale, wistful face looked down on them, great-eyed and sorrowful.

"Such a gentle, patient dear!" he murmured. "You loved her too, of course, Clip. I always knew this!"

"Yes . . . I loved her, Valentine, reverently and with all my young soul, long before she was a wife. But she was so very young . . . her father so rich and cruelly ambitious and . . . Abbeymere was the Earl! So they were married and in that hour . . . part of me died. . . ."

"You hated and feared—him, too,—eh, Clip?"

"God help me,—yes! Fear of him had become a habit . . . for . . . Valentine, I fought with . . . and killed a boy at school, accidentally, as I hope for salvation! But instead of confessing—I was but a lad—I let it seem no more than an accident . . . but Abbeymere, my senior and a prefect, had seen! Through the long years I became his slave, his thing . . . a creature void of all manhood, a poor, spiritless wretch obedient to his nod——"

"Well, he's dead, Clip, he's dead, old fellow, and howling in eternal torment, let us hope——"

"Ah—no, Valentine——"

"Tush! Why not, man, why not? Look on that dear, painted face and think! How often have we seen that gentle head bowed in shame and grief! Those tender eyes dimmed with bitter tears that gathered yet seldom fell . . . while her poor heart broke . . . dying from hour to hour through all those years . . . killed by—him and so slowly—slowly, damn him! But he died in a moment, knew but one pang—ha, the cursed injustice of it——"

"But think, boy, he was snatched to judgment with such dreadful suddenness——"

"And may he be damned everlastingly——"

"No!" cried Clipsby, like one in sudden anguish. "There can be no such thing; God is too mercifully just! No soul is ever lost, for being of God, back to God it goes, purified by suffering, wise by experience, perfected at last."

"A kindly philosophy, Clip, yet what are all such philosophies but a blind and fearful groping in the dark,—the wish fathering the thought? . . . Words and wind! Now as for me . . ." The Earl thrust slim hands into the pockets of his riding coat and turned to gaze up again at his mother's portrait.

"Well," demanded Clipsby, his eyes suddenly intent, "what for you, Valentine?"

"Rest!" answered the Earl softly, and from right-hand pocket, drew a pistol.

"Ah—fool boy!" cried Clipsby, in terrible voice. "There can be no rest in death! Death is but fuller life and vaster effort."

"I wonder?" said the Earl, balancing the weapon in practised hand. "However, being the accursed son of my cursed father and knowing myself such failure in this existence, I intend to put your theory of death to the proof, Clip,—though in fervent hope that at least I shall not be pitchforked anywhere in the neighbourhood of my late departed sire——"

"Valentine——"

"Well, Clip? Were you not better advised to bid me *au revoir* and—go? Your presence here at such a time is a little intrusive and very ill-judged——"

"Valentine, have you—have you ever wondered—how the Earl died?"

"Often, Clip, often! At first with dread, such dread that I contrived it should seem suicide, but now . . . well, there were very many who had just cause for killing him and . . . whoever accomplished it, saved me the noxious trouble of it and, being consequently grateful, I am content . . . to ask no questions."

"Valentine," said Clipsby and stopped, but with such strangely compelling look that the Earl instinctively leaned nearer and in that moment the pistol was snatched from his loosened grasp and hurled crashing through the window; then Clipsby was upon him but, having made sure the Earl bore no other weapon concealed, stepped back, breathless and trembling.

"Valentine!" he gasped. "Dear boy that I love and for whom I'd die . . . this was no way for you to go back to her . . . your hands stained with your own blood . . . Valentine . . ."

The young Earl stared through narrowed lids at this pleading yet so dominating face then, turning away, crossed to the shattered window and, throwing lattice wide, leaned there.

"If," said he, gazing toward the fading western glory, "if, as you think,— my mother yet lives beyond the grave, she would know and . . . were I fouler thing or more sinful and unworthy than I am . . . she would welcome me because she understands. . . . But you . . . you would make me a failure still . . . even in this!"

"I would have you live, for her sake, Valentine."

"And, for her sake, I would die . . . while I am no worse than I am. . . . As a child I often looked down from this window and used to think how very terrible it would be to fall . . . But now——"

"Valentine——" The agonized cry was cut short by a sudden sharp report from somewhere below; the young Earl's slim body seemed to stiffen; then he swung round upon his heels with both hands upraised, as if pointing to the red horror that splotched his face and, uttering a sound that beginning as a laugh ended in sighing groan, he pitched headlong.

And now, as Clipsby knelt to lift his blasted head, into the room came Mr. Shrig at a shambling run and, leaning from the window, thrust fingers into mouth and emitted an ear-splitting whistle.

Ensued a long moment or so of deadly stillness, then from that mazy wilderness below came a second pistol shot followed by another and yet another in rapid succession. Mr. Shrig nodded a little grimly, sighed very dismally and, turning back from the window, stooped to peer into the pale young face that Mr. Clipsby was wiping and wiping with inadequate handkerchief.

"Dead, Mr. Clipsby, sir?" he enquired.

"God forbid! We must get him away . . . bed . . . a doctor. We must get him out of this accursed house. . . ."

"Prompt, sir!" said Mr. Shrig and trotted heavily from the room in quest of Gimblet who met him at foot of the great stairway.

"Eh, Jarsper," he enquired, a little rounder of eye than usual. "Number One—dead, is he?"

"Ar, or pretty nigh, lad . . . and Number Three—not dead too—don't say it!"

"As any red herring, Old Un! A pity, I know, but it was him or me, and there y' are."

"Dog bite it!" sighed Mr. Shrig mournfully. "Number Three should ha' danced the Noogate Jig. How'sever, for Number Vun, my gig—go fetch it, and run, Gimblet, run! Sharp's the vord."

"Sharp it is, Jarsper! answered Gimblet and set off at his best speed.

And thus it befell that in Mr. Shrig's high-wheeled gig, through the dusk of this fragrant summer evening, they brought young Valentine, Earl of Abbeymere, to the care of Charmian and Peter at Holm Dene.

CHAPTER XXXVI

OF A GATHERING SHADOW

THROUGH long weary days and anxious nights the stricken bandaged head upon the pillow had scarcely moved, only sometimes the haggard eyes were open in vague stare, though more often closed as if in troubled slumber or that dreadful unconsciousness from which there is no awaking. And upon this sunny afternoon, down in the garden below a man paced restlessly, staring up at radiant heaven and on the bright world round about him, yet, wheresoever he looked, seeing always that same bandaged head, that death-pale face and slim, motionless form. But as he walked thus, pausing often to gaze up yearningly towards a certain casement, to him amid her flowers came Charmian, soft-treading, gentle of voice, serenely comforting.

"Dear Mr. Clipsby," said she, slipping her hand beneath his arm with loving familiarity, "don't be so terribly lonely in your grief; let us walk together. Speak to me; it will ease your suspense, for in talking with a friend our griefs are sometimes easier to bear."

"Thank you!" he murmured, and yet with something strangely wild and dreadful in his aspect. "I thank you with all my heart for your sweet sympathy, but . . . if he should die——"

"Ah, remember," she pleaded, "remember he is in the hands of God!"

"In God's hands, yes . . . yes. But . . . if he die, then all . . . all is vain! God's hand will be upon me heavily—heavily, for it will have been . . . all vain!" Eustace Clipsby stopped suddenly to stare with awful eyes as one who gazes upon unnameable horror. "In God's hands!" he repeated. "And God is just . . . God is not mocked! Have mercy on him, O God, and—upon me . . . on wretched me in my blindness. . . ."

Gently she compelled him forward; and so they walked together and, in her wisdom, Charmian talked now of other things, of herself and her Peter, of their hopes for the future; of Eustace Clipsby himself, his music and the wonder of his playing.

"And you haven't touched the keyboard for days!" she sighed, gently reproachful.

"No," he answered in wistful apology, "no. There are times when I cannot . . . dare not play, for music is a noble thing . . . holy . . . a wonder of God. And now there is a shadow upon me, an ever thickening darkness. . . !"

"And you play like a master," said she, viewing his drawn features askance and with growing anxiety. "And how very strange," she continued, a little hurriedly lest his attention wander, "how strange that we should have been neighbours all these years, should have seen each other so frequently, and yet only learned to know each other within these last few days."

"Yes," he answered, faint-smiling. "And yet—no! In those dark and evil, ah—those most unhappy days, I was no more than a creeping shade, the very shadow of a man——"

"Ah, no!" she broke in. "You were, ever and always, the gentle soul and great musician we know you for—now! But even in those far-off days you would sometimes play for Valentine and Richard, and they loved it, rogue boys though they were! Richard used to tell me how when they quarrelled you would play them into good fellowship again."

"Ah, it was my only joy!" he answered fervently. "For indeed they both loved music, bless them, even then."

"And do now!" she nodded. "Especially Valentine. The only time he regained consciousness he spoke your name, remember, and asked that you should play. So let us go back to the house and play again—do, it will comfort you and me, yes and perhaps reach Valentine in his dreams and soothe him."

"If you think it would, dear Lady Vibart, oh, if you really think it might, I will play as I have never——" he paused suddenly, his kindling eyes staring at a certain tall hedge, and glancing thither also, Charmian beheld a furtive, lurking shape, round eyes that peered, a wide mouth that chewed upon a straw,—a face that vanished as she looked.

"Some one was watching us, I think," said Mr. Clipsby, turning thitherward.

"Not us," she answered, frowning, "oh, not us. These are spies set to watch my Peter and Richard."

"Spies?" he echoed in wondering amazement. "But . . . may I ask why?"

"Windictiveness, sir!" answered a voice unexpectedly near and Mr. Shrig stood beaming at them from the rosy portal of a little summerhouse. "Windictiveness, Mr. Clipsby, sir," he continued, "is a-trying wery 'ard to prove as how Sir Peter, or Mr. Richard, or both, killed—or as you might say—committed The Fact upon the person o' the late Lord A. And vot do ye say to that, sir?"

"That Vindictiveness is purblind and crassly ignorant as it usually is, Shrig. The mere idea is preposterous, of course, and out of all reason."

"Vell, I dunno, sir. Windictiveness 'appens to ha' got plenty o' reason for suspecting either or both o' said gen'lemen, since both on 'em was at Abbeymere on the wery night and in the wery hour as the Fatal Act was committed, Mr. Clipsby, sir."

"To be sure they were," nodded Mr. Clipsby; "I know all this, Shrig. But what of it, man——"

"Might I make so bold as to ax 'ow you know, sir?"

"I learned of it from Mr. Richard himself and Miss Rosemary, of course. But pray what or whom do you mean by 'Vindictiveness'?"

"Afore I answers you, sir, I'd like to ax you just vun o' two questions. F'r instance, sir, veer might you ha' been at the time o' the shooting?"

"Oh, but, Mr. Shrig," said my lady, a little impatiently, "why trouble him now? Mr. Clipsby is very greatly distressed as I'm sure you will understand. And besides, I have asked him to play for us——"

"Ma'm," quoth Mr. Shrig, squaring his broad shoulders, "you likewise axed me to help you by lookin' into things and I'm a-looking, m' lady."

"Certainly, certainly!" said Mr. Clipsby, almost gaily. "Anything I can say or do to help you and Sir Peter shall be my happiness, dear Lady Vibart. So pray suffer Mr. Shrig to question me . . . indeed, we have had some talk on this grim subject before and in another place."

"Why then, I'll go and tell Peter you have consented to play again at last. So, Mr. Shrig, please don't keep him too long, but come and hear him too, if you will."

"Vith j'y, me lady, thankee! I'm wery partial to music, used to tootle a tin vistle, ar, and scrape a fiddle too ven a care-free lad, ma'm. . . . And now, sir, vereabouts," he enquired in the same breath, as Charmian moved away, "vereabouts might you ha' been the night the Earl got shot?"

"In my bedroom——"

"Then you heard said shot, sir?"

"Quite distinctly."

"And then vot?"

"I got dressed again."

"And then, sir?"

"Something struck my window and I saw Miss Ford down on the terrace below."

"So down you vent to her; and vot did she say?"

"Her exact words I don't recall; the poor child was terribly distraught, but I remember she told me something dreadful had happened to his lordship . . . that she thought he was dead."

"So you hurried off to take a peep at him, eh, sir?"

"Oh, dear, no! You see, Miss Rosemary needed all my care just then;— she was alive and if the Earl was dead, well—he was dead."

"Sir, you didn't exackly love the old Earl, eh?"

"Shrig, your surmise is perfectly correct; I did not!"

"In fact, Mr. Clipsby, sir, you come pretty near disliking him, eh?"

"Shrig, I detested him from my soul, I hated him with all my heart . . . God forgive me—and him!"

"That sounds wery frank-like and open-'earted, sir."

"It is also Gospel true, Shrig."

"So then you helped Miss R. Ford to run off . . . and vy, sir?"

"Because she was determined to leave at once; indeed she seemed quite wild to go."

"And then, arter she'd gone, did you go and take a look at Lord A.?"

"I did. As I deposed at the inquest."

"And found the old Earl dead and the young Earl drunk, eh, sir?"

"Not drunk, oh, no!"

"Vait a bit, sir!" said Mr. Shrig, whipping out his notebook, from the pages of which he drew a newspaper clipping. "This is a report o' the inquest, sir, and it says here: The Coroner axes the question: 'Upon seeing your unfortunate father dead, vot did you do?' Answer: 'I scarcely remember, I was drunk as usual.' Sensation in Court. And vot do you say to that, Mr. Clipsby, sir?"

"That the Earl takes a perverse delight in making the very worst of himself sometimes, poor boy."

"Do you think as Lord A. shot himself, sir?"

"No, Shrig, I do not."

"Verefore and vy, sir?"

"He was never the person to wilfully harm himself under any circumstances."

"Oh!" murmured Mr. Shrig, turning to watch the airy gambols of a hovering butterfly. "And do you think or suppose as he died in that cheer . . . or even in that room, sir?"

"No."

"But, sir,—your evidence at the inquest——"

"Since then, Shrig, certain highly suggestive facts have been pointed out to me by Sir Peter Vibart which might cause any one to think otherwise."

"Har!" murmured Mr. Shrig, his gaze now upon his companion's elegant boots. "Sir Peter, eh, sir? Her ladyship tells me as how Sir Peter suspects some one."

"Indeed? Well, I'm not surprised."

"The question is—oo? For, though suspecting, Sir Peter von't mention no name, not to her ladyship nor yet to me, not 'aving sufficient proof."

"Why, there's the difficulty!" sighed Mr. Clipsby. "It is one thing to suspect but quite another to prove those suspicions true. And Sir Peter, being the soul of honour, would naturally be silent."

"And silent he is, sir—as any tomb! Dog bite me, but he says to me as he'll never speak without proof positive,—not even if they arrests him and his son—and there y' are, sir, and vot d' ye say to that?"

"Admirable, Shrig. But Sir Peter, being Sir Peter, could do no other. And, between you and me, Shrig, I verily believe the person he suspects is—myself."

Mr. Shrig actually jumped, his keen gaze flashed to the impassive speaker's face and his eyes grew rounder than ever to see that Mr. Clipsby was smiling at him quite happily; but this smile was banished suddenly by look of quick anxiety.

"Why, there is Richard," said he, "I wonder if——" But, even as he spoke, Richard espied them and began to run, calling as he came:

"Clip . . . Clip old fellow, he's conscious! Valentine is conscious and whispered your name——"

Clipsby was off and running towards the house with Richard beside him while Mr. Shrig, staring after them with mouth agape, took off his hat, blinked at it, put it on again and, staring round upon creation in general, exclaimed hoarsely:

"Vell . . . blow my dicky!"

But up in that silent, darkened chamber the head upon the pillow had stirred at last, the tired eyes were gazing up into Eustace Clipsby's anxious, gentle face, while from those death-pale lips stole a broken whisper:

". . . dmother . . . God. Clip . . ."

"Valentine, oh, dear boy, what . . . what is it?"

"That be all as 'e'll say, sir," sighed the nurse; calls on his mother and God, he do, pore dear——"

"Hush, pray hush! . . . Valentine, tell me again."

The eyes closed wearily, the dark, slim brows knit themselves, the whisper came fainter:

"Rose—mary. She'll—know."

So Rosemary was summoned and swiftly, silently she came, to kneel with head bent so low that her bright hair touched the young Earl's pale cheek, whereat he opened his eyes and, looking at her, smiled:

"Frayne . . . solved the . . . riddle . . . for us!" he whispered brokenly. "And now . . . I want . . ." Breath seemed to fail him, his eyes closed again, but Rosemary's gentle fingers touched and smoothed the frown from his brow.

"Yes," she murmured, "yes, dear Valentine, tell me what you want; only tell me." Once again that pitiful broken whisper and then Rosemary was on her feet.

"His Fairy Godmother!" said she gently, her eyes dimmed by sudden tears. "He wants little Jane . . . you need our little Jane, don't you, Valentine?"

The pallid lips contrived to smile.

"Then she must be brought to him, of course," murmured Charmian.

"I'll go for her at once," said Clipsby, turning towards the door.

"I too, if I may," sighed Rosemary.

"And I," said Richard.

CHAPTER XXXVII

TELLETH HOW THE EARL SMILED AND WENT A-JOURNEYING

"THREE doctors!" snorted Miss Janet, albeit very softly, as Charmian closed the bedroom door gently behind them. "Three! Why not three dozen or three hundred?"

"Well, you heard them, Janet,—what do you think of him this morning?"

"I'm thinkin' o' yon nurse," quoth Miss Janet, scowling back at the closed door.

"Martha Betts? But, my dear, she is such a gentle, kindly soul, as you know quite well, Janet."

"Ay, she mebbe a' that, but I'm tellin' ye the wumman's a gowk. Suppose Valentine has an interval o' consciousness, d' ye think she'll ha'e the *nous* to act at once and send for us in time to ask him the dredfu' question we must?"

"Oh, Janet . . . the poor boy lies on the very threshold of death . . . how can we ask such question?"

"Charmian Sophia, we must! If you won't, I will, I will—for the sake o' Peter and Richard. We know, you and I, how fiercely Valentine threatened his father's life; there was death in his look, his voice and every gesture, he was mere rampant Murder!"

"And now I—fear he is dying, Janet. Yes, my dear, in spite of all the doctors can say or do."

"The more reason to ken the truth frae him then. . . . Valentine good as told us he would kill his father; it was long ago but I could speak ye the vera worruds he used——"

"Then don't—don't!"

"But guid heavens, Charmian, in your heart you must be vera sure 'twas son killed wicked father as he vowed——"

"But I'm not sure, Janet, I'm not;—no, no, I wish I were. I have gone over it all in my mind, oh, many times . . . recalled his looks and dreadful words and, God forgive me,—even tried to believe his indeed the guilty hand, yet . . . when I remember the dear, shy gentle boy he was—and as you must remember also, Janet—so very like his little, tender, helpless mother . . . when I look upon his poor, stricken face as it is now, all sweet boyish gentleness again, I cannot, no, I cannot possibly believe it of him."

"Well I can—and do!" said Miss Janet grimly.

They had by now reached the sunny garden and were pacing slowly among the fragrant roses; and here Miss Janet paused to stamp her determined belief so violently that she clashed.

"Charmian, I believe he killed yon sinfu' Earl as he vowed he would. And, mind ye, here was no' juist an ordinar' brutal murder; this was an act o' justice, ay—but I would like fine tae hear him confess till it . . . afore witnesses, y' ken, for our menkind's sake. And besides, m' dear, if yon puir laddie is tae die indeed, it were better he made due confession and . . . My gracious me—will ye look at Peter!" she exclaimed, in such sudden amazement that Charmian turned and opened her beautiful eyes very wide at the unwonted, nay, the astounding spectacle of her dignified husband abroad thus and striding towards them in his shirt sleeves, cravat untied and fluttering, hair ruffled, face smudged with dust and grime but his eyes bright and eager.

"Peter—Peter, what on earth!"

"My dear," said he, "my dear, a most remarkable discovery! You know how often I have considered the removal of that corner bookcase in the library, the one so awkwardly placed and such an odd shape? We accomplished it this morning, Mordaunt and I. . . . My dear, that bookcase was definitely so built and shaped to hide a small, secret cupboard and in it I found . . . aha!"

"What, Peter? For goodness' sake, don't tantalize!"

"Money, is 't, Peter? Jewels?" enquired Miss Janet.

"Better than either! Come and see."

Giving an arm to each, Sir Peter brought them triumphantly into his library where Mr. Mordaunt, amid piles of books and ruins of the dismembered bookcase, bowed them welcome.

"There!" said Sir Peter, with dramatic gesture.

"That?" cried my lady in instant dispraisal. "Oh, goodness me, Peter—merely that old, rusty sword?"

"My certie!" snorted Miss Janet. "Is this all?"

Sir Peter sighed deep and plaintively, shook his ruffled head at them in weary rebuke and, taking up the grim-looking weapon almost reverently, spoke:

"A silver-hilted broadsword of the Parliamentary Wars, the blade marked 'Andrea Ferrara——'"

"But such a very frowsy old thing, Peter, and all rust, and I was hoping you had found something really wonderful."

"I have reason to believe," he continued patiently, "this wonderful sword was presented to my great-grandfather by Oliver Cromwell after the battle of Edgehill, and used by him somewhat frequently afterwards; you will observe how notched the blade is."

"Still, Peter dear, it is not a thing of beauty or any value is it——"

"I am endeavouring," sighed Sir Peter, "I am patiently attempting to inform you that this sword once, in all probability, was borne by Oliver Cromwell himself."

"But then, Peter, at school I never liked Oliver Cromwell. I used to think he was a bloodthirsty old wretch."

Dumbly Sir Peter laid the old sword gently upon the table and lifting grimy hand to ruffled hair with an almost hopeless gesture, proceeded to set his hair more on end than ever.

"However," sighed he at last, "despite such unreasoned strictures, Oliver Cromwell was, is and I dare to think, will ever remain, one of our England's greatest."

"Did you find anything else, Peter?"

"I did," he nodded. "I found—these!" and he indicated four stout leather-bound volumes.

"More books!" sighed Charmian.

"These, my dear soul," he explained, sighing like one utterly hopeless, "are a record kept and very painfully set forth by my great-grandfather, John Vibart——"

"Well now, this really is rather wonderful, Peter! Let us look."

"It is—very wonderful!" he answered, dark eyes kindling. "See now this beautiful penmanship! And from brief snatches I have read, it tells much intimate detail of Oliver, his looks, habit, and manner, his fierce hatred of injustice and his deep and obvious sincerity . . . by heavens, the man himself seems to stand before you alive and vigorous! Then here too is an eye-witness's account of the battles of Edgehill and Naseby, with skirmishes and sieges. . . . If you care to sit down and listen, you shall hear how this wonderful record begins."

So down they sat forthwith; then Sir Peter, opening a certain volume with that tender care which ever bespeaks the true lover of books, began to read on this wise:

"The Narrative of John Vibart, heretofore Fifth Baronet of Barcomb, in the County of Sussex and sometime Colonel of Horse in the late wars. Begun this fifth of April in the year of God 1665.

In these sad, degenerate days when faith in Mankind yea and in God Himself seemeth dead, when prayer is jeered and piety become a mock and scorn; in this grievous day when great Oliver's dishonoured bones do, even now, lie rotting with the dust of unnumbered malefactors at shameful Tyburn, I John Vibart bereft of all but life here in this humble cottage that looketh on Dering Tye here forgot yet therewithal content, even I John Vibart that knew this English Oliver as few men might, do take up my pen meaning, in these days of his so bitter dispraisal and wanton mis-judgment, to set down the very truth of him in so far as by God's help I may so do, that when I am safe marched through and beyond Death's Valley, men yet unborn shall, reading these my true and faithful words, learn therefrom and know at the least in some part, what manner of man this Oliver Cromwell truly was."

Sir Peter had paused here and glanced up to ask their opinion when borne to them came a sound of hoofs and wheels.

"They are here!" cried Charmian, rising.

"Ay, and—with the child!" quoth Miss Janet, peering from the window and away they sped together, leaving Sir Peter gazing after them, the open book in his hand.

"It is a strange thing, Mordaunt," sighed he more plaintively than ever, "that women, yes, even the very best of them, are singularly devoid, indeed entirely lacking in reverence for the abstractions of life . . . what are you staring at, pray?"

"Miss Rosemary, sir, Mr. Clipsby, Mr. Richard and a little girl."

"You will see them better if you go out to them, Charles, and when you have greeted them, have the goodness to ride and engage Hurley the carpenter to reconstruct this bookcase." So saying, Sir Peter leaned back in his chair and became lost in the narrative of his long-dead ancestor John Vibart. Time passed, clocks chimed, the light began to fade yet he read on and on like one enthralled, until he became aware the door had opened and frowned, glanced up impatiently and glimpsing Charmian, smiled.

"My dear," said he enthusiastically, "this is a very wonderful history; it is a tale the world must read. It shall be published! We will edit it together, you and I. There are one or two pages gone. I regret to say . . . well, we must bridge those to carry on the story. You and I, Charmian, it will be a labour of love, my dear, and with your assistance, doubly so. . . . Eh? Why . . . what now? Oh, my dear——!" Down went the volume and up leapt Sir Peter, for Charmian was weeping, silently but very bitterly, the great tears falling all unheeded as she stood; then Peter's comforting arms were about her, folding her close.

"Is it—young Valentine?" he murmured.

"Yes—he is—dying, Peter. It has come at last. . . . But so young—so young—so young! He asked for you—come wth me."

And yet, when they reached his bedside, the Earl, it seemed, had no thought for Sir Peter or any one except little Jane, who sat beside him on the great four-post bed, weaving a daisy chain very deftly with small, quick fingers.

"Light!" gasped the Earl. "Draw the curtains . . . give us . . . light! Now little Jane, dear . . . small Fairy Godmother . . . cast me a spell before you go . . . a 'triffic' spell and . . . turn me into . . . a Fairy Prince for ever . . . and ever . . ."

Very solemnly little Jane, screening herself in the bed curtains, waved the flowery chain above and about him, whispering the while her childish incantations, then caught her breath in quick alarm:

"Oh, Fairy Prince, do something hurt you?"

"No!" he gasped. "Ah, no, Sweetheart, it . . . is just the spell . . . the charm is . . . working. So now . . . kiss me, little Godmother and . . . go. Rosemary, take her, God bless her always, take . . . her away." So the awed and wondering child was led from the room and he lay silent awhile; then suddenly:

"Dick," said he, in voice strangely loud and clear, "all's well between us at last, eh, old fellow . . . all's well?"

"Why, of course; always and ever, Valentine——"

"Then Dick . . . so . . . am I!" said the Earl and closed his eyes, but upon his boyish lips was smile so bright, so strangely glad and ineffably joyous that Richard smiled too.

"That's the spirit, dear old fellow!" said he gently. "See Clip, he's better, much better."

"Yes," answered Clipsby, bowing his head between quivering fists. "Yes, he is very well . . . he is with his blessed mother . . . Valentine is dead."

CHAPTER XXXVIII

OF JASPER SHRIG, HIS SCHEME AND VERY BRIEFLY

TIME sped; a clock chimed and chimed again in the silent house below, but Eustace Clipsby stood there motionless, a bowed and stricken creature, staring with wide and awful eyes upon that pale young face so glad in death.

The door opened stealthily but the watcher never so much as moved; a hand touched him gently yet still he nothing heeded; then a hoarse voice spoke close beside him:

"Mr. Clipsby, sir, there aren't . . . never no vords . . . for this here, but——"

"None!" muttered Clipsby. "None! Valentine is dead! The youth I . . . wrought for . . . hoped to see become the great and noble man he might have been . . . is gone . . . above and beyond all help of mine. God has adjudged me! It is thus God has answered my prayers . . . crowned my very desperate efforts! This young life, so much more precious than my own, has been taken from me . . . far beyond my reach. . . . Ah, but . . . so young, so young!"

"He'll be therefore spared a deal o' pain, ditto sorrer and vorry, sir, ar— a lot o' pain and grief too,—him being dead. But, sir, Mr. Clipsby, how about—the living? Sir—I ax you! Jest come and take a peep out o' the vinder, a moment, pray do now, sir, do."

Obedient to the gentle suasion of Mr. Shrig's hand, Clipsby turned and, looking down from this eminence, beheld three furtive-seeming men, who, themselves hidden, kept stealthy watch upon the house.

"You sees 'em, sir?"

"To be sure. What are they doing?"

"Mr. Clipsby, sir, I shouldn't be saprised a bit if to-morrer about this very hour,—the death hour, sir, Sir Peter and Mr. Richard Wibart should be took . . . arrested, sir, and dragged off to gaol, Mr. Clipsby!"

"You think so, Shrig?"

"Sir, I'm pretty sarten sure on it."

"Then reassure yourself; neither Sir Peter nor Richard can ever possibly suffer such indignity."

"Eh? Sir,—you mean——?"

"Exactly what I say. Now please leave me with his lordship yonder; we . . . we are to be parted a while very soon . . . though only . . . for awhile, I pray God." So saying, Mr. Clipsby turned back to the bed and stood there motionless again, staring down at that young, smiling face.

Noiselessly Jasper Shrig crept from the room and as silently stole downstairs and out into the sunset glow; reaching a certain very remote corner of the garden well hidden from the house, he whistled softly, whereat Gimblet appeared from behind the summerhouse.

"Done, Jarsper?"

"Ar! You can send them lads back to town."

"Will it work, Jarsper, your scheme?"

Mr. Shrig appeared to ponder this question, his usually placid face strangely troubled.

"Ar—I reckon so," he nodded at last, "but—I'm vondering jest ven it'll vork and—how, Gimblet, how?"

"What be you a-thinking now, Old Un?"

"Gimblet, me b'y," answered Mr. Shrig, shaking his round head, "I'm a-thinking as Death aren't finished hereabouts yet."

"Jarsper, I don't twig."

"No more don't I!" sighed Mr. Shrig. "Hows'ever, you can get back to London . . . the job's finished—or pretty nigh."

"Then you'll be coming back soon, Jarsper?"

"Ar. Though tell Corporal Dick to expec' me ven he sees me. Good-bye for the present, Gimblet; 'member me to your vife."

Slowly and heavily Mr. Shrig walked back to the house and, being there, paused some while to stare with troubled eyes up at the curtained window of that dim and silent chamber where Eustace Clipsby still kept his watch beside the dead.

CHAPTER XXXIX

TELLS HOW EUSTACE CLIPSBY SAW THE DAWN

OLD SOL, rising in majesty like the beneficent god he is and has ever been, was making a glory of the world, or rather this small part of it,—this South Country of lush meads, shady coppices and bowery lanes backed by the green soft swell of the gentle Downlands with a far-glimpsed splendour beyond that was ocean. Yes, up came the sun in glory and at his joyous advent, dewy turf, hedgerow and tree decked themselves in flaming gems while from these spangled thickets rose—first a vague stir, then a drowsy twittering . . . a blackbird tuned his pipe and thereafter from a myriad small throats rose that glamorous chorus to acclaim the new day and give sweet welcome to the new hope it ever brings.

In this so magic hour it was that little Jane (this child of Destiny) peeped forth of the open lattice and, seeing all things so wonderful, dressed herself with small, nimble fingers, and, leaving Rosemary still fast asleep, stole away down the great staircase and out into the fragrant morning.

And in this same fateful hour Eustace Clipsby, seated in the shrouded chamber of death by the beam of guttering candles, was inditing a letter with rapid quill. His task accomplished, the letter folded and sealed, he crouched awhile, staring dull-eyed on vacancy. At last, as if roused by the blithe morning carol of the birds, he rose, drew back the heavy curtains and, leaning out into the early sunshine, breathed deep of the fragrant air; and as he looked from sweet green earth to radiant heaven, his sombre eyes brightened; from pale, lean face the lines of pain and grief and care were all smoothed away, and upon his features grew a light not of the sun. With eyes thus uplift he raised one hand to his breast to feel and make sure of that which lay hidden there and gazing thus heavenward, spoke in hushed voice: *"In manas tuas, Domine."*

Turning back into the chamber, he extinguished the candles and, kneeling beside the bed where the sun's level beams made a glory, he touched that young, still face,—the cold cheek, the closed, long-lashed eyes, the tender-smiling mouth; he smoothed the curling golden hair very gently as a mother might have done, and with this last, mute farewell, rose and went silently from the chamber, closing the door softly behind him.

For a long moment he stood hearkening to the deep, slumberous stillness of the great, old house, then downstairs went he into Sir Peter's library.

And presently, hat in hand, he (like little Jane) went out into the sunshine.

He walked at leisured pace, stopping now and then to inhale the fragrance of some rose heavy with dew or to watch the soaring flight of songful lark mounting as it were in a very ecstasy.

Walking thus and careless of direction, he presently espied the Home Farm, the trim old house, the thatched and roomy barns grouped about wide rick yard where rose the great stacks fragrant and orderly. Suddenly, out from one of these well-cared-for barns stepped Sir Peter with a sturdy, rosy-faced man who scratched his head and shook it like one in some perplexity. Thus stood they in earnest talk until Sir Peter, chancing to espy Mr. Clipsby, waved hand in greeting and dismissed the rosy-faced man with friendly nod.

"You are early abroad, Sir Peter."

"I often am," he answered, glancing back at trim barns and goodly ricks with a certain complacency; "a farmer who really farms must be up early and late. This morning Giles, my cowman yonder, is having trouble with a young, prize heifer; we are rather worried about her. . . ." Thus Sir Peter and was pensively silent until, glancing at his companion and struck by something very wistful and desolate in the whole man, he forgot his heifer and, laying comforting hand on Mr. Clipsby's drooping shoulder, took his slim, cold fingers into his own warm and vital clasp. So they stood awhile gazing mutely upon each other, eye to eye, while in the sunny air above and around them larks carolled faint and sweet.

"Sir Peter, I thank you with all my heart," said Clipsby at last, "such true sympathy affects me, comforts me, and . . . besides, I . . . feel you do me honour in taking my hand considering, well . . . let us say—the past."

Sir Peter's bronzed cheek flushed beneath the speaker's serene yet very eloquent regard and, instead of answering at once, he tightened his clasp upon this thin yet shapely hand ere he let it go.

"Mr. Clipsby," said he then, "the past . . . is past. I pray that in the future you may find a mede of happiness greater, sir, far deeper than you have ever known."

"Sir Peter, I think—yes, I dare believe I shall!" said Clipsby gently, as they paced on slowly side by side. "For, sir, The Destiny that rules Mankind is often kindly and always just . . . in the end. And to-day I feel a promise of Life . . . see how glorious the world is! On such a morning the haven of our cherished hope and dream shows very near. The very air breathes of Fulfilment . . . the promise of a greater living. In that riotous bird song . . . voices long-hushed may speak again,—calling, calling! Yonder where the shadows play the loved and vanished hand may beckon."

"Yes," answered Sir Peter, glancing at the speaker's rapt features a little anxiously, "it is well to be alive on such a morning."

"Though better to dream or die, Sir Peter, for in death only is realization."

"You are still thinking of Valentine,—poor, tragic boy?"

"Valentine! Of course!" murmured Clipsby, lifting hand again instinctively to the bosom of his modish coat. "Valentine is truly alive at last. . . . For what is this we name Life but a poor, visionary thing where nothing is or can be ever perfect, a waking dream to prepare us in some sort for the reality of True Life to which the thing we call Death—wakes us?"

"Hum!" murmured Sir Peter, beginning to rub at his chin, "I am, to be sure, convinced the abstraction we name 'soul' cannot die, since it is, as I believe, of the Infinite, that is to say,—of God, but——"

It was at this moment that Mr. Shrig suffered himself to become visible as, stepping out from shady hedge, he saluted them hat in hand.

"A very good day t' ye, sirs," quoth he, beaming from one to other. "As fine a morning as ever I see . . . and Sir Peter, I'll ax you to read this here very a-nonnymous letter as I chanced to come by—no, by your leaves, I'll read it to ye!" And forthwith, staying not for yes or no, he drew forth, unfolded and began to read, thus:

"Let Sir Peter Vibart take and instantly heed this friendly warning. Powers are in motion while he sleeps. Messengers ride post for London. An indictment is to be sworn and himself arrested at any moment. Oh, the shame of it! Sir Peter Vibart arrested for murder——

"The Capital Act is wrote in werry large Capitals, sir!

"Consider the odium, the stigma, the undying scandal. Therefore let him act at once to save himself if he can by any or every means. This the advice and warning of—a Friend.

"And vot d' you think o' that, Sir Peter?"

"That you may tear it up, Shrig."

"Ho!" murmured Mr. Shrig, shaking his head. "And vot do you say to it, Mr. Clipsby, sir?"

"I agree with Sir Peter that it is not worth while troubling about."

"Har!" murmured Mr. Shrig, folding the letter very carefully. "But, Sir Peter, lookee now, sir, if powers are in motion vile you sleep—though they'll have to be up precious early—but if men are riding to London——"

"They may ride, Shrig, they may ride——"

"And you still refuse to say, to tell, to visper or to 'int oo it is as you suspects, Sir Peter?"

"I do! Shrig man, I tell you finally and once for all that I am determined now that never under any circumstances will I——"

"Sir Peter . . . oh, sir . . . !" panted a fearful voice and to them ran Giles the cowman, his usually rubicund visage pale, his eyes wild.

"What is it, Giles? Good heavens, man——"

"The bull, sir . . . the noo, gurt, black . . . bull be escaped! Bruk 'is chain, sir, and 'e's away——"

"Rouse all the men," quoth Sir Peter, buttoning his coat. "Get poles and ropes . . . let your son give the alarm. Come on, man, and hurry . . . hurry!"

"Me too, sir," nodded Mr. Shrig.

"Why, what's become of Mr. Clipsby?"

"I vonder!" quoth Mr. Shrig, as they hurried along. "Is that theer bull fierce, sir?"

"Turble fierce!" groaned Giles. "Bruk 'is chain 'e did like so much cotting and——"

"Let us run!" said Sir Peter.

Meanwhile Eustace Clipsby, though in no haste, walked like one with some definite purpose, now and then pausing to glance about him and choosing always such paths as seemed more remote and solitary. So came he to a small stream whose soft ripple and pleasant, murmurous chatter seemed to lure him, for he followed this companionable rill until it brought him into a wood, a shady place, its green glooms shot athwart by Old Sol's radiant arrows and all athrill with the piping song of birds; through this wood he sauntered until beyond green boskages he beheld a wide and sunny meadow. Reaching the edge of this wood, he paused and from the bosom of his coat drew the small pistol had lain hidden there, examined the priming, cocked it and, with death thus ready, glanced slowly round about upon pleasant, sunny countryside and up at the cloudless sky. From this serene contemplation he was startled by a sudden, furious bellowing followed by a child's shrill, breathless scream, and glancing thitherwards he beheld little Jane fleeing towards the shelter of this wood with a trampling, snorting, fiery-eyed destruction close behind. Little Jane tripped and fell . . . the great bull thundered nearer, but Eustace Clipsby had leapt to action.

And now ensued a wild race between man and beast, two legs against four —and two legs won, though by scarce a yard. The child was snatched up, set upon her feet, and:

"Run!" gasped a voice. "The wood . . . run!"

Then heroic man turned to front raging monster,—leapt to grasp those murderous, terrible horns with desperate hands and so checked and, for a moment, held the maddened beast; he was jarred and shaken by that mighty head, yet still for a brief while he clung . . . but he was whirled aloft . . . trampled . . . saw the huge, merciless head lowering above him and, as death transfixed him, from dying lips sped a last cry . . . faint . . . inarticulate, yet a cry this that might have been—gratitude.

CHAPTER XL

WHICH, THOUGH IT SHOULD END THIS NARRATIVE, DOES NOT

GASPING voices . . . shouts . . . quick, stern commands . . . a wild and furious trampling to and fro and the great animal, conquered at last, is dragged away.

"Dam—midged—S'Peter?" gasped Mr. Shrig. "Your coat's nigh—tore off ye, sir."

"No, Shrig, no—but Clipsby—oh, my God,

"Sir, I've see!"

"Poor—poor fellow. It was heroic, Shrig!"

"Ar!" nodded Mr. Shrig, stooping above that dreadful, trampled thing.

"Cover him up, man! Oh, for kind mercy's sake—cover him! Here, take my coat!"

"Very good, Sir Peter, but—first——" Mr. Shrig's deft and nimble fingers became exceeding busy awhile, then, sitting back on his heels, he stared up at Sir Peter in a rather horrible bewilderment.

"What is it, Shrig—what now, man?" demanded Sir Peter, easing his bruised body out of his close-fitting coat.

"The letter, sir! There should ha' been a letter . . . a letter as I worked for, schemed for . . . there should ha' been a letter and—there ain't!"

Unheeding, scarcely hearing, seeing only the awful thing that soaked the trampled grass, Sir Peter knelt and very reverently covered this broken, battered thing with his torn coat and, still upon his knees, summoned divers of his men who came forthwith, bearing a hurdle whereon they laid all that remained of Eustace Clipsby.

"Take him—to the Home Farm," said Sir Peter hoarsely, "and bear him gently, good fellows." Then he arose and, turning where little Jane crouched, mute and shivering beneath a tree, he lifted the small, trembling body and bearing her thus cradled in his arms set out for the house, with Jasper Shrig ambling beside him. They had trudged thus some while in silence when suddenly from beneath Sir Peter's chin, a clear, childish voice spoke suddenly:

"Oh, please . . . will you tell me——" here a stifled sob.

"What, Sweetheart?" he enquired gently.

"Is he . . . gone all dead . . . too?"

"My dear," answered Sir Peter, bowing his head above the weeping child, "he has gone up . . . to be with your Fairy Prince . . . he has risen above us."

"Gone aloft!" added Mr. Shrig murmurously. "Ar,—and by goles, letter or no letter, he done it like a gen'leman . . . troo-bloo . . . noble! And— vich is more—like a proper man!"

Early though the hour, Charmian met them in the garden, where she was snipping roses with busy scissors and on her arm a basket abrim with fragrant blossoms; but, catching sight of them, down went basket and scissors and she came hurrying in quick alarm.

"Peter,—the child, is she hurt?"

"No . . . no . . . poor Eustace Clipsby. . . . The child is well enough, he saved her from the bull . . . but . . . "

"You mean . . . oh, not . . . dead?"

"Yes, dear. Oh, but Charmian . . . by God, it was noble! He fronted those murderous horns almost serenely . . . he seemed almost . . . too calm. Let us go indoors; the poor little maid has had a shock, see how she trembles."

"The poor darling! Give her to me, I'll take her to her beloved Rosemary."

Now scarcely had they reached the house than Jarsper Shrig met them and he was beaming almost bright as the morning, for in his hand was a letter.

"Sir Peter," quoth he jubilantly, "this here, as I reckon, is the letter as I've expected and vorrited over. Sir, I took the liberty o' peeping into your libree and there I found it . . . on your desk, vere nobody couldn't miss it. And sir, and ma'm, it is superscribed to 'Sir Peter and Lady Vibart, to be read together.'"

"But whose, what letter is it, Mr. Shrig?" enquired Charmian, stooping to kiss the small elfin face now pillowed on her bosom.

"Ma'am, it vas wrote by the late Mr. Eustace Clipsby. So if you'll get somebody to take charge o' that theer little innocent, p'raps Sir Peter 'll oblige by reading same and suffer me to 'ark."

"I won't be a minute," said Charmian and hurried away with little Jane.

"So then you expected this letter, Shrig?" enquired Sir Peter, turning it over in his hand.

"I did, sir. Since you ax me s' p'inted, I'll tell you as I schemed to get it wrote or the fac' spoken by vord o' mouth."

"You are extremely mysterious, Shrig."

"Though only now and then, sir." As he spoke, back came Charmian and closing the door:

"Now," said she, "the letter, Peter."

Slowly, and almost as though unwilling, Sir Peter broke the seal, unfolded the letter and read this:

"I, Eustace Clipsby, being about to front my Maker, the God of life and most just yet merciful Judge of poor humanity, do, in this my last hour of life, most solemnly avow that Charles, Earl of Abbeymere, died by my hand. I killed him with good cause. I shot him down as I would have slain any other merciless, ravening animal. Whether or no my act was justified I leave to the Omniscient Judge before whose awful tribunal my soul shall so soon appear to answer for this and every act I have committed in the body.

"Living, I suffered and endured much, yet wrought, as I ever hoped, for the best and would yet have lived to serve a little longer; but dying to such good purpose, I die very gladly. I shall commit execution upon this my corruptible body, leaving my soul, that I believe eternal, to the judgment and abounding mercy of my God. And to this true statement and voluntary confession I for the last time subscribe my name in the hope of pardon and a life of loving service hereafter.

"EUSTACE CLIPSBY."

For a long moment after the reading was done they were silent and utterly still, all three; then Charmian spoke in hushed question:

"But . . . he didn't . . . ?"

"No, ma'm, he didn't kill hisself," said Mr. Shrig as softly; "he meant to do it, he valked out to do it . . . here's the vepping as vas to ha' been the means. I found it primed and loaded, ar—'twas laying vere 'e dropped it as he run to save that theer little innocent from the bull. . . ."

"Ah, yes . . . yes . . ." murmured Sir Peter, folding up the letter reverently, "now I understand!"

CHAPTER XLI

THE LAST

BEYOND all doubt it has been an extremely trying day for certain slumberous owls and bats inhabiting the ancient church tower, for the bells (these clamorous monsters) have been hard at it for hours; and though through the ages they have rung joyful benediction on many and many a wedded pair, surely never in all their vasty length of days have they clashed more merrily or rung a blessing with heartier good will than to-day for the wedding "o' Squoir Vibart's Mus' Richard."

Yes, undoubtedly it has been a peculiarly disturbing day for these particular bats and owls.

It has been a great day in the village, as witness the floral arches, the fluttering ribbons, the flags and—the painted tea tray set off tastefully by garlands in little, old Mrs. Lethbridge's cottage window.

It has been a greater day at Holm Dene, where Sir Peter's many tenants,—farmer, yeoman and hind—have turned up to a man (and woman) sisters, sweethearts and wives, to drink health and happiness to bride and groom with three times three.

And here too was the County (most of it) surprisingly and almost ostentatiously hearty, in especial Squire Golightly and his sprightly, youthful lady.

Squire Golightly has risen (superbly Ajaxian) glass flourished aloft (rather as it had been a javelin) to "toast the happy pair" and thereafter (nose extremely Roman) to "hurl defiance in the Eye of Slander and dare the Tongue of Calumny to ever alienate from their esteemed and highly honoured host the heart, the soul, should he say—the clinging tendrils of true Neighbourliness and enduring Friendship. Sir Peter, as one of themselves, as indeed a shining light in The County, stood to-day higher in public esteem and deeper in the . . . um . . . ah . . . hearts of his peers and neighbours than ever before" . . . *et cætera.*

Mrs. Golightly, backed by the grim and faithful three, has kissed and clung about "her ever adored Charmian," has cooed ecstatic over the young bride's glowing beauty and "perfectly ex-quis-eet toilette."

The Bishop has beamed; the little General, jingling imaginary spurs, has kissed the bride; the Honourable Bob, emboldened by "strong waters" (having exceedingly honoured every toast) has proposed "The ladies" in terms and with metaphors (slightly mixed) somewhat reminiscent of the Fancy and the hunting field; old gentlemen have hobnobbed in corners remote from ear-trumpeted dowagers,—in fine, the County has almost enjoyed itself and now departing, sadly cuts up Sir Peter's neat, smooth drive with stamping hoofs and grinding wheels. . . .

And after some while Miss Janet appears to tell them the carriage is at the door and waiting.

"Oh," says young Richard, glancing a little shyly at his young wife, "then I suppose . . . perhaps . . . we'd better . . . go?"

"Why, of course, my dears!" says his mother, laughing rather shakily.

So Richard and his father shake hands, looked very hard at, and away from, each other, shake hands again and say—nothing. Rosemary kisses Miss Janet, kisses Charmian, goes out to the carriage on Sir Peter's arm, comes running back for a last, whispered word with Charmian and, leaving a tear on her cheek, flies back to hide herself in the carriage; in jumps Richard, waves his hat . . . and they are off and away upon that road which shall lead them—whither?

Thus all are gone, leaving the old house to bask drowsily in the afternoon sunlight . . . and Charmian pacing slowly amid her roses, leaning on Peter's arm. And both are very silent until catching each other's sighing, they look and smile upon each other, though very wistfully.

"Alone again, Peter!" she murmured. "Just you and I, my dear. . . . Our boy is gone."

"To his happiness, Dear Heart."

"But . . . to make another home, Peter!"

"Though not ten miles away, Charmian. . . . And a fine estate—properly managed, of course."

"She will, Peter. Thank goodness, Rosemary has the art of management."

"Eh? Rosemary? My dear, I'm thinking of Richard."

"Yes; well, she will manage Richard—well!"

"Manage him? Now, my dear soul, you know and are perfectly aware that our Richard is an extremely determined fellow, very resolute, perhaps a little too much so, indeed even a little headstrong——"

"Like his sire Sir Peter, Peter—exactly! A dogged, dogmatic man creature and consequently needing the utmost ruling, the sternest management,—and, my dear, Rosemary will!"

"Will—what, pray?"

"Manage him, rule him, guide him, mother him and bully him frequently, I hope. In fact, my man, Rosemary will manage son as I manage father,—not quite so deftly perhaps, but——"

"Well, God bless my soul!" exclaimed Sir Peter, "do I understand that you can actually believe such highly extravagant fallacy even for a moment? Good heaven! Am I not master in my own house?"

"Certainly not!" she answered serenely. "Of course not, never for a single hour, my poor deluded wretch; I merely contrive that you shall—think so. . . ."

"Amazing!" gasped Sir Peter. "Charmian, do you mean to tell me that I——"

"Would have been quite lost, ruined, destroyed, dismal and dead—but for me,—oh, frequently!"

"Preposterous!" he exclaimed, his indignation mounting. "Absolutely ridiculous! Then perhaps you will even tell me that all these years——"

"Yes!" she snapped. "All these years I have ruled you, managed you, do manage and shall manage you, so long as you are my poor, purblined, stately, blundering, frightfully dignified Peter and I . . . remain your most submissive, very devoted Humble Person."

Sir Peter smiled a little wryly, then he laughed, then, halting suddenly, he caught her in his arms and kissed her—her smooth brow, long-lashed eyes and ruddy, sensitive mouth.

"Thank God for it . . . and you!" he murmured. "And may it be long . . . long!" Then they went on again more slowly and with his arm about her now.

"Ah, you dear Peter," she sighed, "you are still such a boy you make me feel . . . older than I am."

"And when you tremble and flush," he retorted, pressing her closer, "you seem such a girl that upon my soul, I feel like a boy again."

"Dear child!" she giggled; yet very presently sighed tremulously.

"What now?" he enquired.

"The little summerhouse!" she answered tearfully.

"I see it, my dear, but what on earth——"

"I used to sit there . . . and teach . . . our Richard . . . his alphabet. . . ." Here she must stop to reach Sir Peter's handkerchief and dab her brimming eyes therewith. "Peter dear, it seems only yesterday that he was my tiny, clinging baby, needing me every moment. . . . I was his very life! And then my wonderful child . . . toddling . . . tumbling about all over the place and running to be kissed well again. . . . I was his consolation! And now——"

"Now, Sweetheart, you have . . . only me again. But Charmian, upon my life and soul . . . you are as much life to me as ever you were to Richard. Yes, my dear, without you I should be lost in the dark and perish indeed! And then, God bless you, I know you are my comfort and consolation . . . always, Charmian, always!"

"Oh, my dear," she murmured, rubbing her cheek against his sleeve, "how you comfort me—now! You can be . . . very wonderful . . . now and then."

"Well, now," said he, with sudden very youthful laugh, "suppose you get into your riding habit and boots, while I——"

"Peter . . . you mean . . . ?"

"That we ride for Sissinghurst; my dear, I ordered Old Adam hours ago to see our horses saddled——"

Round his neck came her loving arms, drawing him to her lips and, kissing him, she murmured:

"Now, my Peter, you are wonderful, because hours ago I sent to old Mrs. Westly to have the cottage ready for us to-night. . . ."

And thus it was that, as evening deepened to glimmering dusk, they rode into little, sleepy Sissinghurst together and drawing rein before the old inn, Sir Peter gestured towards the weather-beaten sign with his whip; quoth he:

"There he is, dearest, our old bull, as fiery-eyed and high-spirited as ever."

"Though fading!" she sighed.

"Then I'll have him painted for you brighter than ever——"

"Ah, no, Peter, let him fade untouched for old times' sake——"

Suddenly the inn door opened to sound of rustic voices and out to them hurried Old Simon.

"Be that you, Sir Peter?" he piped. "And you too, m' dear leddy! Well, well, this do be prime! Mrs. Westly told as you was on the road; she be over tu the cottage now, she be. Will ee come in and set a spell?" Now as the old man spoke, there rose upon the drowsy, fragrant air the sudden clang of hammer and anvil.

"George works late, Simon, surely?"

"Ay, Sir Peter, 'e du so. Jarge doant du nowt else, these days, Jarge be a gloomsome soul; 'is 'eart be buried along of our Pru, I du believe."

"Poor George! Let us go to him," sighed Charmian. "Is he there all alone, Simon?"

"No, m' leddy. Jarge aren't never alone since Tom come back wi' un from Lonnon; him and Tom's gurt friends, puts up wi' his black looks an' ways wonnerful, Tom du. Will my lad take an' stable your 'osses, Sir Peter?"

"Please, Simon. Come, my dear, we'll have a word with George." So they crossed the wide road and, standing in the gathering shadows, looked in at the smithy where Black George laboured with ponderous, clanging hammer, while Tom Lethbridge, a very black and grimy yet withal cheery Tom, leaned to the bellows shaft, whistling softly; and when the ringing hammer was still, Peter spoke:

"George," said he, "since you wouldn't visit us, we've come to you."

"Eh, be that you, Sir Peter?"

"It is both of us," answered Charmian softly.

Down went George's hammer, off came Tom's dingy hat and for a moment was silence; then, stepping into the smithy, Peter held out his hand, but George shook his shaggy, golden head.

"I be too black, Sir Peter," said he, while Tom Lethbridge, erstwhile poacher, shy of Sir Peter and overawed by his lady, stole furtive away.

"Nonsense, man! And call me 'Peter'; we're related now."

"So . . . they'm man an' wife, then?"

"Of course they are. Why didn't you come to the wedding as I wrote and asked——"

"Here be my reason," answered George, twirling his heavy hammer "And you now, you've come to stay a bit at th' owd cottage, they tell me, eh?"

"Yes, George."

"Being . . . lonesome p'raps . . . having lost your son——"

"Good heavens—no! We haven't lost him," said Sir Peter sharply; "on the contrary we've gained a daughter. And then, beside," said he, feeling for and clasping Charmian's hand, "having each other, we can never be lonely."

"Ay—having each other!" repeated Black George, very bitterly. "Each other . . . ay, there it be! Well, I've got my hammer . . . ay, and Tom yonder, so I be just . . . waitin' . . . I've lived my life, worked an' slaved and don't owe a penny to no man and . . . what's it brought me?"

"Achievement and Friendship," said Sir Peter; "your best work is masterly . . . like that church screen . . . and will endure and . . . well we have always been friends, George. What do you say, Charmian?"

"That life has brought him Love," she answered. "A great, wonderful love and . . . Memory."

"Ah!" growled George, like some fierce, wounded animal. "Ah—memory! . . . Ay, there be allus memory and 'tis such pain that I be . . . just waiting . . . till the morning breaks." Now, and even as he spoke, Charmian leaned near and before he might prevent, caught his mighty blackened hand, cherishing it between her two soft white ones.

"George, my dear," said she, looking up into his grim, yet sensitive features, "I knew and loved your Prudence also, and I am very sure such bitter grief would grieve her too. Cannot her sweet memory comfort you . . . even a little, George?"

"No!" he answered, averting his head.

"Have you never felt her gentle presence near you sometimes in your dreadful loneliness?"

"Ay!" he muttered. "Though 'twere only fancy, Lord! I've seen her sweet face . . . smile up at me from my forge fire many a time . . . but I know 'tis only a vision as comes and goes and leaves . . . only ashes——"

"Ah no, George, no! These are more than idle fancies, for I believe there is a . . . a way beyond our earthly sight where those we have truly loved so long, and lost . . . for just a little while . . . may come when least we know to touch and wake us to better life and hope for the future . . . to comfort us, guide and shield us . . . oh, George, can you believe this?"

"I can . . . try," he answered, with a new gentleness. "Yes, I will try for my Prue's sake and . . . yours, for Prue loved ee mighty well and . . . ecod . . . no wonder!"

"Now for that . . . Oh, George, stoop—stoop!"

Wondering, he obeyed and so she kissed him.

"Lord!" he whispered, and into his fierce blue eyes came such tenderness as few had ever seen, a gentle light dimmed by sudden tears.

"Lord!" he gasped again. "And so—turble grimy . . . as I be!"

"Because you are our own Black George," she murmured, "and will come and sup with us—to-morrow."

"Nay now, I aren't used——"

"To-morrow at eight!"

"Nay but I can't nowise——"

"I'll cook a rabbit!"

"I'll come!" said George and, smiling suddenly, reached out a hand to each. "Such friendship——" said he, and choked. "Friendship be a rare, good thing, Peter. . . . Friendship be a very . . . mighty good thing!"

"Yes," said Peter. "Friendship is . . . mighty!"

"Up there," said George hoarsely, "aloft on the beam yonder is your old hammer, Peter; I . . . hung it there when you went away; nobody aren't touched it since."

"Eh—my hammer?" quoth Sir Peter, his dark eyes kindling. "By George, George, old fellow, we'll have it down; to-morrow I'll come and strike for you and we'll chant the old anvil song—you remember:

"Strike! ding, ding!
Strike! ding, ding!
The iron glows
And loveth good blows
As fire doth bellows
Strike! ding, ding!"

"Peter . . . oh, Peter, Lord love ee, I aren't heard or sung that through all these weary years!"

"Then—to-morrow, George!"

"Ay, to-morrow . . . old friend!"

Night had fallen and they walked slowly, these two, and very close together —this husband and wife, this father and mother—walking as only true lovers may, in a perfect mutual content.

"In a leather apron again and black from the fire—my stately Sir Peter!" said Charmian and laughed very happily.

"And, by heavens, I shall thoroughly enjoy it!" he answered, clasping vigorous arm about her. "Thank Venus you don't wear those whalebone things and busked abortions!" he exclaimed.

"Goodness—me!" she murmured. "You would never have stooped to dare to say such thing when you were my very demure, extremely pedantical Mr. Peter—Smith!"

"Perhaps not . . . I was a bit of a stick,—but I knew it; oh, yes, I was quite aware of it, none the less."

"Why, Peter, how in the world——"

"Never mind."

"But I do mind. . . . I was so careful and quite excessively modest,—so how on earth could you——"

"However!" he chuckled, and they went a while in a very pregnant silence.

"I wonder?" said she suddenly. "Peter, do you suppose our children are as happy as we?"

"No, of course not!" answered Sir Peter with his tone of sweeping finality. "But they think they are, so God bless them! . . . Aha, and there's our old cottage, all aglow and winking at us through the green like the sly old rogue it is, for, of course—it knows, Charmian."

"Ah, what, Peter—now what?"

"Just how beautiful you were . . . and are, and how exactly the one and only woman . . . and why."

"The dear, sly, knowing old thing!" she laughed, a little shakily. "Do you wonder I love its every brick and beam? See, how cosy it looks! Mrs. Westly will be there—and supper, Peter!"

"But there," said he, pausing to draw and hold her close, "there will be . . . my Charmian!"

Then Peter kissed her.